Life Goes on After the Turning

Ella Robertson

THE **Beckham**
PUBLICATIONS GROUP, INC.
Silver Spring

ACKNOWLEDGMENTS
(Blessings)

I would like to give special thanks and recognition to the Creator for bestowing a multitude of blessings on my life. I've been blessed with a mother, Ocie who has shared 90 years of wisdom, hope and love with her family. She has been the wind beneath my wings and the ultimate motivator. I've been blessed with a wonderfully supportive family, my sisters Ruthie, Phyllis, Michelle and Denise, who have always believed in me and constantly challenged me to complete this project. I've been blessed with a wonderful husband Eddie who lets me be me and gave me the time and space to be creative without complaining. I've been blessed with brothers, Ron, Arthur, Carson, Mark and Larry who encouraged me to bask in the glory of being a Black woman.

I've been blessed with good friends, Eileen, Erick, Tasheena and Roscoe who read my first draft, listened to my ranting and gave me feedback and encouragement. I've been blessed with even older friends Cathleen, Nellie, Ernestine and Shirley who would have been my sister circle, if one existed. I've been blessed with my personal mentor, Ernestine who taught me to rise in the face of adversity, stand strong, accept a challenge and create my own destiny. I've been blessed to be introduced to Barry Beckham and the Beckham Publications Group to make my dream a reality. Last but certainly not least I've been blessed to be a Child of God.

CHAPTER 1

June 28, 1958 was her personal Independence Day. It was early on a Saturday morning, as they waited quietly in what seemed like an endless sea of people. Sunrays streamed through the train station's tiny windows, mixed with the steam engine's vapors to cast an eerie, yellowish light over what appeared to be hundreds of black people crowding the station—families waiting to board the northbound eight o'clock train. They stood anxiously by, knowing that finally they were going to be reunited with fathers, sons, and grandparents who years earlier had gone north to find work. She often heard folks say "They got plenty good jobs up north" and "Black folks is living real good up north." It really didn't matter to her where this train was going as long as it was leaving Alabama and taking her to her mother.

At the crowded station, she heard men telling teary-eyed children not to cry, that Daddy would be back to get them as soon as he found work. Women stood tall and strong, knowing that they would have to hold the family together, with or without their men. Many black men left the South never to be heard from again. She could see the pain in the faces of these men about to leave everything that was near and dear to them. They were leaving to make a better life for their families. The train pulled into the station like a cruel slave master coming to claim his goods, without regard for the pain and suffering his arrival may cause.

As she stood there listening to the people around her saying their good-byes through tears and uncertainty, she wondered how many of those men would ever be reunited with their families. She held on tightly to the stranger's hand, thinking that if she let go even for a moment, the stranger would disappear and she would be trapped in Alabama for the rest of her life. She couldn't tell you the stranger's name, only that she was a tall dark woman, neatly dressed, soft-spoken and smelled of Ivory soap. She knew that the stranger was sent by God to rescue her and bring her back to her mother. Her name wasn't important; it was only important that she was going to be with her mother. She would have followed Lucifer himself if he promised to take her away from this place. The only thing that mattered on this day was that she was leaving.

Cynthia had been away from her mother for the past five years, shortly after her father died. Those were very uncertain times for her mother; and not unlike many families during those days, her grandmother stepped in. The extended family was critical to the survival of black people during those times. Many families were torn apart by death, unemployment and, in some cases, desertion. Sending children south to live with grandparents was very common, while the parents struggled to get back on their feet.

Everyone, including the adults, called her grandmother Mama. She was a short, round, dark-skinned woman who rarely smiled and always looked as if she carried the weight of the world on her shoulders. As Cynthia grew older she learned that Mama had witnessed the lynching of her husband and oldest son during the "Red Summer" of 1919.

Her grandfather was a large strapping man who worked from sunup to sundown to feed his family. On a stifling-hot August evening in 1919, a blinding light suddenly appeared outside her grandparents' bedroom window. Her grandmother knew that something horrible was about to happen. As she moved through the darkness, gathering her children, she saw a flaming wooden cross burning in the front yard. She later said her heart nearly stopped beating. She heard two shotgun blasts followed by hooded men bursting through the front door. Grandfather handed her grandmother a small brown burlap bag, which held all of his worldly possessions, then kissed her on the forehead before the intruders dragged him from the house. Family lore has it that his final words were "Iona, take care of my babies." Her oldest son, Willard, ran screaming from the house to help his father as his mother huddled in darkness with the other five children. There was nothing else she could do. She cried and prayed throughout the night, and at the first sign of dawn found a ladder and cut her husband and son down as they dangled from a large tree. From that moment on, her grandmother rarely smiled; she would say, "Life ain't gave me much to smile about."

Her grandmother was a widow at an early age, with five young children to raise and only one hundred and three dollars given to her in a brown burlap bag. Using a combination of employable skills that included domestic work, washing clothes, and selling vegetables, her grandmother managed to support her family. She ruled her home and everyone in it with an iron fist. Her word was the gospel and no one ever challenged her authority, even when she was wrong.

Their meals were very basic, and she made sure that Cynthia was clean when she went to school and church. She followed the old saying, "Feed them and let them grow." Cynthia's memories of Mama are hazy, but she did recall that her grandmother went to church on the first Sunday of every month and wore a black felt hat, cocked to the side, with a feather in it. She looked as if she were the most important adult in the church. She carried herself that way. Her grandmother didn't hug and kiss, she didn't show emotion of any kind, she never told Cynthia that she loved her and she never talked about Cynthia's mother.

Although she was only five years old when she left her mother, Cynthia remembered her loving smile, her warm and tender hands, and her soft voice that tenderly sang to her every evening at bath time. Those were the most loving times of her life, and that memory was all she needed to know that she was loved. Alabama has never held any pleasant memories for her, but she remembered vividly the long, hot days and lying in bed at night listening to freight trains that ran along the side of her grandmother's house. The railroad was the lifeline that held America together. Sometimes the train was more than fifty cars long. She often heard groups of men singing and working on the nearby railroad tracks.

Her uncle told her that these men were working on the chain gang and would have to work until the white man freed them. He never told her what these men had done to be put on the chain gang. She would watch them sweating and straining with picks and axes for many hours during the day under the hot Alabama sun.

There was always an older man in the group who would begin to chant and sing. The other men seemed to answer him. This chanting and singing was always in time with the picks and axes as they hit the cold steel of the railroad tracks. They sang for hours, and she often wondered what men working on the chain gang could possibly have to sing about, chained together at the ankles as they worked in the hot sun day after day.

The trains that ran on these tracks seemed to be endless and taunted her every evening as they chugged along. The sounds of the train caused her to make up a song that often put her to sleep at night. The only lyrics that stayed etched in her mind were "Get away . . . get away . . . get away," and she would sing this song over and over to the rhythm of the train. Her hopes and dreams were connected to one day getting on that train and getting away. It was then that she understood why the men on the chain gang chanted and sang their songs. Perhaps, like hers, they were songs of freedom.

She was not allowed to venture outside of the back and front yards. There were three things that she could count on every day in Alabama. They were the sun, the heat, and boredom. With this constant trinity, she quickly learned to use her imagination and entertain herself. Her imagination took her to places she had only read about, and she could get lost in those places for hours. She blocked parts of her Alabama experience from her mind for many good reasons; the most important one was that it would allow her to move forward and forget the past.

The crowd at the train station began to slowly move forward. She tightened the grip on her black angel's hand. She couldn't let her get away for fear that this would end up being just a bad dream. She felt a mild vibration coming from the ground, a sure sign that the train was getting closer. Soon she saw a large black engine coming toward them smoking and spitting bursts of steam from a large black tube on the top. It rolled slowly like a tired field hand after a hard day's work. Cynthia thought this must be what freedom looks like. Once the train entered the station, the smoke lodged in the back of her throat; this had to be the taste of freedom.

When the train rumbled to a complete stop, a round black man stepped from the train and placed a wooden box on the platform next to the door. People were moving everywhere: porters carrying baggage, people scurrying to say their last good-byes and to greet those who were getting off the train. A tall black man wearing a black suit with a red vest stepped from the train, blew a whistle and shouted, "All aboard!" Her black angel held her hand as they stepped up to the handrail to board the train. When she touched the cool steel railing, she thought this must be the feel of freedom.

She ran to an empty seat and sat near the window. She wanted to watch Alabama move into her past. Her angel quickly grabbed her hand and led her to another section of the train and allowed her to sit near the window. Little did she know that her blackness would not allow her to sit in any coach of her freedom train. As the train pulled out of the station and slowly began to pick up speed, she watched Alabama move past her with increasing speed. She began to recognize a familiar sound, the rhythm and the chug of the freight train that ran past her grandmother's house. She bounced in her seat to the rhythm of the train and sang her freedom song: *Chugga, chugga, chugga, chugga, get away . . . get away . . . chugga, chugga, chugga, chugga, get away . . . get away.* Her angel smiled and tenderly patted her head as if she could feel her happiness. June 28, 1958, was the best day of Cynthia's life. That day she felt, saw, and tasted freedom.

Boston is a long way from Alabama, much farther than Cynthia had imagined. She felt as if she had been on the train forever. She saw wide-open sugar cane and cotton fields slowly change into smaller garden plots. Even the soil changed from red to dark brown.

Living in the South she had learned that talking to adults required deference and diplomacy. It didn't take much for adults to consider you "grown" or "fast." She was neither, just inquisitive. She wanted to know what was going on around her.

Her black angel seemed to be different than the other adults she had known in the South. She smiled often and made Cynthia feel that she was pleased to be with her and Cynthia was not just a burden. Her black angel finally asked Cynthia why she had been so quiet; and Cynthia took that as her cue that her black angel was willing to listen. Like most ten-year-old children, Cynthia was full of questions, and her black angel patiently attempted to answer them. She told Cynthia that her name was Maggie and she was a close friend of her mother's. She had been visiting her family in Florida and agreed to pick Cynthia up on her way back to Boston. She said that Cynthia's mother had been working hard over the years to save enough money to send for her.

Cynthia asked her angel to tell her about Boston. She cradled Cynthia's head in her lap and told her about the occasional snow that would blanket the city between November and April of each year. She also told her that everything in the city was concrete, with an occasional patch of grass and trees. Then she told her about the trolleys that ran throughout the city on rails and hung from wires like puppets. Trolleys seemed to be the way that everyone traveled. The apartment buildings really caused Cynthia's imagination to take over. Maggie said they were tightly stacked one against the other, reaching as high as five stories.

When they finally arrived in Boston, there was a chill in the air. Cynthia's mother was waiting at the train station, holding a light blue sweater. No one needed to point her out to Cynthia. She would have known her anywhere—a petite, pretty woman with skin the color of gingerbread. When she saw her Cynthia grinned from ear to ear. She ran from the train right into her arms and thought that heaven could not be better than being in her mother's arms.

They held each other, and her mother cried. Cynthia was much too happy to cry and couldn't understand why tears fell from her mother's eyes. Her mother said that she had waited so long for this day and sometimes thought it would never come. Her tears were tears of joy.

They left the station and got into a big yellow taxi that brought them to Cynthia's new home. The streets of Boston were busy with traffic and filled with noises. Compared to Alabama, everything seemed to be moving fast. She held her mother's hand on the cab ride home and thanked God for hearing her prayers. She knew then that nothing in life would ever be harder than being without her mother.

They pulled up to a large red brick apartment building nestled between a row of other buildings that seemed to be identical.

"You're home," her mother said.

They entered a dimly lit hallway and walked up two flights of steps to their apartment. It had a long hallway, and on the right was the living room. On each side of the hallway were the bedrooms. At the end of the hall was the kitchen.

In the living room was a large overstuffed sofa and chair that sat on what looked like large wooden animal paws. The floor was covered with gray linoleum that was covered with large red and white flowers. The sun was shining brightly through the three windows, which made the living room look bigger and brighter than it actually was. Everything was neatly in its place and smelled of pine and ammonia. It was clear that her mother had worked hard to make a home for her.

The apartment wasn't what Cynthia had envisioned, but it was home and she knew that she would be happy there. She spent the next few days watching her mother, never more than four steps behind her, asking questions and getting acquainted with her new environment. She would wake up in the middle of the night, tiptoe down the hall to peek into her mother's bedroom, just to make sure that she was still there.

In many ways, her mother was an extraordinary woman. She found good in every situation and beauty in all things. When others would talk about a bad situation, or an evil person, her mother would always chime in to say "We are all the Lord's children" or "It will get better in time." Most of her time was spent doing for others—cooking, cleaning, and taking care of everyone else's needs.

She taught Cynthia how to evaluate every situation and to see the big picture. She told her that life was not always going to be fair and that it was important that she always have alternative plans, just in case.

"Cynthia, I want you to learn through my experiences. You have a chance to be all of the things that I only dreamed of," she once told her.

Her mother was a constant giver and rarely put herself first, even when she needed to. Cynthia knew then that she wanted to be like my mother in many ways. She wanted her patience and her loving, caring ways, but she didn't want her tolerance of useless people. Her mother could not hold a grudge, and would always forgive and give what little she had to those she felt were less fortunate. Like many black women during those times, she worked in a factory downtown and didn't earn much money. Nonetheless, she managed to keep a roof over their heads and food on the table.

Neighborhood residents acted as if they were in one big family. For example, when her mother was away at work, Mrs. Henry made sure that Cynthia followed all the rules. After school, Mrs. Henry would be waiting to make sure that Cynthia had a snack, changed her clothes, and did her homework before going out to play. Mrs. Henry was the neighborhood grandmother, sweet and loving, who didn't tolerate disobedience, and would give you fair warning before she got the switch.

Mrs. Henry came to live with her daughter, Ruby, and granddaughter, Vivian, after Mr. Henry died of pneumonia. Vivian was about eight years older than Cynthia and managed to always find time to listen to her problems, answer her questions, and help her adjust to living in the city. She spoke very softly and reinforced Cynthia's mother's lessons about being the best that she could be and always having plans B and C. Vivian was a pretty, brown-skinned woman with long dark hair. Many men in the neighborhood courted her, but she always found time for Cynthia.

From the age of ten to fourteen, Cynthia jumped rope, played other games, and ran every day, all day. She was so happy to have young people her age to interact with. The neighborhood children played Double Dutch, Hot Peas and Butter, tag, and her favorite game, Aunt Dinah's Dead. Aunt Dinah's Dead was an old southern game played by young girls in a circle. One young girl would stand in the middle of a circle and say "Aunt Dinah's dead." The girls in the circle would respond with "How'd she die." The girl inside the circle then reenacted the death with exaggerated moves while reciting, "Oh, she died like this." The girls in the circle would imitate the pose saying, "Oh, she died like this." After one or two poses, the game would end with everyone shaking their little bodies, clapping their hands, and chanting:

Oh, she lived in the country, had to get out of town,

'Cause she shook it, shook it, shook it when the sun went down.

To the front, to the back, to the side, side, side;

To the front, to the back, to the side, side, side.

It was common, on any warm day, to look out of your window and see young girls swaying to the rhythm of street games. Her neighborhood was full of children of all ages—brothers, sisters, and cousins—but very few fathers. She wondered where all the neighborhood fathers had gone, and finally decided that they must have died, just as hers did.

They were all poor, but most of them didn't know it. It was a way of life; they didn't have anything to compare it to. They entertained themselves with simple things—discarded cardboard boxes, bottle caps, and old milk crates.

In the summer they got together outside and found creative ways to entertain themselves. The young boys would overturn empty trashcans, boxes, plastic containers, and anything else that would make a sound. They used sticks and hands to develop a beat, and they would dance as if they had a full orchestra. Double Dutch had a rhythm; Hot Peas and Butter had a rhythm. There was a rhythm to everything happening in the street.

When she was fifteen, Cynthia began to take an interest in boys. Her mother made it quite clear that Cynthia would not be allowed to date until she was sixteen, and even then only on a limited basis. At sixteen she began dating Wesley, a pecan brown, well-mannered, neatly dressed young man. He had a quick chipped-tooth smile and often smelled of canoe cologne. He was a relatively shy young man. While the other boys were running around talking dirty and trying to touch the girls, Wesley usually stood on the sidelines and watched. Occasionally, he would apologize for the other boys' behavior.

She couldn't remember how Wesley became her boyfriend; he just was. He soon moved out of her neighborhood. They were both from families that did not allow young people to come and go as they pleased, so they didn't get to see very much of each other, usually no more than once a week. They both had curfews. Wesley would come to her house and they watched TV together. There was always someone home; they were never left alone, but that didn't stop them from taking every opportunity to kiss, fondle, and rub up against each other. They would do that as often as they could. She remembered a song in the 1980s that had the line "hormones jumping like a disco." Well, that was she and Wesley, one big hormone.

She believed that Wesley still holds the world record for being able to unsnap a brassiere in less than ten seconds, with one hand. In the 1960s there was very little discussion about sex. There was no sex education in the classroom or at home. Parents refused to talk about sex and would make horrible assumptions about you if you asked. Most of the information that Cynthia had about sex came from unreliable sources—the street and her girlfriends.

She never had a problem making friends and fitting in. There were six of them who grew up in the same neighborhood and played together since the age of ten. Sharon, who was the oldest and seemed to know everything, would often control the conversations. Sharon lived with her mother and three older sisters. She was quick to tell them about the things she saw and learned at home while spying on her mother and siblings.

Tina, another neighborhood friend, was quiet and very sensitive. Her feelings were often hurt by their sense of humor. She was an only child. Her mother was a very pretty woman, always with a different man in her life. No man ever stayed for long.

Juanita was the fast one in our group. As early as ten she was chasing boys and was very aggressive about it. She had two younger brothers and was often left in charge of baby-sitting. When her mother allowed her to come out and play, Juanita was determined to have as much fun as possible in a short period of time.

Gwendolyn was a big girl for her age and wanted to become a singer. She also wanted to be in their group and would do whatever it took to fit in. She was definitely a follower. Gwendolyn was the only one of them who had a father at home, at least they all thought that he was her father.

The bully in their group was Phyllis. She came from a family of bullies. Everyone in the Canter family had the reputation of being a fighter, including the mother and even the dog. Phyllis would only bully those who allowed it.

Cynthia floated in and out of the group. When the other girls were doing something she wanted to do, she was right in the middle of things; but if she wasn't interested, they knew not to count on her. She had never been a follower or moved by peer pressure. She never understood why the rest of the girls tolerated this, but they did.

Her body was maturing and she became more and more inquisitive about sex. She remembered one evening while she and Wesley were hugging, kissing, and rubbing each other, she had an urge to see what a penis looked like. She unzipped his pants and pulled it out. Once she got it out, she thought, *Oh my god! What the hell is this? What am I supposed to do with it?*

Like most young girls, her friends would get together to gossip. The next gossip session was scheduled for the next Thursday after school. She couldn't wait to get to this session. Finally, she had something to contribute. She saw a penis! Usually she was just a listener; the other girls were the ones having experiences and almost always had something to share. This time she had something to say. She saw it and she touched it.

As they sat around gossiping and telling stories, she told them her story and the room got quiet. "What you so excited about?" Sharon asked sarcastically. "You didn't get none." Everyone in the room laughed.

"What do you mean, I didn't get none?" she asked. What was she supposed to get, and how was she supposed to get it? She didn't have a clue.

Everyone in the room began to talk at the same time.

"If you didn't give him none, it don't count," Sharon barked.

"But you gotta do it standing up so you don't get pregnant," Juanita contributed. "But if you do it lying down, you got to jump up and down after, then you won't get pregnant," Sharon added.

This went on for a while, and the directions for "getting some" got more and more confusing. Cynthia couldn't talk to her mother about sex, and there was so much that she wanted to know. She had to find someone older that she could trust to tell her the truth about sex. She decided that she could confide in Vivian, who would not judge her and who would tell her the truth. One day she waited for Vivian to come home from work, and she told her about her discovery and the conversation with her girlfriends. Vivian talked to Cynthia for more than an hour explaining sex and answering her questions.

Sex sounded like the most painful thing that a person could do; and to top it all off, you ran the risk of getting pregnant. Why would anyone want to do that? After Vivian explained penetration, Cynthia quickly excused herself. She then went into the bathroom, got a mirror and began to examine her vaginal area, trying to find the entrance that would be big enough to accommodate what she saw in Wesley's pants. She didn't find anything that could possibly stretch that big.

The possibility of getting pregnant was certainly the straw that broke the camel's back. Early in life she equated babies with poverty, and she was determined not to be poor all of her life. She decided at that very moment that intercourse was much too risky. Vivian told her that if she was not ready to do it then she shouldn't, and that she should not let anyone pressure her into it. She said, "If you want to remain a virgin, you can still have fun."

She began to explain all of the other ways to enjoy sex without penetration. Cynthia listened intently, not wanting to miss anything.

Vivian concluded with this advice: "Don't let him convince you to let him put the head in; that's the most dangerous part. Don't ever agree to have intercourse to prove that you love a man. If he loves you he will wait. This is your life. You must make the right choices for yourself. Don't allow anyone to pressure you." Wesley never pressured her for sex. She wasn't sure if he had a better understanding of sex than she did. He never talked about it; as she thought back, she didn't remember him being much of a talker about anything. One evening as he was getting ready to leave, they were doing what they enjoyed most—hugging, kissing, and rubbing—and he quickly got an erection. She decided to experiment with one of the options to penetration that Vivian had given her.

She pulled his penis out again, this time she put her hand at the base and moved it out to the tip. She realized that it was even bigger than she originally thought. She pulled her skirt up and gently placed his penis between her legs, inside her panties. Wesley didn't object. He just went along with it and pulled her closer. She believed that she was a lot more aggressive than he was regarding sex. He slowly moved his penis back and forth between her legs and she knew that she was about to have a new experience. At this point they were both oblivious to everything around them. They were caught up in the moment, and she didn't want that feeling to end.

They continued this back-and-forth motion with increased speed as if this would be their last opportunity to have this feeling. They were both breathing faster and were lost in what she now knows as the pursuit of an orgasm. She really couldn't remember much, except the room started to spin, her knees got weak, and she had the most awesome feeling throughout her entire body. She had her first orgasm, and life would never be the same again. She was pretty sure that Wesley had as much fun as she did because of the evidence that was left in her underwear.

Over the next few months they continued to experiment without penetration. She knew that she was in love. It had to be love; nothing else could have made her feel that good.

Wesley came to visit her one day and astonished her with the news that he no longer wanted to be her boyfriend. He never really said why. She was devastated. What did she do wrong? Was she not pretty enough? Was it because she wanted to remain a virgin? What was it? For days she was confused, hurt, and needed to talk to Vivian. Vivian explained that the first love is the most unconditional love that she would ever have. She would eventually get over this. She would have to let him go and move on.

"Cynthia, whatever you do, don't try to keep a man when he wants to leave," Vivian advised her.

These were words that she would remember for the rest of her life. Moving on was the easy part. She never let go of those feelings of her first love. Shortly after their breakup, one of the young girls in the neighborhood came to her to express how sorry she was that she and Wesley had broken up. Carolyn said she thought Wesley and Cynthia were an ideal couple. Cynthia had seen Carolyn before, but she really didn't know her. She was a petite, brown-skinned girl who dressed in complete matching outfits, down to her purse and shoes. While most of them were struggling to put together stylish outfits, Carolyn seemed to do it with very little effort, and each outfit was always different.

She said that she wanted to be Cynthia's friend and, as a friend, she would talk to Wesley and help her get him back. It was a nice thought and an even nicer thing for a friend to do. She would see Carolyn and Wesley talking on occasion and felt secure that she was negotiating on Cynthia's behalf. Very soon it was apparent that Carolyn and Wesley were a couple. Cynthia had her first, last, and most significant experience with the treachery of a woman.

She didn't see much of Carolyn and Wesley after that. They all went on to different neighborhoods, different high schools, and different lives. She will always remember Wesley. Years later she would understand the significance he had on her life.

After high school, everyone seemed to scatter in different directions. Most of her high school girlfriends were pregnant by the age of seventeen. Cynthia had the reputation of being the oldest living virgin. They would still get together for their gossip sessions, and Sharon could not wait to share the latest news: Carolyn and Wesley got married. Although Cynthia acted as if it wasn't a big deal, deep inside she knew that Wesley would always have a special place in her heart.

Cynthia was the brunt of the virgin jokes. They would laugh and say "What are you saving it for? You can't take it with you" or "Your cherry is so far back up in you, it looks like tail lights." Everyone would fall on the floor laughing. Cynthia would laugh right along with them. It really didn't bother her. She knew what was best for her, and she was not prepared to risk being a poor unwed mother. It wasn't difficult to get a date. She dated all through high school. Unfortunately, after three or four weeks, her dates would realize that sex was not an option and they moved on. Separation became easy and an expected part of her life. It really didn't faze her after a while. She learned to build pleasant memories in every relationship and move on.

During the first summer after high school graduation, she met Gregory. Gregory was a smart young man who had aspirations of playing college football. He was like a big Teddy bear with far more patience than any of the other young men she had dated. He was about five feet eight inches tall, with a dark complexion, and built like a NFL linebacker. Everything in his life revolved around getting to the gym in order to stay in shape. At eighteen, he was very proud of a sparse mustache that had finally begun to show. He believed it was the first sign of manhood.

Gregory had been accepted, with a football scholarship, to a small southern college and was scheduled to enroll in January of the next year. Cynthia and Gregory dated all through the summer of that year. In October they were engaged. She really didn't know why they made that move. They thought it was the right thing to do.

Gregory's mother was a very opinionated woman who expected everyone to see things her way. Cynthia spent much of her time avoiding her. She and Gregory both lived at home with their mothers. Gregory's father left when his son was about eight years old. After meeting Gregory's mother, Cynthia understood why his father might have left home. Gregory's mother was good at making you feel guilty if you didn't comply with her wishes. She played Gregory like a baby grand piano.

Gregory never pressured Cynthia for sex. He understood her desire not to be an unwed mother, and he also related to the concept of babies and poverty being synonymous. By Thanksgiving, however, his discussions began to shift toward sex. He gave her all the standard reasons why they should move forward.

It was Thanksgiving Day. Gregory's mother was going to visit family for the holidays, and she pressed Gregory hard to join her. Under normal circumstances Gregory would do whatever his mother wanted, no questions asked. This time he was adamant about not going along. As she headed for the airport, his mother pressed one last time. Gregory was a little snappy with her for the first time. She shot Cynthia a resentful look. She knew what Gregory had on his mind. For the first time in their relationship, Cynthia and Gregory would be alone for four days. They got together on Thanksgiving eve and had their first sexual encounter. She found out that evening that Gregory, like her, was a virgin. He brought condoms and tried to set a romantic tone for the evening, but they lacked passion.

Their romantic holiday proved to be a case of the blind leading the blind. He continually told her how much he loved her, while pushing, pulling, poking, and groaning. It was over as quickly as it started. Her knees didn't get weak, and she didn't get that awesome feeling all over my body. There were no fireworks. At that moment she had a horrible thought, *What if Wesley was the only one who could make her knees weak?*

She could think of no good reason to continue having sex. It wasn't fun, and it certainly was not worth running the risk of getting pregnant. She knew that Gregory would not be happy with her decision and it would be only a matter of time before their relationship would end. He left for college in January, and by March she got her Dear Jane letter. In it he wrote that he had found someone who had an "appreciation for sex." In many ways she was relieved. She didn't know what sex should feel like, but she knew that it had to be better than what she felt that night in November.

As Cynthia grew older, she and her mother began to have more serious adult conversations. Cynthia's grandmother passed away quietly in the summer of 1968, and that somehow freed her mother to talk more about who she was and what she wanted.

Cynthia's mother had always wanted to be a schoolteacher. However, she yielded to her mother's decision that she should get married. Her mother decided who, what, when, and where. Cynthia's mother followed her directions. Although her life was different than she wanted, she did not regret the fact that she obeyed her mother.

"Cynthia, this is a new day," her mother said, "and I want you to be what you want to be. I don't want you to have any regrets in your life; and I don't want you to have to wonder if you could have been a success. Unfortunately, I can't do much to help you financially, but emotionally and spiritually I will always be in your corner."

While working on a secretarial job in the spring of 1969, Cynthia became overwhelmed with a feeling of failure. She had only a high school diploma, a half-assed job with no upward mobility, and she still lived with her mother. Living at home with her mother wasn't a bad thing. Her mother was still the sweetest woman in the world, but she was keeping company with a man that Cynthia felt had a very dark aura. He treated her mother well, but she didn't like the way he looked at her. There was something about him that she knew wasn't right.

Although she continued to work in her secretarial job, Cynthia couldn't shake the feeling of failure. She had developed a predictable pattern of taking the same train every day to downtown Boston, and reversed that pattern in the evening. Her life had become mechanical, predictable, and quite boring. It was clearly time for an evaluation. What did she want out of life? More important, how was she going to get it? She knew that she needed to have a plan and set some goals. This was the beginning of her "list of things to do." There were at least five items on this list, and one was to get a degree. If she ever expected to escape poverty, she would need to get an education.

CHAPTER 2

September 1970, Cynthia began studying at Northeastern University. It was the place to be if you were a black college student in Boston. She lived on campus because she needed to put some space between her and her mother's new friend. He still made her feel uneasy.

While waiting for her room assignment, she watched as crowds of young people from all over the Northeast moved into their new spaces. She had never traveled outside of Alabama or Boston and wondered what it might be like to live somewhere else. She pushed the thought from her mind. Once she completed her degree she could think about that again.

She was assigned to a suite with two other freshman women. The suite consisted of three small bedrooms, two bathrooms, a kitchen, and what was known as a common area. The suite was beige, cold and colorless; she added some personal touches to make it feel like home.

She struggled desperately through the first year. She had no idea that her B average in public school had not prepared her to handle college-level work. She was determined to compensate for her mis-education. Short of death, she was going to earn this degree. She was approximately three years older than her suite mates, and she wondered if this housing arrangement would work.

By Thanksgiving her suite mates had all gotten to know each other much better. They spent many evenings sitting around discussing family, men, school, and their aspirations.

Sandra was a southern belle from Georgia and often complained that they talked too fast. For her Georgia was the center of the world. She came north because her mother was convinced that Boston was the hub of the universe for higher education. Sandra was a dark-skinned sister with a great set of legs. The miniskirts and hot pants she sported were definitely her friends. They teased her because she was, according to their standards, flat-chested. She would put her hands on her hips, strut around the room and say, "I please my customers; damn you window shoppers."

Sandra was full of southern colloquialisms taught to her by her grandmother. Sandra adored her grandmother and told them that they would miss a chance of a lifetime if they did not get to meet her. She called her grandmother Mama Lee. Her grandmother was a colorful old lady who had lived through the dark days of the South. She had a keen outlook on life and often put life and its pressures in perspective for Sandra.

Sandra was the oldest of three children and well trained by her mother in the art of getting and keeping a man. Her parents were affluent and lived in the Atlanta area. Sandra's father was considered a black real estate tycoon. He bought and sold property in and around Atlanta much like a Monopoly player, and he was damned good at the game. Her mother stayed home and played the role of a tycoon's wife, a role she mastered. Although Sandra was academically sharp, her primary objective at Northeastern was to find Mr. Right, get married, and start a family. She was the only one in the suite with domestic skills, so of course they designated her as the suite cook.

It didn't take long for Cynthia to realize that she was the poorest one in the suite. If it were not for the federal aid program she certainly would not have been there. Most of the black students on campus were as poor as she was, but the concept of unity was real in those days. They worked together to survive.

For poor students it didn't take long for the news to travel that they were eligible for the government surplus food program, and they all went to sign up. Once each month they went to the welfare office and picked up their monthly allotment of surplus food. Sandra was the only person they knew who could take that surplus food and make a delicious meal out of it. She was an all-around traditional woman. The men in the building used her as an example of "quality wife material."

Robin was her other suite mate. Cynthia particularly liked Robin because she was strong and knew exactly what she wanted out of life. She made it perfectly clear to anyone who would listen: Nothing and no one would interfere with her goal of financial freedom by being at the top of her profession. There was no gray area in her life; it was black or white. Robin was never at a loss for words when it came to her feelings or beliefs about any issues. She was very opinionated.

Robin was born and raised in Hackensack, New Jersey, as an only child. Her mother was head nurse in an area hospital and worked long irregular hours. Robin spent a lot of time with her grandparents. Robin's mother was only sixteen when Robin was born. Her father was a high school basketball player who went on to college two years later and never looked back at Robin or her mother. Robin never talked much about him except to call him a sperm donor. Her mother would only say that his name was Walter. She thought he lived in California. Robin called her grandparents Mom and Dad, and her mother Doris.

Her grandparents were well established in their community, owning a chain of liquor stores and living in a home that was considered by some as a showpiece. It was a large brick, six-bedroom home on two acres of land with a heated pool. Robin had her own bedroom and always considered it home. Her grandparents were known for their elaborate parties.

Robin never needed or wanted anything that her grandparents couldn't provide. The suite mates called her their Black American Princess. She was what Sandra called "paper sack brown," with a thick head of well-kept hair. While most of them wore faded or used jeans and T-shirts, Robin wore designer outfits and shopped at the best stores. She never flaunted her family's wealth. She had it, they knew it, and that was that.

The suite mates were the campus social butterflies and would often have a suite full of people. Northeastern University was one of many colleges and universities within a five-mile radius of each other, but everyone came to their campus when it was time to have fun. Their suite was always the center of activity. If you wanted to party and socialize with black folks, you had to come to NU.

The suite mates had friends from Berklee, Boston College, Harvard, and M.I.T. Their parties were definitely standing room only. They didn't need much to throw a party; a can of chipped beef, onions and potatoes would make a great pot of what they called "welfare stew." They all made jokes about the stew because they knew it was all very temporary.

They would pass the hat to buy a few bottles of Ripple, Boons Farm, or whatever wine was less than five dollars for a bottle. A key ingredient for these parties was the standard party whistle worn around the neck. They would party until the early hours of the morning, dancing, blowing party whistles, and chanting, "The roof . . . the roof . . . the roof is on fire . . . we don't need no water; let the motherfucker burn."

It didn't matter what you wore to these parties; being cute was not the agenda. They just wanted to have fun. The style of the day was hip-hugger bell-bottom pants, T-shirts, halter-tops, and platform shoes. The suite mates were not hard drinkers; they just loved to throw parties and gossip the next day about who was doing whom. Between the parties, gossip sessions, dating, part-time jobs, and study time, it was a miracle that they were able to survive. For their first two years, their friendship grew. They were a team. Although their personalities were quite different, they learned to trust each other and to respect their differences. During the last two years, they promised to work hard to keep the friendship together.

Sandra began to date Jason the end of their second year, and it seemed to be quite serious. Jason was the oldest of three children, from an upscale neighborhood in Connecticut. His father was an engineer, and his mother a housewife. Sandra was exactly the kind of woman for whom Jason was searching. She pampered him in every way and even tolerated his chauvinistic attitude.

Robin and Cynthia had very little tolerance for a chauvinistic man and often initiated serious conversations with both Sandra and Jason. They wanted to be sure to raise all of the questions that Sandra would never ask. They wanted to help Sandra understand exactly what she was getting in a man. In spite of his attitude, Sandra loved Jason and was willing to deal with it. She honestly believed that he would change as he got older.

It was the beginning of their third year in college when the frequent parties, lack of privacy, and constant noise began to take its toll. Privacy had taken on a new value in Cynthia's life. It had moved up to second place on her "list of things to do."

Her suite mates were wonderful women. They had grown surprisingly close over the years and felt that they would always be friends. In spite of this, Cynthia needed her space.

During one of their many gossip sessions Cynthia informed Robin and Sandra that she was not going to renew her residence contract for the coming year. She assured them that their friendship was as strong as ever. After a series of questions, they finally understood her need for privacy and wanted to be a part of her apartment search. After all, they would treat this apartment as their new home away from home. Within three weeks of that gossip session, Cynthia found an affordable apartment about four miles from campus. It was located in a quiet, tree-lined neighborhood. It was exactly what she had been looking for. It had a large eat-in kitchen, living room, dining room, and two bedrooms. Two bedrooms were important, just in case she needed to get a roommate. The apartment was on the second floor in one of Boston's traditional three-family wooden homes. Her biggest challenge would be furnishing the place. What she lacked in money and resources she more than made up for in creativity. She visited a nearby second-hand furniture store located in the South End of Boston. The store abounded in broken and discolored pieces of furniture that would be considered junk by most people.

For her, an old broken dresser held the promise of a beautiful antique; a bruised coffee table promised to be a great conversation piece; a sofa and armchair that appeared to be a throwback from 1959 served as a retro living room set with just the right fabric. She spent most of her savings on her newfound treasures. Pillows, paint, fabric, and sweat turned her apartment into a fabulous bachelorette pad that would have made any single sister proud.

Living alone gave her plenty of time to study and to develop plans for the future. She got together with Robin and Sandra at least once a week, mostly at her apartment. They realized that they had outgrown the gossip scene and focused on each other's lives. They shared opinions and helped each other solve current problems. They called their weekly meetings the "Sister Circle" and promised themselves that they would continue this circle after they graduated.

Between studying for school and working, Cynthia had limited time for dating, but managed to fit it in occasionally. She had a body that got plenty of attention. Everything was tight and well proportioned. Getting attention from men posed no problem. Getting attention from decent brothers for the right reasons did pose a problem.

The Vietnam War had taken a heavy toll on the available black men. The country was losing black men in record numbers to the war. If you were going to find a young black man, college was the place to be. They were dealing with the Black Power movement, the Revolution, drugs, and the hippie love phase; almost anything was acceptable. This was the 1970s.

Birth control was widely available. Sex lost some of its intimacy and became just something to do—and everyone was doing it. Women became more aggressive and, for the first time, were doing the choosing, not waiting to be chosen. Even though they were more aggressive, they were still subtle. It was common for women to talk about a brother's sexual ability, or lack thereof. A brother who bragged too much was often the brunt of the jokes, especially if he proved not to be a great lover.

Robin, Sandra, and Cynthia were getting close to graduation and were a little uncertain about their futures.

Sandra and Jason were in love, and she talked about marriage after graduation. Her mother had already begun the preparations for an elaborate southern wedding as soon as the date was set. They were just waiting for Jason to make his move.

Robin seemed to be certain of her future. She had done her fair share of college dating and partying, but always made it clear that she was not looking for a husband. Making money was her priority. She applied to several brokerage firms and banks in the New York and New Jersey areas and felt sure that she would get at least two job offers after graduation.

Cynthia, however, was about to get a degree in business and had no idea what she wanted to do.

CHAPTER 3

May 1974 brought the second most significant event into Cynthia's life. Upon the request of a friend, she contacted Eastern Airlines to arrange a Disney World trip for her and her son as a birthday present. After maneuvering through the standard business telephone system, she waited for the next available sales representative. In about thirty seconds, a very deep baritone voice came on the phone.

"This is Jackson Douglas. How may I help you?" The voice was deep, soothing, mesmerizing.

For a moment Cynthia was caught off guard. She pulled herself together, explaining that she needed information for a trip to Disney World for one adult and one child. The calming voice of Jackson Douglas listed her options, the costs of each, and concluded by asking the age of the child with whom she would be traveling. She told him that the information was for a friend and her seven-year-old son. Jackson Douglas didn't skip a beat and continued to give options and costs. Jackson Douglas's voice then took on the characteristics of a salesman proclaiming that rates to Disney World were excellent this time of year and suggested that she consider taking her family along.

Instinctively, she felt he was fishing for information. Of course she let him know that she was single and had no children.

The soothing voice of Jackson Douglas made its move. "How's the weather in Boston?" Without hesitation the deep tones sped on. "No matter what Boston's climate is, I'm sure it would be a relief for you to bask in Florida's sun."

"It might be a relief for you, but you don't know anything about me. I might be a snow bird, and I know even less about you," she said coyly, hoping he picked up that they should disclose a little more information about each other.

"That's easily solved," he shot back. "I'm the public relations manager for Eastern Airlines. I'm not often in the office and almost never assist the customer service representatives. Today, because of increased call volume, I pitched in."

"I guess that qualifies this conversation, our meeting on the telephone, as unusual," she quipped.

"No, special," he said in a voice laden with tenderness.

"Special indeed!" she retorted. "Do you live in Florida?"

"No! I live much closer to you than that. I live in a small town in northern New Jersey. I'm not there often, though. I spend a great deal of my time traveling for the company. What about you? I only know your name." "There's not much to tell," she offered cautiously. "I attend Northeastern University in Boston and will be graduating in the next year. Even so, I'm still unsure of what I want to do for a living."

"Hold on a minute! Why not consider the airline industry. I suggest this not because it's the industry I'm in, but because it's a growing industry," Jackson Douglas offered forcefully.

"Are there really many opportunities for African American women?" Cynthia asked somewhat incredulously.

"You can count on it," he all but screamed into the telephone. He spent five or six minutes citing career opportunities in the airline industry. Finally, his voice slipped from sonorous to soothing.

"I'm not usually this forward," the voice purred, "but you sound like a very interesting young woman and I'd like to talk to you again."

Cynthia was smiling from ear to ear. "Of course; let me give you my number."

He asked if it would be okay for him to call her on Thursday evening around eight o'clock.

That evening Cynthia called Robin to tell her about the man with the mesmerizing voice that she met over the telephone. Robin laughed and said, "If he's as mesmerizing and interesting as you think, why is he picking up women over the telephone? I'll bet you a dollar he's a six-legged toad, and you're the fool who will get warts." She chuckled along with her. *Robin may be right,* she thought.

She convinced herself that it really didn't matter if he called or not. At 7:45 the next Thursday she sat by the telephone reading. At 8:05 the phone rang. It startled her for a moment, and then she heard that voice.

"Hello Cynthia, this is Jack." After the standard pleasantries, he let her know that this was the first time that he had ever met someone on the phone and felt a connection that he wanted to investigate. She had to admit she felt flattered, but she still didn't know who he was. All she knew was that this man had the most sensuous voice she had ever heard. He said he wanted to know more about her. She definitely wanted to know more about him.

He liked jazz, Italian food, good conversation, cognac, and he had a great sense of humor. He professed a desire for honesty in a relationship. It all sounded good to her. They talked about relationships, friends, careers, dreams and aspirations. They discovered that they had a lot in common. Four hours later they were still deep in conversation. They agreed that they would continue their conversation next Thursday when he would call again.

For the next six months, Jack and Cynthia spoke each week on Thursday evening. He recognized and understood her financial constraints and decided that he would make the call each week. Although Robin, Sandra and Cynthia continued their Sister Circle, they realized that graduation would soon send them their separate ways. Robin was headed to New York City to a major brokerage firm. Sandra would return to Atlanta, the only place she ever wanted to be. Cynthia still hadn't decided what she wanted to do. Commencement would be here in a flash. Where did the time go? They had great parties, gossiped a lot, and laughed all the time. They experienced every known emotion together over the last four years and, most important, they developed a friendship that would last a lifetime.

When Jack and Cynthia spoke on their weekly conversations, he actually listened to her as if he really wanted to know what she felt and thought. He wanted to know things that the average man just wasn't interested in, and that was refreshing. His deep baritone voice reminded her of Barry White without the moaning and groaning. His quick wit and thunderous laugh, coupled with his sincere desire to know more about her, allowed her to open up to him in a way that she had never done before or since.

He wanted to know her dating patterns, who was the man, or men, in her life, why she had chosen to be with them, or why she chose to leave them? She told him about her first love, Wesley. And they talked about the imprint that a first love can leave on your life. He also had a first love that he would never forget, and he understood her feelings.

Their conversations were getting more intense, and she was very comfortable with this man. He offered a male perspective on the whole dating game and life in general. She never realized how important the male perspective was in developing, or keeping, a relationship. Over the next few months, Jack enlightened her to the many facets of relationships and the thought process sometimes used by men. It was early November when Jack suggested that after six months on the telephone, perhaps it was time for them to meet. Their telephone relationship had been such a perfect and informative one, a part of her did not want to risk a personal meeting. What if he were a six-legged toad? Jackson Douglas had caught her attention. Now it was time to put a face with a voice.

They decided to spend Thanksgiving together, even though he knew she wasn't much of a cook. After a few digs and jokes about her cooking, she told him that she would use her resourcefulness and friends to help prepare an edible meal. He assured her that as long as there were restaurants and grocery stores in town they wouldn't starve.

The plan was for Jack to take the first shuttle out of New Jersey on Thanksgiving morning, which would put him in Boston at 9:30 A.M. After another twenty minutes of conversation, they agreed that Jack would stay in her guest room since they were much too early in their friendship to be intimate.

Since they hadn't met, Jack wanted to add a little intrigue to their first meeting.

"I will be wearing a chocolate brown suit and carrying a dozen red roses," he told her. "But I would never want you to feel compelled or committed to meeting me, so you will have the option to identify yourself, or walk away."

Cynthia pulled out all of the stops for this Thanksgiving dinner. She spent hours on the phone with Sandra, who was in Atlanta for the holidays, getting what culinary directions she could.

Cynthia had always been a literal person, especially when it comes to directions, so when she was told to wash the turkey, that's exactly what she did, soap and all. When she called Sandra for seasoning and baking directions, she said, "Girl, you really don't have a clue." She scrapped the turkey for a pre-cooked turkey from a local caterer.

On Thanksgiving morning she met the 9:30 shuttle from Newark, New Jersey. As she watched the passengers leave the plane she became apprehensive. What the hell was she doing? She moved toward the exit and stood behind a large column and waited as the passengers continued to leave the plane. When the crowd began to thin and she saw no chocolate brown suit, her heart sank. *Maybe Jack decided not to come,* she thought. Finally, the last few passengers entered the waiting area, and she saw a striking black man wearing an impeccable chocolate brown, three-piece suit, carrying red roses. She thought, *Damn, that brother sure is sharp.* He was wearing the hell out of that suit. It was clear that he took a lot of time and energy and spared no expense in putting his outfit together, down to his keenly polished Stacy Adams shoes.

He was no Billy Dee Williams, but possessed an intriguing aura. He was about six feet two inches tall, medium brown complexion, and about two hundred twenty pounds. He sported a neatly trimmed mustache and a low-cut Afro. Jackson Douglas walked into the room as if he owned it. He was the type of brother that would certainly make you look twice.

She had to step back and reassess herself. Did she look like the kind of woman that a man like this would be interested in? That morning she had gotten up and put some extra time in putting together her outfit. After all, she wanted to make a good impression at their first meeting. She had on a pair of neatly pressed hip-hugger jeans, a bright orange angora sweater, and a pair of suede boots complemented by a matching suede jacket.

She thought she looked damn good. One thing she knew for sure, she had a serious body and she could always get a man's attention, whether she wanted it or not.

She finally mustered up the nerve to leave the shelter of her column. *What the hell, let's go for this.* She dusted off her confidence, stepped out into the middle of the room, strutted up to him, and extended her hand.

"Hello! My name is Cynthia." If this had been a movie, the music would have risen to a crescendo.

He looked at her with a set of beautiful brown eyes, and a big smile came across his face as he handed her a bouquet of red roses.

"Hello Cynthia. I'm Jack, and I'm so very pleased to meet you. I saw you walk across the room and knew exactly who you were."

She began to think that this meeting had the potential to be something special. They gathered his luggage and headed back to her place.

After six months and countless hours on the phone, Cynthia realized that most of their conversations had been about her. Jack knew everything there was to know about her, even things that she had not shared with close girlfriends. This was going to be her opportunity to learn more about him.

Her apartment was sparsely furnished; she could never stand clutter. What she lacked in furniture, she made up for in rugs, throw pillows, color, texture and creativity. She had a flair for color and decorating on a very small budget. The apartment had beautiful hardwood floors, the kind you can see yourself in. The color scheme ignited the apartment; it was composed of tan, orange, white and splashes of red.

She had received many compliments on her apartment, and she knew it was a comfortable place to be. When Jack asked for a tour of the place, she laughed. How much of a tour can you give in a two-bedroom apartment?

They had a beautiful Thanksgiving dinner. She borrowed stemware and china from a friend and, with her own hands, made linen napkins and a linen tablecloth. The atmosphere, the color and the aura were all there. She even bought a bottle of cognac, even though she was not much of a drinker. Jack had mentioned in one of their many conversations that he enjoyed cognac.

He seemed to be really interested in her apartment's decor. Why did she choose these particular colors? Did they have a special meaning for her? She was quite surprised by his questions even though the colors were all chosen for a reason. Who would have expected a man to be insightful enough to notice? Most men who came to her apartment had only one thing in mind and didn't give a damn about the colors that were around them.

She explained the tranquil effect that the muted colors had on her temperament, and the splashes of red represented the fire and excitement that occasionally sparked her life. He understood the impact that color could have in a person's life and added that his goal was to provide a reason for her to add a little more red to her décor. They talked and laughed until the early hours of the morning. Occasionally, he would hold and massage her hands and fingers in the most sensuous way. His touch was deliberate and tender. She learned that he had gotten divorced about three years earlier. He explained it was a mutual agreement to divorce—the best thing for both of them. He had a twenty-year-old son who was a sophomore in college. Jack, to her utter amazement, had recently celebrated his forty-second birthday.

"So! Is that a problem?" he asked at the mention of his age.

"I'll answer that once we define the terms of this relationship," she retorted in an attempt to be witty.

He flashed that beautiful smile, chuckled and said: "I can see why you might be a little apprehensive, although we have talked over the phone for the last six months. This is the first time that we've actually been together, so I can understand that you would be leery of what this relationship could mean. There is one thing about me that I think you should know." He hesitated a brief moment before continuing. "I believe in being honest. I believe in cutting to the chase and hope that whatever relationship we define, you will be equally as honest and get straight to the point."

No problem! Being direct was her style. Over the years she had learned to temper that in order to deal with young men in her age group. Often they didn't want to hear the truth and certainly couldn't handle her directness without becoming offended, or intimidated. Now there sat a man who wanted the truth. She liked that.

"Cynthia, you're an attractive, educated, creative, and articulate woman with a strong future. Your only challenge at this point in your life, baby, is the dating game."

She was surprised at how easily he slipped "baby" into that remark. She was just as surprised how happy she was to hear it.

"You've got to learn to master it. A woman who masters the art of dating will eliminate a lot of unnecessary grief in her life."

His sultry voice took on a seriousness she had not expected. "Because there is almost a twenty-year difference in our ages, I'm not the mate you want for life. I am, however, prepared to be, most important, your friend. I didn't come here to take anything from you. I came to give you what I have: experience, knowledge and a trusting friendship. Let me make this clear, I won't make any sexual advances toward you unless you ask me to."

She didn't know what he expected her to do or say after such a long confessional. Her initial thoughts were negative: *What a cocky dude. What makes him think he's so fine that I would want sex with him? Why does he believe he knows so much that he can just come into my life and teach me everything he believes I needed to know?*

Then she thought, what the hell, she was finishing up her last year in college. She didn't have a lot of time; she was either at school, at work, or studying. A long-distance relationship might be exactly what she needed. Such a relationship doesn't require a lot of time and might add a little spice to her life. As quiet as it's kept, Jack may be just the man to teach her something. It could be worth a try. They agreed it would be a friendship. He would be her teacher, confidant, and friend.

They talked about his views on life, women, success, marriage, children, and friendships. His views were not so drastically different from hers, but she could clearly see that they were tempered by experience. By the end of the evening they found themselves sitting across from each other, Indian style. A combination of the wine, the music, the atmosphere and that sensuous baritone voice made her want to investigate what was under those impeccable clothes he wore. Only the fact that they had agreed that this trip was only to get to know more about each other—no intimacy—kept her restrained. They continued to talk and laugh about almost everything. His sense of humor was great, and laughter was very easy for them. After about fifteen minutes they both agreed that it might be smart to get a little sleep so that he could get to see a little of the city the following day. He gently kissed her forehead and headed for the guest room. As she went to her bedroom, she wondered what she was getting herself into?

Early the next morning, she heard Jack moving about and wondered why he was up so early. She looked at the clock on her nightstand and realized that she had only gotten four hours of sleep. The smell of fresh brewed coffee filled the apartment and was the encouragement she needed to get out of bed. She dragged herself into the bathroom to freshen up and caught her reflection in the mirror. She was wearing one of the sexiest negligees that she owned. She was determined that Jack would at least get to see it. She washed her face, brushed her teeth, and combed her hair; looking good early in the morning was not an easy thing to do, so she added a touch of makeup.

She went into the kitchen and found Jack busy making breakfast and wearing black silk pajamas. The silk bottoms formed a tight mold around an ass that would get any woman's attention, and the black silk T-shirt exposed the body of a man in good physical shape. It was clear that this forty-two-year-old man took great care of his body. He turned to say "Good morning; I hope you had a good night's sleep" and handed her a hot cup of coffee. She learned to drink coffee in college during those late-night study sessions and found that she needed coffee each morning to get her started.

"I hope you don't mind me invading your kitchen; I thought you might like a little breakfast this morning," he said. She sat across the table from him with her silk robe slightly open to expose a black lace teddy, which lifted and displayed her breast. She knew "the girls" would get his attention. Cynthia and Jack chatted for a while about the agenda for the day. Then he said, "Baby, do not assume that I don't notice that beautiful negligee and how damn good you look in it. But you must remember, we've established the rules of the game."

They had a wonderful day, shopping, browsing, and watching people. He seemed to be looking for something in particular. As they toured the mall he took her hand and guided her into a candle shop. The shop was full of candles of all shapes, sizes, and aromas. They left the shop with a bag full of candles. When they got on the escalator she asked him when and how he developed such an interest in candles.

"Candles are the centerpiece of creating atmosphere, and an absolute necessity when developing the senses. I have a house full of them."

Jack was scheduled to leave on the 8:00 P.M. shuttle that evening, so they tried to make the most of the hours they had together. The more he talked, the more she believed that there was a lot he could teach her. During the course of the day he managed to make several gestures that she found sexy and inviting. He would lightly touch her hand, or the small of her back; he would stand very close to her so that she could float in the aroma of his cologne. These were subtle gestures, done in a crowd of people, but she was the only one who could recognize them and she found that refreshing.

When she took him to the airport that evening and he was about to board his plane, he smiled and said, "This has been a wonderful two days." He asked if he could kiss her good-bye. He gently pulled her into his arms; they were a perfect fit. His kiss was soft, tender, and long. She had to admit, it took her breath away.

"I left the candles on your dining room table," he whispered in her ear. "I'll call you Thursday evening; we'll talk about them."

CHAPTER 4

They talked about everything in the Sister Circle, and the first order of business was an update on Cynthia's date with Jack. She told them that dinner was a success and they really enjoyed each other's company. It was a relationship worth developing. By nature Cynthia was still a very private person. She didn't find the need to tell her sisters everything about Jack, at least not yet.

The Thursday following Thanksgiving, at about 7:30, she made herself comfortable and prepared for Jack's call. At eight o'clock sharp the phone rang. When she picked up the receiver, she heard that deep voice.

"Hey, baby, how are you doing?" She closed her eyes and seemed to float outside of herself; that was very scary. When she spoke to him on the phone, her voice changed, her temperament changed, her attitude changed. Could it be that she was trying to be as sensuous as he was? To this day she didn't know if she succeeded, but she tried real hard. After about five minutes of general conversation, he asked her about the candles he had left.

"They're beautiful and have aromas that I've not experienced before."

"I'm glad you find pleasure in them. Light the red candles, dim the lights, and relax."

She did what he said and returned to the phone.

"You know, we human beings don't use our God-given senses effectively. The sense of smell is probably one of the most unused senses in life. When used effectively it can trigger pleasure and pleasant memories," Jack all but chanted. "When you learn to associate aromas with pleasant experiences, you can often use your imagination to re-create parts of that experience. For example, I've always enjoyed coffee, its taste and smell. However, after my visit to Boston the aroma of coffee triggers images of you wearing that black negligee that framed your perfect golden breasts. Approximately two inches above your cleavage was a gold link chain with a small diamond teardrop. The seductive split on the left side of your negligee revealed long shapely legs that wore a small gold ankle bracelet and freshly painted toenails. I mentally photographed your body in that negligee and can recall that image whenever I choose. We have been blessed with five senses, and when used together they can provide many mind-blowing experiences."

Jack was excited, his voice rising on the telephone before he stopped for a moment in his monolog. When he continued, he had the deliberate tone of a teacher.

"Now, let's work on sharpening your sense of smell," he announced over the phone. "Take each of the four scented candles and memorize the aroma of each. To do that, you will need to burn one candle each evening, even as you sleep. You will find that in no time the aroma will be imprinted in your mind. Then you will need to attach a pleasant memory to each of the scents. Use your imagination and have fun with it. As you find new scents, or body oils, add them to your collection. I have given you four candles: Jasmine, sandalwood, Amber, and Narcissus. I have found them to be relaxing and seductive."

She had to admit that there were certain aromas that triggered pleasant memories of people and events in her life. Jack suggested that she take the time to use those aromas and her imagination to fully develop those memories. Her first thought was Canoe cologne and Wesley.

Graduation was approaching fast, and the Sister Circle grew tighter every day. Sandra and Jason had gotten engaged over the Thanksgiving holiday and planned an August wedding. She asked Cynthia and Robin to stay close to her during this time, to help her through the pressures of their last semester in college. Her mother had already made wedding plans Sandra didn't like. Sandra was determined to have two maids of honor. Her mother thought it proper to have one. She pressed Robin and Cynthia to go with her to wedding expos, various bridal shops, and had them look through wedding magazines to find just the right bridal gown and dresses for the bridal party.

However, Sandra's mother convinced them to try Atlanta; she was sure that Sandra would find exactly what she wanted there. For years Sandra had described Atlanta as her own piece of heaven. Finally, they were going to see for themselves.

Jack arranged three round-trip tickets from Boston to Atlanta at an excellent price, and on February 10 they arrived in Atlanta. Sandra's parents met them at the airport, and they headed to her home in Decatur, just outside of Atlanta. Sandra's mother was a petite woman who clearly took great pride in her appearance. She wore a tailored winter white wool suit. She moved with an air that made her seem aloof and cold. Sandra had often told them about her mother's public image, and they witnessed it.

They finally pulled into a long driveway lined with magnolias. Robin and Cynthia were awed by the size of Sandra's home—a huge brick with eight white columns lining the front. There were extra large multi-paned windows on the first floor.

"I wonder where the slave quarters are?" Robin whispered to Cynthia. They both laughed. They entered this antebellum-style mansion through two large oak double doors that were adorned with large brass knockers.

The foyer was done in beige and white mosaic tile with a large crystal chandelier that hung high above a set of cascading stairs. At the top of the stairs on the second floor was a very large picture window, which allowed the sunlight to bounce off the chandelier. The living room, or public area, was decorated with French provincial furniture resting on a white carpet. Robin and Cynthia smiled at each other.

"Now, this is what money can do for you," Robin whispered in her ear.

"I'm sure you would know," Cynthia shot back at her.

Later that evening at dinner, they met Sandra's mother's other side. In reality, she is a very warm and graceful woman. She embraced them as Sandra's sisters and thanked them for being a part of Sandra's life while she was in Boston. By the third round of drinks, Sandra's mother told them that basically she was just a poor southern girl blessed to run into a man who loved her and could provide her with all of these material things. The first few years of marriage were rough. She developed an outside and an inside image, felt she had to. By the time Sandra was born she had perfected these images and was prepared to live this new life. She wanted Sandra to live the best of both worlds and wanted to be sure that she remembered where she came from. She believed that Boston was a wonderful experience for Sandra and thanked them for keeping her rooted in her heritage.

It was a whirlwind five days of shopping and trying on dresses all day. In the evening they held Sandra's hand, made jokes, and assured her that everything would be okay. On the fourth day Sandra found her dress. It was spectacular—pricey, but spectacular. Robin said Sandra looked like Scarlet O'Hara in *Gone with the Wind*.

Sandra's mother, who finally accepted that there were going to be two maids of honor, made sure that their dresses met her approval. At last, they had a free day to see Atlanta. Sandra took them everywhere. They couldn't help but notice that there were black folks in Atlanta who were well-off. They also noticed poverty in the South was more exposed than it was in the North. Shotgun houses, red dirt, and heat made poverty uniform in the South. At least in the North there were seasons that would sometimes mask poverty, if only for a moment during a slow-moving winter snowstorm.

Sandra had spent the last three years telling the sisters about her grandmother, Mama Lee. Naturally, they wanted to meet her. They were scheduled to spend the next evening at Mama Lee's. They packed their overnight bags and headed toward a small town outside of Atlanta called Eatonton. Mama Lee had no use for the city and made it perfectly clear that she would never live there. Her house was a small two-bedroom that clearly was a throwback to the shotgun houses of the old South. Sandra's parents made sure that Mama Lee had everything she needed. They made regular improvements to the house. The exterior had recently been painted, and the lawn was neatly kept.

Inside the house were the family's memorabilia. Mama Lee guarded them like a sentry at a military camp. Mama Lee was a beautiful woman in her day and had the pictures to prove it. She was everything that Sandra had described, a petite gray-haired woman with light brown skin and light eyes. Her sharp nose and thin lips implied that there was a Caucasian connection to the family. She held the wisdom of the past, understood the issues and concerns of the present, and gave us great insight and suggestions for the future. Mama Lee welcomed them at the door.

"Y'all ain't no strangers. I've talked to each of you enough that y'all are family now," she said. She had never personally met them. However, they had spoken on the phone many times over the last few years, and she had given each of them some sound advice. After dinner, they sat around her fireplace and talked for hours.

She told them about her life as a black woman growing up in the South and about the lack of opportunities for women, especially black women. Robin and Cynthia were captivated by her stories, stories that Sandra had heard many times; but for the first time Sandra was really listening. It was almost like having another sister in the circle. They talked about choosing men, a topic that they disagreed on. Mama Lee gave them her views.

"I've been listening to you girls for the last three years, and I can tell that y'all have grown a lot. But Mama's gonna tell y'all some things I think you need to know. Don't let your life stop for no man. You got careers, something that I could never have. Live life, go places, see things, and build pleasant memories. When you get my age that may be all you got. If something ain't working, fix it or let it go. Don't spend your time trying to make something happen that ain't. Remember, whatever you do, y'all ain't gonna change no man. He is gonna be who he is. Watch how he treats his mama. He won't treat you no better than that.

"Now! That boy Jason, I like him. He's a good boy, but he ain't gonna let Sandra grow. Y'all been friends a long time; don't let silly things come between that friendship. If something goes wrong, talk to each other and forgive each other. You will be lucky to have three real friends in your entire life. Stick together! This life is rough, and y'all gonna need each other. Now the last thing that I'm gonna tell you is to celebrate life each year that the good

Lord gives you. Don't wallow in self-pity and past mistakes; get up, dust yourself off, and move on with your life."

It was a beautiful experience to sit with Mama Lee and watch the pain and joy in her face as she talked to them. Over the years, they fell back on her words on many occasions.

On the evening before they left Atlanta, they went to a place called Underground Atlanta to party southern style. Robin and Cynthia were a novelty for the southern men; and they took advantage of the attention. Nevertheless, they decided that between the heat, the slowness of the men and the status consciousness of the people, Atlanta was a nice place to visit, but they wouldn't want to live there.

When they got back to Boston, they continued their weekly Sister Circle and agreed that they were a little concerned about their lives after graduation. They would always need each other's support and insight, so they decided that the first Sunday of each month would be the day that each of them would talk to the other two. Because they would not all be in the same city, they vowed to meet in 1980 when the youngest one of them turned thirty. Thereafter, they would meet every ten years at what they called the "Turning."

Over the next few months, Jack and Cynthia continued to talk every Thursday evening. They had profound conversations about the five senses, and she learned to appreciate each sense more. She began to hear music a little differently as she was introduced to new jazz artists such as Julian "Cannonball" Adderley, Ramsey Lewis, Norman Connors, and John Coltrane. She now had a wide selection of music and could establish moods for almost any situation through music. She began to truly experience and appreciate sunrises, sunsets, full moons, and colors. She widened her vision and learned to capture mental pictures of things that she wanted to remember.

Their most memorable conversation was related to the senses and their impact on the brain. For the first time Jack wanted to talk about her previous sexual experiences. She had become so comfortable with him that it was easy to disclose her uneventful and often unfulfilling sex life. He listened intently as she told him about her first awakening with Wesley, her disappointing experience with Gregory, and her last year of celibacy. She explained that she was celibate only because she didn't have the time to develop a relationship. She just couldn't get into random sex.

Jack believed that most women spent their entire lives chasing an orgasm, with little knowledge of how their bodies need to be handled and how a brother needs to be directed. Every woman's body and desires are different, and a brother whose intention is to make love to a woman really needs directions.

"Sex, like clothing, comes in different styles," Jack said. "There's basic fucking that requires a penis, a vagina, and little else. Then there's having sex that requires at least a connection between two people. Then there's making love; that requires a physical, emotional, and sometimes spiritual connection. At the core of lovemaking are the five senses.

"Baby, it's now time for you to tell me how to make love to you. I will have no problems telling you what I need."

For a moment she was speechless. No one had ever asked her that question before. He knew she was stumped for an answer.

"We'll get back to that question a little later," Jack said and moved the conversation forward. "Right now I want you to take off your clothes."

She wasn't sure that she heard him correctly. "What did you just ask me?"

"This might sound strange, but believe me, I know what I'm doing. Take off your clothes. Light two of your favorite candles, dim the lights, get comfortable, and let's resume this conversation." She followed his directions and returned to the telephone.

Jack's voice took over. "I'm going to take you on an imaginary trip. In order to enjoy this trip you will need to do as I ask. Please don't ask questions, just answer those that I give you. I need you to close your eyes and try not to think about anything other than this moment. I don't want you to think about school, money, your Sister Circle, or anything else that goes on in your day-to-day life."

He spoke slowly with long pauses between his directions. "First, I want you to lightly massage the back of your neck in a circular motion. Close your eyes and appreciate the feeling. You should feel some of the tension leaving your body. Now slowly move your hands down the front of your neck, out to the left, and continue the soft circular movements on your shoulders. Now move slowly to your right shoulder and continue the circular movement. I want you to continue to follow my directions as I take off my clothes and lay down beside you.

"I want you to guide my hands over your left breast, very slowly, applying just the amount of pressure that will please you. Now move to the right breast and lightly circle the nipple. How does that feel? I can't hear you, baby. I need to know if this pleases you."

"Yes, Jack, it's very pleasing."

"As my tongue gently circles your navel my hands are caressing your tight waist and moving to your smooth round buttocks. I could stay there forever, but I've got this urgency to taste more of your body. Now guide my hands down to your vagina; don't forget to apply pressure where you want it. You know this area much better than I do. Put my hands, or tongue, where you want them to be. I've got all the time you need, and I'm prepared to do whatever you want. What do you need from me? Come on, baby! Talk to me!"

She regained a little composure and realized that she had passed the point of being shy or inhibited. She needed to tell him what to do. She began to tell him how to touch her body, and he verbally followed her directions. Within minutes she had the second most intense orgasm of her life.

Jack was quiet for a while.

"It's nice to know that you can be very verbal about sex when put in the right circumstances," he said.

They both chuckled.

"I now have the answer to my original question," he sighed. "Good sex begins in the head, and a brother who can't get into your head and stimulate your brain should not be given the pleasure of getting into your panties."

The Sister Circle continued and they decided to have one last party before graduation. After all, they held the title of campus socialites for the past four years and wanted to go out in a big bang. Robin found an area nightspot that fit their budget. The evening before graduation, they began to party at about 10:00

P.M. and had a full house. They invited everyone they knew to celebrate with them—old boyfriends, new boyfriends, and prospective boyfriends. Cynthia contacted some old friends and found out that Wesley was no longer in town. She really wanted him to attend, particularly since she had just put him on her "list of things to do"; maybe next time.

Robin knew the club owner; therefore they were still partying hard at 4:30 in the morning, which was not standard in Boston. By 10:00 the next morning they sat dressed in their caps and gowns, many of them still hung over from the night before, waiting for commencement to begin. Sandra had applied for a teaching position and was packed and ready to go back to Georgia. She still had a wedding to plan. Jason had accepted a position in Georgia with a major engineering firm that offered a great salary and plenty of company perks. Robin had moved back to New York and came back just for graduation. She accepted a job on Wall Street and began training as a trader.

Cynthia, however, had applied for a few positions, but had not yet received an offer. Commencement was not a happy occasion; they were all going in different directions, were expected to make their mark on the world, and were wondering if they could live up to the expectations. Finally, their Sister Circle would be spread out over three states, and they knew they would truly miss their weekly meetings.

Cynthia finally got a few job offers and chose to work for United Parcel Service in the customer relations and sales department. They offered an excellent salary; she wasn't confined to an office, and the package included stock options. She was scheduled to begin July 1. That gave her a month to get herself prepared. She decided to revisit her "list of things to do." It was time to check off her accomplishments and add new ones. Life was moving on.

CHAPTER 5

Cynthia wanted a different look. Perhaps it stemmed from Sandra's pending wedding, or her introduction to the corporate world. Whatever the cause, she felt the need for a change. The Afro was definitely the style of the 1970s and she truly enjoyed the low maintenance it provided, but time for the Afro was up. She contacted several friends, looking for a good hairdresser; they suggested Tracy's Hair Salon.

The salon was located in the heart of a black neighborhood and had a two-week waiting list for new customers. According to everyone, Tracy's was the best shop in town, so Cynthia took her place on the new customers list. For the first time in four years she had three weeks all to herself. It was time to decide which of the few short-term items on her "list of things to do" would get accomplished during those three weeks. There was only one of two things on the list she could accomplish in such a short time—find Wesley, or learn to give full body massages. Learning to give a full body massage seemed like the thing to do; she really wasn't ready to find Wesley.

She thumbed through the telephone directory and found a great offer for instructions on the art of massage offered by a downtown massage parlor. The classes lasted over a five-day period and promised to put magic in her hands. After registering, she was scheduled to begin at 9 A.M. on a Monday morning. She was really looking forward to it.

Public transportation was the only sensible way to travel downtown. As she waited for the eight o'clock bus, she gave a special thanks to God that she would only have to do this for five days. It was summer; as she rode the bus that evening, she got flashbacks from 1958 of children playing street games, and mothers sitting on stoops discussing the day's events. She could still hear the rhythm of the street.

During the 1970s brothers seemed to have a fascination with their dicks and would stand around on street corners, prancing and hollering at the women while the brothers fondled their dicks. A friend once told Cynthia that the black man held his dick so the white man wouldn't try to take it, like he took everything else. The last thing Cynthia needed in her life was a dick-dancing brother.

On the way home that evening, she stopped in the corner store to get the newspaper and literally ran into Sharon, the loudest sister from her high school gossip group. They hadn't seen each other for almost seven years and decided that they needed to catch up on each other's life. She said that most of the old group still got together once a month on Friday evenings. She invited Cynthia to join them. She thought that it might be fun to see old friends and agreed to meet at Sharon's house at eight o'clock that very night.

Sharon lived in one of Boston's many public housing developments. Her apartment was on the fifth floor. As Cynthia got on the elevator the stench of urine was overpowering. A combination of graffiti, trash, and neglect made it clear that financially Sharon was struggling. Once inside the apartment, she could see that Sharon worked hard to keep her apartment neat and clean in spite of the surrounding conditions. It was a wonderful reunion. They laughed, joked, drank, and dug up old memories.

Cynthia found out that Wesley and Carolyn had gotten a divorce. *What comes around goes around*, she thought to herself. Carolyn needed to pay for her past treachery. Cynthia hoped there was another woman involved.

They finally began to talk seriously about where they were in their lives and where they wanted to go. As the conversation continued, the evening got a little depressing to Cynthia. Sharon had two children and never completed high school; but, oddly enough, she seemed okay with that. Juanita had four children, all with different fathers; and she didn't see a problem with her life.

Gwendolyn had just moved back to town after a two-year stay in New York, chasing her dream. The only thing she found in New York was drugs and promises. She had been clean for six months and intended to stay that way.

Phyllis was not able to join the group; she was finishing a twelve-month sentence for assault and battery. She found her man with another woman, beat the hell out of him with a baseball bat, and made the woman watch. They had to laugh, because that was her style; she always wanted an audience when she performed.

Cynthia didn't want to seem pompous or better than anyone, so she simply told them about her new job with UPS. She knew at that moment although she liked these women and could enjoy their company occasionally, they had very little in common and would probably not spend much time together.

Cynthia told them that she was in the process of changing her style to fit corporate America and had decided to give up her Afro.

"If you're gonna get a new style, you would really want to go to Tracy's; that sister can really hook up a head," Gwendolyn chimed in as if she were a personal advocate for Tracy's.

Cynthia told them that she was on a two-week waiting list for new customers.

"Girl please! Tracy's my girl; I can get her to do you faster than that," Sharon said. "As a matter of fact, let me see if she wants to join us for a few drinks this evening."

She called Tracy from another room and then returned to tell them that Tracy was going to join them after her last customer.

Everyone in the room was a comedian. They laughed until they cried. About 10:30 P.M. Tracy joined them. The famous and elusive Tracy was just hanging out with Cynthia's home girls. She was a striking woman with smooth, dark skin and wore little to no makeup. She really didn't need it. Her skin was flawless. Her hair was expertly cut into a very short-layered style that complemented her face beautifully. She wore two diamond studs; and it was clear that she took pride in her appearance.

Sharon introduced Cynthia to Tracy. "This is my home girl. You can look at her head and tell that she needs your help. Can you hook her up?"

"How about tomorrow evening, about 8 P.M.? I can fit you in as my last customer," Tracy said, smiling.

Cynthia had just moved up eight days on the new customers list.

She met Tracy at 8:00 Saturday evening and was surprised at the décor and professionalism of her shop. Cynthia had in her head that old stereotypical image of a beauty parlor—storefront, bootleggers, loud women, and gossip. Tracy's shop was decorated in black, white and silver; extremely neat, with light jazz playing in the background. She asked if Cynthia would mind being shampooed by another stylist and said she would finish her personally.

By 9:00, Tracy was blow-drying Cynthia's hair and talking about the tough day she was having. The shop was clearing out, and Tracy and Cynthia were the only ones left.

"This business ain't easy. People think I've got it made 'cause I got plenty of customers. They don't know how hard I have to work."

Tracy wasn't complaining. She just needed to vent, and Cynthia had always been good at listening.

"Girl, I'm sorry for laying all that on you," Tracy said. "But sometimes it gets to be too much."

"I know that's right."

As Cynthia listened, Tracy talked about the long hard hours, the attitudes of some customers, keeping good staff, and trying to cultivate a social life. Before she knew it, they were sitting with their feet up, sipping wine, listening to jazz, and deep into conversation about life, life choices, and outcomes.

Cynthia learned that Tracy had a bachelor's degree from Howard University and ended up in Boston after a bad relationship. Cynthia had only known her for a few days, but she found that they had at least one thing in common—the need to succeed. Tracy didn't need a lot from Cynthia; she just needed someone to listen and talk to. They talked until midnight, and she began to understand why Tracy worked as hard as she did. Cynthia had always been a good listener; people tended to bare their souls to her. But more important, she had always been able to help others think through tough situations. Finally, after midnight they exchanged telephone numbers and promised to get together for dinner.

Cynthia continued with her standing Thursday evening dates with Jack, and truly looked forward to them. She kept him apprised of what was going on in her life, her new job, and reconnecting with old friends. Jack and Cynthia had become good friends; he kept her grounded, focused, and inquisitive. She didn't tell him about her massage classes, she wanted it to be a surprise when they met again. Since meeting Jack, she had become a little more selective about the men that she dated, which reduced the numbers of groupers and braggers. A man had to be able to hold a reasonable conversation to get her attention; no matter how good he looked.

Her new job proved to be an excellent choice. In August, the company gave her the time she needed to attend Sandra's wedding. Cynthia was a regional sales representative and enjoyed not being chained to a desk from nine to five each day.

The regional office was downtown and had the whitest environment that she had have ever experienced, including being a black college student in a predominately white college. After all, it was the 1970s, and black folks were just beginning to get the training they needed to compete in corporate America. The pay was excellent and the possibility of promotion was good. She took full advantage of the employee stock options, with the strong urging of Robin.

Sandra's wedding was scheduled for August 20. Robin and Cynthia had agreed to be in Atlanta a week before the ceremonies to help Sandra keep her sanity and deal with the last-minute details. Cynthia drove to New York to spend the weekend with Robin. They left for Atlanta early Monday morning. Robin and Cynthia were up all night catching up with each other's life. Robin was having a wonderful time working on Wall Street. Her career and money were still her priority.

For Robin the best thing about a relationship with a man was the thrill of the hunt. When the hunt was over she got bored very quickly. Her dating style was considered very masculine. She let a brother know in no uncertain terms that just because she slept with him, that didn't make her his woman. She chose her men the way most people choose an outfit—for the occasion, for the style, and for the fit.

She was a regular in the New York social scene, from formal events to weekend cocktail parties, but not often with the same man on her arm. After about thirty minutes of trying to convince Cynthia to go out and see the city, they settled in for the evening. Cynthia had been to New York many times and had seen about as much of the city as she wanted.

They were still a little concerned about Jason's chauvinistic attitude, but decided that they would support Sandra no matter what. Robin talked about the climate on Wall Street and the rush she felt watching the market each day. Cynthia told Robin about her position at UPS, and she reminded her again to take full advantage of the company's stock options.

Robin truly believed that she would be ready to retire in her early fifties and took every opportunity to prepare for it. She didn't want to leave her sisters behind. After all whom would she have to party with? She was determined to make Sandra and Cynthia smart investors. With Robin's knowledge and determination, they knew Robin could do it.

Jack came through again. He arranged two round-trip tickets from New York to Atlanta, first-class.

"It looks like that old man has a little class," Robin said. "When you begin to earn a decent living, you won't have to travel in the ass end of a plane."

Once in Atlanta they gathered their luggage and met Sandra. They were all happy to see each other and screamed like high school girls in the middle of the baggage claim area. Sandra had a full itinerary planned for their six days in Atlanta. She didn't plan anything for the day they arrived. She knew they needed to catch up in the only way they knew how, the Sister Circle.

Sandra was very excited that evening and insisted on going first.

"I got so much to tell y'all," she told us. "I can tell my man is going to one day be a six-figure man," was the first thing she said about Jason. As for herself, she had taken a teaching position and would be responsible for twenty-three, fifth-grade students in September.

Her parents gave her an early wedding gift, a reasonable down payment on their first starter home, and she was going to enjoy a month of house hunting before starting work. She then began to tell us about the changes in the wedding plans. The original plans were simple but elegant: one hundred and fifty guests, two maids of honor, and three limos. Her mother took charge of the wedding as soon as Robin and Cynthia left last February. Even though her mother turned the occasion into the wedding of the century, Sandra and Jason let her have her way, with a few exceptions. The wedding now had a guest list of two hundred people, horse-drawn buggies, and a much larger church. Sandra held firm on two maids of honor.

Jason chose groomsmen he thought Robin and Cynthia might be interested in ("I really want Robin and Cynthia to have a good time," he told Sandra). Over the next four days they visited every shop, boutique, and mall in the area trying to add the finishing touches to the wedding. They set aside Friday as spa day: hair, manicures, pedicures, and massages for the ladies. All of the bridal party, including Sandra's mother, her aunt, and Mama Lee, joined them for this relaxing experience. Mama Lee pushed her chair back from the table, looked at Robin and Cynthia and asked a direct question.

"Okay, when y'all gonna do this?"

Robin laughed out loud before answering. "Mama Lee, right now my man is my career and I need to figure out what I want to do with my life."

Mama Lee looked at Cynthia, smiled, and said, "Baby, you don't have to say nothing; I know what you gonna say. You're gonna tell me that getting married is not on your 'list of things to do.'"

"Mama Lee, you're right. Maybe one day; but right now I need to know exactly who I am and how I could fit into someone else's life. I don't want to be an unhappy wife or mother."

Unfortunately, most of the married women she knew were the loneliest women that she knew. They were always home being a wife and mother, while their husbands were busy attending the clubs and social gatherings. There was one thing that Robin and Cynthia could say for certain. When they were alone, they were not lonely; and being alone was usually a choice.

Mama Lee entertained them with stories about the childhoods of Sandra and her mother. She told them more stories about the South, and some funny stories about her dating years. There were four girls growing up in her house. Her father had a hard time remembering the names of their suitors, so he called them all Jam Buggas. They laughed, not so sure what a Jam Bugga was, but felt certain that they knew a few.

The wedding went off without a hitch. Directed by Sandra's mother, everyone was in place, on time, looking good and following directions. Cynthia's escort was one of Jason's new southern friends; he was a very dark, clean-shaven brother about six feet two with a deep baritone voice. Later that evening Cynthia thanked Jason for the effort, but the brother just had no style or flair. The brother was quite infatuated by her breasts; even in conversation he never looked her in the eye. Robin thought it was hilarious and pulled Cynthia to the side to say, "You let the 'girls' out and you got that man feigning." Robin was right; the "girls" were definitely out that night.

Robin was paired with a smooth, light brown brother who was a little too beefy for her style. He was finishing up his MBA at Howard. She said the brother was just a little too cocky. Robin and her escort spent most of the evening challenging their knowledge of the business world, and occasionally it got a little heated. Cynthia spent the evening trying to get her escort to look her in the eye. In spite of it all, they were determined to celebrate the event, laughing, dancing barefoot, and having a blast. Jason and Sandra were right in the middle of the celebration. About two o'clock in the morning everyone said good-byes to Jason and Sandra. They wouldn't see Sandra for a while. They were headed off on their honeymoon.

Robin and Cynthia went back to Sandra's mother's house to get some sleep before their early-morning flight home. They had just gotten into bed when Sandra's mother came in, sat on the bed and wanted to talk. Again, she thanked them for being Sandra's friend and hoped that they would always be in her life because Sandra seemed to thrive when they were around.

"I believe that Jason is a very good man and that he will be good to my child; but if he's not, don't let my child wallow in self-pity," she said. "Sandra is a tender-hearted woman. She will tolerate things much longer than the average woman. When she gives, she gives all that she has."

They promised her that they would always be there for Sandra, just as she would always be there for them.

On Sunday morning they were headed back to New York. Robin convinced Cynthia to attend a "Making Millions" seminar on Sunday evening and head for home on Monday. On Monday, by 7 A.M., Robin was gone. Rush-hour traffic in New York is a nightmare for anyone, so Cynthia decided to take her time, have some breakfast, and get on the road at about 10:00 A.M., just behind the morning rush. She arrived home at about two o'clock, kicked off her shoes, and sat down to read her mail.

In the mail was a small envelope the size and shape of an invitation. *This must be another reason to spend money on a gift,* she thought. This year had been unusually full of birthdays, bridal showers, and other reasons to spend money. She opened the envelope and read the note: "I got your address from Sharon and would just like to thank you for listening and allowing me to bend your ear. It is not often that you find a woman you can connect with and is willing to listen to what's going on in your life. Thank you very much, Tracy."

Cynthia thought, *Now here's a woman that everyone in the city thinks has her life together. She makes damn good money, owns a lucrative business, but she has no one that she can relate to. That could be me, if I had not been blessed to have Robin and Sandra.*

Cynthia's mother finally remarried and moved back to Alabama. Cynthia took great care not to let her know that she thought her new husband was shady. He treated her mother well, and that's all that was important. Her mother knew and understood that Cynthia didn't want to go back to Alabama, so they spoke on the phone at least once each week. Vivian, who had been Cynthia's lifeline for so many years, married and moved from Boston; they lost contact. Her Sister Circle was always her sounding board, so there was always someone there for her when she needed an ear. Apparently, Tracy needed caring people around and was having a hard time finding them.

On her next Thursday night telephone date with Jack, she thanked him for the tickets and told him about her trip to

Atlanta. He listened intently as he always did and occasionally asked questions. He wanted to know if she had met any interesting young men on the trip. She told him that she met several young men, but the one she thought might be the most interesting was her escort for the wedding. She described him and told Jack that for a very brief moment the young man reminded her of him. But, like many young men, he didn't have any style or finesse and spent the evening talking to her breasts. One day he might be a decent catch, but right now he was still a little rough and immature.

Jack chucked. "Well, how would you know? You didn't give the young brother a chance."

"It doesn't take long to know if you have anything in common with a man. I talked to him and watched him move. I knew it wouldn't work." After about ten minutes into the conversation, she just couldn't keep her little secret any longer. She had to tell Jack about the massage classes.

"What prompted you to make that decision?" Jack asked.

She had been doing her homework and remembered their conversations about the five senses. Her imagination was active and didn't need a lot of work. Her sense of smell had become much keener. Her sense of sight had developed so that she saw angles, curves, and colors she hadn't imagined before. She learned to appreciate sound and developed an ear for many types of music. Taste was probably her biggest challenge. However, even there she had experienced a wide range of new flavors and textures and even learned to like oysters on occasion.

She always thought that touch was a simple and very direct sense. She figured if you could feel the difference in textures that was all there was. She learned that touch is multifaceted. It includes not only understanding how you want or need to be touched, but also understanding how to touch others. So she took a course in the art of a sensuous massage. She learned that there are probably eight to ten areas of the body that are especially sensitive to touch.

"Baby, you've become quite a perceptive young woman," Jack said. "You've really been on top of your homework. I'm impressed. You know it's been a long time since we've seen each other."

"You're right. I don't know much about sports, but I've always thought that a good coach needs to be in contact with his players so that they understand how the game is to be played. You've been coaching me for quite a while, and I think it's time to play the game," she said, being quite forward.

"I think I understand what you're saying, but let me be sure," Jack countered. "Are you saying that, as your coach, I can come to Boston, hold you in my arms and make love to you?"

"You're right, the only way I can know if I have skills in the game is to get my coach's approval."

"Baby, you don't know how long I've been waiting for you to tell me this. I didn't think you were ever going to be ready."

They both laughed, then she realized that she had been ready for quite a while; she just didn't know how to tell him. He asked her to check her schedule to see if she could get away during the Christmas holidays. He said he wanted to spend Christmas and New Year's with her. That would give them about eight to ten days together; he hoped that wouldn't be too long.

"If you can get the time, I'll make sure that you are entertained for eight to ten days."

"I'm pretty sure that I can arrange it. I'll get back to you on Thursday."

CHAPTER 6

Tracy kept popping up in Cynthia's mind. So Cynthia decided to stop in to see her on her way home from work one Friday, just to see how she was doing. As usual, the shop was full of sisters. It seemed that everyone had some place to go that night. The place was jumping. Tracy was working on a petite woman who almost disappeared under the covering used to protect customers' clothes. Tracy introduced Cynthia to Rosa, an old friend. They exchanged greetings.

"Girl, it's been like this all week long. All I really want to do is kick back, take my shoes off and relax a while. What you doing Sunday?"

"Actually, I don't have any plans."

"Good! Let's get together for dinner. I'll meet you at Sidney's at six o'clock."

Tracy was looking tired that day and seemed to have a lot on her mind.

Cynthia had a date with William, a big country boy who had a reputation as a ladies' man. The brother was definitely fine, and his initial approach wasn't bad. He had tickets to see Stevie Wonder. After the show, they had drinks at one of the neighborhood bars. The bar was a very popular social attraction, and black people were out, dressed and having a good time. She was actually having fun. She hadn't danced that much in quite a while.

A few hours and four or five drinks later, her date lost some of his cool. He told her what he had planned for the rest of the evening: specifically, take her back to her place and "knock it out . . . ride it . . . kill it . . . tear it up."

At this point, she had to tell the brother that her body wasn't available for his entertainment. He looked quite puzzled and wanted to know the problem.

"Look! I'm not the kind of woman to be ridden, killed, knocked out, or torn up. It sounds as if you need to get to a horse stable for your riding pleasure."

The date went quickly downhill after that.

Sunday at six o'clock she met Tracy at Sidney's, one of the better restaurants in the South End of Boston. They sat down to have dinner, and the first thing that Tracy said was "I really need a drink before dinner." Cynthia ordered a glass of wine, and Tracy ordered Scotch on the rocks and began to chat.

"Cynthia, it ain't easy. Every time I think things are going to be smooth, shit happens. I've been in this business a long time, and I do pretty good at it. Whenever I feel like I'm getting control of my life, something, or someone, pops into it. Did you notice the young woman who was sitting in the chair when you came into the shop Friday?"

"Yes."

"She's a very old friend. We met years ago in high school and became very close, but the friendship became draining and brings back bad memories for me. She's married to an abusive man. Every time I see her it seems there's another scar or wound. She says she loves him. They have two children, and she can't afford to leave. It makes me extremely angry, what this man is doing to her."

"Tracy, I can clearly understand why you would be angry, but she has made the choice to stay with him," I said, trying to be objective.

"You're right, Cynthia. "But you don't understand. I lived in the Midwest most of my life with my mother and stepfather. My stepfather was a vicious, heartless man. He hit my mother often, and there was nothing I could do. I was only twelve years old at the time. He was just an all-around mean and hateful son of a bitch. One day I came home from school at about three o'clock, and my mother wasn't home. I came in to do what I normally do: change my clothes, do my homework, and do the chores that my mother expected. While I was in the process of changing my clothes, my stepfather came into my room.

" 'You're twelve years old now, and it's time you learned a little about life,' he snarled at me. Before I could say anything, he unzipped his pants. I wasn't sure what he had in mind, but I knew that I was scared as hell. Before I knew what was happening he threw me on the bed and continued to take off his clothes. I guess I was about to learn a little about life. I was breathing harder and sweating when I jumped off the bed and ran for the door. He grabbed me by the hair and threw me back on the bed; he was all over me cussing and spitting. I began fighting and crying.

" 'No sense in you carrying on like that.' His voice actually sounded tender. 'Hush!' He hissed into my ears while pressing his hardness on my body. 'One day you will thank me for this,' he said.

"I fought and cried, but he wouldn't let me go. He pressed on. My body was not only violated, my spirit would never be the same. I was twelve years old. When it was over, I crawled under the bed crying and frightened. I promised God that I would never allow another man to touch me that way.

"When mother came home, she knew something was wrong. Usually, I met her at the door. This time I was locked in my room praying for the strength to kill this man if he came into my room again.

"She knocked on the door and called my name several times. She looked at me and asked what happened. Through my tears and anger I told her what my stepfather had done.

"She gritted her teeth, and her face turned into something I had never seen before. Her voice changed into something that was calculated and measured.

" 'Tracy, I want you to lock this door behind me, and whatever you do, do not leave this room until I come and get you.'

"Then, she stormed out of the room, slamming the door. I heard her yelling at the top of her voice. My mother never cursed, but then she cursed, screamed, and threatened to kill my stepfather.

"He responded to her in his usual angry and disrespectful way. I can hear him now: 'Bitch, are you losing your mind?' All of this was played out while dishes and glasses were crashing, and mother screaming at him in a way I had never heard before. She sounded like a wounded animal. I couldn't stay in that room. Mother needed me. I ran downstairs into the kitchen and saw my stepfather standing over mother, beating her unmercifully. He kept hitting her over and over again. Blood was everywhere. Through her pain she must have seen me because she kept yelling: 'Run, Tracy! Run, Tracy! Get out of here!' I couldn't move. Fear paralyzed me as I watched him beat my mother viciously on her head and face. Like a machine, he struck her over and over. Finally, she stopped screaming.

"Only then did he stop hitting her and calmly walked over to the kitchen sink, washed the blood off of his hands, grabbed his coat and walked out of the door. I looked at my mother as she lay on the floor. She wasn't breathing, and blood was everywhere. When I finally got control of myself, I ran for help; I ran to our next-door neighbor's house. I ran past the hedges that divided the property, and a hand reached out and grabbed me. I just knew that it was him—my stepfather! I began fighting and screaming. *He would have to kill me this time*, I thought. A voice kept pleading, 'Calm down! Calm down! It's me, Mrs. Cole.'

"Mrs. Cole was our next-door neighbor. She heard the fight and had already called the police.

" 'Mama is hurt and needs help,' " I told her.

"The police arrived, and shortly after a city ambulance. Within minutes they had placed my mother on a stretcher, covered her body with a white sheet, and took her away. She was dead and I had watched her get beaten to death. Since then, life for me has never been the same.

"Aunt Mimi told me the police found my stepfather in a neighborhood bar, drunk, shortly after the murder. He was scheduled to go to trial, and Aunt Mimi was concerned that I might not have the courage to testify. I told her that I really wanted to be there; I wanted to do everything in my power to make sure that this man paid for what he did to me and to my mother.

"The trial was very quick. I stepped to the witness stand and told them exactly what happened. I looked him straight in his eye as I told the story. He stared back at me and I refused to turn away. I stared directly in his face. I wanted to look directly into his soul and snatch out his heart. If looks could kill, he would have been dead on the spot. I had such intense hatred for this man, nothing else mattered. At twelve years old I promised myself that if they did not put him away for life, then I would kill him. He was sentenced to twenty-five years to life in the Ohio state penitentiary. I made a mental note to check with the Ohio state penitentiary in 1986, just to be sure that he was still there.

"Aunt Mimi is my mother's oldest sister; she took me in to live with her in Cleveland. She was a sweet and caring woman who lived in a small house with her husband and two children. Both of my cousins were a lot older than I and were rarely home. It was usually Aunt Mimi, Uncle Joe, and me.

"Uncle Joe was a nice man and did his best to make me laugh, but little did he know that I would never trust another man in life. I didn't want to be left alone with Uncle Joe, even though he had never done anything to frighten me or make me uncomfortable. He went out of his way to assure me that everything would be all right.

"Every day after school I would convince at least one classmate to come home with me to play. I didn't want to be home alone with Uncle Joe. Soon my friends wanted to do other things and I had to figure out other ways to get them to come to my house after school. I was about thirteen at the time, and all thirteen-year-old girls wanted to be pretty. I learned at an early age how to take care of my hair, and I was pretty good at it. I could braid, press, and curl hair, and I quickly learned to use clippers to cut hair. I would arrange to do someone's hair every day after school, just to ensure that I wouldn't be home alone with Uncle Joe. I would finish the last head just about the time Aunt Mimi came home.

"I continued to get better each year; and by high school, doing hair became my part-time job. I did at least two heads a day after school and earned about $40 a day. That was very good money back in the 1960s.

"Aunt Mimi had always been encouraging and supportive. With her help, we turned a part of the garage into a small hair shop. After high school I didn't know what I wanted to do. Aunt Mimi suggested that because I did such a good job doing hair, that maybe I should become a licensed beautician. In less than a year I had far too many customers for the garage and rented my first storefront salon.

"My business was thriving when I met Elizabeth. *Life couldn't get much better than this*, I thought. Elizabeth was a few years older than me; and she was comfortable being a lesbian. I knew that I didn't want a man to touch me, but I never considered a woman. Shit, girl! I was touching myself by that time. I guess she saw in me what I had not been able to embrace, and she became my lover.

"I never asked much about her past, and she never asked me about mine. We were together and it was wonderful. Then, out of nowhere, Elizabeth said she had to leave; she wouldn't explain why or if she was ever coming back. She said, 'Tracy, trust me; this is the best thing for both of us.' I was devastated and alone again."

At this point Cynthia just had to interject. "Tracy, you know the same thing happened with my first love. He just went away, and I never really knew why."

"So you have an idea of how I felt," Tracy said, looking at Cynthia somewhat surprised. She continued. "I later found out that Elizabeth had just completed a two-year sentence for fraud and had violated her parole. "I knew I needed to leave Cleveland; the memories there were just too painful. So I packed my most valuable belongings in the back seat of my Chevy and headed east. I didn't know where I was going, but Boston seemed a place as good as any other."

Cynthia looked at Tracy and could see that there were tears in her eyes.

"Tracy, life has not been easy for you; so it's okay to cry."

"Cynthia, I've got no more tears. I've cried too many times about the hand that I was dealt. I just can't cry anymore. But what I can do is make sure that I will never be put in a bad situation again; I will never be the victim again.

"It wasn't easy when I first came to Boston. I had to establish my own clients and make a name for myself in this town. I started doing hair in a small shop on Shawmut Avenue in the South End of Boston. I got a few good customers and felt that I could make it. As time went on, I got more and more customers and was able to move into a larger shop.

"The harder I worked the less time I had to think about things, and to remember. I just worked and saved money. I believed that if I had money I would always be in control of my life. By then I knew that the touch of a man frightened and nauseated me; it only brought back horrible memories. I had come to grips with the fact that I would never like men.

"Yes, Cynthia, I'm a lesbian. But I'm not your stereotypical lesbian. I'm very picky and I require class, style, and honesty in a woman; she has to be as fly as I am, and every day of my life I'm gonna work to be fly."

They both laughed. She went on to say, "I know that I'll find that woman in my life. Right now it's not a big deal. I need to wait for the right one. I thought I needed to let you know, just in case that would present a problem in our friendship."

Cynthia's response was straight to the point. "I hear what you are saying and I understand that life has been tough, but I need to let you know that I'm straight and hope that won't affect our friendship."

Tracy laughed and said, "Girl, you are all right, but you're not my type." They both had to laugh.

Tracy moved from her personal situation to that of Rosa, the petite lady Cynthia had seen in the salon earlier that week. "The main reason I stay in contact with Rosa is that I keep thinking that if I move out of her life, she will stay there until he kills her," Tracy said. "I know I can't protect her; but I can talk to her and try to convince her that she doesn't deserve to be treated that way. So, on one hand, I was happy when she came to Boston; I could keep working on her to make her understand that she didn't have to be abused. On the other hand, I would have to feel the pain of looking at her every time that man blackened her eyes and kicked her ass.

"Cynthia, you don't know how many times I've wanted to kill that bastard myself, just to put Rosa out of her misery. I want to make him feel the pain he has inflicted on Rosa. I want to beat him the way I saw my mother being beaten. I know this is not my fight and that Rosa has to come to grips with the time and conditions under which she will leave him. I just hope it will not be as they carry her out, covered in a white sheet."

They talked for hours. Tracy said, "Cynthia, I've never met anyone that I could talk to this long and bare my soul; there's something special about you."

Cynthia told Tracy that she wasn't a psychiatrist or therapist, and the best that she could be was a sympathetic friend who would always want the best for her.

"That's all I could ask for in a friend," she said. That was the beginning of a great and lifelong friendship.

Tracy was like Robin in a lot of ways—preoccupied with money and very straightforward and direct. The only difference was that Tracy could get a little raw. When she expressed herself, she left no room for you to say that you didn't understand. She believed that a few well-placed swears insured that she would at least get your attention. As raw as Tracy was, she had plenty of class and style when it was needed.

Tracy was the kind of woman you could take from the White House to the outhouse and she would adjust appropriately. Much like a chameleon, she could fit into any setting and change to fit her surroundings. Over the years Cynthia would have a chance to watch Tracy in a classy environment, holding court like the Queen of England, and in the neighborhood dive ready and able to kick ass. She called that "shit-kicking time." She would say, "I'm not the kind of sister to start shit, but when the shit jumps off, I'm the bitch to finish it."

Ten days at Christmas, that's the time Jack and Cynthia arranged to spend with each other. He would arrive in Boston early on December 24. He didn't want to tell her what to wear during those ten days; he thought that she had excellent taste in clothes. He did request that she have a red formal outfit for New Year's Eve. He reminded her of the conversations that they had regarding the splashes of red in her apartment's décor and how it represented the fire and excitement that occasionally sparked her life. Jack also reminded her of his promise to provide a reason to add a little more red to her life. Plans had already been made for the holidays, and all he wanted her to do was to be ready to go. She had three weeks to find a red outfit for New Year's Eve, and she went on an extensive hunt throughout the city.

Cynthia called Tracy and told her that she was looking for a breath-taking red dress.

"Girl, I can show you where to go to get a dress that will make the brother's dick hard."

The next Saturday morning, Tracy took Cynthia to a boutique hidden in the suburbs. The shop had one-of-a-kind outfits that were just that. Cynthia tried on several outfits without much luck when Tracy came running from the back of the store with a red dress.

"This is you," she said. "Put this dress on! You can make it work."

Cynthia went into the dressing room, put the dress on, and looked in the mirror. Damn! She had to admit, she was working this red dress. The dress fit in all the right places and flattered the hell out of her breasts. It was a red sequined form-fitting dress with a little gold trim; it brought out the color of her skin. This dress was going to get plenty of attention. She came out to show Tracy, who said, "That's it; you're gonna have the brother walking with a limp all night."

The dress was a little pricey, but well worth it. They found a red sequined evening bag and had a little trouble coming up with the right shoes. She finally settled on a pair of red satin, sling-backs with a four-inch heel. The outfit was now complete.

Early Sunday morning Sandra called to give Cynthia the good news. She was pregnant. Sandra and Jason were very happy about the pregnancy, even though they had decided to wait at least a year before having children. But then they realized that if the plan was to have four children, she needed to get started because Sandra wasn't getting any younger. She asked Cynthia not to tell Robin. She wanted to give her the news personally.

Sandra was also excited about their new home. She and Jason had worked feverishly over the last few months getting the house the way they wanted it. She was surprised that Jason was handy around the house; she didn't think that he had it in him. Together they worked tirelessly to make a home. They were prepared for the baby. Although Sandra and Jason both worked long hours trying to establish their careers, Sandra's hours were more flexible and she was always home when Jason got there.

"Are you still cooking meals, washing drawers, ironing sheets, and carrying the happy banner?" Cynthia asked her.

"Yes, that's the way Jason likes it," Sandra chuckled.

She had gotten the wedding pictures and said that they looked spectacular. Sandra said her mother had finally calmed down after the wedding and decided to give her and Jason some time alone.

Sandra did have some bad news. Mama Lee had a stroke and wasn't doing well. The family had moved her into a nursing home. Sandra believed that Mama Lee had given up her will to live. She was always such an active woman, and the stroke had made it hard for her to get around.

Cynthia brought Sandra up to date on her life and told her that she was really enjoying her job. She also told her about Tracy and the rough life that she lived, and about her friend Rosa.

"Damn! Where do you meet these people?"

"I don't know; they just kind of find me. The world is full of people like that. We were just blessed to have an uneventful life." That was Cynthia's honest reply.

"Cynthia, you know I don't know what I'd do if Jason became abusive."

"What do you mean, you don't know what you would do?"

"Well, it's not in his nature; he's a very mild-mannered person, and I just don't know what I'd do."

"You know what, Sandra; if Jason became abusive, you would do what you had to do. I would like to believe that you would not allow yourself to be beaten."

Robin and Cynthia spoke later that evening. They were both happy about Sandra's pregnancy. They agreed that they would take a trip to Atlanta as soon as the baby was born. Cynthia told Robin that she and Jack finally decided to spend some time together and that they were going to hang out for about ten days over the Christmas holidays. Robin thought that was funny.

"Well it's about damn time. I never understood what y'all were waiting for. I hope you have fun."

"I intend to. I've made all of the necessary preparations to have a hell of a good time," Cynthia gloated.

"You know, I met this fine brother at a trading conference," said Robin. "He was the guest speaker, and he caught my attention right away. I obviously caught his attention too, because he invited me to dinner that evening. We've dated a few times. The brother got it going on in many ways, but he has one problem."

"What's wrong with the brother?"

"Girl, his dick is on backwards."

"How the hell can a man's dick be on backwards?" Cynthia laughed.

"If you've ever noticed, when a man has an erection his dick often curves up but always out. Well, this man's dick curves backwards, toward his balls."

"Well damn! I didn't know that could happen."

"Neither did I, 'til I saw it."

"That sounds like it could be a problem and possibly painful."

"Yeah, girl, it's a real problem. I'm gonna have to cut him loose. On a lighter side, I think I found my condo," Robin said. "It's a really nice two-bedroom condo in Manhattan. It's a little pricey, but that's what it takes to live in Manhattan. My grandparents are going to help me with the down payment. When I finish negotiating the deal, you've got to come see it."

Cynthia told her about Tracy and her friend Rosa, and how rough their lives had been.

"Girl, as long as I can remember, people have always brought their problems to you."

"You're right; and I really don't know why. I think Tracy is a really nice woman. If I can be there to help her in any way, I'm gonna try."

"Cynthia, you're a trip. You are a young, single woman, and in your life you've got an old man and a lesbian. Girl, you need to get some spice in your life."

Cynthia told Robin that there were plenty of young black men out there and she was dating quite regularly. "I just haven't found the one that fits what I need. So I'd rather not have one unless he's a good fit."

"Yeah, I guess I understand that. I can't really say much 'cause I haven't found Mr. Right either. But you know what, sister; I'm having a damn good time searching for him."

CHAPTER 7

Jack was due in Boston in three days. Although Cynthia had spent significant dollars rearranging her wardrobe, getting new loungewear, teddies, and underwear, she was still filled with nervous energy. She got a pedicure and a manicure, and Tracy hooked her hair up nicely.

"This should last for ten days," she told her, "but you might be in trouble if you let the brother sweat your hair out; that's on you."

Just when she finally got her wardrobe the way she wanted it, Cynthia realized that she needed a classy piece of luggage. She went to one of the area shopping malls and, as she was looking around for just the right garment bag, she saw Wesley. He was walking toward her, and for some unknown reason her heart began to pound. She thought it was going to leap out of her. It had been almost ten years, but he appeared happy to see her. She knew that she had a big grin on her face. They embraced and had a brief, non-descript conversation. She reached into her purse, took out her business card, put her home phone number on the back and asked him to give her a call. Although he was still on her "list of things to do," she really didn't have the time to stop for him now. She was on a bigger mission, and that was preparing to spend time with Jack. She would get back to Wesley another time.

He gave the appropriate exit lines and she continued to browse. These are slightly different times, and it seemed to her that most of the brothers out here are getting accustomed to being seriously chased by women. Brothers don't have to do much anymore. Sisters come after brothers, and come after them hard.

Now, she had never been a chaser and could not imagine becoming one. A high-maintenance man is generally too much trouble for her. She could understand why women would want to be with Wesley, but if he is a high-maintenance brother and needs to be chased, Cynthia and Wesley would probably never get together.

She found a very nice leather garment bag with a matching suitcase and headed home. When she got home she checked the apartment to be sure that everything was in order. She had plenty of groceries, candles, wine, and cognac. She kicked back, put on some smooth music, poured herself a glass of wine, and began to read. It wasn't long before she fell asleep. Tomorrow was going to be an early day.

Jack was one of the last passengers off the plane. When he entered the room, she smiled. The brother was looking just as good as he did the first time she saw him. He was wearing a charcoal gray suit, carrying a black cashmere topcoat and, again, he was wearing the hell out of that suit.

As they moved toward each other with big smiles on their faces, he put his bag down and pulled her into his arms.

"Baby, I promise you one of the most memorable Christmases of your life." For the first time she recognized his cologne. It had the aroma of Sandalwood.

On the way from the airport they laughed and talked. Jack was a very witty man, in a mild low-keyed kind of way. He had an excellent command of the English language and could easily turn a phrase that would sometimes take her a moment to understand.

"Baby, I believe I know what you're thinking. Don't worry about time for the next ten days. I'll be your clock and calendar; so don't worry about where we're going, or when. I've taken care of that, and I promise you that it will be memorable. I just want you to relax and enjoy."

She felt that she knew this man better than she had known any other man. She felt comfortable letting him take control. As they entered her apartment and he put his bags down he said, "It looks like you've been quite busy." She said, "Yes, I have; and it's been a lot of fun."

The apartment was quite a different place than it was when Jack first came. She changed the color scheme, and there was now a little more red in her decor. She now had a job that produced available dollars, and she used those dollars to redecorate. Of all of the rooms that had been transformed, her bedroom had been changed the most. She found a wonderful black lacquered, queen-sized bedroom set. She saw it while on a shopping trip with Tracy. She fell in love with this mainstay of the bedroom. It fit ideally into her space. She dressed the bed in white satin sheets, covered with a white cotton comforter. She found the contrast of black skin on white sheets arousing. Around the room, in strategically placed areas, were four black lacquer and glass pedestals and on each pedestal were four to six candles, arranged by color and aroma. She'd learned not to merge colors and aromas. That just didn't work.

She had truly learned to appreciate images. Consequently, she attached two four-foot mirrors to the ceiling. She had an old contractor friend come over and install the mirrors to be sure that they were attached properly to the ceiling. Once he got the mirrors secured tightly, he said, "Damn, baby, what you trying to do up in here; you gonna kill a brother." She thought that kind of funny. Her only intention was to make sure that whatever happened in that room would be memorable.

She finally threw away the used furniture in the living room and replaced it with an off-white sofa and love seat. In the middle of the room was a large leopard-skin rug. The only thing missing in the room was a fireplace. On her last trip to Atlanta, she came across a unique chess set that she knew would accent the room. It was carved out of black and white marble, and she hadn't seen anything like it before. She learned to play chess during her second year in college and had gotten pretty good at it. Unfortunately, she didn't run across many chess players after college. She was pretty good for a beginner and had plans on getting better.

"You are quite a creative lady," Jack said as he entered the bedroom. "I particularly like the way you have arranged the black lacquer bedroom with the mirrored accessories. This room definitely shows your creative side."

He enjoyed the Christmas holidays almost as much as she did, and neither of them could remember not having a Christmas tree each year. There was always a large tree in her home, even when there was nothing under it. They both recognized the commercialization of Christmas; oddly enough, neither of them was a big Christmas gift giver. Jack said he gives gifts all year round, and Christmas is not a special time to express your feelings for someone. She was certainly happy to hear that. In all of the excitement and preparation for his arrival, she had forgotten to get him a gift.

It was about 12:30, and Jack wanted to see a little of Boston, claiming the only thing he knew about Boston was what he heard on the news. According to the news, the city was full of crazy, racist white folks defending forced bussing. It had been a pretty rough time for race relations in Boston. Although many black folks were not in favor of forced bussing, Cynthia had to admit that she was proud of their ability not to resort to violence. Black people clearly understood the issue to be one of poor quality public education, citywide. Race became more of an issue for white folks, and they were determined to protect their poor white neighborhoods and poor quality schools from "the niggas". The busses that transported black children were stoned and in many cases almost turned over by angry mobs of South Boston residents as the nation looked on. Rarely was there any violence shown toward the busloads of white children that came into the black neighborhoods. She was proud of the restraint shown by black people. She knew that it would be just a matter of time before black people got tired of turning the other cheek, and obviously the mayor knew that too. In an effort to retain order in the city the mayor activated the National Guard.

She took Jack first to see the black neighborhoods of Roxbury, Dorchester, and the South End. They made a quick dash through the predominantly white neighborhoods of South Boston and Charlestown. After seeing both neighborhoods, he asked what she thought was a very valid question.

"Baby, what are folks in Boston fighting for?" Jack asked after seeing both black and white neighborhoods. "It seems to me that poor white folks are being bussed into poor black neighborhoods, and poor black folks are being bussed into poor white neighborhoods. What is the purpose of that? When it's all said and done, you still got poor dumb black and white kids who are probably a little dumber because the children couldn't possibly learn much with all the violence swirling around them.

It seems to me that the people in Boston are as dumb as they are racist."

She thought about it for a moment, and he was absolutely right. Boston really wasn't going to gain much from this effort. Since Jack had agreed to prepare dinner that evening and he wanted to stop and pick up a few items that he needed. The supermarket was full of last-minute holiday shoppers. She was thankful that he only needed a few things. They grabbed what they needed and sped through the eight-items-or-less express line and got back to her apartment by 4:30 P.M.

Jack was an excellent cook and had a new dish that he wanted to try. He knew that she couldn't cook, and seemed not to have a problem with it. Cooking just wasn't something that interested her.

"You know, I'm not trying to make you a cook or anything," Jack said. "But I've got a recipe for a great meal that is so simple, even you could make it. Come on in the kitchen and I'll show you how to put it together. But before we get started, maybe we need to get into something a little more comfortable," he said with a chuckle.

He came back into the kitchen wearing a pair of silk pajama bottoms, Kelly green.

"You know, baby, I'm really not a pajama person, but when you visit someone's home, you usually don't want to walk around naked."

"If naked is what you want to be, please feel free," she shot back. "However, it might be a little dangerous in the kitchen."

"We've got a few days left to run around naked," he answered softly.

He prepared a beautiful dinner of chicken Marsala, asparagus, and potatoes, and suggested that they might have a little wine with their meal. She pulled out her best wine glasses, set an impressive table with her best china, and poured two glasses of wine. They sat down for dinner.

Jack and Cynthia had never had a problem talking, whatever the topic, time of day, or personal mood. They enjoyed each other's company. They finished dinner and moved into the living room with their drinks and listened to some smooth jazz. Her collection of jazz recordings had become impressive.

"I didn't realize you played," Jack said, noticing the marble chessboard in the corner.

"I'm not that much of a chess player. I learned in college, but didn't often find others to play with."

"Let's see how much you know about the game."

She got comfortable across the table from him and watched him take the first move.

"I enjoy playing this game because it's so much like life," Jack acknowledged. "As a new chess player, there's probably a lot about the game that you are still learning. The most critical part of the game is to protect your king. You've got to have a good defense, much like life. You've got to have a plan, and you've got to have a strategy. You've got to know what you want to accomplish and be aggressive about moving these pieces on the board so that you can accomplish it. More important, you need to have patience and you have to watch the game in order to seize your opportunities. The primary difference between chess and life is that you don't get to play life over again.

"I want to teach you to win at this game, just as I want you to win at life, but I also want you to savor the game and enjoy every moment."

As she listened to him she realized that this chess game was more than a simple game, he was also teaching her about life.

"I play chess the way I love a woman—slow, easy, methodical, and seeking every opportunity to enhance the game. I want you to learn to play this game the way you will learn to love a man. If you play too quickly, the game can be over much too soon, leaving little to remember. Checkmate!"

She had a bewildered look on her face. That must have been the quickest game in history, and at that point she could only laugh.

"We're going to play this next game slow and easy," Jack said.

Indeed, the next game was much better. She played slowly. She watched the way he moved and anticipated his next move. She thought through situations. That allowed her to use her defense and offense when needed. When she made a move that was deliberate and enhanced her position, Jack cheered her on:

"That's it, baby," he would say. They sipped wine and cognac and played over and over again; each game got more and more intense. They lost track of time.

"You've got the potential to be an excellent chess player," Jack said, "but I think we've played enough chess for one evening. I know we've sipped enough cognac and wine."

When she stood up to clear the table she realized that she had a little too much to drink. She had never been much of a drinker, and that evening she had at least five glasses of wine, which is more than she had ever drank before. Jack must have noticed too.

"Baby, why don't you get in bed. I'll clean up and be right behind you."

She got up and went into the bedroom, put a little water on her face and realized that she was quite tipsy. She crawled between the satin sheets and quickly remembered how cold they were, especially when you were in bed alone.

Her mind began to race. She thought, *What a lousy first impression, drinking too much on our first night together.* It wasn't long before she felt the heat from Jack's body. He pulled her closer to him, cradled her head in his arms and said, "You know, baby, I think we both had too much to drink."

"Jack, I'm really sorry. I hadn't intended to drink this much."

"Don't worry, baby, it's not a problem. I'm a seasoned cognac drinker, and I think I drank a little too much also; but we still have nine days and nights to make up for this."

She must have gone to sleep in less than sixty seconds. When she awakened the next morning there was the smell of coffee floating in the air, and the sound of water flowing in the shower. For the first time in her life she had a hangover. As she lay in bed trying to get her thoughts together, it dawned on her, she had finally gotten this wonderfully sensuous man in her bed and she was too drunk to remember. She would have to find a way to apologize for falling asleep on him; but right now what she really needed was a hot shower and a cup of hot coffee.

She left the bedroom, headed for the bathroom, and met Jack standing in the doorway wearing only a towel. He had the body of a thirty-year-old.

"Good morning. How about some coffee?" Jack asked.

"Give me fifteen minutes in the bathroom, and coffee will be exactly what I need."

She got into the shower and slowly returned to her senses. After showering and primping she moved into the kitchen for coffee. A part of her thought that she needed to apologize again for falling asleep last night, but another part of her thought, *Why draw attention to the obvious.* As usual, Jack was in her head.

"Baby," he said, "I know what you're thinking, but you must remember that last night neither of us was ready to fully enjoy each other. I had a wonderful time just holding you in my arms all night."

She thought to herself, *I sure wish I could remember that.*

After coffee, breakfast, and analyzing items in the *Boston Globe*, he suggested that they go out and see a little of the town. She had to remind him that this was Christmas day in a white Irish Catholic town; there really wasn't anything to do.

He laughed and said, "You know, I forgot that we were not in New York or New Jersey. Boston still has those archaic Blue laws."

They decided to catch an evening movie and spend the day lounging around the house. This would be her opportunity to do something nice for him. She would show him how much she'd learned in her massage class. He was definitely a willing subject.

After cleaning up the breakfast dishes, she told him, "Now I want you to take directions from me. I want you to relax, listen, and follow my directions. He chuckled as if she had just told him a good joke.

"You know what, baby, I'll do whatever you tell me to do."

She asked him to give her a couple of minutes to prepare the space for the massage and then they would begin.

She prepared the bed by pulling back the comforter and placing a large terry cloth towel over the satin sheets. She moved two of the pedestals to each side of the bed and lit four narcissist candles on each one. She turned on the massage oil warmer and added about a quarter of a cup of the ultimate massage oil, "Joy." She found the combination of scents hypnotic. She changed into something a little less restrictive, so that she could freely move around his body. She chose a short white teddy, a terrycloth robe, and put on some soft mood music in the background.

The room was set, and she went to get Jack. He was sitting in a terrycloth towel reading the news. She walked up behind him and began to lightly massage his neck and shoulders.

"Let's take this to my massage parlor." She walked him into the bedroom and asked him to lie face down on the bed. He followed her directions, still wearing the towel. She straddled his body and whispered in his ear, "If you're feeling inhibited, you can have a slightly clad stimulating massage. However, if you are uninhibited, you can have a totally nude, full-body experience."

"Baby, I don't think I've ever been inhibited. I've kept the towel on for your sake." He got up and let the towel drop to the floor. He must have heard her catch her breath. If her eyes had been a slot machine, they would have read "Jackpot!"

He got back on the bed, face down, totally naked. "I'm all yours."

This was her big chance to work her magic. The massage oil was heated to just the right temperature. She began the massage just behind his ears and down to the back of his neck. She massaged in an upward motion from the top of his spine to just under his earlobes. She talked to him as she massaged his body. She told him why she started at this part of his body and that he needed to relax and enjoy it.

She moved from the back of his neck to the top of his shoulders and asked him to concentrate and feel the tension leave his body. She massaged the back of his biceps moving down to his forearms. As she moved to his back she began to give him breathing directions. Breathing is important in a full-body massage. As she worked each of the muscles in his back she told him what the muscle was and how it functioned in the body. She told him to let here know if she was being a little too rough.

"No, baby, you've got it just right."

She continued to apply hot "Joy" to the muscles of his back down to the bottom of his spine. At this point he began to let here know that he enjoyed the massage. She worked each of the vertebrae down the spine to the top of the buttocks.

As she began to massage his buttock she was quite surprised at the tightness of his body. She asked him to relax because she was feeling tension. She continued to massage his buttock down to the top of his thigh. She massaged the back of his thigh in an upward motion, pushing blood toward the heart. She applied a little more "Joy" and began to work the back of his knees. This is one of the many areas of the body with heightened sensory receptors. As she massaged the back of his knees, she felt his body tighten, she quietly asked him to breathe deep and relax.

She moved down to the calves and began to loosen his leg muscles, continued to his ankles and to the soles of his feet. The soles of the foot can be a ticklish area, yet if massaged properly it is one of the many sensuous parts of the body. She massaged the soles of his feet as she had been taught in her massage class.

"Damn, baby, that's nice."

She asked him to take two deep breaths and slowly roll over on his back. As he rolled over, she asked him to keep his eyes closed and take the spread eagle position. This was also a test. She knew that a man would not allow himself to be in that position unless he trusted you. She straddled his body and began to massage his jaw and upper neck. Again, she asked him to relax, take a deep breath and let the tension leave his body. She applied hot "Joy" to his shoulders and upper chest and used a circular motion to increase the blood flow to the heart.

She continued down the chest to the stomach, using reduced pressure and spending a little extra time around the navel. His penis was no longer flaccid, it was definitely responding to the massage. She moved from the lower stomach to the top of his thigh, taking care to avoid the genital area. She was told that once you begin to massage the genital area, sex, or masturbation, should occur next. They had plenty of time for that. She explained why she avoided that area.

"We can always get back to that," he said.

She continued down his thigh to the inner thigh, down the shin to the ankles and top of the feet. She threw in a toe massage just to top if off. His entire body smelled like "Joy," and he said that he had not felt this relaxed in years. After finishing the full-body massage, she moved up, allowing her body to rest on his and whispered in his ear that she was going to clean up the massage oil, pick up around the bedroom, and that he should continue to relax.

She cleaned up the oil and began to put the room back together. She couldn't help but wonder if he really enjoyed the massage. When she returned to the bedroom, Jack was asleep; the massage had worked. She let him rest and went to tidy up the kitchen and pick up in the rest of the house.

Her mind kept wandering back to that great body and that beautiful penis. She thought about their previous conversations regarding anticipation as a wonderful aphrodisiac. The anticipation of connecting physically with this man was definitely an aphrodisiac.

She still had a few things to do around the house and put on a little Christmas music. She found Nat King Cole's greatest Christmas hits and played "The Chestnuts Song," one of her favorite Christmas songs. Although it was only four o'clock, the sun had set. That's what happens in New England in the winter. She decided to light the Christmas tree and enjoy the season and the music. She stood back to admire her handiwork; she had done a good job with the tree decorations. As she stood there enjoying the Christmas aura, Jack quietly moved behind her, put his arms around her waist and pulled her close to him.

"I guess it's my turn to apologize for falling asleep on you. We seem to have that effect on each other; but that's a good thing, because very few women can relax and calm me to drift off to sleep. Baby, you've got some damn good hands. Speaking from one masseuse to another, you have learned well."

She didn't know that he was a masseuse. He told her that for about two years after he graduated from college he earned his living as a masseuse. He said he didn't know what he wanted to do with his career, and a black masseuse was a novelty and paid very well. She told him that she thought she was being impressive by showing and telling him something new.

"Believe me, baby, you were impressive."

They decided to grab some dinner and catch a movie. She took him to Sidney's. She was sure that he would like the atmosphere and the food. They got downtown in time to catch the 8 P.M. show. She found it interesting that wherever they went, Jack made it perfectly clear that they were together. She had always been a very private person and never would be caught in public displays of affection. With Jack, it was a public display of affection that was so subtle and meaningful that she found it intriguing.

They decided to catch *Mahogany* featuring Diana Ross and Billy Dee Williams. They were in the middle of the 1970s and blaxploitation movies were everywhere. They were standing outside the theater, waiting to pick up their tickets, and it seemed that most of the black people in the city had decided to see *Mahogany* on the same night.

During the 1970s most black folks spoke to each other, but she found it most interesting that women, who barely spoke to her on a daily basis, found a need to greet her that evening as if they were old friends Women approached her with big smiles on their faces and said, "Hey girl, how are you doing? I haven't seen you in a long time." She greeted them back and ignored them as they waited to be introduced. She refused to do it; and after a few awkward moments, they walked away. "Baby, is there a reason that you continually ignore these women?" Jack whispered in her ear.

"Those women find it necessary to speak to me only because you are here, and I refuse to play into their games."

He pulled her closer. "Your honesty is one of the many things that I like about you."

When they left the theater the weather had gotten colder and a light snow was falling. They parked the car at one of the major hotels and waited for the valet to return it. They stood in the doorway of the hotel waiting for the car, and out of nowhere Jack gave her the most intense and passionate kiss that she ever had. They had kissed each other before, but never like this. Curiosity got the best of her and she wanted to know what prompted it.

"Baby, just being with you makes me want to do that. I've wanted to do it all evening."

He volunteered to drive, if she would give directions. That was perfectly fine with her. When they entered the apartment and began to take off the heavy winter clothes, Jack got right to the point.

"There are three things that I'd like to do right now: First I'd like to get into something more comfortable, then I'd like to have a cognac, then I'd like to feel your body next to mine. They are not in the order of their importance, but the first two will prepare me to be at my best when we do the third."

She was determined that there would be very little wine sipping for her. She was not going to fall asleep this time.

Comfortable to Jack meant a pair of pajama bottoms; and if getting sexy was the agenda for the evening, she was definitely going to participate. She put on a short bright red lace nightie that barely held "the girls" in, poured herself a small glass of wine, and joined Jack in the living room. The room was dark with the exception of the Christmas tree and two red candles burning on the coffee table. Jack was on the sofa and asked her to come over and join him. As she approached the sofa, he parted his legs and motioned for her to sit. As she sat between his legs he gently pulled her back against his chest; it was a very comfortable position.

They laughed about the movie, the people they saw and the things they did. Then he got serious.

"You know, baby, I'm really having a wonderful time with you. When I first met you on the telephone, I felt then that there was something special about you. When I told you that I would never come to Boston to take anything from you, I mean that more now than I did then.

"You have matured in many ways, and I admire your willingness and openness to learn and experience new things. I've listened to your sensitivity as you talk about your old friends, and the new friends that have just recently come into your life. I truly look forward to our Thursday-night telephone dates.

"You need to understand what a special woman you are. Because you're so special, you should have a special man. I hope that I can show you all of the things that you will need in that special man. I wanted to tell you this before we become intimate, because I don't want you to think that being intimate with you will change, or reshape, my opinion of you. Cynthia, sex with you will be a mind-blowing experience for both of us because we've prepared for this.

"I must admit that my heart has gotten into this a little more than I expected, but not enough to make me lose sight of reality. The reality is, and always will be, that there is almost a twenty-year difference in our ages. That may not mean very much to you today, but in the long run the difference in our ages would pull the relationship apart. I hope to always be in your life in some form, and I will always be there for you no matter what. I don't ever intend to marry again, but I know at some point you may want to. You may even decide that you want to have children. So, baby, we will enjoy the time that we spend together, however long it may be. We will build pleasant memories; and when we leave each other's life, we will leave it better than we found it. I love you, Cynthia, and I love you not with the kind of love that's going to make us go out and become husband and wife, buy a little house with a white picket fence. I've passed that stage in my life. You are all the things I needed in a woman ten years ago."

"I'd like to believe that I'm a realist," she finally responded. "I try very hard to stay connected to reality; but I have to admit this is going to be difficult because you've shown me things that have enhanced my life. You've shown me sides of a man that I've not known before. I agree with you, that when we become intimate it is going to be earth shattering and that's going to make it more difficult for me to stay connected with reality. That's when I'm going to need your help."

"Baby, we'll have to keep each other rooted in reality." He got up, pulled her from the sofa. "Meanwhile, let's see if we can make the earth move."

They went into the bedroom, and she intentionally lit all of the Sandalwood candles. She had already imprinted Jack with Sandalwood. He turned on the massage oil warmer and said, "Now it's my turn to give you a massage; and I brought my own massage oil. I don't want you to take your clothes off; I'll do that for you. I just want you to lie on the bed, comfortably on your stomach and let me do what I do."

Her mind said, "Oh shit!" as she climbed on the bed. Jack massaged her body from the top of her head to the tip of her toes, and it was an exhilarating experience.

"Baby, I need you to roll over on your back."

Jack's need was explicit but gentle. She was almost in a trance, but she heard his directions and did as he told her. Once on her back, she realized that he had already removed her nightie and had began to massage her temples down to her jaw. He didn't have to tell her to breathe deeply, he didn't have to tell her to relax. She had already done that. He worked her shoulders, her arms, and began to work on her chest. His touch was tender, and he used just the right amount of pressure as he massaged her chest, her breast, and upper stomach. As he worked her abs and her inner thigh she noticed that her body began to tense; he noticed it too. In his deep baritone voice he quietly said, "Relax, baby, relax." He moved past the genital area.

"You know why we've passed that area, but we will get back to it later."

He gently massaged her thighs and her calves, even to the most fantastic foot massage she'd ever had.

"It's now time to get to serious business," he said and gently pulled her legs apart so that he could lightly massage the genital area. She had never had this done before, and it came as quite a surprise. As he massaged the area tenderly her legs began to tremble. Abruptly he stopped; he knew that too much of this would have brought her to an orgasm.

As he lay down beside her, she reached over to embrace him. He kissed her again in that deep passionate way. This time she responded. It wasn't the sloppy, urgent kisses that she had been accustomed to having from men. This was a slow meaningful kiss, and there was nothing urgent about it. She responded by kissing him back the way she wanted to be kissed, and the combination of the two made her head light. There was no fumbling, prodding, and pushing involved. It was just soft tender meaningful kisses.

"Jack, it's now my turn to complete the full-body massage that I started this morning."

She straddled his body again. As she moved down she slowly removed his pajama bottoms. Using the warm massage oil, she gently massaged the genital area. She directed him to lie on his back and lift his legs in the sitting position.

"Lie back and relax. It's time for you to let me do what I do."

She massaged his penis for a brief moment before she moved to the testicles and the scrotum. She could hear soft moans as his penis began to get more and more erect. It was a beautiful penis, perfectly sculptured, and she enjoyed just watching it. She continued to massage from the tip of the penis to the bottom of the testicles, and again in the opposite direction. She did this for a short while and was quite amazed at the self-control he showed. Eventually he put his hands on hers to hold them still. "Baby, I have practiced self-control most of my life and my self-control is better than the average man's, but we all have our limits."

He pulled her up onto his chest, and as she lay prone over his body she could feel his erect penis throbbing while he held her tightly rubbing her back and neck. He asked her if she was ready to do this. Her body answered him as she moved up on her knees and prepared to be entered. Jack was never in a hurry to do anything. However, she was much more aggressive than he was at this point. He gently lifted her and laid her next to him on the bed. As they faced each other he lifted his leg and put it over her body, which allowed his erect penis to lie between her legs.

He talked to her about the significance of allowing a person to enter her body, and the significance of becoming one in the full sexual act. He went on to explain how slow and easy intercourse should be, particularly when your heart and soul were involved in the act. Now Jack was not a little man; he said he thought it was important for her to talk to him and to let him know if at any point it became uncomfortable. He said it would always be in her best interest to have control with a new partner.

He slowly rolled over on his back and pulled her back on top. "Now you control how you want to do this."

As he entered her body she could feel her head getting light. He moved farther and farther into her body, and it was awesome. He continuously brought her to the edge of orgasm, but knew exactly when to stop. They changed positions several times; he was always slow and tender. They were both lost in the experience. The world disappeared.

The muscles in and around her vagina began to tighten and release over and over again, and it frightened her. She had never before had an experience like that. Jack obviously felt the contractions and told her to go with it, enjoy it, and to know that he was right there with her. Her entire body began to shiver almost like a person having convulsions; it was a true outer-body experience. Jack held her close to his body as the orgasm moved from her body into his.

As she lay there next to him, her head feeling very light, she realized that she couldn't hear out of her left ear. She told Jack about the deafness. He laughed and said, "Baby, that's obviously the sign of an earth-shattering orgasm. Let's wait a moment, it will be okay."

When her head began to clear, the hearing returned to her left ear. She smiled when she realized that Wesley was not the only man that could make her knees weak.

She was lying next to a man who was what many women searched for—slow, sensuous, methodical, and determined to please a woman. As they both drifted off to sleep she thought, *How the hell am I ever going to be able to walk away from this man?* The next few days were truly unbelievable; she was in a constant state of arousal. It didn't matter what the time of day, this man constantly aroused her.

They spent the day sightseeing all around town and enjoying each other's company. They spent the evenings exploring each other's body. Jack continuously talked to her; there was nothing that they couldn't talk about. He helped her to understand the male body, how it works, how to make it feel good, and how to relax it. He also helped her to learn more and more about her body and what pleased it. By the sixth day she had developed new skills.

Jack told her that they were scheduled on a flight out of Boston on the morning of December 29, and that she should pack the clothes she thought she would need and be prepared for a formal event on New Year's Eve. He still wouldn't tell her where they were going; but it really didn't matter.

By three o'clock in the afternoon of December 29, they were checking into the Sands hotel in Las Vegas. She was excited about being in Las Vegas, but for some unknown reason she had gotten a little airsick. Jack spent the day pampering her. They had a light dinner through room service and spent the evening watching the massive neon light show over Las Vegas. The next day they went shopping, visited several casinos, and marveled at the amount of money moving through that city. Jack made sure to point out that although they were in Las Vegas, their primary purpose was to be together.

Jack was an expert swimmer. She watched as that beautiful body swam laps in the hotel pool. They had a wonderful time in the hot tub and the Jacuzzi, and ended with a great massage. That evening she got a pedicure, manicure, and even found a hairdresser that could put a little order to her hair. On New Year's Eve she was going to wear her outstanding red dress.

During the day on New Year's Eve they had an early dinner to allow them time to get ready for the formal event that evening. It was difficult getting dressed because Jack and Cynthia could not keep their hands off each other. They needed to be dressed and ready to leave by ten. He looked absolutely fabulous in his black tuxedo, and it fit him like a glove.

As she continued to dress she couldn't help but think, *Will I look good enough to be on this man's arm?* Once she had gotten dressed she left the bedroom and walked into the living area. Jack stood up and looked at her with a big smile on his face.

"Damn baby, you look good."

The dress was working. He asked her to turn around a few times and just stand there. He wanted to imprint the vision in his head.

They went downstairs to the grand ballroom; heads were turning. Her breasts have always fascinated white men, and this was no exception. As they waited to be seated in the grand ballroom, an older couple stood next to them. The man seemed to have a difficult time looking past her breasts; finally he just gave up and stared. Jack smiled, got his attention and said, "They're beautiful, aren't they?" The man turned beet red, and his wife pulled him toward their table. Cynthia and Jack both laughed at the man's inability to control himself.

The New Year's Eve show featured Roberta Flack. Jack chose her because she could sing all of the things that he wanted Cynthia to hear. Roberta Flack was notorious for her ability to sing meaningful love songs; and she did just that. It was a fantastic show. As the New Year came in she sang "Tonight I Celebrate My

Love for You." Jack and Cynthia danced, and he stroked her neck and back. She didn't ever want this evening to end. He kissed her passionately. She looked into his eyes and said, "Remind me that there is almost a twenty-year difference in our ages."

"I'll remind you, baby, but not tonight."

It was New Year's Day and their ten-day dream world was pretty much at an end. They would leave in the morning. She would be headed to Boston, and he would be headed for New Jersey. Although they laughed and played most of the day, they both knew their time together was coming to an end, and they had no idea when they would see each other again. There was one thing that they both knew for sure: there is no amount of time and nothing in this world that would ever make them forget these last ten days.

They got to the airport at about 10 A.M. Her flight left at 10:30, and his left at 11:00. They sat there waiting for the plane, holding hands, and not saying very much. When the plane began to board, he helped her gather her things and then held her in his arms.

"This is not over," he said. "There is no way that I could let you walk completely out of my life right now."

"It is my hope that there will never be a time when we can walk completely out of each other's life." She kissed him good-bye and boarded the plane. When she finally arrived home, everything in the apartment reminded her of him. She needed to keep busy, so she started picking up things in the house, vacuuming, and doing all the chores that she hadn't done for the past ten days. She could not bring herself to change the bed.

Cynthia missed her Sunday Sister Circle calls, so she got in touch with Sandra and Robin just to catch up. After speaking with Sandra, she found out that her family had a wonderful Christmas, but she was having morning sickness. Her grandmother, Mama Lee, wasn't doing too well. Sandra wondered if Mama Lee would make it another month.

Of course Cynthia discussed her holiday vacation with Jack.

"The only thing that I can tell you is that it was a journey of a lifetime."

"You really like that man, don't you?"

"Yeah, I do."

"Well, what are you going to do about it?"

"I'm not going to do anything, just continue to do what we're doing."

"Well, if it was me, I'd go get that man."

Sandra promised to keep her posted on Mama Lee's condition. Cynthia promised to catch up with her next Sunday. When Cynthia spoke to Robin, Robin humorously chastened her. "Well, I'll be damn! You finally came back from dreamland."

Cynthia told her as much as she dared to about those ten days.

"Girl, that sounds fabulous," Robin said.

"It really was."

"Well, I'll be honest. I don't know if I could handle a relationship like that."

"Girl, believe me, if you ever came across a relationship like this, you would handle it."

A few days later Cynthia stopped by the salon, and Tracy looked like she was having a rough time.

"Has business really been that rough?" she asked.

"Yeah, business has been tough, with the holidays and all. I've had back-to-back customers for the last five days."

"That's what happens when you're making money hand over fist."

"But I'm beginning to realize that there's got to be a limit to what you're willing to do for money."

She told Cynthia that Rosa had been in the hospital for about three days with three fractured ribs, a punctured lung, and her left knee dislocated.

"I really don't have to tell you what happened. Of course you know he beat her again. Cynthia, this time, that crazy man beat her because she asked him to come home for New Year's Eve."

"I'll stop by after work, and we can both go down to visit her."

"Thanks, I really didn't want to face her by myself."

Cynthia thought about Rosa most of the day. It must have been a horrible experience for her children to watch their mother being beaten by their father. It must have brought serious flashbacks for Tracy, too.

When they got to the hospital, Rosa was sitting in a chair looking out the window. She clearly looked as if she'd been beaten. Her left eye was swollen shut and her left leg was in a plaster cast and heavily bandaged. Her hair was matted to the back of her head. The wrinkles in her brow were a true indictor that she was in pain. When they entered the room, Rosa looked at Tracy and said "Oh Tracy, I'm so glad you came" and tears began to roll from her eyes.

"Cynthia, thank you for coming, too."

Tracy couldn't look her in the face; she kept pacing around the room while she talked to Rosa.

"Rosa, when are you going to take control of your life and stop allowing this motherfucker to beat you?"

"Well, it really wasn't his fault, I shouldn't have—"

Before she could finish her sentence Tracy shouted, "Damn it, Rosa! There's nothing that you should or shouldn't have done that would make you deserve to be beaten like this."

Cynthia reached over to hold Rosa's hand. She really didn't have much to say. She didn't know Rosa well, but she held her hand while she cried. They left the hospital, and on their way home Tracy ventilated.

"Cynthia, I really want to kill that motherfucker. He deserves to die."

Tracy suggested that they get dinner on Sunday; she had to get back to work, and they really didn't have a lot of time to talk about Cynthia's ten-day visit with Jack. Sunday was the only day that Tracy refused to work. When they did meet for dinner at Sidney's on Sunday she looked a lot better.

"Cynthia, I'm so glad you're here because sometimes you can bring sanity to very insane situations. I was feeling real bad about Rosa, and I know you could tell because it showed in my face and body. I realize I can't save her, and Lord knows I don't want to see her die."

"Tracy, the only thing that I can do is work with you and try to convince Rosa to want a better life."

"If you can do that, it might make a difference."

Cynthia and Tracy decided to include Rosa in their Sunday dinners. They were going to have to convince her that they would be there for her no matter what.

"Okay, that's enough about Rosa. Tell me about your ten-day vacation, and if that red dress had the brother limping."

"Tracy, it was ten of the most fantastic days of my life."

"Girl, was it really all that?"

"I spent ten days with a man that transformed me into a hell of a woman. This brother took me places and taught me things that most women never learn. He had unbelievable talent and unbelievable patience."

"Well damn, sister, you need to package that brother and sell his ass. We could make big money. All kidding aside, Cynthia, there's a part of me that is envious of you. I would love to have someone in my life that made me feel that way. But then there is another part of me that is happy for you, because at least someone that I know is having a good time."

"Tracy, you work six days a week from eight o'clock in the morning until sometimes ten o'clock at night. Where do you expect to meet someone who can change your life? Even if you do, you don't have time to cultivate a relationship."

"You know you're right, but that's going to change and it's going to change soon. I've been thinking about expanding my business. I want to franchise because I don't want to work as hard as I'm doing now. I really need to get connected to somebody with a business head to help me develop a franchise plan. I've got the ideas, but I need to develop a business plan to take to the bank."

"Tracy, I may have just the person who could help you work that out. Give me a little time and let me see if I can arrange a meeting."

They finished dinner, and Tracy brought Cynthia up to date on what happened in town over the last ten days.

Jack and Cynthia continued their Thursday evening dates; his warm soothing baritone voice became her weekly tranquilizer. She kept him appraised on what was going on in her life, her Sister Circle, her new job, and her new relationship with Tracy and Rosa. She also realized that she knew very little about what went on in his life on a weekly, or monthly, basis. He never volunteered any information and she never asked. So she decided to ask him the same question that he asked her every time that they talked: Had he met any interesting women?

"Baby, I meet women all the time, but rarely do I meet women who can hold my attention. She would have to come with some very special things to get and hold my attention. I date occasionally but all too often, after the second date, I realize that we don't have much in common."

"It sounds as if it's going to be as difficult for you to find your second wife as it will be for me to find my first husband."

"The difference is I'm not looking for a second wife. One was enough for me." He laughed.

"How's your son doing?"

"That's odd; you have never asked me about him before."

"You're right. I really do want to know more about you."

"He's doing fine; he's off stumbling around trying to find himself, much like I did at his age. We get together occasionally, and it's generally when he needs some advice or some help. I guess that's what a father is supposed to do. But when he does ask me for advice, he takes it very seriously. I would not want him to make the same mistakes that I did. I want him to take a little more time to weigh his options. When I see him, I see myself at his age; and I'm trying to prepare him to recognize what he needs as opposed to what he wants, and to recognize when the wants and needs come together. He's a work in progress."

Tracy and Cynthia decided to visit Rosa in the hospital again; they wanted her to know that they were thinking about her. Rosa looked much better and felt that she would be leaving the hospital very soon. They asked her if she wanted to join them for dinner on Sunday. It was something they did as often as possible. Dinner on Sundays gave them a chance to catch up. Rosa said she would join them if she could get a babysitter.

While they were talking, the nurse came in to check Rosa's vital signs.

"Rosa, you're looking real good. The doctor thinks you will be discharged tomorrow."

"That's great news!" Tracy all but yelled. "You'll be going home."

Rosa looked at them, and the smile left her face. Going home didn't seem to excite her.

Within minutes a tall, thin, dark-skinned man entered the room. He wore a black leather jacket, bell-bottom pants, and a white turtleneck sweater. His face was clean-shaven with the exception of a neatly trimmed mustache. When he whizzed into the room, the entire mood changed. Tracy looked at him, rolled her eyes, and turned her back. Rosa suddenly looked down at the floor. Cynthia was the only one in the room who didn't have an immediate negative reaction to him.

"Carlton, this is Cynthia. And Cynthia, this is my husband, Carlton."

She extended her hand, and he stepped back, looked her up and down, and shook her hand.

"Hello, Cynthia."

She heard the evil in his voice. He looked across the room and saw Tracy and said hello, but Tracy refused to respond. Cynthia watched him as he talked to Rosa. He never asked her anything; he just barked directions and demands.

He told her that the kids were doing fine and that he was picking them up tomorrow before he came to get her. He warned her to be ready when he got there, he didn't want to have to wait. Cynthia observed his mannerisms and saw his attitude. There was something sinister and unhealthy about Carlton. He had a foreboding aura around him. Tracy and Cynthia left, but not before telling Rosa that they would see her at another time.

As they left the room Cynthia said good-bye.

"Nice meeting you, Cynthia; and bye, Tracy," Carlton blurted out.

Tracy was silent. While Cynthia and Tracy were on the elevator, Cynthia asked her why she refused to greet Carlton.

"I have absolutely nothing to say to that motherfucker. Every time I see that man the only thing I want to do is to hurt him, and he knows it. The only reason he talks to me is that he knows how much it bothers me."

As regional sales representative, Cynthia found herself all over the city at various times during the day. She was just leaving an appointment with a new customer when she ran across Thomas, a very old friend. They had dated for a short while when they were teenagers, around seventeen and eighteen. Men didn't date very long back then without the promise of sex. Thomas was different. He was a virgin, as she was at the time, and was okay with his virginal status. She remembered him as being respectful and enjoyed his company until he went away to college. He had returned to Boston to take a job with the Internal Revenue Service. She was glad to see him. He had matured quite nicely. They exchanged phone numbers and he invited her out to dinner. Naturally, she accepted. It would be nice to catch up with an old friend.

At dinner it was obvious that Thomas still had a great sense of humor. What Cynthia remembered most about him, though, was that in his own way he was quite smooth. Over dinner they laughed and joked about dating and how different it had become. When he was younger, Thomas considered going to a seminary. According to him, he had very strong religious beliefs but wasn't so sure that he wanted to commit himself to God in quite that way. They talked about finding mates, getting married, and having children. Thomas wanted to find the right woman and have at least two children.

That wasn't for Cynthia and she told Thomas so. Marriage was not on her "list of things to do" and she didn't really want to be a mother. He didn't understand that. He thought she would be an excellent mother. They enjoyed each other's company. They went to movies and plays, and just hung out having fun. He wasn't a groper, or a puller. He was consistent and patient. They had not gotten to the point where they were ready to become sexually involved, and he didn't press hard.

Now neither of them were children, and they both had sexual desires, so at some point they knew that they would at least try to see if they were sexually compatible. Thomas was a great kisser and understood foreplay. When it came down to actually having sex, he was relatively smooth. At an earlier point in her life he would have been quite acceptable, but the passion just wasn't there. She also knew that ultimately he wanted something that she didn't know if she could give—a wife and children.

She learned early in life that you can't make a person into someone they're not; so before they got to the point that either of them would be unhappy, it was best that they moved on. They chatted occasionally on the phone, but they never dated again.

When she told Jack about the reunion with Thomas, she heard two things in his voice. Part of him was saying "Keep trying because you'll find the right man" and another part of him was saying "I'm glad he wasn't the one." As long as "the one" was not in her life Jack knew he was "the one."

Late on Friday evening Sandra called. Mama Lee had passed away in her sleep.

"Cynthia, I know I'm asking a lot, but I really need you to be here. The funeral will be Tuesday."

"Of course I'll be there. Take care of yourself. I'll probably get there by Sunday morning."

Cynthia hung up and called Robin. She had also gotten the call, and Sandra asked her to please try to be there.

Robin and Cynthia arrived in Atlanta on Sunday and went straight to Sandra's house. Sandra was a wreck. Between sobs she kept asking, "Who's going to keep me grounded? Who is going to be there for me? I don't know what I'm going to do."

Robin and Cynthia hugged her and assured her that they would always be there for her. If she needed to be grounded they would do that also. They knew that they couldn't replace Mama Lee and wouldn't even try, but Sandra needed to know that they would always be there. She wasn't alone.

It was a beautiful going-home ceremony in one of Atlanta's larger churches. It was clear that Mama Lee had a lot of people that cared about her, and she was sent home in a grand fashion. Sandra asked Robin and Cynthia to go with her and her mother the next day to clean out Mama Lee's house. This was a trying experience for them all. They helped to pick up and pack all of the family pictures and other memorabilia and began to move them out of Mama Lee's house. Sandra's mother had arranged for all of her mother's belongings to be brought to her house for storage. Sandra asked if she could have the family pictures.

That evening, after dinner, Jason knew that they wanted to spend some time together, and he left the house for a while. They spent a lot of time consoling Sandra and talking about their individual lives. They raised questions and asked for opinions and feedback, just as they had always done. Sandra told them that she was pregnant again. Her first child, a daughter, was about two years old. Sandra hadn't planned this pregnancy, it just happened.

She and Jason agreed that if they were going to have three children, they might as well accept this blessing and get it done and over with. Robin and Cynthia felt that it was awfully early for a second child, but they also knew that Sandra needed their support. They congratulated and hugged her and wished for a boy. Sandra said that she enjoyed her job and had gone back to school to work on her master's degree because one day she hoped to be a principal.

Robin brought pictures of her new condo. It was beautifully decorated. Cynthia promised her that one weekend she would come down to visit. Robin was still dating quite actively, but said she still had not found anyone who held her interest for any length of time. She still found men to fit the occasion and felt that was the best way to deal with men at that point in her life. Of course Cynthia had to tell them again about her ten-day experience. Sandra sat on the edge of her seat and exclaimed, "That sounds so romantic."

"While it's romantic, I still don't understand what you two are doing," Robin said.

Cynthia told her that she and Jack were enjoying the hell out of each other, and that was all that was important.

Since Cynthia had them both together, she thought this would be an appropriate time to tell them about Tracy and Rosa and how she thought that they could benefit from having other women with whom they could talk.

"Well, I understand that these women are having problems, but we've been together a long time, and the last thing we need in our Sister Circle is someone who can't commit the way that we have committed to each other," Robin said, putting her feelings right up front.

"It's very simple to me," Sandra chimed in. "If they can't commit, they just won't last very long. But I realize that if I did not have my sisters I don't know what I would do. I would hate to believe that there is someone out there who needs love and support, who needs us, and we're not there to help them."

Cynthia expected to hear sensitivity from Sandra because she was always the most caring and inclusive one in the circle. Robin was still a little unsure and was trying to understand why there needed to be any other women involved in the Sister Circle. Cynthia suggested to Robin that before she completely closed her mind to these two women, perhaps she should meet them.

"I'll meet them, but they really need to be special to fit into this circle."

Cynthia told Sandra that she would really like for her to meet them, too. Any woman who would come into this circle needed to be approved by all of them.

"I'm fine with bringing women into the circle as long as they understand who we are and can commit in the same way that we do. I won't be able to come and meet these women right now. Whatever you two decide will be all right with me."

They spent the rest of the evening laughing about old times and some of the fun they used to have. They thought about the time they spent with Mama Lee and all of the stories and life lessons she shared with them. Robin was the one to remind them about the "Turning."

Mama Lee had told them to celebrate each year and be happy the Lord continues to bless their existence. They agreed to celebrate the "Turning" each year on their individual birthdays, and every ten years they would celebrate the "Turning" together.

Time was moving quickly. Within the next few years the youngest of them would be thirty, and they needed to figure out where their first group "Turning" would take place. They all had ideas about how they should celebrate. They were brainstorming, and laughing because some of their ideas were pretty extravagant.

"I don't care what we do; but one thing is for sure, it's got to be classy with a lot of style. We've got to be among the finest sisters in the room," Robin said. "So that means we have to celebrate in New York. Where else can you find the venue and the style that we would need? Now Georgia is all right, but it doesn't have the atmosphere that New York has."

Sandra became parochial, saying, "Anything they got in New York, we got twice as much in Georgia, and we add a lot of sunshine."

Over the years they had made many friends and associates and wanted them all to be invited to this "Turning." They wanted old boyfriends, new boyfriends and prospective boyfriends to be present and accounted for. There were only two possible sites, New York or Atlanta. Boston was not considered as an option because they knew it was not the high point of travel for black people.

They decided that Atlanta would be the most economical for Sandra, after all she was the only one with children, and they could use Sandra's mother, the "Queen of Flair," as their official party planner. If it was going to be a gala event, Sandra's mother knew where to hold it and how to plan it. They decided to invite Sandra's mother to lunch the next day and get her excited about planning their first group "Turning." It would take her mind off of her recent loss.

At lunch the next day they giggled like schoolgirls preparing for the prom. Sandra's mother said, "I guarantee you that I can give you an event to remember. And if you leave it up to me, everyone will have a wonderful time."

They figured that they had fewer than two years to plan this event and they would leave no stone unturned. Robin and Sandra headed home that evening. Cynthia promised Robin that she would be in New York in two weeks to see her condo.

CHAPTER 9

One Sunday when Rosa, Tracy, and Cynthia were having dinner, Cynthia mentioned the Sister Circle and how good it felt to be back with it. The circle had brought her through some rough patches. Being with her sisters was always invigorating and caused her to move on with her life.

Tracy understood. "It's rare, girl, to find even one, or maybe two women, you can develop that kind of relationship with. Doing it with more women than that seems to me to be damn near impossible."

Rosa sat there quietly eating her dinner. So Cynthia asked her how she felt about networking with women willing to support her and stand by her side through the good times and the bad times.

"I've never really thought of that," Rosa said in almost a whisper. "I've been by myself for so long I never thought of having anyone that I could talk to."

"Having someone to talk to can make a world of difference in your life. I can testify to that," Cynthia said trying to encourage Rosa.

"Cynthia, if they are your friends they must be pretty decent people, and I'm certainly open to meeting new people," Tracy said. "I need to broaden my horizon and become more sociable. I'm really looking to find that special person in my life one day. I've never had any social time. It would be nice to have women that I could talk to, who might understand some of the problems women have."

"There will only be one problem for me. I don't think Carlton's going to like this," Rosa said.

"Fuck Carlton," Tracy snarled. "Who gives a damn about what he likes?"

Rosa lowered her head in what seemed to be embarrassment. Cynthia knew she would have to work with Tracy to help her understand that attacking Rosa's husband was not the best way to get Rosa's attention. After all, Carlton was her husband, right or wrong. More important, Rosa loved him. It was going to take a little work, but she would have to show Tracy how to work with Rosa so that her friend could see the light. And yes, she understood why Tracy might want to kill Carlton; she was sure that the more she learned to love Rosa the more she might want to hurt him herself. That wouldn't resolve the problem, would it?

Cynthia promised Robin a visit at her New York City condo, and she always kept her promises. So she left Boston one Friday afternoon about two o'clock and headed for New York City. She got there about seven o'clock that evening. Traffic was unbelievably heavy. Robin had cooked dinner.

"You know, girl, you must be all right with me 'cause you know I don't normally do this shit," Robin joked.

Cynthia knew no matter how hard she tried, Robin would want to take her to at least one social event whether she wanted to go or not. Usually she would go.

New York and New Jersey had a reputation of having great supper clubs. Robin was a regular at a place called Small's in Harlem. After dinner, they got dressed, jumped in her car, and headed to 135th Street. When they arrived at Small's, they saw that the Four Tops were performing. Now in Boston the Four Tops performing would have been a big event. It didn't seem like a big deal to the folks in New York. The club was full of all kinds of people, but she noticed the bar area seemed to be reserved for an assortment of black men dressed in colorful suits and shoes doing what they called "business." She mentioned it to Robin.

"You know, sister, everybody's got to make a living," Robin hipped her. "If there's a pimp out here who can find a dumb-ass woman to sell her body and give him the money, I say more power to him."

"Well you know, Robin, some women just find themselves in a bad situation and that's how they earn a living."

"I can understand tricking; I just can't understand tricking and giving your money to someone else. If I were ever going to trick, I'd be a damn good whore. But all of the money would be mine." Robin was emphatic.

They ordered drinks and sat at the far end of the bar for a while talking to the brothers who came back and forth with a different line. The lines of the 1970s were so lame, but they seemed to work for these brothers. There was the toothless brother who stepped to the bar and told them he wanted to sop them up with a biscuit. Then there was the dick-dancing brother who stood in front of them with his hands on his penis, twitching and fondling himself. Believe it or not, there was the brother with no game at all. He just kind of stood around trying to think of something to say. Cynthia prided herself on her ability to mix in with most crowds, so she laughed and joked with all the brothers. They danced, but she made it clear that she was not in town looking for a man.

A handsome satin-skinned brother tending bar overheard her comment and said, "You know, sister, I could tell you weren't looking for a man. You don't have that aura about you." She wanted to know what the aura was.

"Well sister, I don't know how to explain it, but any brother who's out here playing can look at a sister and tell if she's looking for a man and if she's desperate. The sisters just can't hide it. You just don't have that look."

The brother's name was Sam. He claimed to be co-owner of Small's and said it as if it was meant to be impressive. Sam was what she considered a pretty boy—about six feet tall, two hundred and twenty pounds, with dark silky skin and a thick black mustache. His clothing was rather conservative, top quality, and they fit his body quite nicely. They sat at the bar just talking in general and it was clear that he could walk and chew gum at the same time. That prompted Cynthia to continue the conversation.

He asked if she had children, how many, and why she was out without her man. She told him that she didn't have children, or a husband, and that she was alone by choice. He looked at her with a straight face and said, "Well, what's wrong with you?"

She had to laugh at the brother and told him that there was nothing wrong with her, having a husband was just not on her "list of things to do." She had a direction in her life and, personally, she was a little too straightforward for the average man. Besides, there is no real challenge to having a husband or children. Some of the most stupid people in the world have accomplished that. She did not believe in bringing children that she didn't want or could afford into this world. There are enough fatherless babies in this world.

"Sister, you know you're right, and I'm sorry if I offended you in any way. It's just that 90 percent of the women I meet have at least one or two children somewhere. When I meet them in the club, I often wonder what the hell they are doing here."

"Brother, I'm sorry to disappoint you, but I'm probably not your average woman."

"The more I talk to you, the more I realize that you're not."

She knew then that there was something different about Sam. Whenever another brother came to the bar and showed the slightest interest in her, Sam would look at him, shake his head, and the brother would walk away. She wondered how he had the power to make people disappear. When Robin returned, she asked her how much she knew about Sam. Robin said that he was co-owner of the club and had other business dealings going on in the city. He was a real nice brother, but he didn't take any shit; and everybody in the bar knew that.

"From what I can see, he's put a claim on you this evening," Robin said. Cynthia laughed because no one had ever staked a claim on her in such a nonverbal way. "Talk to the brother; you might like him. He is smoother than the average New York brother."

Out of sheer curiosity Cynthia decided to talk to him a little more and found that he had a few things going in his favor. He looked like he stepped out of *Gentleman's Quarterly* magazine. He had a decent command of the English language. Getting into her panties did not appear to be his only goal; and last, he knew what he wanted and went after it.

The club was pretty loud and it was difficult to have a conversation, so he asked if she would like to sit in the club's conversation room. The conversation room was just to the left of the bar, and there were several people there having drinks and talking. She let Robin know where she was going and followed

Sam into the room. He offered her another drink. She told him that she'd had her limit but would like a ginger ale. He lifted his finger slightly above his head, and a waitress virtually ran over to see what he needed. She had to smile because he seemed to enjoy wielding power. The waitress came back shortly with the drinks. They talked about who they were and what they liked. He had a decent sense of humor and managed to catch the puns and innuendos that she occasionally tossed at him.

After about the third drink he suggested that they go back to his place to continue the conversation. She told him that she enjoyed their conversation where it was.

"However, if you really need someone to go home with you this evening, you might want to spend your time and energy on someone else."

He continued to press indirectly by telling her how influential he was, how much money he had, and how many women were seeking his attention.

She told him that she was a very open and honest woman; and if honesty was a problem for him he might not want to talk to her too long. Like most brothers, he said, "An honest woman is hard to find, and I certainly would welcome and appreciate it." She thought to herself, *It's on now.*

"Look, brother, all the money and prestige that you have don't necessarily make you a better quality man."

"You are absolutely right, but usually those are the things that will impress a woman," he said with a chuckle.

"You know, Sam, I just may be a little different than most of the women you know."

"So I can see; but one thing I have to let you know, and that is, rarely have I not been able to convince a woman to share in my bed."

"There is a first time for everything, and I need to let you know that I won't be going home with you this evening. A brother has to get into my head and stimulate my mind before he could get into my panties," she quipped.

"I believe that I can get into your head," he said with a sly smile.

They talked a lot that evening. She thought that maybe there was something worth investigating in Sam. When the evening ended for them he suggested that they exchange phone numbers. As they exchanged numbers she thought that this brother probably doesn't even know that the ball was now in his court. He was clearly accustomed to women chasing him, and this would have to be a different game.

Robin and Cynthia danced, flirted, and had a good time that evening. As they were leaving the club, Sam stopped Cynthia and said, "You're a very interesting and refreshing woman, and I really would like to get to know you better."

"You've got my number, give me a call."

On the way back to her condo, Robin felt a need to tell her more about Sam.

"Girl, do you realize how much money that brother's got and how much property he owns? There are sisters out there trying to get with this brother, and you act like you're not even that interested."

"I know all about his money. Sam was not shy about his market value. It's not that I'm not interested, there are some interesting things about the brother; but money and material things really don't impress me. I want to know what kind of man he is."

"Well girl, don't be surprised if he doesn't call. You're making it too hard for him."

"That's the idea. If he's not willing to come for it, he certainly doesn't deserve it."

Robin's condo was beautiful and certainly got Cynthia's stamp of approval. Robin agreed to come back to Boston with her to meet Tracy and Rosa. They left Sunday morning in order to get into Boston around four o'clock. Tracy and Cynthia usually had dinner on Sundays around six o'clock. She invited Rosa to join them. It would be a great opportunity for Robin to meet them both.

The first thing that Robin noticed when she entered Cynthia's apartment was how drastically it had changed .The second thing she noticed was the candles.

"Girl, what's going on with the candles? Are you having a séance in here?"

"No girl! Candles are therapeutic, and each of these has a different scent. Each scent, depending on the individual, can create a different mood."

She tried to explain the concept of scent and how it stimulates the body in different ways. Robin wasn't getting it. So Cynthia gave her four candles to take back to New York.

"The next time you're about to get busy with a brother who turns you on, light these four candles, turn off the lights, breathe in deeply and see how the atmosphere changes."

Robin laughed. "I'll try it. I just hope it don't scare the brother away."

"If the brother has any level of sensitivity he won't be scared."

They got dressed and headed for Sidney's. When they arrived, Tracy and Rosa were already there, seated at their favorite table. Cynthia walked over to the table, greeted them and introduced Robin.

She had already told Robin that she thought Tracy was a lot like her—straightforward, frank, and quite graphic with her language.

"I can respect that. I'll respect any sister who is straight with what she's got to say," Robin said.

She also told her that Rosa was mild, meek, and generally kept her head down. Once she got to know you she would open up, and you could carry on a conversation. Robin also knew that Tracy was a lesbian. Robin's only concern was, "Girl, as fine as I am, I hope she doesn't try to hit on me." They chuckled, and Cynthia told Robin that she didn't think Robin was Tracy's type.

"Girl, I'm everybody's type."

When they sat down, no one seemed to have anything to say. Cynthia felt a lot of tension at the table and tried to change the mood. She figured at least over dinner they could get through the pleasantries. She watched Robin and Tracy, and it seemed as if they were trying to size each other up, almost like two fighters getting ready to enter the ring. Rosa did what she always does, sat with her head down. Cynthia asked about her children and if she liked her new job. She had just taken a job with the Department of Youth Services. Tracy and Cynthia thought it was ironic that a woman who is being abused in front of her children would take a job with D.Y.S. Cynthia realized at that moment that she knew very little about Rosa. They never had a deep or meaningful conversation the way that Tracy and her had. All Cynthia knew was that Rosa was being abused and had two children. She didn't know where she came from, what her life was like when she wasn't being beaten, and why she lived this way. Cynthia figured that they had a lot of the evening left and sooner or later she was going to get her to disclose.

Cynthia told Tracy and Rosa how she met Robin and Sandra, and how they became fast and lifelong friends. The three of them were connected in a powerful way. She told them some of the funny and silly things that they did together. She talked about the rough times and how they were there for each other. Sometimes they even cried together.

"Yeah, these sisters have been my lifeline," Robin chimed in.

Cynthia asked Tracy about the business and how things had been going. She told her that Robin was the person she wanted her to meet. Robin had a business head like no other. She could put together a business plan and get most banks to finance it. She always had an idea and a vision. She was damn good at what she did. Tracy brightened up.

"Girl, I really need to know somebody with a business head," Tracy spoke up. She was animated.

If you ever wanted to get Robin's attention all you needed to do was talk about business or money. By the time they got to coffee and desert, Robin and Tracy were doing their own thing. Robin had all the questions, and Tracy had all the answers. Robin took a small note pad from her purse and began to jot down notes; she pulled out a calculator and began to calculate percentages and compound interest. Rosa and Cynthia didn't know what the hell she was talking about. Tracy was on the edge of her seat and soon began asking all the questions.

Rosa and Cynthia sat there looking at each other, trying to figure out why they were even in the room. So Cynthia decided to take this opportunity to have a one-on-one conversation with Rosa. She wanted to know about her dreams and aspirations. What did she want out of life?

"I used to have dreams before Carlton and the kids came into my life," Rosa said wistfully.

At this point they had finished coffee and desert, and Cynthia suggested that they take this conversation back to her house where they could kick back and relax. As Robin and Cynthia got into the car and headed back to her apartment Robin said, "I like that sister; she's got it going on. She has a damn good business head, and I think we can develop a strong business proposal for her salon."

When they got to Cynthia's apartment, she made cocktails and they kicked back to continue their conversation. Rosa and Cynthia decided to get into the business conversation; it was getting quite interesting. Rosa even perked up a little. Cynthia later found out that Tracy had aggressively coached Rosa on the ride to her place. She told her to lift her head and brighten up, and stop looking so down all the time.

"This is our chance to have a group of supportive women in our lives; don't blow it" was Tracy's advice to Rosa.

It sounded like Robin and Tracy had some good ideas. Tracy asked, "What can we do to make this happen?"

"Let me work on it," Robin said in a cautionary voice. "Before I leave, I want to come by your shop and take a look at what you're doing. I'll go back to New York, put together a business plan, and get a few leads on some financing. We will go from there. I also have an idea for a strong marketing plan."

For the first time in a while Tracy was smiling. Cynthia saw this as an opportunity for Robin to get to know a little about Rosa.

Rosa didn't seem anxious to talk about a lot, so Cynthia had to figure out a way to get her to open up. She asked her where she was from. Rosa said she was from the Midwest, and that's where she met Tracy. Robin picked up on Rosa's hesitancy and took over

"I know that neither of you really know me, so let me tell you a little bit about who I am." Robin then went on to tell them where she was from, a little about her family, where she went to school, what she majored in, what she thought about marriage, life, business and making money. She also let them know that the Sister Circle and her sister friends were her lifeline throughout college and every day of her life.

"For the life of me, I can't understand how women can go through life without someone to lean on. Those of us in the circle have gone through some rough times, but we have always been there for each other. Because of that we've always made it through. Sometimes we look back on those experiences and laugh even though they really weren't funny at the time. So, ladies, I encourage every woman to be a part of a strong circle of women in some form. There is one thing you need to know about us, we try to be open and honest about things, so please know that no one would ever intentionally hurt the other's feelings. However, we will always tell each other the truth. We expect it.

"In our group, Cynthia is the realist. She accepts things for what they are. She either chooses to deal with them or chooses not to. It's hard as hell to hurt her feelings because she is the kind of person who will never allow anyone else to define her. She's got a great sense of humor and is in a strange-ass relationship with an old man."

Everyone in the room started to laugh, including Cynthia.

"But me, I'm a little different. Money is my game. I like men and plenty of them. They all have a purpose and I try to use them accordingly. My agenda right now is making money and seizing every opportunity to build my fortune.

"I don't intend to work the rest of my life. I intend to retire in my early 50s, and I want to be ready. I say what's on my mind; as I get older I try to be a little more tactful, but I'm coming at you and I'm coming straight. There is one thing that I can guarantee, and that is, if you become a part of this Sister Circle and begin to feel the love, I will have your back no matter what. I expect you to do the same for me.

"Now our other sister, Sandra; she's a softy, real tender feelings. She's learned to accept the truth from us. We have tried to find the right words to make it a little easier for her, but after all is said and done we still tell her the truth. She's a loving and supportive person, and she will always be there for you. She's the only one that's married, and she got married pretty early. She seems to be happy and that's all we're concerned with. We try to talk to each other at least once a week and plan to get together a lot more often than we have.

"Birthdays are a major celebration for us. We like to call it the Turning. When we 'turn' we love to celebrate and thank the Lord for giving us another year. In college we were the socialites. If there was a party happening, we were the ones throwing it. We love good people and love good times. Now that's just a synopsis of who we are. I'd like to know more about you."

Rosa continued to look at her drink with her head down. Tracy took a deep breath, looked around the room and said, "I'm gonna give you the short version of who Tracy is.

"I was born and raised in the Midwest. I was sexually molested as a child, and I watched my stepfather beat my mother to death. At an early age I knew that I would never allow myself to be a victim. I've taken the skills that I've acquired as a hairdresser and parlayed that into a business. I will work my natural ass off to keep making money.

"I believe that there is some truth in the saying 'Money talks and bullshit walks.' I'm very honest, sometimes to a fault. My language is a little colorful 'cause when I express myself I need to express myself in a way that everyone understands. I'm not a mean person, so I will never say anything to anyone just to hurt his or her feelings. But I'm not a pussy either. I will never be pushed around and I will never be intimidated. I'm versatile, and I try to fit into any crowd. I think I got a damn good sense of humor. I've never been privileged to connect with a group of women, and I realize that never having had that connection has made life a little more difficult. Open and honest women are exactly what I need in my life.

"As much as I like money, I don't mind spending it. I like nice things. I've only known Cynthia for a little while, but I connected to her spirit because I knew she was genuine. Much like you, Robin, I don't intend to work forever. I'll bust my ass for another few years and put in place the resources I need to continue my life without hard work. Once you become my friend I will always be there for you. Last but not least, I'm a lesbian. No, I do not like or trust men; and I'm a picky-ass lesbian. The woman who comes into my life has to be smart, classy, and fine. She's got to be fine because I'm fine and I deserve nothing less. I haven't found that woman yet, but I know I will. I certainly hope that the Sister Circle doesn't have a problem with a lesbian."

"Well girl, you're a money-making lesbian. I don't have any problem with that, as long as you ain't trying to hit on me," Robin interjected.

"Robin, you're all right and you're a smart sister, but you just ain't my type. Actually ain't none of you bitches my type, just for the record."

After they finished laughing about Tracy's last comment they looked to Rosa. They wanted to hear what she had to say. Rosa began to talk to them with her head down.

"Rosa, if you don't pick your head up and look at us we can't hear what you're saying." Tracy's tone was soothing, gentle.

Rosa lifted her head and spoke in a much louder voice. "I'm from the Midwest, born and raised. My mother was a schoolteacher, and my father was a police officer. I have three brothers and two sisters. I left the Midwest to go to Howard University where I studied sociology and met Carlton, my husband. I came from an abusive family; my mother was abused, and I watched this most of my life. I married a man who turned out to be an abuser. I can't figure out how to get away from him. I don't want my children to grow up that way, but I don't want them to grow up poor and hungry either. My husband is the one with the money.

"I've known Tracy since high school; and throughout my life no matter how bad it has gotten, she has always been there. As I sit here listening to each of you I began to realize that you are just what I need in my life. Each of you has a different strength and a different manner. I believe through the Sister Circle I will grow. I will gain strength in myself and be able to do what I should have done years ago.

"It's not a matter of self-esteem, because I know I'm not ugly and I know I'm not stupid. It's a matter of strength. That's what I'm trying to develop. It is awesome to watch strong women. The more I watch, the more I realize that I can do it. The only thing I ask is that you have patience as I try to put my life back together."

At this point, between the alcohol and what they had just heard from Rosa, they all got a little teary-eyed.

"Don't cry for me. I cry enough for myself," Rosa said with what seemed to be a newfound strength. "What I need from you is your strength and understanding."

Cynthia watched Robin throughout the conversation; she knew her well enough to know that both of these ladies would be embraced in the circle. They continued to do what they did. The Sister Circle now had five women, and the Sunday evenings were spent touching bases with everyone.

CHAPTER 10

Robin and Tracy got along wonderfully. Tracy ventured to New York several times, and Robin traveled to Boston more than ever before. They worked out a business plan that was easily financed by one of the larger Boston banks. Tracy opened two additional salons, all bearing her name. She worked about three days a week on her special customers. Most of her time was spent managing her salons.

She hired some of the best hairdressers in the city and had no problem keeping her customer base high. She was definitely making money. She purchased a house about twenty miles outside of Boston, a place to get away to when she finished in the salons.

Rosa seemed to be doing a little better, too. She didn't get hit as often as she did before. Carlton became very indifferent toward her, only slapping her around every now and then. Rosa admitted that she was happy with his indifference because it gave her a small window of opportunity to try to live her life. Originally, he did not like the Sister Circle idea, but as time went on he became more and more indifferent toward her.

"I don't give a damn if you hang out with those bitches. They can't do shit for you. Just make sure that you take care of my babies," he told Rosa.

The telephone rang exactly at eight o'clock. Cynthia lifted the receiver and heard Jack's deep baritone voice.

"Hey, baby, remind me that there's almost a twenty-year difference in our ages."

"I'll remind you the next time I see you," she said playfully. "Are you okay?"

"I'm doing fine, but I did have an unusually difficult week. This week has been very difficult for me to stay in touch with reality. There were far too many people and things that reminded me of you."

"Well Jack, it's very common that once or twice a day I'm reminded of you. My friends often tell me that they know when I'm thinking about you because I get a dumb look on my face and go into a trance."

"I guess what I'm trying to tell you, baby, is that it's been six months since we've been together and I really need to see you."

"You are absolutely right, Jack. Six months is a long time, and I think we need to figure something out."

He couldn't have missed her more than she missed him, but she couldn't let him know that. It was now the middle of June, and he suggested that they try to get away for the Fourth of July. She could certainly arrange the time, and suggested that he come to Boston.

"Baby, when I see you in July, I need your undivided attention. I don't think I can get that in Boston. You're a very busy lady with a lot of things going on. I don't want to share your attention. I'll tell you what, I'll come and get you in Boston, but we're going to have to leave town. I'll arrange everything."

Why not, she thought. Every surprise Jack had planned for her had been awesome.

Sandra's mother was having a field day planning the first major "Turning," now only three months away. They placed a cap of three hundred fifty persons on the guest list. There were new and old friends, and they wanted them all to join the celebration. The first "Turning" would take about four days so that they would have time to reflect on their past and plan for the future. Rosa found a babysitter who was willing to take her children for the week, and the three of them—Rosa, Tracy, and Cynthia—scheduled the same flight out of Boston to Atlanta.

Sandra's children were now four and two years old. She and Jason chose not to have a third child. Two were enough. One of the most important preparations for this "Turning" was finding outfits that would make each of them memorable. The hunt was on. The three sisters in Boston looked into every nook and cranny, every boutique and shop in the greater New England area, for that special outfit.

Tracy chose a form-fitting black gown that was simple but chic. Now, they didn't know why, but the other sisters thought that her outfit would be a little less feminine, being a lesbian and all.

"Yes I'm a lesbian; but I'm also a woman, and I'm a fly-ass woman," Tracy made it clear for them.

Sandra wanted to wear winter white and searched all over Atlanta to find just the right outfit. She wouldn't tell them what it looked like, but assured them that they would be impressed.

This was the first time in a long time that Rosa had an occasion to get dressed up, and she didn't have any idea what to wear. Tracy and Cynthia stepped in to help her find just the right outfit for the "Turning." Rosa spent most of her life not wearing anything that called attention to herself.

They chose a full-length dress in royal blue, a color that complemented Rosa's complexion. Gold accessories added a little splash to the outfit.

Cynthia chose Kelly green, and Robin chose gold as colors for their outfits. Now, all of these outfits had one thing in common: they accentuated the positive and pulled attention away from the negatives. Cynthia's gown accentuated her breasts. Tracy's gown accented her tiny waistline and height. Robin's gown had a deep split on the left side so that her shapely legs could show. Rosa still wasn't secure enough to show cleavage or legs, but she would be beautiful nonetheless.

Sandra said that her gown was stunning. It would definitely turn heads, but she really wasn't ready to show any particular parts of her body, at least not yet. Jason thought his wife still looked good and encouraged her to show a little cleavage, but Sandra, being the southern belle that she was, she just couldn't do it.

Jack and Cynthia were still having their Thursday evening telephone dates. It was years later that she realized they were having phone sex. It had been quite a while since she evaluated her "list of things to do." She was sure there were things on that list that needed to be deleted. Certainly some things needed to be added. She would be sure to do that before she left for the "Turning."

They finally agreed upon a date. The "Turning" would be Saturday, December 3, and every ten years the "Turning" would happen the first Saturday in December. Sandra's mother sent each of the sisters a large manila envelope full of information and asked them to take a look and decide between them which facility they wanted to use. It was a unanimous decision to hold the "Turning" at the Atlanta Hilton.

It was 1980, and Atlanta was changing. People from all over the country were moving there.

They choose the Atlanta Hilton because it had an elegant grand ballroom, and enough rooms for their out-of-town guests. They still had time to choose their menu, but they booked their hotel reservations early so that they could get the penthouse and the two adjoining suites.

They even requested a large, three-tiered chocolate cake and plenty of champagne. The cake was to read: "To celebrate the Turning of Cynthia, Sandra, Robin, Tracy and Rosa."

Sandra's mother had included four samples of invitations that they might use. Although all four were good, they agreed on one that was black with silver script. Sandra's mother suggested that they begin to put together their individual invitation list. She commissioned a calligrapher who would address and mail them. The invitations wouldn't be sent until the first of November, so they had plenty of time.

When Jack and Cynthia spoke again on the next Thursday he sounded a lot better. He wanted to know if he could pick her up on July 1 and bring her back on July 6. It took her a second because she wanted to count the days. Six days sounded damn good to her. He said they weren't going to do anything formal, so she didn't have to worry about formal wear, just pack some leisure clothes.

"Baby, I'll be at your door by noon on July 1."

"What time shall I pick you up at the airport?"

"Don't worry about that. This time I will be picking you up. Just be home by noon on the first of July."

She told him about the plans for the "Turning" and he thought that the idea was great. She told him where they were going and all of the great plans that they made. He knew that she had been on a massive search for just the right dress for this "Turning" and he said, "Whatever you wear, I know you're going to look good, but would you do me a small favor and not wear that red sequined dress. That dress makes a powerful statement, and I really want to feel that the dress made the statement only for me."

She brought him up to date on the Sister Circle and how well Tracy and Rosa were fitting into the circle and how they thought that the five of them were going to have a great time. Again he asked her the standard question that he asked on most of their Thursday night dates.

"Have you met anyone interesting?"

Of course she told him about Sam.

He asked her what she liked about this man, and she said, "Well, he's probably smoother than a lot of the men I've met. He accepted no for an answer without getting nasty." She told him that she hadn't heard from Sam, so she didn't think this was going to lead to anything special.

"Well baby, this gentleman might be the kind of man you're looking for, but be sure that you ask a lot of questions and find out as much as you can about him. If he still interests you, I say, you've got to try. But he'd better be a damn good man."

"He may or may not be, and I wasn't in a real hurry to find out," she told Jack. "I met him, he caught my attention for a moment and we'll see where that goes."

Little did she know at the time that Jack knew Sam. He wasn't impressed with him and even less impressed with what he did and how he did it. Jack never told her this until much later in their relationship.

He then asked her if she had contacted Wesley. Jack was probably the only person who knew about Wesley. He was also the only person who knew Wesley was her first love and on her "list of things to do."

"Funny you should ask. I ran into Wesley about six months ago. I extended an invitation for lunch and have not heard from him since. I'm not sure why he didn't call. He seemed happy to see me."

"Baby, there could be several reasons," Jack volunteered. "The brother could be in a relationship. He could be a little intimidated by you. It could be several different things. But I'd bet you it wasn't because he was disinterested in you. If he actually saw you, he would have to be interested or there is something really wrong with him. I have a feeling that he has other things going on in his life and just doesn't know what to do about you.

"Baby, I know that you're not a chaser and you will not pursue a man; but I think that this brother, because he meant so much to you, deserves at least one more attempt. You need to find out who he is, what kind of man he grew into, and does he have any of the things that made you fall in love with him at sixteen. Sometimes the memory of your first love is much better than the reality. Don't take him off your 'list of things to do' yet."

"Maybe you're right. I'll keep him on the list and see what happens."

The next few weeks came and went in a flash. It was June 29 and Jack was coming for Cynthia in two days. Anticipation was setting in, and she really couldn't concentrate too long on any one thing. On Saturday morning she got up bright and early and met Tracy downtown for lunch.

"You know, Cynthia, this is the first time since I was fifteen years old that I wasn't somewhere sweating over a head on a Saturday afternoon. I like it," Tracy crowed. "I still enjoy being able to be creative with someone's hair; I especially enjoy doing it when I want to." Then she looked at my head. "Speaking of hair, what the hell happened to yours? That shit looks like a wild wolf's pussy,"

Cynthia laughed until there were tears in her eyes.

"Come on, girl!" Tracy continued.

By three o'clock Cynthia was sitting in Tracy's chair at the salon enjoying her work her magic.

Every chair in the shop was occupied and there were people waiting. This definitely was a busy day. The salon maintained its style and class. Light jazz played in the background, while the women chatted among themselves. The receptionist made sure that the waiting customers were given something cold to drink and something hot to read while they waited. Tracy told Cynthia a while back that the importance of managing three different shops was the element of surprise. They never knew when or if Tracy was coming. As a result, personnel in all three shops stayed on top of their game at all times.

Tracy didn't tolerate panhandling and made it perfectly clear that no one was to come into her shop selling, trading, or buying. There would be no bootlegging or boosting. She also asked customers to keep their gossip to a minimum.

"You know, girl, gossip is something that everyone does, although most people assume it's women who do most of the gossiping," Tracy said. "I got a friend who owns two barbershops, and he says that nobody can gossip like a group of men. So, even though I ask the women not to gossip, I realize they're going to do it anyway. We really want to try to keep it to a minimum. The things I hear in this shop would curl your hair.

"If some of these women knew where their men were and what they were doing, there would be at least two or three double homicides nightly. There are women who come in my shops and make it very clear that the only man they want is a married man. If the man ain't married, they ain't interested. Seems like everybody out there in this world is trying to get something for nothing. Women are no different.

"In all three shops, on any given day, there is always a story being told about who's got the big penis, who's fucking who, and who's fighting with a short stick. Now when they tell these stories they think it's funny and don't really care that their business is being put in the street."

Having finished her monologue, Tracy asked what Cynthia's plans were for the evening. She wanted to come by to get Cynthia's opinion on a problem she was wrestling with.

Cynthia was lounging around the house finishing up some last-minute packing and daydreaming when Tracy came by carrying four or five shopping bags and wearing a big smile.

"I'm not going to stay long; I just wanted to run this one by you." Tracy gave the impression she was dashing in and out. "Do you remember when you told me that I would never meet anybody unless I had some time to get out socially?"

"Yeah, I remember that."

"Girl, you were right. I've been going to the gym recently, and I met a woman while sitting in the sauna. Now, you know in a sauna there generally isn't anything to do. So you often strike up a conversation with whoever is there. I was sitting in the sauna when the door opened and a woman came in and sat down beside me. She didn't say anything. I looked over at her and said, 'Hello.' We began to chat.

"Her name is Brenda, and she was born and raised right here in Massachusetts. We clicked right away, even liked a lot of the same things. As we were leaving the sauna she asked if I'd like to stop and have a drink. It didn't take long for me to know that she had a romantic interest in me. Sometimes I'm pretty slow on the uptake, but I saw this one right away. I checked her out. She was quite nice. Brenda's a schoolteacher, recently divorced. We're scheduled to have dinner on Friday night.

"A part of me wants to follow this through and see what happens. Another part of me is a little wary. I don't want to start a relationship that's not going to last. I don't want to put my heart out there like that. I don't want to miss an opportunity to get to know this woman, either."

"You know, Tracy, there's risk in everything. There was a risk in you leaving the Midwest and coming to Boston, but it paid off. There was a risk in franchising and broadening your business. That paid off, too. Yes, there may be a risk in developing a relationship with this woman, but it might pay off. Even if it doesn't, life has to be lived. You've got to enjoy yourself whenever you can. If it turns into something bigger and better, that's wonderful. If not, you can at least say that you tried. I'm going to share some wisdom that was given to me by an elderly woman. She said, 'Live your life and build pleasant memories.' Nothing comes to you forever. I don't care how much you love it, or it loves you, one of you has to leave the other. I know you're going to make the decision that is best for you, but I say go for it."

"Sister, thank you. You said all of the things that I needed to hear."

About forty-five minutes before noon the next day, Cynthia's telephone rang. It was Jack, and of course she put a big cheese-eating grin on her face.

"Listen, baby, I need you to give me directions from the airport to your apartment."

She didn't ask any questions. She told him exactly how to get to her place from the airport. He took the directions and said, "I'll see you in about thirty minutes."

When she got off the phone she started grinning and dancing. If there had been witnesses to her behavior, they would have thought she was crazy. She lit a few candles, put on some music and finished packing her clothes. Just as she had gotten the last item into the garment bag the doorbell rang. She pressed the buzzer, waited a few minutes, opened the door and there he was. They stood in the doorway holding each other. She basked in the smell and feel of his body. When they let go of each other he guided her by the hand into the apartment and closed the door.

"You know, baby, I've driven in almost every city in the country, but I've never driven in a place where there are no road rules. What the hell is wrong with these people in Massachusetts?"

She had to agree with him. Driving in Boston was like playing Russian roulette.

The temperature was in the 90s over the last few days, and that day promised to be another hot one. The air conditioner had been running all morning so the apartment was nice and cool. Jack sat on the sofa, kicked off his shoes, threw his left leg over the back of the sofa and motioned for her to come sit between his legs and rest her head on his chest. That was one of her favorite positions. They must have sat that way for at least an hour while he told her how much he missed her. He also mentioned what he had been doing the last six months.

What he didn't tell her was where they were going. He did suggest that they get started so they could be there by sunset. He took the luggage downstairs and she closed the apartment. Outside, standing next to a large white Lincoln with the passenger door open was Jack, wearing cream colored linen slacks with a cream and tan linen shirt. Damn, that man looked good.

We all have something particular that we like in the opposite sex. Jack was a tit and ass man, and she was particularly blessed in both of those areas. When Jack and Cynthia were together, she made sure that she dressed to hold his attention. She wore a wrap dress that showed just enough cleavage and fell gracefully over her ass. As they headed north she couldn't help but wonder where they were going. What the hell was north of Boston?

She really couldn't tell where they were. She stopped watching road signs an hour outside of Boston. She was enjoying the easy ride of a luxury air-conditioned car, while Norman Connors sang "Star Ship" and Jack softly massaged her fingers. He exited the freeway and entered a small town composed of a gas station, post office, and general store. She thought that general stores only existed on television.

Jack read her mind and said, "I might as well tell you that we are headed for a mountain cabin that is about twenty miles from here. Everything that we need is there, except groceries." He pulled an old wobbly shopping cart from its rack and began to go up and down the isles. He was an organized shopper. He knew exactly what he wanted and how much he needed. Her job was to pick up fruit and snacks.

In about thirty minutes they had five bags of groceries and were headed north again along winding, narrow roads. They passed farms with cows, goats, and chickens.

"You know, baby, I'll bet you these people haven't seen a black man up in this part of the country since they got rid of sharecropping," Jack observed as they passed one of the farms.

They left the dirt road and turned onto what she thought was a driveway. When she looked around for the house, she saw nothing but trees. Jack glanced over at her and laughed.

"Baby, I can't keep you in suspense any longer," he said. "The cabin is about two miles farther up this road, and I guarantee that you will be pleasantly surprised."

The road took a sharp turn to the left. As they rounded the turn she saw what she thought was an unusual sight, particularly right in the middle of the woods. She would have expected a rustic log cabin, but this was quite different. It wasn't really a cabin at all; neither did it appear to be a summer home. It looked better than many of the homes she'd seen in town.

They entered the front door of a split-level house with a large fireplace in the middle of the living room overflowing with sunlight and plenty of space. At the end of the hall there was a large master bedroom and two smaller guest rooms on either side. Off the master bedroom was an enclosed sun porch with a

Jacuzzi the size of a small swimming pool. Someone had put a lot of hard work and money into this place.

While Jack unloaded the car, she inspected what Jack called the cabin. It had all the amenities of home, plus some. She went into the master bedroom where there was a king-sized oak bed with a matching armoire. The room had the largest television she had ever seen. She found the drawstring of the draperies that covered the entire left wall and pulled them open. Staring at her were two sets of eyes. Now, being the true city girl that she was, she knew when to run. She stumbled backward over the luggage as she tried to flee the room. Jack must have heard the commotion and met her as she came running out of the bedroom. He grabbed her around the waist and lifted her off the floor.

"What's the matter?"

"Jack, I don't know, but there's something staring through the bedroom room window."

"Calm down, baby! Let me take a look." Within seconds she heard his thunderous laugh. He came back into the hallway.

"Come here, baby, let me show you this."

She was a little leery about going back into the room. They walked over to the patio door, and Jack pointed to a pair of skunks leisurely lying in the sun looking at them. She told Jack that she felt sure that this was going to be a wonderful six days with him; she was a little concerned about how scary it could get.

Jack went into the kitchen and returned with a bucket of ice, a bottle of wine, and a bottle of cognac. She asked him where they were, and he said the White Mountains, about twenty miles away from any other human beings. He chose the White Mountains because of its spectacular views.

"Baby, I don't think we will ever be able to get together as often as either of us would like to; but if we can get together at least once every six months, I could live with that," Jack confessed to her. "But, when I do get with you, I want your total, undivided attention. I want to always be able to give you mine. Getting together every six months means seeing each other in July and December. That won't last forever. Sooner or later you're going to find the man you want to settle in with. But if I can get you as my

Christmas present every Christmas day, and if I can hold you in my arms every New Year's Eve, I'll be a happy man."

"Even though I love you dearly, I cannot guarantee you that one day I might not want that little house with the white picket fence. Right now the house and fence aren't important. What's important is that I get to love you as long as I can. You have taught me so much, and I know there is more for me to learn. The more I learn, the closer it pulls me to you; and that's when it gets scary. It's scary when you know that a man that fulfills you in so many different ways will someday walk out of your life."

"Baby, I don't think that I can ever walk totally out of your life. I don't believe that I'm strong enough to do that. But I know there will come a time when I can't fulfill all of your needs. There will be a younger man to take my place. But even then, I still would want to talk to you occasionally, to know that you're okay.

"Now baby, I have to be perfectly honest; there was a reason that I choose Christmas and New Year's as the times when we needed to be together. Not only do I need you during those times, but I also realize that it's a special time for most people. Whenever it gets to the point that you can no longer spend Christmas and New Year's with me, I will then know that there's another man in your life. I don't look forward to that time, but I know that it will happen. Until then, I want to be everything to you that I can, and I want to give you everything that I have."

Although they were high in the mountains, the temperature was still quite warm. Jack assured her that it would cool down quickly by evening. It was about six in the evening, but neither of them was really hungry. They had a light salad for dinner and waited for the sunset. Jack really wanted her to see this sunset. The sun was just beginning to set, and it was the most awesome sight she had ever seen. She moved in behind him, put her arms around his waist and rested her head on his back. She could hear his steady heartbeat.

"I don't want to talk about where we are going anymore. I just want to talk about right now, where we are in this moment."

"Whatever you want, baby; we'll be in this moment for the next five days," Jack whispered to her.

They needed to lighten the mood, so she challenged him to a game of chess. The winner would get a full-body massage, which was a bet wherein they both would be winners.

They were both competitive people. She had been working on her chess game for months and thought that she might be good enough to take him this time. He suggested that they take the game out to the Jacuzzi. The mountain air was getting colder so they added a little heat to the Jacuzzi, pulled out the chessboard, and lit a few candles. So began one of the better chess games of her life. She was slow and methodical. She had a strategy going into the game that she believed would baffle him just long enough for her to gain an advantage. The game went according to her plan and in the next six moves she had him in checkmate.

"Baby, that was a damn good game. Where did you learn to play like that?"

She told him that there were some old men who played chess in Washington Park every Sunday morning during the spring and summer, and they would let her play with them occasionally. Gus, who was about eighty years old, told her that when you play this game you need to understand that there are moves and there are countermoves. Sometimes if you do the opposite of what people expect you to do you can baffle them just long enough to win the game.

"Baby, your game has improved considerably. Gus is right. You can sometimes baffle them, but what he failed to tell you was don't try to baffle the same person twice. And baby, that also holds true in life. But fair is fair and you did win the game, so come into my massage parlor and let me do what I do."

Everything that Jack did was slow and deliberate. Massages were no different. He was the only man she knew who really understood the connection between the head and the vagina. Whenever he was touching here he talked to her, particularly during sex. He would talk to her before, during, and after the act. The more he talked, the more aroused she became. He asked her what she knew about oral sex, and she told him that she didn't know a lot about it. She'd heard people talk about it, but just couldn't figure out why anyone wanted to do that.

"The physical connection between men and women is excellent for making babies, but it's not necessarily the best fit for having orgasms," Jack explained. "For a man it's a good fit; after all, you can't make the baby without the sperm. For a woman it's not necessarily a good fit because there is limited clitoral stimulation.

"I know you know these things and I'm being very elementary with this information. I want to be absolutely sure that you don't miss anything," Jack went on to explain. "There is an art to oral sex, and if you're going to do it you need to do it right. For me, it's not a standard part of sex; it's not even a standard part of making love. It only happens when I'm making love to a woman with my heart, my mind, my body, and my soul. Now that has occurred with only one other woman in my life, but I have had that feeling with you and held back. I needed to prepare you, and I needed to have you open for the experience."

His massage put her in a trance-like state, but she heard every word he spoke.

"Baby, I want you to forget everything that you've heard about oral sex. I want you to get rid of every myth and every story and know that it is the ultimate pleasure that a man and woman can give each other."

He massaged the genital area, slow and deliberate. She thought if oral sex is more intense than the orgasms that Jack had been giving her, then she may not survive it. She closed her eyes and went with it.

She felt as if she was losing control as Jack parted the lips of my vagina and softly with his tongue made slow circular motions. Her senses went into overload. He pulled her legs farther apart and told her to relax and go with the feeling. At that moment she felt if she went with the feeling she would lose her mind.

"It's okay, baby, go with the feeling and lose your mind. You'll get it back, I promise."

As his tongue danced over her clitoris, she did indeed lose her mind; and at that moment she knew never in life would she find another man who would make her feel this way. As she lay in his arms, deaf in one ear and trying to catch her breath, she knew that she wanted to learn how to bring a man to the ultimate orgasm.

For the first time in her life she woke up horny as hell. She moved over to get closer to Jack and realized that he wasn't in bed. Jack was on the sun porch sipping coffee, reading the newspaper, wearing a T-shirt and boxer shorts. Early mornings in the mountains could get quite chilly, so she grabbed a blanket and a cup of coffee and snuggled in close to him.

Some people are just not cut out to go back to nature. She might be one of them. There are things in the woods that she really didn't care to meet, but they all seem quite anxious to meet her. There are raccoons, possums, rabbits, but the most vicious of all is the mosquito. In the White Mountains they were the size of jet planes and came out at night. You could hear them coming even if you couldn't see them. It didn't take Jack long to recognize that he could teach her some things, but that he probably would never teach her to appreciate Mother Nature.

One thing you can count on in the mountains is a significant temperature drop in the evening. On their second night there, after dinner, she grabbed a blanket, a glass of wine, and followed Jack onto the sun porch. They cuddled closely under the blanket and watched another magnificent sunset. She told him that, after having the ultimate orgasm, she had a much better understanding of oral sex.

There were times when she felt that she was loving him with everything that she had—mind, body and soul. During those times she wanted to give him the ultimate pleasure, but she remembered his warning: "If you're going to do it, do it right."

"I need you to teach me how to do it right."

"Baby, I think I also told you that you should do this only because you want to, not solely for the pleasure of someone else."

"This is something that I want to do."

Jack and Cynthia found fun and laughter in everything that they did, and this was going to be no different. He went into the kitchen and in about five minutes he returned with two peeled cucumbers in a bowl of warm water and a glass of fruit punch.

"Baby, there are a couple of things that you should know about oral sex. The most important is that the penis is a very delicate organ. It can be handled firmly but not roughly. That means no tooth marks."

That brought a chuckle from both of them.

"For starters, take this cucumber, put it in your mouth and move it back and forth a few times," Jack began his instructions.

She did exactly what he said.

"Now, let's take a look at the cucumber," Jack said and pointed out the tooth marks and scrapes along the side. "Now, baby that will hurt. We're going to try it again and I'm going to give you a little more direction this time.

He took a paring knife and removed the tooth marks from the cucumber. "This time I want you to take your tongue and flatten it against the bottom of your mouth covering your teeth. Now try it again."

She followed his directions, and this time there was only one tooth mark on the top of the cucumber. He asked her if she could see and feel the difference. She told him yes, and they tried it again.

"Now I want you to put the cucumber as far into your mouth as you can without gagging," Jack said.

She tried to get the whole damn thing in her mouth and, of course, she gagged. They had to laugh about that for a while.

"Baby, it's not necessary to put the whole thing in your mouth. You put in only what you can comfortably handle."

She tried it a few more times and realized that she could do this. They moved on to the next stage.

"I want you to use this next cucumber a little bit differently." He handed her the cucumber; there was a drinking straw inserted through the middle.

"Well, this is different," she said.

"It has a purpose," Jack said as he put one end of the cucumber into the glass of fruit punch. "I want you to sip the fruit punch through the cucumber and the straw, being careful not to leave any teeth marks." She worked at it for a while, but nothing came through the straw.

"Remember, baby, flatten your tongue against your teeth and form your lips around the cucumber and gently suck."

For some unknown reason she thought that was hilarious. After they laughed about it for a while, Jack asked her to try it again. She put the cucumber in my mouth, flattened my tongue against her teeth, tightly formed her lips around it and began to suck. The fruit punch came through the straw. She realized that she had to make a seal between her lips and the cucumber in order to make it work.

After about fifteen minutes of laughing and experimenting, she felt that she was ready.

Later that evening as they were engaged in hot and heavy foreplay she tried her new skill. She began by kissing his neck and moving down to his chest, then to his navel. Playing with Jack's navel with her tongue had always gotten him excited very quickly, and it was no different this time. By the time she reached the penis it was fully erect. She held it firmly in her hand and lightly circled the tip with her tongue. That got his attention. Now it was time to get down to real business and show him what she'd learned.

She flattened her tongue, laid it against her teeth, and put the tip of his penis back in her mouth. She played with his penis with her tongue. He said, "That's nice, baby." She continued this for a while and then began to apply a light sucking motion to the penis. He began to move with her. She reached down, cupped his testicles in her left hand and gently squeezed. Although Jack had unbelievable control, this seemed to be the one thing that he wasn't able to handle as well as he might want to. It wasn't long before she knew he was about to have an orgasm.

When she began the process of learning about oral sex she hadn't given much consideration to the fact that a man's ejaculation must go someplace. She continued to work Jack's penis with her mouth, and suddenly there was a rush of semen with enough force to make her gag.

Five full days and nights with a man who kept her in a constant state of arousal was more than most women could hope for.

Neither Jack nor Cynthia knew where their relationship was going. They did know that when they were together, they willingly entered a fantasy world. On the evening of the fifth day they knew it was time to help each other back to reality. Ultimately, they knew that Jack was headed back to New Jersey and she was headed back to Boston. They were going to get together again for Christmas and New Year's, six months away.

CHAPTER 11

As Cynthia unpacked her suitcase from the trip, memories of the last six days flooded her mind and she smiled. While putting away her toiletries, she noticed that there were three birth control pills left in the package. This had to be a mistake. She looked again and realized that for the last three days of this trip she had forgotten to take her pills. How could this have happened? She'd always been careful about taking these pills. How could she have made such a stupid mistake? She sat on the side of her bed in the middle of a brief panic attack. What if she got pregnant? What the hell would she do? She had been so faithful with these pills for the last eight years; maybe, just maybe she didn't get pregnant over the last three days. She decided to take the pill for the current day, as if that would correct her mistake, and she prayed that everything would be okay.

She checked in with the Sister Circle.

Rosa was still being ignored by her husband and loving every minute of it. Robin had just been introduced to a new man who sparked her interest; and she said he might be a keeper. Tracy told her that she didn't know where her relationship with Brenda was going, but she knew they both enjoyed each other. Sandra was doing fine and helping her mother plan the gala set for the "Turning."

Cynthia told Tracy about her weekend with Jack and her introduction to oral sex. Tracy laughed and said, "I'll be damned, girl! You finally got and gave some head."

At dinner on Sunday, Rosa, Tracy and Cynthia were talking about the preparations for the "Turning." Rosa asked Cynthia if she had invited Jack to come along. Cynthia thought about it for a moment and realized that she didn't even think about it. She told Rosa that it was probably better because the "Turning" was designed primarily for the Sister Circle. She and Jack had plans to get together for Christmas. As she prepared for bed that evening she thought about Jack and the fact that she didn't even think about inviting him to the "Turning." She thought about the fact that he always called her and she didn't have a number to call him. She thought about the fact that he comes to Boston, or takes her away, but she had never been to his home. She decided that she would need to raise these questions with him the next time they talked. After all, they prided themselves on having an open and honest relationship.

It was the second week in August, Friday morning, as Cynthia prepared to go to work, when she got this overwhelming feeling of nausea. As she went into the bathroom to barf her brains out she really wanted to believe that it was something that she ate. The rest of the day was fine, but by early evening on Friday the nausea returned. Her period was about four weeks late, and her breasts were getting tender. She had to face reality. She was probably pregnant. She needed to know for sure, so she called her doctor. He scheduled her for a pregnancy test on Tuesday morning.

She didn't want to jump to conclusions before the results of the test, but her mind wandered for the next few days. She didn't want to be a mother. Although she knew that Jack loved her in his own way, he had made it perfectly clear that he was not prepared to take on another wife, or additional children. They were in agreement on that. How could she make such a mess out of this perfect relationship?

By Thursday afternoon the results were in. She was pregnant. Her worst fear was a reality—the fear of becoming a poor unwed mother. She tossed and turned until the early hours of the morning before she finally fell asleep. When she woke on Friday morning she wanted to believe that this was all just a bad dream. She had another wave of nausea and she knew that her pregnancy was real. For the first time in a long time she prayed. She asked the Lord to forgive her for what she was about to do.

She spoke to her doctor and got a pre-abortion meeting for the next Monday morning. She really didn't understand the need for this pre-abortion meeting. She knew what she had to do and, more important, she knew what she wanted to do. The pre-abortion meeting was scheduled with a hospital psychiatrist. She was a pompous, stuck-up white woman. Cynthia knew she looked at her as just another black statistic. She asked Cynthia a series of what Cynthia thought were very silly questions. Questions like, Do you know who the father is? Do you have a job? Could you support the child? Do you believe that you have given this abortion serious enough thought? It took every ounce of Cynthia's energy to keep from cursing at this pompous woman. Cynthia knew what she was doing. She just needed to have it done. She didn't need to be judged or reprimanded. She would do that to herself.

The abortion was set for the next Friday morning at a small clinic on Beacon Street. Cynthia was told that the abortion could not be performed unless there was someone to accompany her home. She had not planned to tell anyone about this, but it seemed as though she wouldn't have a choice. She had to choose someone that she could trust to share this horrible secret.

On Wednesday evening, after her regular bout with nausea, she sat back to have a glass of wine and catch the six o'clock news. The headline topic was anti-abortionists who had rallied around a small clinic on Beacon Street in an effort to shut it down. She got nervous. She needed that clinic, and she prayed that these anti-abortionists would not succeed. She sat there watching television and saw a crowd of intense and very aggressive women demanding that the clinic close. They were parading back and forth with signs that quoted scriptures from the Bible, and one that read "Baby Killers." She sat glued to the demonstration; these women truly believed in their cause.

She was determined to have this procedure, and she knew that she had the heart to face that group. She needed to choose someone to accompany her who also had the heart to face this crowd. She realized that the person with the heart and the person whom she could trust was Tracy. Tracy would clearly understand why she would choose not to have a child. She wouldn't judge her; and the anti-abortionist who got in her face would have hell to pay. Cynthia immediately got on the phone to Tracy and told her that she had a problem and needed to talk to her. She told

Tracy that she had made plans to have an abortion at a small clinic on Beacon Street. She told her about the anti-abortionists that had surrounded the building. She also told Tracy that she thought that she was the only person that could be trusted, with the courage to see her through this. She made Tracy promise that both of them would take this secret to their graves.

By 7:30 Friday morning, Tracy and Cynthia were walking toward the abortion clinic. There must have been thirty or forty angry men and women ahead of them blocking the way with picket signs while chanting. Cynthia looked at Tracy.

"This ain't gonna be easy," she whispered to Tracy.

"Girl, this is gonna be easier than you think. Just follow me." Tracy grabbed her hand and they moved toward the crowd.

As they got closer to the building a young woman flashing an anti-abortion sign jumped in front of Tracy screaming, "Do you realize you are killing a human being? You can't go through with this!" As she said this several anti-abortionists joined her and began to circle them in an attempt to keep them out of the clinic.

"I'm gonna tell you this and I'm gonna tell it to you one time: Get the fuck out of my face! Back up, we're going in! The next bitch that gets in my face is gonna get slapped!" Tracy was loud and convincing.

The first woman backed up. She saw the seriousness in Tracy's face. The other women kept moving forward. They could clearly tell the leader, a woman in her late forties. Tracy grabbed the woman by the back of her shirt and pulled her close. "Bitch, I'm gonna give you thirty seconds to call these people off; otherwise I'm gonna act the fool out here and you're gonna be the first one that I act out on. It won't be pretty."

With one simple wave of her hand, the woman moved the crowd backward.

In one last attempt before they entered the building, an older gray-haired man about sixty years old stepped forward and called them killers.

"What the hell are you doing here?" Tracy yelled at the old man. "This is a woman's right issue. When was the last time that you dropped seven pounds out of your asshole? When was the last time that you sat up all night trying to figure out how to feed a baby that you couldn't afford? When was the last time you had a labor pain? More important, every woman, and I mean every damn woman, has a right to determine what happens to her body.

"This is about the right to choose. And if I have the right to choose, the thing I would choose most, right now, is to shoot that dead piece of meat hanging between all you motherfuckers' legs, so women would never have this problem again."

While they sat in the waiting room, Tracy held Cynthia's hand.

"I will only ask you this question once," she said. "Are you sure you want to do this?"

Cynthia told her she wanted to do it and she had to do it. "This was not a choice for me to consider. It is my worst nightmare." Just as she finished the statement a tiny little blond-haired nurse in a crisp white outfit called her name. As she got up to follow her, Tracy smiled.

"Go ahead and handle your business," she said as encouragement. "I'll be right here when you finish."

By eleven o'clock Tracy and Cynthia were sitting at a downtown restaurant having brunch. They chatted through their meal, and Tracy talked about everything but the abortion. To be honest, Cynthia was waiting for her to raise the topic.

"You know, Tracy, I've been on the pill for over eight years and I've been very faithful with it. I just don't know how I allowed this to happen. I really didn't want to be a mother," Cynthia said.

"Yeah, and your old man is too damn old to be a daddy," Tracy said with a chuckle. "By the way, does he know about this?"

"You're the only person who knows about the abortion. Jack doesn't know and he never will."

CHAPTER 12

The rest of the summer was fairly uneventful. Socially Cynthia was as busy as she wanted to be. There were picnics, birthday celebrations, cocktail sips and all kinds of outside events. She flirted a lot, but didn't find anyone who held her attention more than ten or fifteen minutes into a conversation. Of course everyone she knew thought she needed to have a man in my life. She was often set up on dates; everyone had a friend they thought she should meet. She made it perfectly clear that she would not participate in blind dates. That was the problem with most women, they dated blindly. She had her eyes wide open and knew exactly what she wanted and was not ready to settle for less.

Around the middle of October on a Saturday, around nine o'clock in the morning, her telephone rang. *Who the hell was calling this early?* She picked up the phone and heard an unfamiliar voice.

"Good morning, Cynthia. How are you?"

She listened for a moment, still not able to recognize the voice.

"You're a hard person to catch up with. You're never home."

She never functioned well in the dark so she had to put a halt to this conversation until she knew who it was. She said, "I'd like to have a reasonable conversation with you, but I'm really not sure who you are."

He laughed. "Cynthia, this is Sam. I met you in New York while you were visiting your friend Robin; it seems like ages ago, but if you can remember, I told you that I would call."

"Oh yeah, I remember you. It's so nice of you to call."

"I know it's been a while; but when I met you I said I'd really like to get to know you better. I didn't think I'd have such a hard time catching up with you. I took a chance this morning because many people like to sleep late on Saturdays. Unfortunately, I'm just getting in.

"Cynthia, I was wondering if you would come to New York for Thanksgiving. Before you say no, Robin and I have been talking and she said she'd like to make Thanksgiving dinner and have us both over."

"That might not be a bad idea, but I would need to reschedule a few things to get a few days off. I'll get back to you. Give me a number where I can reach you."

"I consider this a good sign. When we last met, you wouldn't take my number." His sarcasm was apparent.

"I wouldn't take your number because you hadn't put any effort into getting to know me."

"You are definitely a different woman," Sam offered. "When we first met, you told me that you liked to associate with honest people. You also said an honest man was important to you. So I'm going to be honest and hope your feelings won't be hurt."

"Don't worry about my feelings," she shot back. "I am not a thin-skinned sister."

"I don't know how you deal with other men, but with me you seem to act like you're the only woman around."

"No! Sam, that's not it. Believe me, that's not it. I know that I'm not the only woman around, and I certainly know that there are plenty of fine sisters out there. But I also recognize that I'm not in the top 10 on the dog list either. More than that, I'm very secure in who I am and in what I bring to a relationship. I watched women come after you that night at your club, and that's just not my style. A brother has to make the effort and I'll respond. I'm just not a chaser."

"I guess that's fair; you certainly sparked my interest, and you can consider this my effort. If you call and don't get me, please leave a message on my answering machine. I do look forward to having Thanksgiving dinner with you."

She immediately got on the phone with Robin. "Okay heifer, what have you gotten me into?"

"So, Sam finally got in contact with you."

"I just finished with him. What's up?"

"Well Cynthia, I know you got my back, but this is what happened. Sam has a business partner, Sonny, and the brother is fine. I've seen him in the club many times, and I really haven't had a chance to get his attention. So Sam and I were talking the other night at the club, and he was saying how difficult it was to get in contact with you. You really got his attention. So I told Sam I'd deliver you for Thanksgiving dinner if he'd deliver Sonny. He laughed and called me a conniving bitch. I told him that he was absolutely right, but did we have a deal. He agreed to deliver Sonny."

"Robin, I don't believe that you just pimped my ass."

"No, sister, it really ain't pimping 'cause you can choose to do whatever you want. I didn't tell him that you would lay up with him. I just told him that you would have Thanksgiving dinner with us."

"You know that I am agreeing to Thanksgiving dinner primarily because you're my girl."

"That's why I love you."

Cynthia left a message on Sam's answering machine letting him know that she would be at Robin's for Thanksgiving.

At dinner on Sunday she told Tracy and Rosa about the Thanksgiving arrangement. Tracy thought it was hilarious.

"You just might have a good time," she said.

Rosa gave her a shy look before commenting. "I don't think I could ever do that."

"It's only Thanksgiving dinner and a chance to talk to someone who had already gotten my attention."

"I don't think I could do it because I'd be too afraid," Rosa confessed.

Tracy and Cynthia chuckled a little and told Rosa: "You're going to get better. You're going to stop being afraid of everything; trust us."

Rosa was getting prepared to host Carlton's family for the holidays, and she felt that the most difficult part of this Thanksgiving was making these people believe that she really gave a damn. For the sake of harmony in the house and the fact that her children needed to know their grandparents, she would make dinner for the family and suffer through it.

Tracy and Brenda seemed to be getting along quite nicely and decided to have an intimate Thanksgiving dinner together. Sandra, of course, was doing her wife-and-mother thing, preparing Thanksgiving dinner for both sets of parents. There would be a house full of people in Atlanta for the holidays.

Cynthia was on the highway headed south to New York on the eve of Thanksgiving. Before she left, Tracy called to say, "If you're going to New York to check this brother out, make sure your hair looks good and pack your working clothes."

Robin worked over time preparing Thanksgiving dinner, even though most of it was catered. She dressed the condo with the feel of Thanksgiving, and a cozy fire going in the fireplace ignited the living room.

Dinner was scheduled for six o'clock. At 5:30, Robin and Cynthia were having cocktails.

"You know I never intended to pimp you, Cynthia; it was just an opportunity that I couldn't pass. For some reason Sam is quite infatuated with you. He thinks that you're a refreshing change to the women he knows."

"I'm not sure what Sam is looking for, but I do know what I need in my life. We'll see what happens."

"Cynthia, what are you really looking for in a man?"

"He needs to be sensitive and able to show it. I need a man who can connect to my head as well as my vagina. A brother really needs to be able to talk to me. He needs to be mildly aggressive, yet patient. When it comes to sex he needs to be slow, smooth, steady and verbal. Robin, what are you looking for in your men?"

"Well, he needs to be fine, hung like a horse, and knows what to do with it. A brother who can't lay it down is useless."

"Damn Robin, is that all you want?"

"Oh yeah, I forgot, he's got to have a place to live other than with me. Damn Cynthia, you want a hell of a lot out of your men."

"At this point in my life I'm not asking for a lot; I just want to be treated like a human being. A brother doesn't need to profess his love for me, but he's got to care about me. I've got to be treated better than just a piece of pussy."

Robin laughed, but Cynthia knew Robin understood what she was trying to say.

The doorbell rang at about ten minutes before six. Robin answered, and there was Sam carrying flowers and a bottle of champagne. He gave Cynthia flowers and a hug.

"You're a hard woman to catch up to."

She accepted the flowers and thanked him. Sam, Robin and Cynthia continued with cocktails and talked about New York City, the bar scene, how much money Sam makes, and what he intended to buy.

Robin kept chiming in to make sure that Cynthia understood that he wasn't lying. He was really all that. She sat there and listened for about ten minutes and was relieved when the doorbell rang. It was Sonny. During their conversation she couldn't help but wonder why Sam didn't just put a sticker price on his forehead.

Sonny came in with a bottle of wine, greeted everyone and then noticed the flowers. He looked at Sam and said, "Damn man, since when do you bring flowers? You're making a brother look bad."

Sam looked at Cynthia and said, "A brother's gotta do what a brother's gotta do."

After dinner Cynthia suggested that Sonny and Sam take their drinks into the living room while she and Robin cleared the table. Sam said, "I've got a better idea; Robin and Sonny can go into the living room, and I'll help you clear the table." Sonny thought that was very funny and left the room laughing as Robin followed him.

Sam and Cynthia cleared the table and chatted. She asked him to tell her about himself, not his business, money, property, or fame. She just wanted to know about Sam the man. He seemed quite surprised by her request.

"Cynthia, you'll have to excuse my surprise. No one has ever asked me about Sam the man." He went on to tell her that his family was from North Carolina and he came to New York as a young kid. His family was dirt poor, and he was determined that he was going to make something out of his life. He met all of the right people at the right time and ended up in the nightclub business. She asked if he had children. He said that he didn't have any that he knew about. One thing he knew for sure was that he was not the marrying kind.

She told him that she could seriously understand his position on marriage, because she didn't think that she was the marrying kind either. He laughed.

"That's kinda hard for me to believe. I've never met a woman, except you, who wasn't. They will tell you that they're not interested in getting married, but given the opportunity they will corner you as quick as they can."

She told him that might be true for some women, but it wasn't her style. She realized that in order to corner a man she would have to get in the corner with him; and she didn't like being cornered either.

They grabbed a drink and went back into the living room. When they entered the room it was clear to them that Robin was hard at work on Sonny. She was determined to have Sonny for desert, and it looked like Sonny was going to accommodate her. Cynthia had to give her girl credit. When she went after something, she usually got it.

Sam and Cynthia sat on the sofa, propped their feet up and continued learning more about each other. For the first time he wanted to know where she came from and what she did. She kept it short but gave him the truth. They laughed and talked about growing up in the 1960s and 1970s. They talked about their first love, their first kiss, and she was beginning to feel that there was a decent man in Sam. He told her that people in general had a very warped concept of who he was. If you watched him on his job, running the club, he seemed like a hard-line asshole. That was the front he believed was needed in order to survive in business and New York City.

"I'm not an asshole by any stretch of the imagination. Actually, I think I'm a pretty nice guy, but I can't let my guard down. I can't let people see that side of me. You know, if you lived in New York, I probably wouldn't let you see that side of me either."

Sam's attitude was that in a town full of users and opportunists, it was difficult to find someone he could trust. There was only one place that he could go and be himself, and that was his apartment. His apartment represented him in a way that most people could not appreciate. He called it his corner of the world. Few people got invited in.

Sam told her that he had recently turned forty years old and begun to slow down a little bit in terms of the nightlife. He still enjoyed going out and socializing and having a good time, but he finally understood moderation. He bought a boat and sneaked off to go fishing on occasion.

"Cynthia, I would appreciate it if you wouldn't tell too many people about this side of me. After all, I have a reputation to uphold."

He asked why she was so hard on men. She told him that it was not her intention to be hard on a man. She was very picky, but not picky about the things that most women are. She believed that a woman should not ride in on the money, prestige and wealth of a man. If a woman does the things that she can do, she can acquire those things on her own.

"Cynthia, you are quite unique. I hope at the very least we can be friends. Meanwhile, I'm going to continue to try to stimulate your mind."

It was about three in the morning. Robin and Sonny had left them at about midnight. For some reason Robin had been playing that old bump-and-grind music of the early 1970s, and Sam asked Cynthia to dance. As far as bodies are concerned Sam had just the right height, was neatly packed, and their bodies were a perfect fit. He lightly stroked her back.

"You know, Cynthia, I haven't had a date like this since I was sixteen."

The door to Robin's room opened, and Sonny came out looking a little stunned.

"Damn man, looks like you were in a fight," Sam said to Sonny.

"Man, it was a hell of a fight. But you know me, I don't back away from a fight," Sonny said with a big grin on his face. "I handled it. I hate to leave y'all, but I got things to do, and I've got to get at least three hours sleep."

"You know, it is kinda late. I want to let you get some sleep, so I'm going to leave with Sonny. Before I go I'd like to invite you to spend a little time with me tomorrow, since you're going to be here another day."

"What do you have in mind?"

"I would invite you down to the club, but I understand that you're not much of a clubber. So how about you meet me at the club at nine o'clock, and I'll take you to a little place that I enjoy. I'll have you back at a reasonable hour."

She agreed to meet him at nine o'clock at Small's.

After they left, she picked up the house a little and figured that she needed to check on Robin. When she entered Robin's room, the candles that she had given her months ago were burning all around the room and Robin was laying face down on the bed wearing a white nightie. For a brief moment Cynthia panicked, she thought, *What the hell happened in here?*

"Cynthia, I can see why those women are lining up in the club trying to get next to Sonny. Girl! That brother certainly knows how to handle business. I felt like I was in a rodeo. I know that it must have gotten a little loud in here. I'm sorry, girl; but, damn, that brother had me howling at the moon."

Cynthia laughed until she cried. "Robin, I would never mess with a brother that rode me like a horse and left me looking like I was in a fight."

"Girl, isn't it wonderful that we all don't like the same things? There wouldn't be enough to go around."

The next morning Robin came out of her room looking like she had been on a three-day binge. Cynthia was sitting at the kitchen table having a cup of coffee when Robin stumbled in. Cynthia handed her a cup of coffee and told her to sit down and tell her what it was about that man that made her feel like she had to howl at the moon.

"Girl! This brother turned my ass every way but loose. His dick never went down. I think he left here with a hard dick. Take my word for it, the brother worked tirelessly. That's the kind of brother I need to keep in my stable, 'cause he's all right."

She told Robin that she agreed to meet Sam at nine o'clock at Small's and that she and Sam were going to hang out a little before Cynthia left.

Robin smiled and said, "Looks like brother man's got your attention."

Now Cynthia knew the atmosphere in Small's, and the women in there were jockeying for their position with Sam. You could see them circling, flirting and flaunting their bodies. It was clear what they had to offer. They left nothing to the imagination. She was determined that she was not going to be one of the horses in the race. So she put on a very sophisticated, low-keyed outfit. She wanted to be as inconspicuous as possible. Robin was pleased to take her down to Small's since it gave her another opportunity to run into Sonny. She wasn't finished with that brother yet.

When they arrived at Small's Cynthia saw Sam standing at the bar having a drink, while a young woman was climbing all over his body. She smiled because that's the way it was in that kind of business. When he saw her he winked, peeled the woman off of him and walked over to greet Cynthia. If looks could kill, Cynthia would have been a dead sister that night.

"Cynthia, give me two minutes and I'll be ready to go." Sam walked behind the bar and spoke to the bartender, walked into the back room and came out with his coat. While waiting for Sam, the woman who had been draped all over him said, just loud enough for Cynthia to hear, "Well I'll be damned, that motherfucker don't know what he wants." Cynthia wasn't trying to antagonize her, but the cat in her made her smile as Sam gently led her toward the exit.

As they were leaving, Sonny asked him, "Where you going, man?"

"I'm taking the rest of the evening off. You can handle this."

"Man, if I didn't know any better I'd think your nose was wide open." Sonny was serious.

Sam took her to a small out-of-the-way spot for dinner in a part of Harlem that she had never been to before. After dinner they got in the car and headed toward Manhattan.

"Cynthia, I'm taking you to one of my favorite places. If you ever tell anyone that I took you there I will deny it to the bitter end."

They ended up parked in a rather secluded area. As he backed the car up to turn around they were facing a fantastic view of the George Washington Bridge and Upper Manhattan.

"Sometimes I come here just to think and to be by myself. When I come here I seem to be able to think through situations and problems in a much more sane and rational way." He reached in the back seat of the car and pulled out a chilled bottle of champagne and two glasses. Now that was a pretty nice touch, she had to admit. They sat overlooking the George Washington Bridge, sipping champagne and talking.

Although she was a very picky person, occasionally a sister just has to get the monkey off her back. When those times come, you want to at least choose a person who appears to have some of the qualities that you're looking for. At that moment Sam was close enough. She didn't want to be Sam's woman, and she definitely didn't intend to spend any significant time in New York with him; but he had managed to stimulate her mind just enough to get a tingle in her panties.

Sam was an excellent kisser, and after a few moments the kisses became more passionate. Between kisses Sam asked, "Have I gotten your attention yet?" She chuckled and told him, "You've got my attention, at least for today." They went to his penthouse apartment in Brooklyn. They had already had the discussion about sex. He knew that if it wasn't working for her too, it wasn't happening.

Sam turned out to be a pretty good partner. She had to keep reminding herself not to compare him to Jack. He was very attentive, vocal in a limited kind of way, and he took directions fairly well. It was clear, however, that he wasn't accustomed to getting directions from a woman, especially regarding sex.

"You know, in all of the years that I've been fucking, a woman had never before given me directions," Sam whispered to her.

"You know, Sam, if we were just fucking, I probably would not need to give you directions. I would be in it just for the bang. But we were having meaningful sex, not that slam-bam-thank-you-ma'am shit."

"Cynthia, you are absolutely right, and I didn't mean to imply anything different. I've really enjoyed your company. I hope we will get to spend a lot more time together."

It wasn't earth-shattering, but one thing was for sure: Sam could certainly keep the monkey off her back, and she enjoyed his company.

CHAPTER 13

It was now one week before the "Turning," and several of Cynthia's friends called to say they had received their invitations. She put out a few feelers, trying to see if anyone knew where Wesley was, so that she could be sure to invite him. Everyone had an idea of where he might be, but no one could give her an address. She stopped and assessed her continual infatuation with Wesley. That was almost twenty years ago, but there was still a part of her that wanted to know what kind of man he had grown into. She realized that the primary reason she wanted to see Wesley was to show him that she wasn't the frightened sixteen-year-old girl he used to know, and that sexually she had developed too. She really wanted to see if Wesley could rise to the occasion. She didn't want to keep him, she didn't want to marry him, and she didn't want to take him from another woman. She just wanted to roll the brother over one time.

Tracy, Rosa and Cynthia arrived in Atlanta early in the morning and arranged for a limo to take them directly to the hotel. They had so much luggage, you would think they were going to stay in Atlanta for a month. They wanted to make sure that they had an outfit for all occasions. The hotel suites were everything that they hoped for—two large adjoining suites, and four separate bedrooms. Robin was due in about three o'clock that afternoon, and Sandra was on her way.

They spent the evening catching up. There is nothing funnier than five women, all with a few new and different stories to tell. They stayed up until the wee hours of the morning laughing and telling stories. Robin had them all in tears telling them about the brother whose dick was on backwards, and Tracy chimed in with some hilarious stories about her customers.

They reminisced about their college days, music, dances—who wore what and who did who. Everyone in the room could relate to the music and the dancing, especially those red-light parties and the bump and grind. Even Rosa had a few stories about her life, pre-Carlton.

Tracy finally wanted to share her new relationship with Brenda, and she admitted that it had been so long since she had someone in her life that it was difficult to leave Brenda behind for the "Turning." They hadn't met Brenda yet, but they all agreed that if she made Tracy happy she was all right with them. The next morning as they peeled themselves out of bed, they realized that five hung-over sisters ain't a pretty sight. They had lunch with the caterer at noon and spent most of the day browsing and shopping.

The next few days were theirs and they were determined to make new friends and to "turn out" a few nightspots in Atlanta. They soon found out that it wasn't easy to "turn out" a club in Atlanta because southerners really knew how to party. Robin and Cynthia had always been labeled as flirts, and they did just that everywhere they went. Sandra was the old married woman in the group; she consistently told them that they needed to be careful about picking up stray people—"They'll bite you just like a stray dog." Cynthia told Sandra that she didn't need to worry about her. She might flirt and meet a lot of people, but she didn't take them home. Robin said, "Well I don't take all of them home either." The rule for the week was that they all needed to watch out for one another; and that's exactly what they did.

On Thursday night after partying with the after-work set in Underground Atlanta, they closed the club and really weren't ready to stop partying. They brought the party back to the hotel. At least twenty people came back to the hotel with them. They danced and laughed until the wee hours of the morning. At about 3:30 a.m. Sandra and Rosa made it clear that they had enough and went to bed.

They were all in awe of Tracy. For a woman who did not like men she had the brothers gravitating to her. She identified her sexual preference only if they pressed her too hard. Cynthia really wasn't interested in finding another man. Between Jack and Sam, she had enough on her plate. Robin said she really wasn't looking either, but if something real nice came along she wouldn't kick him out of her bed. By 5 A.M. Cynthia was exhausted. She excused herself and went to bed. Robin and Tracy were left holding court and entertaining the hell out of a room full of people.

Sandra and Cynthia got up at about 8:30 A.M. When they entered the common area they saw five men sleeping in the area. They were all good-looking brothers. Sandra asked, "What the hell happened here?"

"Things were pretty tame when I went to bed last night," Cynthia told Sandra. They went into Robin's room and ran into a half-naked brother on the bed. Robin was in the shower. They rousted her out of the shower and told her that she needed to help them clean the place up, that meant getting rid of the bodies.

Robin started laughing. "I tried to get them out of here all night long, and they just wouldn't leave."

Room service arrived just as they pushed the last brother from the room. While they sat having coffee, Sandra asked for a recap of the evening. Cynthia told her that she was in bed by five o'clock, so she didn't know what happened after that. Robin said, "We just partied and had a damn good time." Sandra asked her who the half-naked man on her bed was.

"I don't know the brother's name. I was going to take him on, but he was too drunk to get it up. There's nothing more useless in this world than a brother with a limp dick."

It was Friday morning and they unanimously agreed that they had partied long and hard for the last three days. They needed to rest, if they wanted to be presentable for Saturday's event. Sandra's husband, Jason, had a different idea; he wanted to bring some of his buddies over to meet them. They agreed to meet them as long as they could be in bed by midnight.

Friday turned into one of those cerebral days in which they got together to solve all the problems of the world. They lounged around and talked about welfare reform, the prison system, the state of the nation, and Robin threw in the financial status of African Americans.

Jason showed up around six o'clock with a few of his friends who were engineers. They jumped right into the debate and held their own. After about an hour or so, they somehow got on the subject of male-female relationships, always a volatile topic.

Robin kicked if off. "It is so hard to find a good brother these days."

Cynthia never agreed with Robin on that topic, and obviously the brothers in the room didn't either because the conversation got intense.

Calvin, a short, clean-shaven brother, was probably the brightest and most articulate one in the room. "Women just don't know what they want," he said.

Tracy jumped all over that statement. "You're wrong. Women know what they want; men just don't know how to give it to them."

The women in the group knew exactly what she was talking about, but we weren't so sure the brothers understood.

She continued: "Most women are too shy or embarrassed to ask."

That admission from Tracy caused Calvin to quip, "If a woman is too shy to ask for what she wants, that's not a man's problem; that's her fault."

Up until that point Cynthia had been quiet. She really had to jump into this. She tossed a hypothetical situation at Calvin.

"You and your woman are doing what you do, and you really think you are on top of your game. Suddenly she says, 'Wait a minute, Calvin; stop, you're not doing it right.' How would you feel?"

The brothers in the room started laughing and talking about what they would do and how they would feel.

"This question is not just for Calvin," she continued. "Anybody can answer it."

Butch, a big Mr. T.-looking brother, stood up and said, " Jason tells us that you ladies are easy to talk to, that we could be ourselves and your feelings wouldn't get hurt, so I'm gonna be honest. If it were me I'd be pissed. I been fucking for twenty years and all of a sudden a woman's going to tell me I'm not doing it right. Ain't nobody else ever complained."

All of the brothers, including Jason, agreed.

Tracy chimed in and said, "It sounds like y'all are making the assumption that all women want to be made love to in the same way. That's not true. We have preferences. Some sisters like to have that Wah-Who-Willie rodeo style of love, and other women like to be made love to slow and easy; and some of us like it on the top, while others like it on the bottom. There are many variations. The problem is when you stop a brother and try to tell him what you like, he gets all funky and bent out of shape."

Rosa stood up and said, "Go ahead and teach, Sister!"

Tracy did just that. "Doing it right for one sister doesn't necessarily mean doing it right for the next sister. So if I was going to give brothers some words of advice, I'd say ask your woman what she wants. I would also tell sisters to stop fronting for these brothers. Women are hollering and screaming like it's the best thing since Cracker Jacks, and the shit ain't that good."

Butch jumped in again. This time he walked around the room for effect. "Now, brothers, come on be real; if you gonna lay some pipe, damn it, lay it. You got to let the sister know you up in it. Now think about it, brothers. You got the backboard rattling, and the sisters calling your name and urging you on. You supposed to keep doing what you're doing and, if possible, you suppose to bring it up a notch."

Rosa joined in again, which surprised the hell out of the Sister Circle. "Have you ever thought that when the sister is urging you on, she's trying to get you to finish your business so you can get the hell up off her?"

Jason stood up and said, "Now sisters, there are four men in this room; and on an average we got about fifteen years worth of fucking experience each. That's a total of sixty years worth of experience in fucking, and y'all gonna tell us that we don't know what we're doing."

The sisters looked over at Sandra. She wasn't saying a word. Robin spoke up. "Well, most of you think you know what you're doing; and a sister may not have the heart to stand up and tell you that you've got it wrong. So you go through life believing that you're doing it right."

The brothers spat out to each other how good they were and how they knew what they were doing. They ended by slapping each other five.

Tracy got up and walked around the room. From the look in her eyes the sisters knew she was going to get deep into their shit.

"You know, you motherfuckers are poster children for lesbianism."

The sisters looked at each other and pushed their seats back a little bit. It was on now!

"I'm a woman and I'm a lesbian; and the women that I've been with came to me after being with brothers like y'all. Y'all the kind of brothers who won't eat no pussy."

"Naw man, I ain't going down," Butch jumped in to say. Another brother who had been quiet most of the evening agreed with Butch and said, "No man! I ain't going down either. Hell! I get mad when I slip down." The men started laughing.

Tracy took the floor. "Yeah, but all of you want your dick sucked though, don't you?"

"If that's what she wants to do, I ain't gonna deny her."

Tracy didn't back down. "You know what, brothers, I'm your worst fucking nightmare. I look good and I know how to make your woman feel good."

"Yeah, but you ain't got no dick." That came from Butch.

Tracy started laughing. "Brother, I got about as much dick as any woman would want. You can buy that shit in any store. I can give them six inches, seven inches, eight inches, and twelve inches; thick, thin, black or white. I can even make my shit vibrate. What you got?

"Brothers, I'm gonna give you a message from me and every other lesbian woman in the world. Keep doing what you're doing. Don't ask your woman what makes her feel good. Keep tearing up pussies all over town. Don't try to be sensitive or tender; and whatever you do, please don't eat no pussy. 'Cause it's brothers like you that keep lesbians like me in high demand."

You could have heard a pin drop in the room. Jason said, "I think we need to change the subject."

Calvin said, "Well, it is kind of late and we know you ladies want to get some rest, so we probably need to be going."

They put on their coats and jackets and began to leave the room. It took every once of control for the Sister Circle to wait for them to get outside before they began to laugh. Once the brothers had left the room, the sisters fell on the floor, in tears, laughing and trying to catch their breath. This was the funniest shit they had seen in a long time.

They got a good night's sleep and woke up the next morning relaxed and ready to go. They had a full day of events—saunas, pedicures, manicures, and massages. Tracy brought all of her equipment to help them get their hair tight for the evening. In the middle of the sauna Sandra confided in them that late last night Jason called her and began to ask questions about their sex life. She said he was asking very direct and specific questions, and she told him that they would talk about it after the "Turning."

Sandra's mother had given them directions earlier in the day to be dressed and ready by 9:30 for the "Turning." At about 9:35 she entered the suite. She looked damn good for a woman her age. At fifty-five she still took great pride in her body and appearance. She wore a pink two-piece gown with silver metallic trim and carried a cool, elite image in a way that turned the heads of many men. She wanted to have a little time to thank the sisters again for being such a tight-knit group of women, and she hoped that they would always remain this close.

The sisters got on the elevator and headed down to the ballroom. The Grand Ballroom was eloquently decorated—china, crystal and silver. The sisters felt like celebrities. It was time for the toast, and Tracy said, "If y'all don't mind, I'd like to offer the toast." She picked up the microphone, introduced herself and asked each of the sisters to stand as she introduced them. She then went on to explain the concept of the "Turning" and how blessed she felt being a part of it. She said that all of her life the thing that she wanted most was to be loved and appreciated, and she found that in the Sister Circle. "These women love me for who I am. They don't try to change me, but they force me to be a better me. At this point I cannot imagine not having them in my life. My grandmamma once told me that I would be real lucky to have two true friends in my lifetime. My luck has never been good, so I prayed.

"After the death of my mother, I truly believed that I would have to go through life alone. But the Lord heard my prayers and sent four of his angels into my life, and for that I will be eternally grateful."

Now at this point there was barely a dry eye in the house. She finally pulled herself together and said, "Okay y'all, that's enough of that." Everyone laughed. She said, "This is a celebration, and let's be about celebrating. Mr. D.J., I have one request, and you don't have to do this all night, but at least for a short while. Could you take us back to the 70s?" That's exactly what the D.J. proceeded to do.

He told Tracy, "Not only will I take you back, but I'm going to take you back on the good foot." James Brown began to play. The whole room jumped up.

Between the champagne and the music, it felt like the 1970s all over again. By one o'clock in the morning the place was packed. It was hot, and folks were sweating, you know the kind of sweating that makes your hair go back. Folks were re-introducing themselves to old girlfriends and old boyfriends, and you could tell by the guilty looks on their faces that they were doing something they shouldn't be doing.

The D.J. said, "I'm gonna slow this down a little for you and let you catch your breath." He began to play some old bump and grind. Robin said, "Excuse me, ladies. I got a little work to do." She was going to get a man.

At about 2:30 in the morning they began to close the grand ballroom, but of course black people still weren't ready to leave. They noticed that those that were ready to leave were leaving in the most unusual ways. There were all kinds of sign language, head nodding, winking, people sliding out the back door. Some folks were getting into some deep shit that night.

By the time the sisters got back to the suite they were dead tired. They wondered if they would ever be able to have a "Turning" as successful as this one.

Sandra told them that she was going home that evening to spend some quality time with her husband. It seemed they had a lot to talk about.

It was ten o'clock the next morning before anyone regained consciousness. Tracy, Rosa and Cynthia sat around in their nighties drinking coffee, recapping the evening's events and laughing at some of the funny things that happened. After a few moments of laughing and joking, Cynthia asked if Robin made it in. Tracy said she was probably knocked out in her room. Cynthia thought they needed to wake her up so she could join them for coffee. Rosa nudged her and pointed to a necktie on the sofa, and next to it on the floor was a jacket and a pair of shoes.

Sandra invited the sisters to a late brunch at one of the local jazz spots. Tracy knocked on Robin's door and said, "Just checking, sister; you all right?" Robin came out to join them.

"I'm fine, just dog tired."

"What's the matter, sister?" Rosa asked. "You didn't get any sleep?" They all laughed, including Robin.

When they got into Sandra's car they noticed that she was in a great mood and had a big grin on her face. She turned around, looked in the back seat and thanked Tracy. Sandra said, "For the first time since I've known Jason, he made love to me in a way that he's never done before. He was sensitive, and he wanted to know what I wanted and how I wanted it. I don't know where I got the courage, but I told him and he followed my directions exactly."

Tracy, Rosa and Cynthia had a nine o'clock flight on Monday morning out of Atlanta; Robin was leaving at noon. They said their good-byes, and Sandra's mother promised to send them all personal picture albums of the event. Once they boarded the airplane, they settled back for the flight to Boston.

Cynthia closed her eyes and began to think of Jack. She wondered where they were going this Christmas. She was looking forward to hearing from him on Thursday. Jack had been in her life for a little over eight years now; and every time she saw him it was always as good as the first. Their conversations were still stimulating; he was still attentive, and he continuously told her how much he missed her in between their visits.

Rosa nudged her and asked if she was okay. Tracy said, "If she's got that dumb look on her face she must be thinking about Jack."

Cynthia pushed her seat back, closed her eyes and began to think of all the wonderful times that she and Jack had together. She thought about his hypnotic baritone voice and how he whispered in her ear. She thought about his masculine arms and chest that enveloped her body and made her want to climb into him. She thought about his full-body massages that almost always kept her at the brink of an orgasm. She could feel his hands on her body, and she recognized the scent of jasmine. Her body began to tingle as it always did when Jack was around. Out of nowhere came a voice urging her to wake up. It was Rosa telling her that they were about to land. Cynthia sat in her seat trying to compose herself. She couldn't believe that it was just a dream. It was so real. She could smell him and she could feel him. Even though it was only a dream, somehow she got physically aroused.

CHAPTER 14

Thursday evening at eight o'clock on the nose Cynthia's phone rang. Although she and Jack talked every Thursday, there were still some things that she hadn't told him. She really hadn't told him much about Sam. She wasn't so sure that Sam was going to fit into her life in a long-term meaningful way. On this Thursday she told Jack about the "Turning" and how much fun they had.

He wanted more detail, so she told him about the old girlfriends and boyfriends that got back together; many of them reunited for one night only, most of them had husbands and wives at home. She told him about the Soul Train line and how Rosa had come out of her shell a little bit and had a grand time that evening. He asked her the standard question he asks every other Thursday: "Did you meet anyone of interest?" She told him no. She certainly saw a lot of people she hadn't seen in years, but nobody who struck her attention to the point that she would want to get involved.

"Baby, I think your standards for men are getting harder and harder to match."

"You're right, but I don't think that I'm asking a lot of anyone, at least not any more than I'm willing to give in return."

Then she said, "Jack I've been thinking and trying to figure out why our connection is the way that it is. By that I mean, you call me every Thursday and I look forward to your calls, but I can't call you. You know where I live, you've visited me several times. Yet I have no idea where you live. You don't even talk about it very much.

"Now, this is not said to make you believe that I want a different level of commitment in this relationship. We have an open and honest relationship and I would really like to know more about you."

"Well, baby, I've called you every Thursday totally out of habit. We began the relationship this way. I knew that you were in school, and I was certainly willing to pay the cost to talk to you every Thursday. But now that you're out of school if you would like to change the arrangement, we can. Get a pencil and let me give you my telephone number.

"In terms of where I live, I've got a proposition for you. Let's spend Christmas and New Year's in New York and I'll take you to my place. Now I know that you have other questions, and we will get to those when I see you. And, baby, I really need to see you. Can I get you from the morning of the twenty-fourth of December until January third?"

She thought about the eight years that she and Jack had spent together. She was now thirty-three years old, and Jack was close to fifty-two. She hadn't noticed any significant change in their relationship. He still kept her in a constant state of arousal; he was in great shape and treated her like a queen. What else did she need in a relationship? Marriage was still not on her "list of things to do," and she really had begun to appreciate this long-distance relationship. It gave her time to investigate other people, but it also gave her a sense of security knowing that she had a man like Jack in her life.

She also had to be real. He was fifty-two years old. She decided that this might be a good time to revisit her "list of things to do." There were still things on her list that were undone, like taking a cruise, buying a house, going to Africa, learning to play the piano, and finding Wesley. She wondered if it was really worth her while keeping Wesley on this list.

The next few weeks were kind of hectic, catching up on her customer relations and making sure that everyone had what they needed as they went into the Christmas holidays. Jack booked her on the 10 A.M. shuttle out of Logan Airport on Christmas Eve.

The next Sunday at dinner Cynthia, Rosa and Tracy found themselves laughing at the candid pictures taken at the "Turning." These pictures held memories that could never be captured again. Cynthia asked Rosa about Carlton and she said, "As far as I know he's fine. He comes in and out whenever he feels like it. He doesn't realize that I really don't give a damn."

"Do I detect a little backbone?" Tracy asked sarcastically.

"I don't know if you would call it backbone. I just know that life should be better than this."

Tracy shared that she and Brenda were getting a lot closer, and it was beginning to make her a little nervous because she wasn't so sure that she wanted to put her heart on the line.

"You know, Tracy, I think by the time most people have to decide whether or not to put their heart on the line, it's already out there. Personally, I'd rather put my heart on the line and enjoy the feeling of loving someone than to hold my heart close and miss the opportunity to love," Cynthia said.

"Yeah, I guess you're right, but I really don't want to go through that bad relationship shit again."

"Sister, don't even think about that. Just enjoy what you have while you have it."

Tracy added, "There is another small problem. Brenda doesn't have any friends and I think she resents the Sister Circle. She doesn't understand why she can't be a part of it. I truly enjoy being with her, but to bring her into the Circle would mean allowing her to encompass my whole life, and I can't have that. If y'all don't mind I would like to bring her to dinner just one time so that she can meet both of you. She cannot become a part of the Sister Circle, and I truly hope that she doesn't push me to have to make a decision between her and the Circle."

Cynthia told Tracy that she believed once Brenda got a chance to meet them and realized that they were not trying to take her woman, she would probably be okay. Tracy chuckled and said, "You know I hadn't thought about that. Maybe she thinks there's some freaky shit going on in the Circle."

Cynthia landed at JFK Airport on Christmas Eve at about 11:15 A.M. and, as always, Jack was standing there with a dozen red roses. He looked as good that day as he did eight years ago. He walked up to her, pulled her into his arms and gave her a deep, passionate kiss.

"Remind me that there's almost a twenty-year difference in our ages," Jack said as a greeting.

"I'll remind you on January third."

"Baby, there's been a slight change in plans. I got an excellent opportunity that I couldn't refuse, and I'm sure you'll enjoy it. But you can rest assured that before this vacation is over you will get a chance to see my place."

They walked toward the boarding gate and she noticed to her left a sign that said "Flight 128 to Bermuda." Jack laughed and said, "Okay, I guess my secret's blown. But, baby, I got a deal on a cabana in Bermuda for four days that I really didn't want to pass."

She certainly had no objection to lying in the Bermuda sun in December. Unfortunately, she had packed all the wrong clothes. Jack was in her head again and said, "I know that you did not pack for Bermuda, so I've made arrangements for a few light-weight outfits. By the way, you are a size 10, aren't you?" She smiled and wondered how he could possibly know that.

It seemed as if everyone who worked for Eastern Airlines knew Jack; he got the V.I.P. treatment everywhere he went. Cynthia told him she didn't realize that he was such a big shot. He laughed and said, "You know, baby, I'm really not. But I do know how to treat people right, and in turn they treat me right."

It was a very smooth flight, first-class to Bermuda. The weather was awesome when they arrived. Of course she was overdressed for the climate, but he promised that he would take care of that. It was an extremely well kept island cabana, right on the beach, with air conditioning and large ceiling fans circulating cool air throughout the rooms. She told Jack that she really needed to come out of some of her clothes because it was much too warm. He said, "Baby, that's exactly what I was hoping for." She began to take off her clothes and realized that he had settled in to watch.

She told him that if this was going to be a show, she didn't mind doing it, but she could certainly use a cold glass of wine. He chuckled and said he would bring a cold glass of wine as long as she promised not to start without him. He was back in a flash and she began her show. She had never done a strip tease before, but she'd seen a few; and as far as the bump and grind went, she knew she could do that.

She asked him to put a little music on and began to take her clothes off. Her body was still in good shape for a woman her age; she didn't have any stretch marks, and everything else was fairly tight. He said, "Baby, I don't think you've ever done this before so I want to help you use your imagination. Take a moment, have a drink with me and imagine being a stripper." She sat back, closed her eyes, drank a little wine, and he talked her through a strip routine. She asked him how he knew so much about the art of stripping; he laughed and said he had seen a few shows in his time.

He began to tell her what a stripper does, how she does it and what the customers like. After a half glass of wine, she said, "Okay, baby, I've got this. Turn the music on. I've got a show for you." Slowly she began to take off her clothes with a little light bump and grind in between. She intentionally bent over to remove her panty hose so that she could wiggle her ass. For a first timer, she thought she was doing a pretty decent job. She got down to the bra and panties and took a little extra time removing the bra. Once she removed the bra she took an ice cube from his glass and lightly circled her nipples. This, of course, made her nipples jump to attention. When she got down to her panties, he said, "No, baby, I'll handle those." She continued to dance, adding a little more bump and grind.

Now there's one thing that every sister learns at a young age, and that is how to roll her hips and shake her butt. She told Jack that she wanted to try a lap dance; he laughed and said, "Go for it."

She straddled his lap and began to slowly gyrate in front of him. She continued to roll her hips while she lowered her body onto his lap, being careful not to apply too much weight. As she continued this slow sensuous lap dance she felt his penis begin to rise. Within minutes it was fully erect. As smooth as she liked to believe that she was, she lost all concentration and a lap dance was no longer what she was trying to accomplish. Both she and Jack enjoyed the anticipation of making love and they would often keep each other on the verge of orgasm for long periods of time. But this had gotten very intense, very quickly.

He lifted her with her leg wrapped around his waist and moved toward the bedroom. Before she realized what was going on, they were both standing in the middle of a cold shower. Jack was fully clothed, she stood there in her panties. Within seconds they were laughing like children. He said, "The anticipation of making love to you heightens the experience threefold. And it's been so long since I've been with you, I don't want to lessen that anticipation." Now she probably would have figured out a better way, other than the cold shower, to stop what they were doing, but she also understood what Jack meant.

They had dinner reservations for eight o'clock that evening. Their luggage arrived at the cabana at promptly six. At about 6:15 a garment bag was delivered with a yellow sundress, a black T-strap dress, a multicolored halter-top dress, and a white T-strap dress packed into it. There were two things these outfits had in common: they were all very form-fitting, and they required Cynthia to be braless. Jack was a tit-and-ass man, and these outfits definitely accentuated both. She decided to wear the white T-strap dress and, without a bra, the outfit had plenty of bounce. Jack loved it.

After a romantic candlelit dinner they walked along the beach. They found a lounge chair built for two and settled in, sipping cocktails and watching the evening tide sweep over the beach. The sea breeze and the ocean mist were intoxicating. As usual, they talked about any and everything. He asked her about her love life; she told him that she'd dated a few men but hadn't found anyone who could hold her attention yet.

He was quiet for a moment before he asked, "What do you think of Sam?" He knew she had met Sam through Robin, and she told him that she spent Thanksgiving in New York and had dinner with Sam. Cynthia told him that Sam appeared to be a nice enough man and he was working hard to get her attention, but that she wasn't so sure that he was the type of person she needed in her life right now.

"You know, baby, not long ago you asked me why I had never invited you to my home. I needed to take a little time to be able to explain my reasoning to you so that it made some sense. I never envisioned that you would be so deeply entwined in my life. I can vividly remember every time and every place I've ever made love to you. Those places and times are etched in my mind. Every time we've been together I've always felt that I couldn't get enough of you; and if I took you to my home, it would be the same. The memory of making love to you in my bed would be etched in my mind. When you find that man you may ultimately want to settle in with, I can avoid those places we've been, although the memory will still be there. I can't avoid home. The memory of you in my bed would be too constant and make it twice as difficult to let you go."

She told him that she understood his reasoning, and she really did; but she also told him that she tried not to think about letting him go. She had become reasonably comfortable with the fifteen to twenty days a year that they spent together. She realized that during those days she experienced more love, more passion, more intensity and more desire than the average woman does with her man all year long. She had begun to realize that maybe she was just not the kind of woman who needed a man every day of the year.

"Baby, I don't know how long you're going to feel that way, but as long as you do I want to continue to be that man who gives you everything you need and everything that I've got. I'm fifty-two years old, and I can still deliver; but there's going to come a time when maybe I won't be able to. I don't expect that to happen anytime soon, but if, or when, it does, I want you to have a man in your life that can."

Jack proved beyond a shadow of a doubt that evening that at fifty-two years old he could damn sure still deliver. At three o'clock in the morning while she was lying in his arms trying to catch her breath, he said, "Merry Christmas, baby." It was Christmas day.

Jack had the ability to keep her sexually aroused even when he wasn't touching her. They spent the next three days in Bermuda on their own private fantasy island. On the morning of December 29 they left Bermuda and flew to New Jersey.

It was about twenty-five minutes from the airport to his house. They pulled into the driveway of a very nice split-level, brick-front home. Jack held her hand and said, "I just wanted you to know where I am on those evenings when we are having hot steamy phone sex. Welcome to my home. Put your stuff down and I'll give you the fifty-cent tour."

From the foyer they stepped down into a sunken living room carpeted in a plush caramel-colored carpet. She made a comment about how bright and sunny his house was, and he said that the sunlight was one of the things he enjoyed most about the house. He pointed to the ceiling. A large skylight encompassed most of the ceiling.

"Baby, feel free to look around and browse. I'm going to make a fire to take some of the chill off the house."

To the left of the living room was a fairly large kitchen, with mahogany cabinets and tan and black tile. Down the hall on the right was a medium-sized guest room, and at the far end of the hall was a large master bedroom. In the master bedroom was a king-sized oak bedroom set with a matching armoire. The room was carpeted in a luscious forest green, complemented by antique gold curtains. Off the master bedroom was a medium-sized study, which also served as a music room. Jack had an impressive record collection.

She browsed through his library and noticed that he was an avid reader. As she moved through the house she didn't want to admit that she was looking for signs of a woman, but this was definitely a bachelor's home.

When Cynthia came back to the living room, Jack said, "We skipped breakfast this morning because we were running late, so I'm making a little lunch."

While they were having lunch, she asked Jack about his home.

"You know, baby, it wasn't until I was forty years old that I realized the benefit of owning property. Prior to that, property really wasn't important to me. I found this house about a year before I met you. The sunlight and the openness of the house are really what drew me to it. I've changed a few things since I've been here, but in general it was exactly what I wanted. The only reason I keep a guest room is that occasionally my son comes through and will spend a day or two with me. He's still out there trying to find himself, but I've seen a lot of improvements in him. I think he's going to be ready real soon."

By four o'clock they were on their way to Manhattan to check into the Marriott. She finally had a chance to see where

Jack lived, and it wasn't important that she ever got a chance to go there again.

For the next five days they would be in mid–Manhattan, and there's never a shortage of things to do there. Although they caught a play and had a few candlelit dinners, their reason for being in New York was solely to be together. Jack had tickets for one of New York's premier New Year's Eve events and suggested that they go, even if it was just for a little while. It was times like this that she was so grateful for Tracy, because she was not only a great hairdresser, but she also was a great teacher on how to improvise in times of need.

After being with Jack for almost ten years, she knew that when they were together almost anything could happen. She had to be prepared for as many occasions as possible. So she had packed a simple New Year's outfit and a more elegant one. She chose to wear a black beaded dress with flecks of gold, and there was just enough tit and ass showing to make Jack smile and to keep her modest. They called room service and ate dinner in front of a large picture window that overlooked Times Square as they watched all of the countdown preparations.

"Baby, I need to let you know that this evening's event will be full of people from all over the New York-New Jersey area. There may be one, possibly two, women in the room that I have dated at some point. Because I know how catty women can be, I wanted you to know that in advance."

She thanked him for the heads-up, but told him that she could generally handle herself in those situations.

He said, "You know, baby, when we first met I told you that I loved the Christmas season, but I was never much of a Christmas gift giver. I give gifts all year round and I don't believe that Christmas should be the only time to show someone that you care. Because we don't see each other that often, it's usually Christmas and some time in the summer, I decided that I wanted to buy you a gift this year. Don't consider it a Christmas gift; just consider it something that I wanted you to have."

Jack walked over to a large box on the chair, opened it, and pulled out a full-length fur coat. Cynthia has never been a connoisseur of furs. She always thought it was pretentious, so she didn't know what type of fur it was Jack had given her. She figured at some point in the evening he would either tell her what it was or she'd find a tag that would let her know. She was speechless. He helped her into the coat, grabbed his coat, and headed for the elevator. If there were going to be any women there who had ever been with Jack, they would have plenty to talk about.

The room was full of beautiful women, young and old. There was no shortage of fine brothers either. Jack put his arm around her waist and guided her into the ballroom.

The party had been going on since nine o'clock, and most of these people started long before that. The master of ceremonies came to the microphone; introduced The Dells, and the crowd went wild. Women were jumping up and running toward the stage as The Dells began to perform. Jack and Cynthia, seated at a table in the middle of the room, decided to get out of the way so these women could get to the stage. They moved to the left side of the ballroom. Jack leaned against the wall, pulled her in front of him, and held her around the waist.

The Dells were putting on a powerful old-school show, and you could tell by the screaming that they were really bringing back memories.

Jack then said, "Notice to the left of us, sitting at the second table, the gentleman wearing the gray cummerbund?"

She glanced over at the man, waiting for Jack to finish his story. As she looked closer she realized that it was Sam. She wasn't sure if Jack was asking her a question or just pointing out the fact that Sam was there, so she didn't say anything.

She finally realized that he was waiting for her to respond.

"You know, Jack, that looks like Sam."

"It is Sam. He's been watching us all night. Is there anything you'd like to tell me?"

Her mind began to race. How much did she really want to tell him?

"I've dated him twice. He's a very nice man, from what little I know of him. But, unfortunately, he can't hold my attention. Part of the reason is because I keep comparing him to you. You once told me that it was going to be very difficult for me to bring another man into my life because I put such high standards on a man. I agreed with you. A brother has got to come with at least fifty percent of what you bring. I don't think Sam has that."

This was one of the few times that Jack and Cynthia had ever been out around people that neither of them knew. Cynthia was not one to show displays of affection in public; however, it seemed to be no problem for Jack. He pulled her closer to him and gave her two quick passionate kisses as he caressed her back. She began to wonder if this was all for show. When they left the dance floor he said, "Baby, I think I've shared you more than enough tonight."

While they were in the lobby to retrieve their coats, Sam walked up and wished her a happy New Year.

She returned the greeting and kissed him on the cheek.

"Now I know why it's so difficult to find you," Sam said. She realized that he had too much to drink. "What on earth do you see in that old man?"

"Sam, don't let his age fool you. That old man has what most women would kill for."

"Do you realize who I am? I own property all over New York. I run one of the most successful clubs in the city. There are women lining up to get next to me." Sam was pissed off and it showed.

"Sam, there are certainly women who will line up to be with you, and I told you when I met you that I was a different kind of woman."

As she turned to walk away Jack arrived with the coats.

"Happy New Year, man," Sam said as he extended his hand to Jack.

"How did you get Cynthia's attention?" asked Sam. "I tried to talk to her, but she wanted me to be a punk to be with her."

"Well brother, I don't know what to tell you. I've never had to be a punk to be with any woman."

"Well, good luck," Sam said as he staggered away.

While they waited for the valet to retrieve the car, Jack said, "You really must have caught that brother's eye to make him pursue you to the point that he felt he was being punked."

Once they were back in the suite, Jack called room service for cognac and a late-night snack. They sat in the Jacuzzi having a nightcap and laughing at the events of the evening. Jack said,

"Cynthia, I have to be honest with you, I've known Sam for quite a while. We've never been friends, just acquaintances. I've watched him wheel and deal around some business opportunities that many felt were at the very least shady. Sam has always felt that we were in direct competition in some way. I've never understood how or why, particularly since we didn't frequent the same places. That may explain his attitude this evening. Alcohol and Sam have always been an unpleasant mix. I believe that, basically, he's a decent man but can be quite aggressive when he drinks and doesn't get his way.

"I'm not going to tell you that he may not be the man for you. I just wanted you to know what you would be getting. Cynthia, I'm pretty sure that I'm going to hear about this evening at some point later on." She wasn't so sure what he meant by that, but she decided to let it go because whatever he heard and how he responded to it was going to be his problem. He continued, "Baby, believe me, there is a brother somewhere right now preparing to take my place. And when he comes, he'll be everything that you want. Trust me!"

CHAPTER 15

Dinner with Rosa, Tracy and Cynthia was always relaxing. They looked forward to spending the time together. With Brenda joining them for this one time only, according to Tracy, there was something just a little bit different about this Sunday's dinner. Rosa and Cynthia were at Sidney's when Tracy came into the room. She was alone. Where was Brenda? Tracy stood in the doorway looking a little impatient and obviously waiting for someone. Within seconds after Tracy arrived a tall, medium-built woman entered the room. She was what they called high yellow, and although she had a pretty face, she wrinkled her nose and forehead as if she smelled something bad. She walked with her head held high in the air so that she looked down on everyone she passed. It was what they knew as the "Uppity Black Bostonian attitude." She followed Tracy to their table.

Rosa and Cynthia tried hard to engage Brenda in a conversation, but when asked a question, Brenda would only give short responses. Not enough meat there for a conversation. She didn't ask them anything about themselves, and they didn't volunteer. It was an uncomfortable situation. Tracy was visibly displeased. They struggled through dinner with idle chatter about Tracy's hair salon, Cynthia's job, and Rosa's new position. Their Sunday dinners were usually two hours long and full of laughter. This dinner was so out of character, their favorite waiter, Rex, came over several times to make sure that everything was okay. Cynthia gave it the old college try one more time.

"So Brenda, what do you do for a living?"

Brenda slowly put down her fork, picked up her napkin, and lightly touched the corners of her mouth, waived her finger in the air as if to say "Wait a moment and I'll answer you." Maybe it isn't cool, but they sometimes talk with their mouths full and never give it much thought. Not Brenda. When she finished chewing her last bite she answered Cynthia's question.

"I'm a schoolteacher."

Cynthia thought to herself, *All that time waiting for four damn words.* She was too through. She wasn't going to be the one to try to engage her again.

Rosa took Cynthia's lead. "Well, how do you enjoy teaching, and has that always been your dream?"

After taking a moment to consider the question, Brenda spoke up. "It's okay, and no."

Rosa kicked Cynthia under the table, and they left the entire conversation alone. They could clearly see that Tracy was not pleased with the responses Brenda had given. Shortly after dessert, Tracy informed them that they wouldn't be able to stay. They watched Tracy quickly pull herself together to leave. Brenda scurried to keep up with her. Once they were out of the room Rosa looked at Cynthia and said "Damn, Cynthia, that woman has the personality of a fucking wart toad."

Cynthia almost choked on her dessert. This was a different side of Rosa. Cynthia never would have expected her to say anything like that.

Cynthia came in from work one Tuesday evening absolutely drained. She was working harder than ever; she had to. The transport business was more competitive than ever and more was required from its workers. After a long hard day, she sat down, kicked her shoes off, poured herself a glass of wine and checked her mail. There was a letter with no return address and with a New York postmark. Her first thought was that absent-minded Robin forgot to address the envelope. She opened the letter and it read:

"Dear Cynthia, I hope that you had a wonderful holiday season and that your New Year will be prosperous. I know that you like to get straight to the point, so here it is. It took me a while to get the nerve to send you this letter, and now that I'm writing it I want to be as open and honest as possible. First, I'd like to apologize for my behavior at the New Year's party in New

York. It really was not my intention to be offensive. A combination of alcohol and jealousy made me approach you in an inappropriate way, and I'm sorry. You are definitely a unique and interesting woman, and I hope that I have not jeopardized my chances of getting close to you, which would truly be my misfortune. Now I know you're wondering what right I have to be jealous. Realistically, I have no right. But sometimes you want something and think you're working toward it, but you can't understand why you can't have it. If I have ruined my chances of being more than a friend, then that's something I'm going to have to deal with. At the very least I would still like to be your friend. Again, please accept my apology. Sam."

She thought about the letter for a while. The apology was real nice. However, she saw a side of Sam that did not fit her personality. So if friendship was all that he wanted, she might be able to do that; but friendship was definitely all that they could have.

On their normal Thursday evening date, Jack lifted Cynthia's spirits considerably. She explained how the rush was on to get her company's services into some of the smaller businesses and how hard she'd been moving around the city trying to make it happen. He was very sympathetic and, as usual, they talked about any and all things. Suddenly, he asked her if Sam had apologized yet. She wondered how he could possibly know that Sam would be apologizing.

"Baby, I'm a man and I watched how he looked at you. He's not finished with you yet. Yes, he's going to apologize and he's going to sound sincere and he's probably going to try to make you believe that he only wants to be your friend. He's going to be charming and sincere. He knows the only way he may be able to get to you is through a strong friendship. That's what I'd do."

She really didn't know what to say because it's almost as if he had read Sam's note. She told Jack that Sam had sent a note of apology.

"Be careful, baby."

Over the next few weeks she continued to move all over the city, pulling in new customers and, whenever she could, stealing a customer from a rival company. She was pretty good at selling this service. If she could get a person to listen for a while, she could probably make the deal. It was a warm sunny day, and she was running in between appointments when she pulled into the parking lot to check on one of her clients. She had prepared a strong presentation for a new line of service. She intended to run in, pitch it and be out in less than thirty minutes. She parked her car, grabbed her briefcase and ran into the building. The pitch went a lot smoother than she had expected, and her client saw the benefit of the deal right away. Cynthia was out in fewer than twenty minutes. She sat in her car for a moment, checking the rest of her schedule for the day. She had gotten a lot accomplished; one more stop and she could go home early.

By 4:30 that afternoon she was sitting on her sofa, thumbing through the mail, when she heard a familiar sound coming from the street. She looked out her window. The sun was shining and the street was full of young children playing street games. It had been a very long time since she'd been home this early and she didn't know that there were that many children in the neighborhood.

The young girls were playing Double Dutch, with hips swaying as they chanted. It was the rhythm of the street. The young boys were running, like most young boys do, chasing a ball and playing tag. It was the rhythm of the street. While Cynthia sat there and watched, she realized that it was 1986 and the rhythm of the street had changed. It was no longer the carefree rhythm; it was the kind of rhythm that you get as you looked over your shoulder waiting for something bad to happen.

The rhythm of the street now included street gangs and drive-by shootings. Young people had become desensitized to death and had lost respect for authority. The music had become hard, cold and disrespectful. Whatever happened to the simple love song? There was something bad out there, and it wasn't out there when Cynthia was a child.

Cynthia was now thirty-eight years old and doing well both financially and socially. Most of the women that she knew were struggling. Many were struggling to raise babies made during the Black Power era, when the movement believed that genocide was being used to reduce the black population. Women were encouraged to strengthen the race by having babies, and far too many of them believed it. So, while black women struggled in the 1980s to feed the babies conceived during the revolution, the brothers of the revolution were settling into the suburbs with their new white wives.

Cynthia was struggling in a very different way. She was struggling with the occasional memory of the dishonest way that she handled an unwanted pregnancy. If she truly believed that she and Jack had an open and honest relationship, why did she hide the truth? That question would haunt her for quite a long while.

It was time to revisit her "list of things to do." As she looked over the list she crossed out the piano lessons. She had made an honest attempt at learning to play the piano and struggled with it for more than six months. She had the desire and the will, but fell short on talent. It just wasn't going to work. Everything else on the list needed to stay. She still had intentions of accomplishing them. But what would she do about Wesley? He was still on the list.

She pushed back in her recliner, closed her eyes and tried to remember Wesley. It had been well over twenty years. She must have fallen asleep because she found herself back in her mother's living room hugging, rubbing and kissing Wesley. The intensity was still there, and she again put his penis between her legs inside her panties. She could hear him breathing heavily in her ear as he got closer to an orgasm. An orgasm swept over her body the same as it did the first time.

She opened her eyes in a panic; this experience was just too real. Once she gathered herself together she realized that it was only a dream. She kept Wesley on her "list of things to do." It bothered her most of the day that she could have an orgasm in a dream with a man she had not been intimate with in twenty years.

Sunday evening at dinner, Tracy looked quite bothered. As they sat laughing and joking about the events over the last week, Tracy didn't have much to say.

"Tracy, is there something on your mind? Something we can help you with?" Rosa asked.

"I don't know; the magic is just not there. She doesn't do the things she used to do. And that funky-ass attitude of hers ain't cute no more," Tracy snapped.

They knew she was talking about Brenda.

"When we make love she's just a receiver, and I really don't feel the urge to touch her anymore," Tracy admitted.

"I hate to sound dumb, but this is the first time that I realized lesbians had the same problems in a relationship that everyone else has," Rosa said.

"Yeah, but it is a little different. It's much harder to find a woman that you want to be with," Tracy replied.

"Well Tracy, there's over a million women out there who find it equally as hard to find a man that they want to be with," Cynthia added.

"So what are you going to do, Tracy?" Rosa asked her friend. "It's clear you're not happy."

"I don't know. I'll work it out, but right now I've got something a little more pressing on my mind. I've got to get to Ohio to make sure that motherfucker who killed my mother is still in jail. I want to see his ugly face behind bars."

"Are you sure that you want to relive those unpleasant memories?" Rosa cautioned.

"I promised myself as a child that I would make sure that he either stayed in jail or stopped breathing. Now it's time to see which one it's going to be. I'll only be gone a few days. I'm coming back as soon as the parole hearing is over. Don't worry, I won't do anything stupid."

Cynthia asked if one of them could come along with her.

"Hell no! Y'all don't need to be in this shit."

They knew better. If her stepfather was paroled, he was going to be a dead man.

Meanwhile Rosa had been so removed from Carlton at this point, that when they asked her how he was doing, she'd say Carlton who? Sandra had finished her master's degree and felt that she had a good shot at becoming principal. She said that Jason had just been given a new position with the company and was working long hours in his new six-figure job. The only thing that she didn't like about the new job was that it required him to travel on occasion.

Robin was on her way to California. She was presenting a series of seminars in Los Angeles, and she believed that the outcome of these seminars could take her to the next level. Life was moving on for all of them, and moving at a fast clip.

Robin's trip to California really had her excited. Till this day they still don't know how, but Robin managed to get tickets to the 1989 Academy Awards. Although they were very happy for her, they were all a little jealous because they wouldn't get to go.

They decided to watch the Academy Awards this year just in case Robin got a little air time. Rosa wasn't able to join them. Tracy and Cynthia decided to camp out at Cynthia's house to watch the Academy Awards. Tracy was responsible for cocktails.

"Cynthia, I got some very disturbing news this afternoon," Tracy said to her as they watched television at her apartment.

"I was in my downtown shop this afternoon. The shop was pretty full and everyone had a conversation going on. I was working on a new customer, who came in with two or three of her friends. While I worked on her hair, they began to talk about an event that they attended last weekend, and the fact that there was a bunch of fine brothers there.

"One of them said, 'Don't even get excited about those brothers because none of them like women.' They continued to talk about what a great time they had and how unfortunate it was that all the men in the place were gay. They certainly didn't look like it. Marsha, who was the client that I was working on at the time, said, 'They couldn't all have been gay because there was a fine brother that I was talking to at the bar, and he seemed to be interested.' The biggest and loudest woman in the room said, 'Yeah, I hear what you're saying. But they tell me that some of those brothers are swinging both ways.' Someone else said, 'Yeah, that's what they call bisexual.' The big girl said, 'Bisexual my ass. If you trying to get some boy pussy, you gay.' Everybody started laughing.

"Marsha began to talk about the fellow that she met at the bar. She said that he was a good-looking brother—tall, dark and clean-shaven. He really had it going on, owned a lot of real estate in the city, wasn't one of those standard broke brothers and had a fairly decent rap. She thought she might want to see him again.

The big girl said, 'I know who you were talking to. That's Carlton. Girl! That man's got a wife and kids, and he been switch-hitting for years.' Marsha said, 'Well I'll be damn. That was certainly a waste of my time.' The big girl said, 'You gotta stop hanging around with those people. You need to come out next weekend and go to this club downtown, where the brothers are real."

"Cynthia, it bothered me all day long. I really wanted to believe that they weren't talking about Rosa's Carlton. Now you know I don't like the motherfucker, but I wanted to give him the benefit of the doubt because of Rosa. I know a couple of brothers who consider themselves bisexual. So I threw Carlton's name out there, and they knew exactly who he was.

"I told you years ago that motherfucker needed to die," Tracy barked.

"Well wait a minute, Tracy. Are we absolutely sure that this is Rosa's Carlton?" Cynthia asked.

"Cynthia, they gave me more than enough information to know that it was him. I was really kind of glad that Rosa couldn't make it tonight because I didn't know how to tell her this."

"Tracy, if you're absolutely sure, we still need to figure out what good it would do to tell Rosa. She still doesn't have the heart to leave that man; and if she confronts him he's gonna beat the hell out of her.

"We've got to figure out how to do this to preserve whatever dignity she's got left. We're going to have to work harder at getting her to the point where she can make it on her own. She's come a long way, but she's not strong enough to leave him yet.

"I think the first thing we need to do is figure out if they are sexually intimate. If they are, we're gonna have to tell her quick. If they're not, we have a little time to figure out a plan."

"I hear what you're saying and it makes a lot of sense. But I'm telling you again, he deserves to die." There was no remorse in Tracy's voice.

Tracy then told Cynthia she had contacted the Ohio state penitentiary to check on the parole hearing of her mother's killer.

"I found out that his parole had been denied. A wave of relief came over me; I was really not looking forward to planning his death. Now that's one less thing that I need to think about right now. I'll worry about it five years from now when he goes up for his next parole hearing. You can bet your ass I'll be there."

Robin began making her Sister Circle connections early on Sunday morning. She chatted with Cynthia for almost an hour. She met a brother in California, Troy, who took her every place and introduced her to all kinds of people.

If Robin intended to shock Cynthia, she did when she said, "Saturday night, I found myself in a very uncomfortable position. I met my father. I was in my hotel room changing when I heard a knock on the door. A man on the other side of the door identified himself as hotel security. I looked through the peephole and asked him to show his badge and some other form of identification, which he did. I never really paid attention to the name on the badge. When I opened the door and he stepped inside, I felt that I had seen this man before. He got right to the point.

" 'My name is Walter Connors, and I'm your father,' he said. My first instinct was to laugh in his face, but the serious look on his face kept me from doing so. I stepped back to take a better look at the aged man in front of me. The only image I had of him was his high school picture my grandparents kept of him. He was well over six feet tall with huge feet and hands. His complexion was light brown, and what was left of his hair was graying at the temples. He might have been quite a handsome man in his youth.

"He began to tell me where and when I was born, my mother's maiden name, the hospital I was born in and where I lived as a child. Still, I just stood there with a blank look on my face. He asked me to sit down. He just wanted to talk to me, to tell me why he left, where he'd been, and why he never contacted me. I really didn't give a damn. Too much time had passed. He ended by asking if I had any questions to ask him. I had two: Why are you here? and What do you hope to accomplish?

"He said, 'I just want to be a part of your life. I missed your childhood and I thought maybe we could—'

" 'It's too late for that,' I said. There is nothing you can do for me now. It's been nice meeting you, and I hope you had a pleasant life. "

"He left. I expected to feel something, but I didn't. It was almost as if it never happened. I would definitely have to talk to my mother when I got back to New York, I thought. But I really don't need that man in my life."

"Damn, Robin, that's deep. And you're really not feeling anything?"

"No, Cynthia, I'm not."

"You know, Robin, whatever your decision is about meeting your father, I will support you and so will the rest of the sisters. I want you to think it through, because you may not get another chance."

"I've already thought it through, and I realize that I cannot need or miss something I've never had." Cynthia heard the anger and hurt in Robin's voice as Robin shouted, "Where was he when I needed a father? Where was he when I cried myself to sleep as a child because all of my friends had a father? Whatever happened between him and my mother was no reason to shut me out of his life! I was his child!"

Robin was crying.

That Thursday Cynthia told Jack about Robin's and Rose's situations.

"All you need to do is say the word and I'll be there in less than four hours" was his response.

That's really all that she wanted Jack to say. She just wanted to know that if she needed him he would come. It was more than psychological, though. She really did need him to comfort her. She really did need to rest in his arms. And so, for the first time in their relationship they would see each other outside of their six-month schedule. He would be in Boston by five o'clock.

From five o'clock Friday evening until five o'clock Sunday evening Cynthia was prepared to put the world on hold. For the next three days she wanted to immerse herself in the one thing that always made her feel good—Jackson Douglas. By 6:15 on Friday evening he was holding her. She thought to herself, *Is there another woman in the world that can count on a man like this?*

She had been home from work since three o'clock. She needed something to occupy her mind, so she prepared dinner. It wasn't extravagant, but it was pretty good. Jack spent the evening bringing her back to reality. He knew exactly how to make her focus, particularly on the important issues, and he knew how to make her recognize and accept her limitations. He helped her realize that sometimes it's the little things you do to and for your friends that can help ease them through a bad situation.

Tracy and Cynthia had already decided that the focus of this Sunday dinner would be on Rosa. Rosa was like the bud on a rose bush; every time they saw her she looked stronger. She had begun to wear makeup and was wearing it quite nicely. She thought about her outfits a little more and began to develop a little style and flair. She was definitely blooming. They needed to find out where Carlton was in her life.

Before they could tackle that serious subject, Rosa brought up the "Turning" by asking what they were going to do for the fortieth "Turning."

"Damn, I ain't ready to be forty yet," Tracy lamented.

For a brief moment Cynthia thought about the fact that she would turn forty-two that year and Jack was sixty. Where the hell did the time go? One thing for sure, there was nothing about that man that looked like a sixty-year-old—his body, his attitude, nothing. Tracy took the opportunity to flip the conversation.

"How's Carlton doing?" asked Tracy.

"I guess he's all right," Rosa said.

"You guess? It must be wonderful to have a man right there with you all the time, especially when you get horny," Cynthia said.

"Yeah, at least you don't have to call your man and wait a day for him to get there," Tracy said through chuckles.

"Yeah! But when he gets there, he damn sure delivers," Cynthia volunteered since she thought Tracy was referring to her and Jack. They all had to laugh.

"Rosa's the only one at the table who can talk about getting delivered and served up on a regular basis," Tracy persisted.

"No, we don't do that anymore. We stopped doing that about a year ago, and it was fine with me. The last thing I need is Carlton touching me. I really don't think I want to be with that man. I don't even think I like him anymore."

"Well, sister, it sounds like you need a plan," Tracy offered.

"I'm working on it and I'll share it with y'all in due time. It ain't quite ready yet," said Rosa.

Tracy and Cynthia left dinner knowing that it was only going to be a matter of time before Rosa left Carlton, and they certainly wanted to be there to help her unfold her plan. As far as they knew, Carlton's sexual involvement with men was just a rumor. The Sister Circle had unanimously agreed that they would not bring Rosa this kind of information without being able to prove it. After all, Rosa and Carlton were no longer sexually intimate.

The sisters were now about six months away from the fortieth "Turning," and Jack and Cynthia were having a wonderful summer vacation. Jack had always chosen where they would meet, and she never questioned it. On this trip he told her to pack for the heat.

From JFK they took a flight to Fort Lauderdale, Florida. Fort Lauderdale in July has an unbelievable heat, and Cynthia promised herself, God and three white men that if he let her out of that town, she'd never go back again. The only good thing about Fort Lauderdale was that Jack was there, and they were only scheduled to be there for three days. Everything was air-conditioned, so once inside the hotel they agreed they would not leave for the next three days. Jack said, "Baby, this is just a pit stop; I guarantee that you will enjoy the rest of the vacation."

This vacation was a little different because Jack seemed to take more of a formal interest in the sisters in the circle. He said, "Baby, because these women are so important to you, I want to know more about them." They talked about the sisters, where they came from and what their strengths and weaknesses were.

They talked long and often about many different things, and their conversations were often interrupted by their inability to keep their hands off each other. Saturday evening, over a romantic candlelit dinner, Jack asked Cynthia about her "list of things to do." He asked her about Wesley, and she told him how she thought often about taking him off the list, but somehow he always stayed on.

Jack said, "Baby, don't take him off your list yet. When it's time to take him off your list, you won't have to think about it; you'll just do it."

Jack surprised Cynthia with a seven-day cruise to the Grand Cayman Islands. Their cabin was located on the sundeck and opened onto a private balcony. They sat on the balcony sipping cocktails while the ship left the port. She thought to herself, *Does it get any better than this?*

Every morning they had breakfast on the patio and spent the day enjoying the amenities of the ship, and the evenings enjoying each other. They were both getting older. They both looked great for their ages. She was forty-two, and Jack was sixty-one.

Although Jack tried to hide it, every morning after breakfast Jack would take a little pink pill. Cynthia wondered why he needed medication. She knew that he would tell her when he thought it was important. He still kept her in a constant state of arousal. It was an awesome seven days at sea.

Rosa had been on Cynthia's mind, so Cynthia called her first. Rosa said she had just gotten back from visiting her mother in the Midwest and caught a horrible summer cold. Cynthia spoke to Tracy next. Tracy was doing fine, but the more she thought about it the more she realized that she was really going to have to cut Brenda loose. Cynthia told Tracy that they would certainly support her, whatever her decision was, but she needed to think about her decision carefully because it took her so long to find someone in her life.

Next Cynthia called Robin; she is not always the easiest person to find, so Cynthia had to get her very early in the morning.

Robin said she was doing fine, but the job was getting very intense. The seminars that she had been doing were a great success, so she had been asked to do more of them in the New York area. At least twice a week she would be in various parts of New York doing a seminar. She said, "Although I really enjoy doing the seminars and meeting all kinds of new and interesting people, I really do miss the trading floor. I miss the rush.

"You know, sister, we really need to evaluate our financial portfolios. Since I'm the person who has made most of the investments for the Sister Circle, I want to give each of you an overview of your financial status when we come together at the 'Turning.' If we really intend to retire early and enjoy life, we need to take a look at our current financial status."

Cynthia told her that it sounded like a good idea. They all needed to know how they were looking financially as they moved into their forties. She said, "Yeah girl, fifty ain't but a minute away, and we need to be prepared."

Finally, Cynthia got Sandra on the line. Sandra told her that she felt that she was next in line for a principal position in the fall, and she was really excited about it. She said Jason had become an awesome lover, and she really loved it.

"But sometimes when he's on the road for business, or when he's not at home in our bed, I begin to wonder if maybe I created a monster."

"Don't let your imagination get the best of you," Cynthia added.

"You know, Cynthia, Jason was never a creative lover. He was very basic. But since Tracy woke him and his boys up, he has worked hard to acquire some great skills. He's good at what he does and he enjoys doing it. I just hope that he enjoys doing it only with me." Cynthia heard a real concern in Sandra's voice, and she really hoped that Sandra's feelings were wrong.

At dinner on the next Sunday, Tracy was looking and feeling like her old self. She was laughing and joking and having fun. Cynthia couldn't help but ask what was going on in her life.

"Girl, I finally realized that I could not keep Brenda in my life. I told her all the reasons we couldn't stay together, and the bitch had a hissy fit. She started screaming and hollering and throwing shit. I thought for a moment I was going to have to beat her ass. I finally calmed her down enough to get her out of my house, but I don't know if it's over yet. I think she's going to be a vindictive bitch about this."

"What prompted you to make this decision now?" Rosa asked.

"Y'all, I got to be honest. I met someone else," Tracy said with a trace of guilt.

Within the next few weeks everyone in the Sister Circle knew that Sandra thought that Jason might be cheating on her. It was hard for any of them to believe. Jason had been such a devoted husband and father for so many years. Robin said it didn't surprise her because all they ever knew was each other. Once he became a better lover, it was only a matter of time before he would want to share his new skills. Now that doesn't make it right, that's just the way it is.

They asked Sandra if there was anything they could do. She said there was no evidence that Jason was doing anything wrong; it was just a feeling that she had.

CHAPTER 16

Jack was a very resourceful man. He lived in the New York–New Jersey area most of his life and knew it like the back of his hand. He knew enough about Robin to get a pretty good idea of where to find her. He sat in the back of one of her seminars and watched her work. He watched her take charge of the group with a level of authority, and even the sharpest brokers in the room couldn't make her second guess herself. She moved around the room with great confidence and took control of the situation when the chauvinistic attitudes of the brokers began to surface. Sandra was too tenderhearted. Rosa was much too meek. And Tracy, well, she was just a different kind of woman, the kind he didn't understand. Robin was definitely the one.

As she worked the room he caught her attention. She knew that he was watching her, but she thought that this is business and that she would get to him later. When the seminar was over and people began to leave the room, Jack sat there for a while as the room cleared.

As usual, Jack was impeccably dressed. He stepped up to Robin and said, "I've been watching you conduct your seminar, and I must admit I'm impressed. I wonder if you would have dinner with me this evening."

Robin's ego got fat; he was an impressive-looking older man. Robin responded, "Since we don't really know each other, I'll tell you what, my last seminar is over at 7 P.M. Meet me then and we can go down to the hotel restaurant for dinner." She was immediately drawn to his deep baritone voice and his mannerisms and thought that it might be a pleasant change to be with an older man.

She didn't see him come in, but by the end of her last seminar he was sitting in the back of the room. She smiled. He acknowledged her, smiled back, and by 7:15 they were sitting at a table in the hotel restaurant ordering dinner.

Robin said, "Let's get the preliminaries out of the way." She identified herself.

Jack said, "Robin, I know exactly who you are. My name is Jackson Douglas." She thought about it for a minute with a puzzled look on her face. Jack said, "You may not know my last name, but I'm sure you've heard Cynthia speak of Jack."

"Well, I'll be damn! You're real," Robin said. Jack chuckled.

"Robin, I've invited you to dinner because I need your help, and I think that you may be the only person that can help me."

"It's true; you do cut right to the chase."

He said, "Yes I do, and I just need you to listen for the next few minutes."

Jack began to talk to Robin. Twenty minutes later he was still talking, and Robin was intensely connected to the conversation. At certain points she thought maybe he was pulling her leg, he really couldn't be serious. But as he continued the conversation she realized that this man was very serious. She watched and listened. She could easily understand why Cynthia could be so spellbound by this man.

Finally, he said, "I know that this is a lot to take in at one time. I know you have questions and you need to think about it. Let me give you my number and, please Robin, give it some serious thought and get back to me as soon as you can."

Robin took his number and sat there with her mouth wide open. She couldn't believe what she had just heard. At the beginning of the conversation he asked her to please keep this conversation between the two of them, and he made her to promise. If she had known what he had in mind, she never would have made that promise. But she did, and now she had to honor it.

Cynthia established herself quite nicely with UPS. She had a reputation of being a strong agent for the company, consistently finding new customers and developing new initiatives for old ones. For years Robin had been trying to convince her to make an investment in property. Cynthia decided that this was going to be her year. She contacted a local real estate agent who was anxious to make a deal. She loved living in the city and didn't want to move too far into the suburbs. She gave her agent the specifications of the house she wanted and let him do the work. Jack had given her a lot of advice on the things to look out for as a first-time buyer and how to get the best deal on a piece of property.

One Saturday, after a long day of house hunting, Cynthia came home with every intention of getting some things done around the house. While sitting on the sofa she drifted off to sleep and had another of those scary dreams. She didn't remember the beginning of the dream, only that there was a man touching her body. She became sexually aroused. The man asked her if she was ready, and she replied yes as he penetrated her body. She was on the brink of orgasm. She woke up. She sat there panting for breath and scared because it was so real. She thought, *There must have been someone in this room with me.* It was so very real. She pulled herself together and accepted that it was only a dream. How could a dream seem so real? This was the third such dream.

At her annual physical she told her doctor about these dreams. Cynthia needed to know if there was something physically wrong with her. The doctor asked her to describe the dreams. She felt embarrassed because in those dreams she had actually gotten sexually aroused. The doctor smiled and asked, "Is this the first time you've had an erotic dream?"

"I've never had one before now."

"You're a little late, but have a good time. There's nothing wrong with you. It's quite normal in some women. Consider yourself fortunate."

Cynthia was still too embarrassed to tell anyone about the dreams—at least not yet. She continued to have them occasionally. What was most disturbing was that the man making love to her never had a face. The dreams never led to orgasm, but it was mighty damn close. She decided that since there was nothing physically wrong with her, maybe she needed to see a psychologist. She scheduled an appointment to see Dr. Hendricks, and within two weeks she was sitting in her waiting room.

Cynthia went into her office and was quite taken aback by the number of degrees and citations that lined her walls. Dr. Hendricks introduced herself and asked Cynthia to take a seat. She then asked her why she thought she needed a psychologist. She told her about her dreams and that she had recently spoken to her physician, who said there was nothing wrong with her physically. Nonetheless, the dreams continued. So she thought maybe a psychologist could help her understand what was going on.

"Well, Cynthia, it is not uncommon for human beings to have erotic dreams. Why does it bother you so much?"

Cynthia told her it bothered her because they were new and the man in the dream never had a face.

"It seems that the dreams aren't hurting you. You're not being physically harmed and, if anything, you're having a good time. You just need to go with the dream and enjoy it. If the man has no face, give him a face, but there's nothing wrong with you. To be honest, there are many women who would love to be able to have those kinds of dreams. Enjoy them! If they become violent, or if you are hurt in anyway, then we may need to take a look to see what's going on. But right now it sounds like a normal erotic dream. The dreams will be only as good as your imagination. If you have a great imagination, you'll have a wonderful time."

Cynthia couldn't control when the dreams happened, but she could make the man in the dream do whatever she wanted him to, except to produce an orgasm. Once she knew that there was nothing physically or mentally wrong with her, she felt that she could share her new experience with the Sister Circle.

They were now three months away from the fortieth "Turning." Since this "Turning" would be in New York, Robin had been busy finding locations that suited their needs. Sandra's mother was disappointed that she didn't get to plan another "Turning." Tracy had a new woman in her life but wasn't ready to tell them about her yet. Brenda didn't go away quietly, but finally went away.

Early on a Sunday morning in October Cynthia's telephone rang. She picked up the phone and heard Sandra's voice on the other end. She could tell that Sandra had been crying.

"Cynthia, I was right. He has been fucking around."

Cynthia's heart sank. It seems that Sandra had attended an office party to which Jason had invited her. He really didn't expect that she would attend. When she arrived, she saw Jason leaning against the bar. A woman was all over him, and he had his hands on her ass.

"I just stood there and watched for a while;" Sandra continued. "I wanted to be sure of what I was seeing. Once I was convinced that something was going on, I walked straight through the room, tapped him on his shoulder and told him what a lousy thing to do to his family. When I left, I saw the look of shock on his colleagues' faces.

"Jason followed me home, telling me how sorry he was. Then I asked him about the woman. He claimed he hadn't known her long and had only been with her twice. I could tell he was lying. He finally admitted that she wasn't the only one, but insisted that those women didn't mean anything to him. It was just something to do. Then he tried to assure me that for every woman he was with he always used a condom—almost as if the problem was whether or not he used a condom, and not adultery. He went on to explain how I had been the only woman that he had sex with, and he just wanted to see what it was like to be with other women.

"I was getting ready to be a sucker and forgive him, but he couldn't promise he wouldn't do it again. As much as I love Jason and want my family to stay together, I couldn't live like that. So unless something changes drastically, Jason and I are getting a divorce."

"Damn! I don't believe that," Cynthia said. "Would it help if I came to Georgia?"

"I'm going to be all right, girl. I just need a little more time to process things."

Sandra's parents were devastated by the news that Sandra and Jason were divorcing. Sandra's mother was making sure that Sandra had the best lawyer in all of Georgia. She said she wanted to be sure that Jason could get away but that he couldn't take anything away with him. She publicly guaranteed Jason an ass-kicking in court. Tracy, Rosa, and Cynthia went to see and confirm the arrangements for the fortieth "Turning." With their approval, Robin had hired an events planner to put things together. They went to Robin's condo and were surprised that she had dinner ready.

The next morning they were up and on the move. They met their events planner for breakfast. They wanted an Afro-centric theme to this "Turning," and their coordinator could give them what they wanted.

By noon they were on the hunt for the right outfits. They were trying on clothes all over the city. Tracy and Cynthia were having a blast. They spent much more money than they had intended. Although Rosa kept telling them that she was having a good time, she always seemed to be preoccupied and one step behind them.

Rosa went to bed early, causing them some concern. She had so little energy these days.

The next day they were all headed home, loaded with new purchases and talking about their Thanksgiving plans. Cynthia was going to have dinner with her mother in Alabama. Rosa's mother was coming to Boston for the first time to be with Rosa for the holiday.

Robin reluctantly agreed to have dinner with her mother at her grandparents' home. This would be the first time in over ten years that she would have dinner with her mother. She admitted that she really didn't know her mother well. Once Robin met her father, she knew that she finally had to talk to her mother in a serious way. She wanted to know the truth about her father. Tracy was looking forward to spending her first thanksgiving with her new friend. They would all get together again for the "Turning" in just a few weeks.

They arrived at the New York Hilton, excited about the fortieth "Turning." By 6 P.M. they were settling in with their first round of cocktails. Now they were always loud when they got together, and it was no different this time. Tracy and Robin were telling stories and acting them out. They took their party to the hotel lounge. It was much too early to turn in for the night.

The lounge was full of people having a good time dancing and laughing. They found a table and ordered drinks. The plan was to spend no more than two hours in the lounge and call it a night. Robin was the first to notice that there seemed to be quite a few men out that evening. As it turned out, they were right in the middle of a Masonic convention.

The sisters decided, what the hell, they would dance and have fun for the next few hours. One thing you can count on in the presence of Masons is drinking, partying, dancing and a lot of flirting. One of them took a fancy to Robin, asked her to dance, and for the better part of the evening they seemed to be getting along quite well.

"Damn! I hope she doesn't bring that old man upstairs and kill him," Sandra joked.

Eventually Robin came over to the table, pulled Cynthia aside and said, "Cynthia, I like that smooth old man. What I like most is that we were slow dancing on the floor and the brother's packing."

"It didn't take you long to figure that out," Cynthia said.

"What do you do with an old man?" Robin asked.

"Robin, I wouldn't call the man old, and I don't think you have to do anything different than you would do with any other brother. Oh! But wait a minute, it just dawned on me who I'm talking to. One thing I'm pretty sure that you can't do is rough the brother up. The probability is good that he ain't a rough rider. Think about that before you get in an embarrassing situation."

"You know, Cynthia, ever since you and Jack started hanging out together I've always wondered what it would be like to be with an old man."

"One thing I can tell you is that they are not all the same, and Jack is not an old man. Now I don't know about this old dude and what he's bringing with him, but believe me, sister, they are not all the same."

"Well, I'm forty-one years old, and I'm going to check this shit out."

"Just be careful and use some protection."

"Listen, let the sisters know that I'll catch up with y'all later."

Cynthia told the sisters that Robin had something to do, and they all started laughing.

"She don't even know that man." Tracy laughed.

"I don't think that has ever stopped Robin before," Cynthia said.

"Naw, we can't have that. We gotta know something about this man. What if the bitch winds up dead? We at least need to know who she left with." Tracy snapped.

Tracy got up and strutted over to the brother, introduced herself and asked him his name. He said his name was Roger, he was from Baltimore and he was here for the Mason's conference. Tracy, being as straightforward as she is, said, "Listen brother, I'm not trying to get up in your business, but if I need to find you next week, how can I do that?" The brother smiled and said, "Here's my business card." Tracy brought the business card back and placed it on the table.

"Now, let that bitch go do her thang."

Tracy had a tendency to use the term *bitch* more often than anyone else, but they knew that when she used it toward them it was always in a loving way.

By 10 o'clock the next morning the sisters were up enjoying a continental breakfast when Robin came in. Tracy stood up.

"Damn girl, looks like you got your ass whipped." Robin plopped down on the sofa. She had a big grin on her face.

"It really wasn't a fight. The old dude was smooth. At first I couldn't figure out what the hell he was doing, or when he was going to get to it. When he finally got down to business, damn. I think the old dude did some new shit to me."

"I don't think he did anything new to you; he was just smooth," Cynthia commented.

"You know, I could get used to that shit. I think I have a better understanding why you keep hanging out with Jack."

Cynthia smiled because Robin really had no idea of how smooth an older man could be.

By nine o'clock that evening they were dressed ready to enjoy their fortieth "Turning." They got downstairs; about 10:00 folks were laughing, and having a good time, many of these people hadn't seen each other since the last "Turning," and that was ten years ago. The sisters greeted their guests with hugs and kisses and then joined the party. At about midnight, the D.J. brought in the oldies and the place began to rock. At 12:20 the wait staff brought out the champagne for the toast.

The party was still going strong at three o'clock in the morning. The sisters knew they would catch hell trying to get these people out. By 10:00 in the morning they were all up, looking like something the cat had dragged in. Robin fell into the suite at about 10:15 A.M., grinning like a Cheshire cat, just in time for coffee.

Rosa suddenly got very quiet. Something had been on her mind since they came to New York. She just hadn't said anything about it.

So Tracy said, "Rosa, if there's something we can help you with, please let us do it. We know there's something on your mind."

"Well, there is something on my mind," said Rosa. "It really hasn't bothered me so much. I just need to figure out how to tell you."

"Well just tell us," Sandra implored.

Rosa sat down slowly. "I told you that Carlton and I hadn't been intimate for quite a while. That much is true. I had to confront him and demand that he leave, and he did. He left because he'd been fucking around. I wouldn't mind if he had just been fucking around with a woman, but he's been messing around with men, too."

Tracy and Cynthia glanced at each other, as if to say "Finally, she got the heart to end the relationship."

"How do you know he's fucking around?" Tracy asked.

"He admitted it. I can't stand the sight of him. Carlton has mentally and physically abused me, taken away my self-confidence and, on occasion, made me feel stupid and useless. This was totally unforgivable.

"When I came back from visiting my parents over the Thanksgiving holiday I had a cold that I couldn't seem to shake. My temperature would go up for no reason, and I would have night sweats. Finally, I went to the doctor. After a few tests, he told me I was HIV positive."

The room was absolutely silent. Tears streamed down Sandra's face. Robin and Cynthia sat there in total disbelief. Tracy paced the floor, agitated. They were shocked into consciousness by the sound of glass shattering against the wall.

"I told y'all years ago that the motherfucker needed to die!"

This time there was no disagreement in the room.

Rosa was the only composed person in the room. "I was diagnosed about six weeks ago and I'm beginning to come to grips with this. What I want to share with you is that it doesn't mean that I'm going to die, not any quicker than any of you. It means that I will be medicated for the rest of my life. It means that I have to live a different lifestyle and see my doctor regularly. The virus is not airborne and can only be transmitted through blood and semen. I've still got a lot of life to live, and I intend to do just that.

"When I confronted Carlton, he was very defensive. Even now he refuses to deal with the fact that he's a carrier. He has admitted having sex with men, but refuses to be tested. I know that the only possible way on earth that I could have gotten this virus was through Carlton. Tracy, I felt the same way that you feel, that this motherfucker had to die. When Carlton refused to deal with the fact that he was a carrier of HIV, I went into a rage. I've had a gun for years, and I bought the gun to protect me and my family when Carlton was away. This time I wanted to use the gun to protect my family from Carlton. He was sitting across from me at the kitchen table with a nasty sneer on his ugly face, and I lost it.

"I scrambled across the table. I wanted to feel my hands around his throat. We both fell on the floor. I pulled the gun out of my pocket and pointed it at his face. When I cocked it, we both heard the bullet lodge in the chamber. All I needed to do was to pull the trigger. I had never felt such rage. He knew he was a dead man. I held the gun to his head, trembling as I told him that he was a sleazy, low-life motherfucker who had made my life miserable. As the tears rolled down my cheeks I told him that the only thing that would please me now was to see him dead.

"My oldest son heard the ruckus, came into the room, and talked me back to sanity. He took the gun from my hand and helped me off the floor. Carlton scrambled to his feet and headed toward the door. I told him that he had better get everything that he wanted out of this house because if he came back I would kill him. For the first time since I've known Carlton I saw fear in his eyes. He knew I meant everything I said.

"I don't know if I would really have pulled the trigger, but at that moment I felt like I could. I've had a little time to think about it. Yes, he deserves to die, but all I have left is my soul and I can't compromise that to kill him.

"This is not good news, sisters, but it's not the worst news in the world. I'll survive this, but I think it's a wake-up call for all of us. All I ask is that you not treat me any differently. I've been taking the medications for the last six weeks, and I feel better than I've felt in a long time. The only reason that I'm sharing all of this with you is because the Sister Circle has become such an important part of my life, and if there's ever a point where my spirits need to be lifted, I know that I can count on the sisters to help me do that.

"I intend to be around for the fiftieth and the sixtieth 'Turning.' So don't feel sorry for me and don't count me out."

Her words hung in the air. This was definitely a wake-up call. They were now all single, and they had to do their own personal assessment of how well they were protecting themselves. Cynthia thought about Jack. They had never used a condom; they were going to have to talk now.

The sisters huddled around Rosa and cried.

"Don't cry for me. If you're going to do anything, let's pray."

After the prayer, Rosa stood up, smiled and said, "Let's dry up those tears and let's get sharp. We've got one more night on the town. I want to turn it out."

They were shocked because Rosa was never the partying type. She wanted to party, and they were certainly going to go with her.

CHAPTER 17

Robin was determined to take the sisters to Small's. The club was packed for a Sunday night, and folks seemed to be having a good time. The sisters took a table in the far corner of the club, and Robin went to find Sonny. When she returned, she looked at Cynthia and said, "You can get comfortable now; Sam's not working tonight."

They enjoyed the club until midnight when Robin dropped them off at the hotel.

"Sister, I want you to have a good time, but I want to give you this," Rosa said as she gave Robin a condom.

Now most of the folks in their generation had to get accustomed to the concept of using a condom. They were children of the birth-control era and felt that condoms were no longer needed once they could control pregnancy. They never gave much consideration to sexually transmitted diseases. You could always get a shot for that. But now there was the ultimate sexually transmitted disease, and there was no shot for it. The condom had to become a part of their life whether they liked it or not.

By nine o'clock Monday morning they headed for the airport. Four hours later, Cynthia was sitting in her apartment. She put on some music and began to think about the weekend and all of the events that unfolded.

Tuesday morning she was back at the grind doing what she did for a living. On her Thursday night date with Jack it felt so good to hear his voice. He wanted to know everything about the fortieth "Turning," and of course he asked her the standard question: "Did you meet any interesting young men?" She gave him the standard answer: "Not yet."

She told him about all the fun parts of the "Turning" and then she told him about Sandra and her pending divorce. He was sympathetic and said Sandra was going to have to learn that life goes on. She then told him about Rosa and how devastated they were to learn that she was HIV positive. She told him that after talking to Rosa, they had the conversation about the use of condoms. Cynthia said she thought it was a conversation that she and Jack needed to have. He said, "You're right, baby, we do need to have that conversation and we'll have it when I pick you up for Christmas."

They were roughly two weeks away from Christmas vacation, and she couldn't imagine what the plan would be for this year.

Jack was much more than an awesome lover, he had become an intricate part of her life. Because of him it had become extremely difficult to find Mr. Right. She had become accustomed to having a damn good man without being smothered.

The erotic dreams didn't stop. They became more intense. She had been working diligently to acquire some level of control over these dreams. They went according to her directions. She had given the faceless man the face of all of the men that she thought she ever wanted to be with in life, and the only face that ended in orgasm was Wesley's. In these dreams she made Wesley anything she wanted him to be. She made him do anything she wanted him to do. She dressed him however she wanted to, and she could have him anytime she wanted him. That was power! It was at that moment she knew she had to take Wesley off of her "list of things to do." If she kept him on her list and accomplished the deed, she would no longer have a face to connect to her erotic dreams.

December 23, 1991, Cynthia met Jack at JFK. This time they ended up in Aspen, Colorado. Although Jack told her to pack for the cold, she never expected to end up in ski country. Aspen at Christmas was beautiful. They walked into an impressive ski lodge with exposed wood, a huge fireplace, with brass and copper everywhere. She followed Jack as he walked past the registration desk. He looked at her and said, "This is not it, baby. Follow me." They walked through the lodge, out the other side through a large set of glass doors into a huge courtyard. A combination of the snow and the Christmas lights made this courtyard sparkle. Around the courtyard were five miniature chalets, each with its own walkway and private entrance. When they got to the middle chalet, Jack reached into his pocket, pulled out a key and opened the door.

She knew that she must have looked like a little kid on Christmas day. They stepped into a large living room with a huge Christmas tree in the corner. At one end of the room was a set of French double doors that opened into the master bedroom. On one side of the bedroom was the entrance to a bathroom that was bigger than most living rooms; and on the other side of the room was a glass-enclosed Jacuzzi.

The trip to Colorado was a fairly long one. Both of them just wanted to get comfortable and relax. They kicked their shoes off. Since this was their first night in Aspen, Jack ordered dinner to be served in their chalet. The best position in the world for Cynthia was still snuggling up close to Jack, and that's exactly what she did.

"Baby, tell me about Rosa."

She told him the story even to the point where Rosa thought she could kill Carlton. She tried to hold back the tears. Every time she thought about Rosa she had to fight to hold back the tears. Rosa deserved so much more in life than she was getting. Cynthia told Jack that Rosa had given them all a reality check. They were now five single women, and the HIV virus was getting out of control. They needed to be careful and they needed to use protection.

When the sisters were having the conversation about condoms, Cynthia thought about Jack. She and Jack had been together for a long time and never talked about the use of condoms. It's time that they have the discussion.

"Baby, you know I date occasionally. We both do. But I don't often meet women that I really want to make love to. I agree with you; we need to come to some agreement. I'm prepared to use a condom, if that's really what you want me to do. But if I'm given a choice, I'd rather use a condom with any other woman but you. I want to be able to feel every sensation that your body provides. I want to be able to feel the temperature and the texture of you, and I believe that a condom would limit that.

"I know that you date occasionally, and what I'm about to ask may sound strange. It may even sound a little selfish, but I'm going to ask you anyway. I need to be the one man in your life who touches you in an uninhibited way. Therefore I'm asking that when you date, if you become intimate with other men, that you ask them to use the condom. I can guarantee you that I'll use a condom if I become intimate with another woman."

She needed him to know that his request was not nearly as strange as he thought it would be. She told him that making love to him was one of the few things that she did with one hundred percent of her, and she wanted to be able to feel every part of his body as well. The thought of latex between them was totally unappealing to her, and she could easily give him a hundred percent guarantee that if she became intimate with another man he would absolutely have to use a condom. They both agreed to those terms, and she truly trusted him to do the right thing.

He held her in his arms and consoled her as she cried for Rosa. He made her feel that everything was going to be okay. After dinner they both knew that the mood had to be lightened. She needed more than ever to move into her fantasy world, and the quickest way into that world was through making love to Jack.

For the first time since they had been together Jack was not always ready when she was. Age had crept into their sex life. When he was ready, he delivered as strongly and intensely as ever. When he wasn't ready, he compensated beautifully. She was never left without a smile on her face and the inability to hear out of her left ear.

They brought the New Year in sitting in a hot tub, watching the snow fall. He pulled her close to him and kissed her passionately.

"Baby, it ain't as easy as it used to be. My mind and heart are always willing, but my body doesn't always respond. For years I have asked you to remind me on New Year's Eve that there is almost a twenty-year difference in our ages. This year my body has reminded us both."

She had to let him know that sex with him was still fantastic, and their relationship was built on more than just sex.

"For right now, that's true because I'm not totally out of the game, but sooner or later I won't be able to do the things that you need to have done. Now we came into this relationship knowing that this time would come, and it's time for me to make a little more room for that younger man. I don't want you to get me wrong, I'm not moving out of your life. I'm just moving over a little bit."

So they agreed to call each other once a month on the first Thursday; but if either of them needed the other, they would call in between. Neither of them was prepared to give up the six-month meeting, not yet. They took advantage of every moment they had left, knowing that soon she'd be headed back to Boston and he'd be headed back to New Jersey.

Once at home, she began to ponder what would life be like without Jack. She had plenty of things to keep her busy most of the time. She was still looking for her house. She had a fantastic Sister Circle. She was still dating occasionally, and she still had things left on her "list of things to do."

When Cynthia spoke to Robin she was upbeat and happy. Robin said that she had a wonderful holiday. She and Sonny had been getting along quite nicely, and she was beginning to like him a little more than she liked most men. She said she couldn't define it as love because she had never been in love before, but she really dug being with the brother. Her mood changed when Cynthia asked about her mother, Doris.

Thanksgiving with her mother and grandparents had really enlightened her, Robin said. Her mother was surprised and angry that Robin had made contact with her father. She asked Robin why she needed to know a man who was never a part of her life. Robin began to ask her mother questions about her father. When Robin was a child they never talked about him. Doris kept staring at Robin as the questions came one after another. Finally, Doris stormed out of the house.

Robin said she turned to her grandparents for the truth. They were always protective of their daughter and would never say anything against her. Over the years they had developed an odd way of talking to Robin about her mother. If the answer to Robin's question was yes, they would not respond. But if the answer was no, they would respond verbally, sometimes with an explanation. When Robin questioned them this time, they said nothing. Robin's father was telling the truth.

Robin finally knew why he left and why he hadn't contacted her over the years. Doris had placed a restraining order on him shortly after Robin was born. For the first few years Walter tried everything to see his daughter. Working through her grandparents, he finally got to see her one last time before leaving for California. He sent birthday cards and presents. When they weren't thrown away, they were returned. Robin's mother harbored an intense hatred for Robin's father for leaving, and made her parents promise not to allow Walter to make contact with Robin. When Robin was two years old, her mother had a nervous breakdown and spent two years in treatment. Since that time no one talked about Walter. Robin knew she would have to figure out what role Walter would play in her life, if any.

Robin had been working on the financial portfolios for the Sister Circle, and they were looking pretty good financially. She couldn't see any reason they wouldn't be able to retire when they wanted to. The only one she was concerned about was Rosa, who didn't own very much and had not been able to make significant investments.

"I'll bet that sleazy bastard of hers is worth a lot of money," Robin said.

She asked Cynthia about her Christmas vacation. Cynthia told her, as usual, she and Jack had a wonderful time. She told her that she was a little concerned because his age did appear to be catching up with him a little.

"Cynthia, you knew when you got into the relationship that this time would come. It's probably time for you to begin to date a little more seriously. Keep your eyes open, Cynthia, 'cause I think Mr. Right will be coming along."

"Robin, you wouldn't know Mr. Right if he jumped up and slapped you in the face."

"Yeah, I may not be the sharpest knife in the drawer, but when it comes to men, I may know more about your Mr. Right than you think, even though you're a lot smarter than I am."

When Cynthia called Rosa, Rosa said she was doing great. The kids were all doing well; her baby was now seventeen years old and ready to graduate from high school and would be off to college soon. Rosa was redoing the house, getting rid of every trace of Carlton. She hadn't seen him since she tried to kill him.

"Cynthia, it is in his best interest that I never see him again," was Rosa's cryptic remark.

The new lady in Tracy's life seemed to have her attention. They spent Christmas and New Year's in Atlantic City.

"Cynthia, she makes me happy."

"If it makes you happy, then go with it."

Sandra was getting used to the fact that Jason was gone. Her mother was smothering her and trying to introduce her to new people, but Sandra really wasn't ready for that yet. Her baby was now sixteen years old. Her biggest challenge was her son; he hated his father for leaving. This was her daughter's first year at college, and the longer she was away at school the less Sandra heard from her. Life was moving on.

CHAPTER 18

On May 1, 1993, Cynthia purchased a house. She could have done this years ago, but she really didn't want the hassle. She liked her apartment in the city. Almost every time that Robin and Cynthia were together, Robin would take out her calculator to show Cynthia how much money she was losing by not being a homeowner. She was the last one in the Sister Circle to own a home. On the day that Cynthia received the keys to her new and empty home, the sisters were there toasting with champagne and celebrating.

Everyone came for the weekend to help her move, and they brought their own set of decorating ideas. She took everything from her old apartment that she needed and threw away the rest. The sisters made a list and took her on a marathon-shopping trip. By Saturday evening she had taken all of the suggestions that each of her sisters had to offer.

Robin and Sandra left Boston on Sunday afternoon. Rosa had to get home to check on her young adult son. Tracy fixed dinner for Cynthia. Cynthia knew Tracy well enough to know that she had something on her mind.

After dinner Tracy said that she was still having a very difficult time accepting Rosa's diagnosis. Every time she ran into Carlton all she wanted to do was to blow his brains out.

They were all in contact with Robin over the last few weeks, evaluating their financial status. Robin had made some very wise investments for them over the years, and it looked as if they would be able to retire within the next five to seven years. They were all concerned about Rosa's financial situation; the house, the business and all of the investments were in Carlton's name.

Rosa had a job and roughly four thousand dollars in a savings account.

"Cynthia, when the time comes to retire, we can't just walk away and leave Rosa. We've got to help her develop a plan. As I see it, that sleazy motherfucker has much more value to Rosa dead than he does alive. If he were dead, the real estate and the investments would all become hers. Now I'll bet you that he's got some serious investments. I know his business is a lucrative one. I just need to figure out how to make it all Rosa's. Carlton has wronged a lot of people. There are a lot of folks out there that would like to see him dead, and you can count me in that group.

"I figure that all I need to do is put his business in the street and it would be only a matter of time before somebody takes him out. Rosa will be a wealthy woman. The brothers that travel in his down-low circle would kill him if they knew that he was HIV positive and still chasing boy pussy unprotected. They are smart enough to know what the implications are for them. You can't talk me out of this, Cynthia, it's already been done."

Cynthia told Tracy that this sounded awfully dangerous.

"It's only dangerous for Carlton. I know what I'm doing, and I'll handle this."

Jack and Cynthia had established their new once-a-month telephone agreement, and she couldn't begin to count the number of Thursdays that she wanted to break the agreement just to hear his voice. She found herself making notes so that she would remember all the things that she wanted to say when she talked to him. She kept him up to date on her house hunting, and before she signed the final papers she gave him an in-depth description of the house. He said that it sounded like a pretty good deal and the price wasn't bad at all. They were scheduled to be together from July 1 to July 8, and they were really looking forward to this. He asked her if she would mind spending the seven days at her place. To her it really didn't matter as long as they spent the time together. She and Jack had made so many trips to so many different places that this would be a restful change.

Cynthia still dated occasionally, but it was getting harder and harder to find a man that could hold her attention beyond a couple of dates. Most of the men in her age group were divorced and bitter about it, or overloaded with alimony payments. Since she wasn't in the market for a husband and didn't need a sugar daddy, occasional dating did not pose a problem for her.

She still had erotic dreams in which she could have Wesley whenever and however she wanted him.

Sunday evening dinner found the Sister Circle in great spirits. Cynthia hadn't seen Tracy's spirit that high in a long time. Her new woman was working out. Tracy said that one of the things she liked most was that this woman didn't want to move in with her. Tracy said that the older she got the more she appreciated her privacy and freedom.

"You know, I've never been good at keeping secrets from y'all, and I just gotta tell somebody about my new woman.

"Her name is Carolyn Henderson. She sits on the City Council and is a bad bitch. She don't take no shit. She's financially stable, very secure in who she is, and a hell of a politician. She was born and raised right here in Boston. I met her at a sickle cell anemia fundraiser. You know, since I have all of this free time I've become quite a socialite in Boston. We were seated at the same table for dinner, and she immediately struck up a conversation. By the time dinner was over I was quite impressed with her, and she was obviously impressed with me. We exchanged phone numbers. She is not your stereotypical lesbian. The sister looks better than any straight woman that I know. We do have one small problem, though; she's still in the closet. She guarantees me that after this November's election, when she wins her seat back, she's going to publicly come out. I told her that it wasn't important to me that everyone knew that we were seeing each other, but it was important to me that she recognized who she was and was honest with it."

Rosa looked wonderful, better than ever. She kept her hair and makeup done. The sister could put together beautiful outfits on her limited budget. She often told us that Filene's basement was the poor woman's Sax Fifth Avenue. Her son was now twenty-two years old, and the ladies were constantly trying to get his attention. He was a good-looking young brother and he knew it.

Rosa made it known that Carlton Jr. was a very angry young man at times and kept his feelings to himself.

Her daughter was twenty years old and completing her second year in college. When she was sixteen she told her mother that the only thing she wanted to do was to get away from the fighting and the pain. Rosa realized that Carlton damaged not only her but also the children.

Cynthia was really excited about seeing Jack. It had been a while and so much had happened in between their last visit. She picked him up at 10:00 A.M. at Logan airport. She sat in the waiting area watching the passengers come and go and remembered how nervous she was sitting here almost twenty years ago, waiting to meet Jack for the very first time. After twenty years of unbelievable memories and experiences, she was back at the airport again, waiting for Jack. For a sixty-four-year-old man he was still looking damn good.

They picked up his luggage and headed home. Once on the expressway she realized she was headed in the wrong direction. She was going toward her old apartment. Finally, she pulled into the driveway of her new home.

"Well, baby, so far it looks like you made a good deal."

They lounged on the sofa and talked about everything that had been going on in the last six months. Jack massaged her neck and shoulders. She closed her eyes and felt the tension move from her body.

"You know, baby, you are the most memorable woman that I have ever known. I think about you often, maybe too often. I sometimes wonder what life would have been like if I had met you twenty years earlier than I did."

"No different," she told him. "We would still be doing what we're doing today."

"You're probably right, but right now I just want to hold you and talk to you."

And that's exactly what she wanted him to do. She thought about the last time they were together. Although the passion and intensity was still there, his body didn't always respond the way he wanted it to. She could tell how much that bothered him. She promised herself that on this visit she would not put such demands on his body. She would let him determine when and if he was ready. She would let him determine how often he was ready. They spent the evening cuddling and talking.

For the first time in the years they had been together Jack asked her to promise him that she would honestly give other men a fair chance at proving themselves.

"Baby, you're much too young to be alone. As I've always told you, life goes on."

She heard finality in his voice she hadn't heard before.

Very early in the relationship he told her if ever there was a point where he could not sexually please her, he would have to move out of her life and make room for a younger man. She knew he was thinking that the time was now. She knew she wouldn't be able to convince him that he was still the man she fell in love with almost twenty years ago. She also knew this might be their last visit. She was determined to make this visit as memorable as all the others.

That evening she lit some candles and played some soft music, and they held each other. She told him there was no pressure for him to perform. She was quite comfortable just being held in his arms. He let out a thunderous laugh and said, "Well baby, I can't do it like I used to, but I can still do it. I can't do it as often as I used to, but I can still do it. And I may not be able to do it as long as I used to, but, damn it, I can still do it." By two o'clock in the morning it was clear that Jack could still do it.

She woke to the smell of coffee. Jack was still an early-morning man and knew that coffee in the morning was the quickest way to get her attention. Since he had been up much earlier than her, he took the liberty of looking at the rest of the house. He asked her how she felt about living in what she called the country. She told him that she was getting used to it and felt that everything would be fine as long as Mother Nature stayed outside. He had decided on a house-warming gift, and it arrived on Thursday morning at nine o'clock: a security system was installed. By the end of the day every possible entrance to her home was secured. Jack wanted her to be safe.

This was a sensitive, state-of-the-art system. She had to remember all of the codes it took to operate it. The crew from the alarm company walked her through the entire system and told her what each and every devise did, even down to the hidden panic button.

Jack said he would now be able to sleep knowing that she was secure in her new home.

They had no intentions of leaving the house during this vacation. It was going to be their time, seven full days of loving and being loved. There were times when Jack's body would just not respond. It bothered him much more than it bothered her. She could see it in his face and attitude. Even when his body would not respond, she was never left incomplete because Jack was still a master at improvising.

On at least two different occasions she awoke in the middle of the night and found Jack watching her sleep. He assured her that it was only a little insomnia. On the evening before he left, he wanted to have another serious conversation about her inability to accept another man in her life.

She told him, as she had told him many times, she was not unwilling to accept another man in her life; she was just unwilling to accept a man without some of the necessary qualities. He would need to be warm, smooth and tender. He would need to be verbal, both in and out of bed. He would need to be secure in who he was, and he would need to be open to learning how to please her as much as she would want to please him. Last but not least, he would need to have a good sense of humor. She told Jack she didn't think that was an awful lot to ask of a man, and when that man came along she would gladly accept him into her life.

He said, "Baby, that man is coming sooner than you think, believe me. Now you may not see all of those qualities immediately in this man, but you'll have to give him a chance. Promise me that you will at least try."

She promised him that she would try.

That evening they sat on the patio in her favorite position and watched the sunset. Although he was physically there with her, he felt so distant. There was something very different about this vacation. For the first time in almost twenty years he didn't have a lot to say. At about ten o'clock he said, "Baby, there are only two things that I want to do right now: I'd like another glass of cognac, and I'd like to make totally uninhibited love to you."

And that's exactly what they did. There were times that evening, during their love making, that she wanted to climb into his body because she felt that would be the only safe place in the world. She couldn't hold back the tears. She'd never been a crier. She'd been known to get angry and fight for what she wanted, but in this case all the fighting in the world wouldn't allow her to keep this man. Those were not the terms of the original agreement. At that point she clearly understood that "nothing is certain but change."

They stood in the airport waiting for the ten o'clock shuttle to New Jersey.

"Cynthia, I've loved you longer and harder than I've ever loved any woman, and that will never change."

He then gave her one of those deep passionate kisses that always made her lose her breath, and before she could respond he was gone. She stood there dumfounded. She didn't get to tell him that she loved him equally as much. Throughout the years she had always felt rejuvenated and ready to take on the world after being with Jack. This time she just felt drained.

On the trip home from the airport her mind began to race. What if he didn't know how much she loved him? And if he did, would it make a difference? How much longer could she keep this man in her life? And what the hell would she do when he was gone? That evening she prayed and asked the Lord to give her the strength to take on this new challenge in her life.

CHAPTER 19

News travels fast in the city. At this point everyone knew that Carlton was an HIV carrier. Tracy was getting a little tired of waiting for someone to kill Carlton. There was always a lot of talk about it, but nothing seemed to happen. She knew that she was going to need to stir the pot a little.

Rosa, Tracy and Cynthia had their normal Sunday dinner at Sidney's. They both wanted to know about Cynthia's date with Jack. There was no reason not to be honest. She told them that she sensed that things were coming to an end. She reminded them of Jack's promise to move out of her life so that she could find a younger man when he couldn't keep her happy sexually. At the age of sixty-four it wasn't easy for him to do that anymore.

"Well sister, you knew that sooner or later this time would come."

"Yeah, I work real hard at being realistic," Cynthia retorted, "but reality is a bitch. You know she's coming, but somehow she just manages to sneak up on you. I'll handle this and go through the slow process of healing. On the very bad days I'll remember Jack's words: life goes on."

Cynthia caught up with Robin late that evening. Robin and Sonny had just returned from a weekend trip. She said that the whole relationship with Sonny was making her a little nervous. She wanted to be with him more than any other man in her life, and they had such a great time together. Her biggest problem was that Sonny wasn't ready to commit to one woman. She said that she wasn't trying to marry the man; she just wanted to elevate her status to the woman who gets most of his time. She thought that she held that position but needed him to say it, and he just wouldn't do it.

She, too, asked about Cynthia's vacation with Jack. Cynthia told her what she told the other sisters in the circle.

"Cynthia, you knew this time was coming, and we've talked about this for years."

Cynthia told her that she knew it was coming but she really expected a little more closure.

Robin said, "Well now it's time to give other brothers a little more consideration than you've given them over the years. There's got to be somebody out there who can take his place."

Cynthia told Robin that they would see what happens and that she would keep her up on what's going on.

"Cynthia, I don't normally get into your business," said Robin, "because I know how private you can be sometimes, but I am a little concerned about you. Are you going to be okay?"

Cynthia told her that whatever the outcome was, she would have to be okay with it and that she would adjust.

When the conversation was over Robin needed a nightcap. She made herself a dry martini and sat down to think about the recent conversation with Cynthia. *What was Jack doing? After all this was all his idea.* When they met for dinner she remembered asking him to be clear and concise when the time came, make it quick. She knew that Cynthia needed to begin the healing process. She thought about the hurt and confusion that Cynthia must be feeling at this point and got very angry. She loved Cynthia dearly and never wanted to be a part of anything that was going to make her experience painful, but Robin had bought into this arrangement and didn't know how to get out. She had never kept such a serious secret out of the Sister Circle before; there was no one that she could talk to. No one would be able to understand how she could become a part of this painful experience. The anger overwhelmed her as she hurled her glass against the dining room wall. She would have to talk to Jack, because things weren't going as planned.

It was the first Thursday in August, and it was Cynthia's turn to call. When the dates changed to once a month, they took alternate turns making the call. She spent the last couple of weeks jotting down everything that she wanted Jack to know.

She wanted him to know that she loved him as much as he loved her. She also wanted him to know that although they had a fantastic sexual relationship, that was not all there was to the relationship, and she could accept those times when he couldn't perform.

It was 8:05. She dialed his number. The phone rang three times and a voice on the other end of the line said, "The number you have reached is no longer in service." Cynthia knew that it must be a mistake, so she redialed the number, but got the same message. This couldn't be happening; there must be a mistake. Even though she knew the number by heart she went to her telephone book to verify it. She came back and had to try it one more time. She listened as the voice repeated, "The number you have reached is no longer in service. If you need assistance, please stay on the line." Cynthia waited for the operator and asked her to please check the number that she had dialed. The operator said, "I'm sorry, that number has been disconnected."

The room suddenly became unbearably hot. Cynthia's stomach began to turn and she headed toward the bathroom. After she composed herself, she sat trying to clear her head, which had quickly gotten cluttered with questions. *What happened? Where did he go? Why didn't he call her and give her his new number? Was he okay?* Although she had been to his house, she didn't know his address; so she couldn't even drop him a note. *Was this it? Was it really over?*

She tossed and turned throughout the night trying to make sense of the situation. She thought about his last visit in July and realized that he was trying to give her a message. She knew that this was going to be much harder than she ever imagined. Even if they never got together again, she wanted to know that he was okay.

For the next few days she had a constant headache and life was moving around her in a blur. By the fifth day she knew that she had to pull herself together because life had to go on. However, she would not deny herself those moments when she could think, feel, touch and smell Jack, and relive those many wonderful memories.

It was now 1996, and the sisters were moving on with their lives. The Sister Circle had been immensely supportive because everyone knew how Cynthia felt about Jack. Robin didn't pressure her to come to New York, for she was coming to Boston. She always had a new man in tow; there was always someone she wanted Cynthia to meet. Cynthia thanked the sisters in the circle for keeping a constant supply of dateable men around. She had to let the sisters know that it was going to be very hard for her to find a man she could love the way she loved Jack.

She was now forty-seven years old and had heard all of the rumors about how difficult it was to date after the age of thirty. She learned in her mid-thirties that dating was not difficult but that the concept had to change.

It was very difficult for those women who were looking for a husband or a man with no children or no alimony; that was a pretty hard man to find. But it wasn't difficult for those women who were only looking for a quality black man to spend time with. Cynthia learned that a broke brother is not un-datable. He may not be a keeper, but he's not un-datable. She learned that bitter brothers were not un-datable; you just had to date them differently. She learned that each man was different and could not be lumped into a general category. After the age of thirty everyone seems to bring his or her own baggage into each relationship. The sisters decided that they would work together to be sure that they carried their baggage with style and finesse.

There was a whole town full of black women in Cynthia's general age group that didn't date. They were home tending to grown-ass children, going to work and coming home. Somehow these women believed that they were no longer datable and took very little time with their attitudes, clothing and body. These women had either devalued themselves or allowed someone else to do it.

Dating was even more difficult for women raising young sons. When there was no man in the house, these young sons would often determine whether or not their mothers could date. The sons very often could not accept the presence of any other man. Most women didn't learn until it was too late that their young sons would eventually find their special woman and leave the same way that their fathers did years ago.

Cynthia found that black men in her age group were looking for the same thing that she was looking for. They didn't want a needy sister, and she didn't want a needy brother. They were looking for an independent black woman, and she was looking for a black man who could appreciate her independence. They said that they were looking for an honest and open woman, but that wasn't quite true. Honesty and openness terminated many relationships for her.

It was 7:30 A.M. on a Sunday when she heard her telephone ring. She tried to ignore it because anyone who knew her knew not to call that early on a Sunday morning. The phone would not stop ringing. She finally came out of her fog and picked up the phone. On the other end she heard Robin screaming at the top of her lungs with excitement. It took her a while, but Cynthia finally got Robin calmed down so that she could understand why she was so excited.

"Cynthia, I taught you how to read the stock market, and I taught you how to stay on top of your investments. Why haven't you been doing it?" she barked.

"The stock market just doesn't interest me, and as long as my investments don't lose money I'm fine," Cynthia answered

"Do you realize that UPS. stock has gone public?"

"Actually, I received a memo about that recently."

"Cynthia, do you have any idea what that means."

Cynthia had to admit that she really didn't understand the impact of UPS stock going public.

"I'm going to hold on the phone while you go into your file cabinet and find the folder marked 'Investments' and come back to the phone."

Cynthia was still in a fog. So she asked her if it would be okay if she called Robin back in about a half hour with the investment information.

"Fine, but just do as I told you, and I'll wait for your call."

Cynthia called Robin back in about thirty minutes. While she was having her coffee she asked Robin to please tell her what was so exciting.

"Okay I'm going to get right to the point, because all the explaining in the world is not going to make you understand what I'm trying to tell you. Your stock has gone public; you have over twenty years worth of UPS stock that was bought at a very low discount price. That stock is now selling at well over ten times the price that you paid. Do you realize, Cynthia, that you are a wealthy woman?"

Robin knew that reality really wasn't sinking in for Cynthia on this issue and that Cynthia truly relied on her to keep her apprised of what was happening.

"Cynthia, I'll tell you what. I don't want you to do anything; I'll be at your house Friday evening to try to explain what just happened. As a matter of fact, this might be an excellent time to take a look at everyone's investments. I'll call Sandra to get the information I need from her, and I'll also see if she can come up and join us. You call Rosa and Tracy. Tell Tracy to bring the folder that says 'Stock Options' and anything else that she believes will make up her personal value. I'm not sure what to tell Rosa to bring. But if she has any documents in her possession that she believes have a value, tell her to please bring them with her.

"Now, personally, I believe that you should be the one to make dinner 'cause you're the one that just made a lot of money. It might be really nice if we all stayed at your house. We haven't had a Sister Circle in a while, and we've all got something to share."

It was always nice to be with the sisters. Cynthia prepared to open her house for next Friday evening. It would be a long weekend, but it would be worth it. When she got off the phone with Robin, she called Tracy and Rosa and gave them the directions that she had been given. She then sat back to finish her coffee and think about her life. She was a blessed woman, and it appeared that she was doing better financially than she thought. Her health was good, and her social life was about as much as she could handle. The only thing that she was missing was Jack.

She closed her eyes and she saw his smile, she heard his voice, and she felt his warm embrace. What a wonderful experience to have had him in her life. She lit four sandalwood candles and, as the smell filled the room, fond memories of Jack came with it. She allowed herself to stay in those memories for what must have been at least forty-five minutes. Then the telephone rang again. This time it was Tracy.

"Cynthia, I just realized that Robin could be bringing the news that would allow us all to decide our retirement date. But what about Rosa?

"The motherfucker ain't dead yet. I saw Carlton the other day. He looks dead, but he's still walking. But mark my words, he'll be dead in the next two weeks."

She told Cynthia that she would join them a little late on Friday because she had some business she needed to take care of. Tracy said she would be there by nine o'clock.

Cynthia poured another cup of coffee and kicked back on the sofa to read the morning newspaper. There was a story about Councilwomen Carolyn Henderson, her re-election and her public announcement that she was a lesbian. Cynthia started to turn the page, but something pulled her back to the front-page picture. She stared at the picture for a while and realized that it was Carolyn—not the Carolyn that Tracy had a relationship with, but the Carolyn that married Wesley. Tracy's lover was Wesley's ex-wife.

Cynthia laughed out loud. She wondered at what point Carolyn realized that she really preferred women, and had this impacted Wesley in any way. More important, Cynthia had to decide whether or not she was going to let Tracy know that she knew her Carolyn. She didn't think that it would make a lot of difference to Tracy; after all Carolyn was her woman now. While she sat thinking about the strange turn of events, Cynthia thought that even though Carolyn did her wrong over thirty years ago, she didn't get to keep the man. But Cynthia got to keep him in her erotic dreams.

Over the years Cynthia had gotten a little better at cooking, so by six o'clock in the evening she had a decent dinner prepared. Rosa and Cynthia sat having cocktails as they waited for the others to arrive. Rosa had been a very important part of the Sister Circle, but often she would share things with Cynthia before sharing it with the other sisters. As Cynthia watched Rosa that evening Cynthia knew she had something to share.

Robin and Sandra were scheduled to arrive at Logan Airport at the same time. Robin would pick up a car and bring them both to Cynthia's house. Robin had been to her house so many times that she knew how to get there better than Cynthia did.

Since Jack left, Robin felt a need to spend more time with her. Cynthia had given all of her sisters keys to her new home, and she had keys to theirs. They enjoyed the feeling of having more than one home. Although everyone had keys, the only one that used hers regularly was Robin.

At about 6:15 P.M. Cynthia heard the keys in the door. Five seconds later she heard loud screams as Sandra and Robin came into the room. They were all close to fifty years old, but still squealed like young schoolgirls when they were together. Sandra was looking damn good; she must have lost at least twenty pounds and she said that she really loved life. Cynthia told them that Tracy wouldn't be able to join them until about nine o'clock that evening but that she would be here. The first order of business was dinner.

Over dinner Robin spent time explaining the stock market. She explained the significance of UPS stock going public.

"Cynthia, you've been with UPS for almost twenty-five years and taken full advantage of the stock options over the years. You've made out like a bandit on this deal."

She reached into her briefcase and pulled out an envelope, handed it to Cynthia and said, "As of today this is the net value of your stock in UPS." Cynthia looked at the numbers on the paper in total disbelief. There must be a mistake; this was a hell of a lot of money.

Robin said, "Although the dollars and cents look quite impressive, you still have to consider the number of years that you would need to be able to financially take care of yourself after retirement. I would suggest that you make some reasonable re-investments to carry you through the later years and then eliminate your existing debt. You don't have to make any decisions right away. You certainly have time; your stock prices won't be going down for a while. So think about it, and we will decide what to do."

She told Sandra that she had reviewed her stock portfolio and was very pleased with the stock choices they had made over the years. She took another envelope out of her briefcase and handed it to Sandra.

"This is your net stock value, not including any of your assets received in the divorce settlement."

Sandra opened the envelope, smiled and said, "Damn, girl, I really didn't know that you were as good as you are about picking stock."

Robin smiled and said, "That's my business. What do you think I've been doing for the last twenty-five years? I know this shit like the back of my hand, and I have the ability to call shit quite accurately."

She told Sandra that in order to get her total value Robin would need to see the assets left to Sandra in the divorce. Sandra said as soon as she got home she would put that stuff together and get it to her.

Robin looked at Rosa, and the mood of the room changed.

"Rosa, unfortunately I was not in your life early enough to be able to make strong investments for you. We all know that Carlton is an asshole, but he is a smart asshole. All of his investments and assets are in his name. At this point Rosa, I couldn't tell you what your net value would be. Unfortunately, Carlton controls all of that."

Sandra asked, "Did he at least make her his beneficiary?"

Everyone was in shock, for the sisters would have not expected Sandra to ask that question.

Sandra continued: "Because she is his wife, wouldn't she naturally be the beneficiary of all assets if something were to happen to him?"

Rosa sat quietly, as if she was in very deep thought. She said, "Sisters, don't worry about me. I'm going to be all right; you watch. I'm not gonna let HIV take me out, and I'm not gonna let the lack of money remove me from the Sister Circle."

They all wanted to make it perfectly clear that the lack of money would never remove her from the Sister Circle. They would compensate as much as possible so that she could be a part of everything.

CHAPTER 20

It was now eight o'clock in the evening. Tracy was sitting in a bar nursing a Scotch on the rocks. She knew she had to get this done; it had lingered on much too long. She had run out of patience for the possibilities; she could no longer wait for someone else to make it happen. A skinny little man named Jake, with the remnants of a care-free curl moved in beside her. Jake had the face of a man who was once considered quite good-looking. Time and neglect had taken their toll on his teeth, but that didn't stop him from flashing a tarnished gold-tooth grin. He ordered a Vodka and tonic and lit a cigar.

"Where you been, baby? I ain't seen you in a long time," he whispered in Tracy's ear.

"I've been quite busy holding down my business, but now I need a favor," she said. Jake sat quietly waiting for Tracy to tell him what she needed.

"Jake, do you know Carlton Stevens?"

"Yeah, I know the motherfucker. He stiffed me out of $4,000 on a real-estate deal."

"Did you know that Carlton was an HIV carrier?"

"Yeah, I heard some shit like that. The last time I saw him he looked real bad."

"Well, he ain't looking bad enough. That motherfucker needs to die."

"You gonna have to wait your turn, sista. There's a bunch of them sweet-ass motherfuckers out there looking for him."

"Why is it so difficult to find him? It seems like everyone has seen him in the last week."

"Yeah, but he knows people are out to hurt him, so you'll only see him during the daytime, and with plenty of people around. You can't take out a motherfucker with a lot of witnesses, and he knows that," Jake replied.

"If I could put him in the right place at the right time, do you know anyone who could take advantage of that information and take him out?" Tracy inquired.

"I know some people that will take his ass out in a heartbeat," said Jake. "I know some people that would even pay for that information."

"I'll put him in the right place for you," said Tracy, adding that Jake could pocket the money from anyone willing to pay to know Carlton's whereabouts. "I just need you to get this information to the right people to get the job done."

It was a deal. Jake flashed his tarnished gold-toothed grin.

"I'll contact you next Friday night to tell you exactly when and where; the how is up to you," said Tracy. She finished her Scotch and hoped that this would be the last time she would have to come into this joint to get business done.

"Baby, before you go," said Jake, "I need to let you know I still got a thing for you."

Tracy smiled. "Jake, you know who I am, you know what I am, and you know it ain't never gonna happen."

Jake chuckled, licked his lips, and replied, "Yeah, I know that; but you can't blame a brother for trying."

Tracy looked at her watch; she had time to get to Cynthia's house by nine. She hoped that they remembered to save her some dinner.

When she pulled into the driveway she could hear the house full of laughter. She hated to think of what her life might have been like had she not had the Sister Circle. While Tracy ate dinner, Robin brought her up to date on what was going on financially for the Circle. Tracy and Robin were in the dining room. Rosa, Sandra and Cynthia were in the living room laughing, listening to 1970s music, and remembering the old days.

Robin reached into her briefcase, pulled out an envelope, and handed it to Tracy. "This figure represents your net worth, including assets and investments."

Tracy opened the envelope and read the numbers. "Ain't this a bitch? A poor-ass lesbian from the Midwest, I finally got some shit right in my life."

Robin went on to explain the feasibility of retiring in her early 50s was quite good, but Tracy would need to reinvest to insure an income in her later years. On paper Tracy was looking damn good. Robin told her that all of the sisters had done well in the market; they made some good investments over the years.

She said that Rosa might be a problem because she had no idea of her net value. Everything—the business and the real estate—was all in Carlton's name. Tracy smiled.

"You know, Robin, sometimes shit ain't as bad as it seems," said Tracy. "I think Rosa's gonna be okay."

Robin said, "I hope you're right; but meanwhile why don't we go back into the living room and join the celebration?"

The thought of being considered well to do was a little much for the sisters to take. They broke out the champagne and began the celebration. As usual, they laughed and joked about events that had occurred in their lives. Finally, Sandra said, "You know, y'all, we're only about three years away from the fiftieth 'Turning'; and we decided a long time ago that this turning was going to be the turning of a lifetime. So we really need to begin to figure out what we're going to do."

Robin said, "Whatever we do, it's got to be memorable, 'cause I promised people at the last turning that it would be. We need to do something that we've never done before."

"We need to do something that other people may have never done before as well," said Sandra. "We need to get people hyped up for this event."

Rosa suggested that we take a cruise. "We need to call it 'The Cruise to Celebrate Life.' If we start now we can probably get an excellent deal on a seven-day cruise. It would also allow us the opportunity to get the information out to people at least a year in advance. That means those folks who are working with limited resources could put a down payment on the trip and pay on a monthly basis. Now it's going to cost us a little more money to pull off a cruise, but if we do it right it would be a memorable event."

Rosa continued: "We need to find a travel agent who can put together a cruise package that covers airfare to the port of departure, one night hotel accommodations, transportation to the ship, the cost of the actual cruise, return transportation from the ship back to the hotel, one night's lodging and airfare back to their respective hometowns. Because we have friends all over the country, we'd have to make sure that folks registered early for this cruise so that their package could account for the distance that they had to travel to get to the port."

"Damn girl, you really thought this shit through," Tracy said.

"I've been thinking about this for a while, and I've got some ideas for entertainment on the cruise. We only turn fifty once, and we need to do this right."

"I may have just the travel agent for this job," Robin said.

"I know a sister in Georgia who runs a travel agency that's excellent. She plans wonderful vacations for all the major social clubs in Atlanta," Sandra added.

It was decided. They would ask both agencies to bid on the cruise, then they would use the one that could give them the best deal. The sisters also decided that at fifty they were going to take class to another level.

"Whatever we do, we need to make sure that the folks who join us on this cruise are in a certain age group," said Robin. "The last thing we need is some tight-assed, twenty-five-year-old heifers all up in our mix. I want the competition to be fair."

They all laughed because they knew exactly what she meant by "the competition." At forty-seven, Robin was still going strong and would compete against any woman in her general age group, even some of the younger women. She took good care of her body and flaunted it every chance she got.

They laughed about the idea of young women being competitive with women in their age group, and then the conversation took off. They all had to realize that they were no longer sizes eight, nine, and ten. Personally, Cynthia was waging a battle with menopause. The concept of menopause never frightened her; she actually looked forward to it. She saw it not as an ending but as a new beginning. Tracy believed that she was pre-menopausal. The thing she hated most was the occasional hot flashes.

"Girl, sometimes I'm in the shop, and all of a sudden my whole body gets soaking wet, and there ain't a damn thing I can do to stop it," said Tracy.

Cynthia told her that once she officially gets into menopause, she would be surprised how many different medications could be used to ease the symptoms.

"Well, girl, I'm gonna have to do something because you can't be cool and fly, sweating like a stuck pig," said Tracy.

They spent the evening drinking champagne and talking about the state of the young African American woman.

"You know, I've never considered young girls as competition because there are far too many dumb, broke, fat, and out-of-shape young girls. I don't know what the hell these young girls are eating," Tracy snapped.

"I don't understand it either. When I grew up, everyone I knew was skinny; we ran and played all day. Now the average twelve-year-old looks like she might be twenty-two," Cynthia said.

"Yeah, but these young girls are running around here fucking like rabbits," said Tracy. "They start at twelve or thirteen years old, and the young men are using them like a doormat."

Rosa piped in, stating that birth control was the culprit. "Before birth control a brother had to work to get in your pants. He had to tell you shit, even if he didn't mean it, croon a few love songs in your ear and treat you damn good, at least until he got it."

"These brothers out here ain't got to do shit. These young girls got the pill and they're giving up pussy out of both draw legs, and the brothers know it," Tracy said and laughed.

"One of the things that bothers me is these old-ass men are out here running these young girls," Rosa said.

Tracy pointed out that a lot of the time it's the young girls who are chasing these old-ass men. "They are looking for money and a sugar daddy, and they are using their tight little bodies to get it."

"I still got a tight body for a forty-seven-year-old woman; maybe I need to go find my sugar daddy," Robin said as she pranced around the room in her cocky way.

"Girl, the operative number is *forty-seven*, and I just need to let you know that old pussy don't sell," Tracy said sarcastically.

They laughed, all the while knowing that Tracy was right. They were at the age where a relationship had to be about more than sex. They were blessed; they were considered baby boomers, and they heard that their generation made more financial gains than any generation before or after them. Their parents could not begin to conceptualize the kind of money that they would squander sometimes.

Sandra said she sometimes resented being considered a black baby boomer. "I'm a black woman who has worked hard and made some good investments. When you call me a boomer it puts me in the category with white baby boomers. Now one thing we know for sure, no matter how much money you make and how much you have to spend, traveling with white folks just ain't fun. They often have a different concept of fun."

The conversation then turned to interracial dating. Robin said that she knew far too many black women who were alone because they can't find a good black man and won't date a white man. "But the brothers will date a white woman in a flash. Can you imagine what would happen if black women decided that they were going to start dating white men in numbers?" Rosa asked.

"Yeah," Tracy piped in, "all hell would break loose. That would be the white woman's worst nightmare."

Robin pointed out that there were two issues here: One is the belief that there was a lack of quality black men, with the word *quality* needing to be defined. The other is the decision and preparedness to date outside of the race, if a black woman really and truly cannot find a quality black man.

Robin said, "Quality black men are definitely out there, and all of them ain't running white women. There are brothers out there just as committed to having a black woman as we are to having a black man. The problem is that the quality black men don't know where you live, so they are not going to come to your house and knock on the door to take you out. You got to spruce yourself up, get out, and get involved.

"We also need to recognize that a quality black man does not necessarily mean a doctor or lawyer. There are quality black men driving taxis, buses, and digging ditches, but we have a tendency to overlook those brothers 'cause they ain't in a suit. I met a brother in a lumberyard, a big hard-working, strong brother, and he was telling me how hard it was to meet a quality sister. Sisters have got to decide what qualities they need in a brother other than money.

"And if you really and truly can't find a quality black man, there are plenty of brown brothers out there. If you get a dark-haired white boy and put his ass in the sun long enough, he doesn't look too bad." They all had to laugh.

Rosa jumped in: "Sisters, there's a third issue. A quality black man wants a quality black woman. The same way we don't want a brother stepping to us with absolutely nothing, I can understand why a brother wouldn't want a sister to step to him with absolutely nothing. A quality black man ain't impressed by six babies and a welfare check. Sisters need to spend more time working on themselves rather than working on finding a man. We got to stop having these babies that we can't afford."

Tracy finally said, "I've heard everything y'all had to say. It's four o'clock in the morning; I'm half drunk, and I know the rest of you heifers are half drunk too. We need to get some sleep if we are going to be productive in the morning, 'cause we ain't going to solve all of the problems of the world this evening."

They got up Saturday morning just in time for lunch. Tracy said she wouldn't be able to join them for shopping but she would meet them back at the house by six o'clock. Shopping was something that all of the sisters did exceptionally well. Rosa had gotten good at it. They splurged a little in celebration of their newfound wealth. By five o'clock they were headed back to Cynthia's house.

Tracy knew that there were only two things that would get Carlton where she needed him to be, that was Ramon and money. Ramon was about thirty years old and was from Kansas City. He came to Boston by way of New York, where he thought he was going to be the next Broadway drag queen. When Ramon dressed in drag he was a dead ringer for Diana Ross. He worked in the combat zone as a drag queen, and he was good at what he did. The word on the street was that Carlton had definitely become attached to Ramon and took good care of him.

Ramon lived in one of Carlton's better apartments on the corner of Columbus and West Springfield, which would have normally been out of his price range. When the word hit the street that Carlton was HIV positive, Ramon immediately got tested. The test came back negative. Ramon realized that he had an immediate problem; he needed to disconnect from Carlton as soon as possible.

He managed to convince Carlton to use a condom, but he didn't know how long that would last. Ramon realized that he was either going to become HIV-infected or be beaten to death if he tried to leave. Tracy offered him an out: to tell Tracy where Carlton lived. He had forty-eight hours to decide if he would disclose that information. Tracy added a bonus to the deal: $2,500 for a set of keys to Carlton's apartment.

Ramon met Tracy at the Kitty Kat club in the combat zone and told her exactly where Carlton lived and the times that he would be home. He then exchanged the keys to Carlton's apartment for $2,500 and walked away.

Tracy knew she needed to get the keys duplicated, just in case Jake couldn't handle the job. She wondered how much money Jake would get for this information and then decided that it really didn't matter, that it would be worth it to have Carlton dead.

By seven o'clock that evening they were back at Cynthia's house, again in the Sister Circle. The previous night they had talked about many different things but they didn't get a chance to catch up on each other's life. That's what they did that evening.

Rosa told them she met an interesting man. She had seen this brother occasionally on her way to work in the morning, and they would acknowledge each other and exchange the normal morning pleasantries. About a month ago she was running late for work and hurried to catch the 8:15 train. When she got on the train, a man stepped on immediately behind her just as the doors closed. It made her a little uncomfortable, so she turned to see who he was. He smiled, extended his hand, and said "Good morning, my name is Jeffrey. I've seen you on this train many mornings, but never had an opportunity to introduce myself." She smiled back and introduced herself.

The train was nearly empty because they had missed the morning rush, so they sat together and talked on the way to downtown Boston. Jeffrey was a customer representative with a large insurance company. He said that he'd only been in Boston for a year and was still trying to adjust. Rosa could relate to the difficulties of adjusting to Boston and told him that she was also from the Midwest. They were deep in conversation about the social and economic adjustments necessary to live in Boston when she noticed that the next stop was hers. Jeffrey obviously knew this too and said, "I know you'll be getting off the train shortly and I don't want to miss this opportunity. I'm wondering if you would have dinner with me this Friday evening." Rosa was not sure that she heard him right, so she asked him to repeat his question. He simply said, "Would you have dinner with me this Friday evening."

Her mind began to race; she hadn't drawn the attention of a man in quite a while. If she missed this opportunity she wasn't so sure any others would come. After all, there was not a line of men waiting for her affection. She finally said yes and quickly jotted down her telephone number and told him to give her a call. She didn't want to give him her address yet; she wasn't so sure if he was mentally healthy, and the last thing she needed in her life was a stalker.

Jeffrey called her on Wednesday evening. They talked for what seemed like hours. She agreed to have dinner with him next Friday evening.

He picked her up at seven o'clock Friday evening and took her to a lovely restaurant where they had a leisurely dinner. Jeffrey wanted to know everything about Rosa. For the first time in Rosa's life a man was actually interested in what she thought, how she felt, and what she wanted.

Rosa and Jeffrey agreed to have dinner and see a movie on the next Friday evening. They had been on about four dates, and Jeffrey was beginning to get affectionate. At first Rosa welcomed his affection. It felt so good to have a man's arms around her; she hadn't realized how much see missed that. Within seconds, however, reality slapped her firm in the face: she was HIV positive.

"I don't want to live my life without the company of a man," said Rosa, "and I don't want to have a man around me that I can't touch. It would be very unfair for me not to tell him about my condition. When I tell him, he's probably going to leave; if the tables were turned, I would. For the first time since my diagnosis I cried myself to sleep. I wasn't crying because I had the virus, but because I felt that I would never be able to feel the touch of a man again in my life."

"Why don't you wait to find out where the relationship is going before you tell him?" Sandra asked.

"I think the problem is going to be that it could take six months to a year to know where the relationship is really going, and I just don't know if the brother's going to hang around that long waiting to get a piece," Tracy said.

"Rosa, I agree with you. You've got to tell him so that he can make an informed decision about what he wants to do," Sandra said. "I'm not so sure that there is anything that we can do, but if there is you know we are always here for you."

Tracy said that for the first time in a long time her life was pretty quiet. Carolyn and Tracy were doing fine. Once Carolyn came out of the closet they were able to spend a lot more public time together. As a politician, Carolyn was always invited to various dinners and fundraisers, which kept them pretty busy. Tracy was enjoying it.

"What I enjoy most are the heads that turn when we enter the room. You would think in this day and age people would be more aware of lesbian relationships. They don't say anything, but they look at us like we got four heads.

"Carolyn thinks it's funny and she makes a joke out of it. Sometimes it's funny, but most of the time it's just stupid, especially the times when men will say 'You don't look like a lesbian.' And it takes every ounce of energy to keep from asking them, 'What the fuck do you think a lesbian is supposed to look like?' I promised Carolyn that I wouldn't let these people pull me out of character. Right now, sisters, all I can say is life is good."

Tracy looked at Cynthia and said, "Cynthia, what about you? What are you up to?"

"I agree with you, Tracy, life is good," Cynthia said.

"Well, Cynthia, whose the man in your life?" Sandra asked.

Cynthia chuckled because she knew that's all they really wanted to know in the first place. She told them that she was still dating now and then and that Richard was around to keep the monkey off her back. She told them that she and Richard had been hanging out for the last few years, off and on. Richard had just gotten out of a bad marriage and was totally shell-shocked. He was a very nice brother. He looked good, had great sense of humor, kept his body tight, but he was ass-deep in alimony. He only had one thing to give and, oddly enough, it was the only thing that she wanted from him.

Sandra said, "It must have been very difficult to stop a twenty-year relationship with a man that you were so involved with."

Cynthia told her that it was very difficult, even though she knew it was coming. The most difficult part was the lack of real closure. She often wonders where Jack is and how he's doing, but she had to admit, that man gave her enough pleasant memories to last a lifetime. There was one bad thing about the relationship: he raised the bar so high that it was difficult for any man to measure up. She kept making regular adjustments to her requirements in a man, but there are just some things that she was not willing to compromise.

Just as Cynthia was about to ask Robin how her love life was going, Robin got up and left the room. Cynthia didn't know if anyone else noticed, but Robin seemed to be a little upset. So Cynthia focused her attention on Sandra and asked how she was doing in the dating game.

"I'm with you and Tracy; life is good," said Sandra. "I'm dating and having a wonderful time. I don't know about Boston and New York, but there are quite a few datable brothers in Georgia."

Sandra said that she ran into Jason at a recent cocktail sip, and he had the nerve to get an attitude because she was with a date.

"I've run into quite a few women in our general age group who deal with life as if it's over," Sandra said. "They go to work and come home, go to church and come home, and in the middle they pray for God to send them a good man. That's got to be such a boring existence. I must admit, if it had not been for my sisters I would probably be just like those women. I'm forty-seven years old, full of life, and I got a lot of living to do. I'm not going to crawl into a hole and die because I don't have a husband or a man. I have to tell you that I'm not mad that these women aren't coming out; it leaves many more options for me. I've been seeing George fairly often, and I may have to introduce y'all to him soon."

Just about that time Robin entered the room. Sandra and Cynthia had known Robin long enough to know that something wasn't right. Sandra asked her if she was okay; Robin said she was fine. They knew she was lying.

Robin could still hear the pain in Cynthia's voice when Cynthia talked about Jack. She thought by now there would be someone else in Cynthia's life to take the pain away. The last time that Robin visited Jack he was wearing those famous silk pajamas, and his age was beginning to show. Jack was a wonderful person to talk to, and every time Robin saw him she understood why Cynthia was so connected to him. Robin also understood why Cynthia was in pain when he left. Robin was now beginning to feel the pain of keeping a secret from the people that she loved the most, things were not happening quickly enough.

Robin told the sisters that she was having a very new experience in her life; she thought she might be in love.

Rosa said, "Sista, you are going to tell us that at forty-seven years old you don't know if you're in love or not."

Robin said, "I have to be honest, I really don't. I've never been there before, but I do know that I want to be with Sonny every chance that I get."

They were spending much more time together. She had even done the unthinkable: she allowed him to keep some of his things at her condo. He was at her apartment at least two or three times a week, but she still wondered what he was doing the other four or five nights. She said she was considering monogamy for the first time in her life and hoped that it would not come back and bite her in the ass.

It had gotten fairly late. Sandra and Robin had an early flight out of Logan Airport in the morning.

Robin said, "There are a few things I want to tell y'all, and one is, this is 1998 and you old heifers gotta keep up with modern technology. Get a damn cell phone. I'm getting tired of having to wait till y'all are home in order to contact you."

The rest of them couldn't figure out why they needed a cell phone, but they knew that if they didn't get one they would have to continuously hear her mouth.

She continued: "There is no excuse; you can all afford it, so let's do it. Another thing, the fiftieth is coming up soon, and all of us need to get in the gym and get these bodies in shape. How y'all going to be fly, looking like a busted can of biscuits?

"And third, we need to pin down this travel agent within the next couple of months. I'm going to do my thing in New York, and I'll have a proposal in the next thirty days. Now Sandra, I know them folks in the South are kinda slow, but see if you can do the same thing. We need to be able to compare these plans very quickly and make a decision."

They looked at each other and smiled. Robin was using her serious business tone.

As they prepared for bed that evening, Robin came and sat at the foot of Cynthia's bed. "Sister, I need you to be okay."

Cynthia told Robin that she was quite okay; she was living nicely, had a decent man around her, and was financially stable. She told Robin not to worry about her. Robin sat quietly for a while.

Finally she said, "You know, Cynthia, I love you. You've been the most stable part of my life, other than my grandmother, and I would kill before I allowed anyone or anything to hurt you. Just tell me again that you're all right."

Cynthia told Robin that she felt the same way about her and asked her to please believe that she was okay. Something was definitely weighing heavily on Robin's mind.

CHAPTER 21

It was Monday morning, and they were back to the same old grind. Each of them had something she needed to accomplish in a short period of time. Rosa sat on a bench in the station waiting for the eight o'clock train. Jeffrey weighed heavy on her mind; she knew she had to tell him she was HIV positive. She had sat on this bench many mornings waiting for the train, but that morning she was much more in tuned to her surroundings.

She noticed that the station was full of people, and everybody seemed to be in a hurry. For the first time she noticed that, among those people struggling to get to work in the morning, there were a large number of school kids. They were carrying large backpacks, listening to loud music, and seemed to be coming from everywhere. The young boys were playing, pushing and punching each other; and the young girls were sitting around giggling. It was very much like a three-ring circus.

She could hear the train squealing around the tracks, heading toward the station. She knew it was time to get up and take her place, if she expected to get on this train. It was clear that everyone was not going to be able to board the train. She was standing perilously close to the white line and knew that she needed to move back before the train came in. When she took a few steps backward, several people took her place on the white line. She thought how dangerous it was to be so close to a moving train. The young kids continued to play, run and push. When the train finally entered the station and opened its doors, there was a mad rush to get on board. She decided that she still had time and would wait for the next train.

While waiting, she thought about the scene she had just witnessed. One misstep, one misjudgment, and there could have been a disaster. She never realized how dangerous it was to get to work each morning. During the day, thoughts of the crowded train station kept running through her mind. By noon she had a pounding headache. She was scheduled to see her doctor on Wednesday and decided that she would ask him about her recent headaches.

By 12:30 the pain had grown almost unbearable, so she made a quick call to her doctor's office. Dr. Kennedy suggested that she come right in. Her doctor's office was only four blocks from where she worked, so she decided to walk, thinking that the fresh air might do her some good. By the time she reached the doctor's office she was wet with perspiration.

She sat in the waiting area thinking about her life and how different it could have been had she not met Carlton. Dr. Kennedy called her in and began the examination. He quickly decided that since she was due for a blood analysis anyway that he would do it that day.

After the examination, he asked her a series of questions and said that he didn't believe that her headaches were directly connected to the virus. He said he believed that she was allowing stress to dictate her life. He said he would give her something for the pain and told her to go home and rest. He told her that, once the lab results were in, he would contact her if her treatment needed to be changed.

He told Rosa not to worry and to take a moment to relax while he went to find the pain medication. She looked around the room; the walls were lined with degrees and citations. Dr. Kennedy was tops in the field of infectious disease. Rosa noticed on the corner of his desk a stack of blank stationery. Instinctively she reached for it. She didn't know why she needed it or why she even wanted it, but she put several pieces of the blank stationery into her purse.

After leaving the doctor's office, she called her office to let them know that she would be taking the rest of the day off. She headed toward the train station. As she sat waiting for the train she noticed an unusually large group of school kids running, playing and laughing all through the station. She looked at her watch and realized that it was 2:10 and schools were letting out all over the city. The kids pushed and shoved each other, oblivious to others in the station. The 2:20 train came barreling out of the tunnel into the station. The crowd pushed forward hoping to position themselves in front of one of the doors when the train came to a stop.

There must have been at least eight cars on this train. As the train moved through the station Rosa could feel a forceful breeze being created. The doors of the train opened, and the crowd pushed forward; people were being swept up into the train. Although the train was crowded, Rosa was determined to get on it; she really didn't feel like waiting.

That evening, about an hour after she had taken the pain medication, she felt much better. She decided to have dinner and think about how she would eliminate the stress in her life. She knew that Jeffrey would be calling and that she was going to have to tell him that she was HIV positive.

Jeffrey and Rosa chatted for a while. She noticed that Jeffrey seemed a little distant. He told Rosa that he really appreciated her company and wanted to spend more time with her. He said that he had something very important he needed to talk to her about and that he should have had this conversation long before now.

Rosa seized the opportunity to tell Jeffrey she believed their relationship was developing to the point where they needed to be honest with each other. She said she realized that everyone has baggage going into a new relationship and that she needed to share her baggage with him.

Jeffrey said, "Rosa, that is exactly why we need to talk."

The cell phone was a wonderful invention; it meant they no longer had to wait for Sunday to get in contact with each other. Sandra and Robin were in constant contact regarding the preparations for the fiftieth "Turning." Cynthia enjoyed being able to contact her sisters whenever she wanted, but unfortunately the cell phone took away her ability to sometimes disappear.

She and Richard planned a three-day getaway to Gloucester, Massachusetts, which had some of the most beautiful hideaways on the East Coast. When she first met Richard he was a very bitter man and had a limited ability to converse with women.

The fact that she could take a man or leave him was probably what prompted Richard to want to get to know her.

When they originally exchanged phone numbers she thought Richard expected a chaser. After about four weeks he finally called her. On their first date she thought it was important for him to understand who she was, and it was equally important for her to know who he was. She explained to him that she was not a chaser and that if he hadn't made the first move they would not have a relationship. She told him that it was important for her to feel that when a man was with her it was because he wanted to be, not because she coerced and convinced him to be there. Four years later Richard and Cynthia were still hanging out together.

Tracy was sitting in the neighborhood bar waiting for Jake. She swore to herself that this would be the last time she would do this. It was a Friday night, and the place was packed; folks had just gotten their paychecks and were willing to spend it. She found a seat at the far corner of the bar and watched the entertainment as it unfolded in the room. You could tell who the regulars were because they greeted each other in a very matter-of-fact way. You could also tell the newcomers because folks in the bar began to whisper. Some of these folks in the bar didn't even go home after work and were prepared to hang out until the wee hours of the morning.

As Tracy watched the men and women hitting on each other she remembered something her Aunt Mimi told her: "Tracy, if you meet a man in a bar, you need to leave him there." Although Tracy wasn't interested in men, she always vowed that if she met a woman in a bar she would always leave her there.

Just as that thought left her mind a relatively large woman pulled up a stool next to Tracy. You had to look carefully to know that she was a woman; otherwise you would have thought she was a big man. She wore no makeup, one earring in her left ear and a short-cropped Afro. She wore those stereotypical lesbian khaki pants and navy blue V-neck sweater. Tracy looked at her watch; Jake was due in five minutes. Tracy was going to have to tolerate this until Jake got there.

When Tracy's drink arrived, she pushed a five-dollar bill across the bar. The woman sitting next to her put her large hand on Tracy's and said, "I got this." Tracy thought, *Oh shit, what the hell am I supposed to do with this big bitch?*

The woman introduced herself as Sarah and asked Tracy why she hadn't seen her in the bar before. Tracy told her that she doesn't normally come in the bar and that she was waiting for a friend. Sarah took the most direct approach Tracy had ever seen; she pushed her barstool close, leaned toward Tracy, looked directly in her face and said, "I can offer you much more than your friend can." Tracy took a moment to decide how to handle this situation. She had one of two choices: she could cuss this big bitch out and run the risk of a fight, or she could cordially decline her invitation.

Tracy decided to take the high road and cordially declined Sarah's invitation. Sarah got the message, but it didn't stop her from staring at Tracy the rest of the night.

Jake was one of those brothers left over from the 1970s, the kind that rode around in the big Cadillac with the diamond in the back, leaning so far to the right that that you could barely see his head. She met Jake back in 1975; somebody had to keep his processed hair tight, and that was her job. Although Jake was in the pimping business, he thought he was a bigger pimp than he really was. He ran a small stable of about three or four women; most people considered his women second-rate whores. But Jake was out there every day trying to be the best pimp he could be.

It was now 1998, and Jake failed to understand that pimping was dead. He couldn't put together a stable full of women, but he still wanted to keep the image. Jake was like a bad memory; he just popped up out of nowhere. He always seemed to be standing in the shadows waiting for an opportunity to jump on something. That night wasn't any different; suddenly out of nowhere Jake appeared.

As old as Jake was, he was still a dick dancer. He stood in front of Tracy holding his dick and twitching. Tracy smiled because Jake was never going to change his style. He told Tracy that he had watched the big dyke try to rip her off.

"I gotta give you credit," said Jake, "you handled that shit well. But she's still watching you, so let me buy you a beer just in case you gotta fight your way out of this joint."

Tracy laughed and said, "Don't worry about me, I'll get out of here. But I'll take that beer anyway."

She handed Jake an envelope and told him that inside he would find the place where Carlton could be located and the time, along with a set of keys to Carlton's apartment. It would be up to Jake to use this information the best way he could, and it was also up to him whether or not he could get paid for it.

Jake looked at Tracy and said, "You know you're a ruthless bitch."

Tracy smiled and said, "Yeah, but this ruthless bitch is surviving." Jake moved back into the shadows and disappeared.

Tracy stood to leave and felt someone standing much too close to her; she turned and saw Sarah standing there. Sarah said, "Please don't tell me that you were waiting for that old tired-ass pimp. I know I can do more for you than he can." Tracy was getting quite annoyed with Sarah and decided at this point she needed to come on a little stronger.

"How many ways do I have to tell you that I'm not interested?" Tracy asked. Sarah made Tracy feel like new meat in a woman's prison. Tracy did something she hoped she wouldn't regret; she turned and walked away.

Rosa knew that the next meeting with Jeffrey would make or break the relationship, but she really didn't have a choice. She invited Jeffrey for dinner on the next Friday evening. He arrived at about seven o'clock bringing flowers and wine. This was the first time that Jeffrey had ever brought her flowers. Rosa and Jeffrey tried to keep the evening as light as possible, but they both had something heavy on their minds. Although Jeffrey said he had something important to say, he found it very difficult to say it. Rosa thought she would ease his suffering by self-disclosing first.

She told Jeffrey how much she enjoyed his company and how she would love to continue the relationship, but in fairness to him there was something he needed to know about her.

"There's no pretty way to say this, and there's no need to beat around the bush. I'm HIV positive."

She told him about Carlton and watched Jeffrey carefully for some type of response. He sat there quietly, listening; his facial expression never changed. When she finished the abbreviated version of her story, she sat back in her chair, relieved that he knew but frightened that this would be the end of their relationship.

Jeffrey pushed his chair back from the table, stood up and poured himself another class of wine. He began to pace the room; it seemed like an eternity before he finally spoke.

"Rosa, you cannot enjoy this relationship nearly as much as I do. You are a wonderful woman, a joy to be around, and I've thought of so many wonderful things that we could do together. The next level of our relationship would be a long-term commitment. Rosa, to be honest, I don't know what long term would mean for us, because I'm HIV positive also.

"I lived a pretty fast life in Kansas City. I was all over the place, all of the time. I don't know when I got infected and I really don't know who infected me, but I do know that I'll have to live with this for the rest of my life. I thought if I packed up and left Kansas City that I might have a chance of starting my life all over again. But I failed to remember that although I left Kansas City, I brought the virus with me, so life would be pretty much the same wherever I went. Of all of the things that I should have been angry about, I was most angry about the possibility of living my life without the love of a woman."

He reached across the table to hold her hand. "I don't know what this means for us, Rosa, but if you're willing, we can go through this together. But before we attempt to do anything we need to each talk to our doctors to find out the implications of two HIV-positive people having a meaningful sexual relationship."

Rosa felt like the weight of the world had been lifted from her shoulders. Whether or not they could maintain a sexual relationship, he still at least wanted to be with her and that was more than she ever thought she would get out of life. That evening as Rosa sat in her bed she thought, *There are only two stressful things left in my life: my angry son and Carlton.*

Carlton had made her life miserable for the past fifteen years, and left her with the HIV virus and no money. She couldn't even get him to appear in court for child support. Carlton was not looking back at the damage he had done not only to her but to his children. She was going to have to make it right. She reached into her purse and pulled out the stationery she had gotten from her doctor's office and then looked through her files to find the letter she received from her doctor after she had been diagnosed with HIV. This was going to be how she would get Carlton's attention. The heading on the stationery read: "Massachusetts Infectious Disease Unit."

She sat at her computer and composed a letter to Carlton:

"Dear Mr. Stevens, According to our records in the Massachusetts Infectious Disease Unit, you have been identified as an HIV carrier. Our records do not indicate that you have chosen a doctor and are currently receiving treatment. Your current status makes you an excellent candidate for a new FDA-approved virus blocker. This new treatment was designed to reduce the current HIV virus in your body and, over a period of time, we hope to eradicate it. This is the most aggressive, lifesaving treatment that has been developed in our fight against AIDS. We have arranged for you to meet with Doctor Mendelson, September 10, 1998 at 2:45 P.M. at the Massachusetts Infectious Disease Center. We hope that you will agree to be a part of this major medical breakthrough. Sincerely, Dr. Kanowski."

As she printed the letter on the letterhead, she thought this should get Carlton's attention. She knew that there was only one way to get to the disease center in downtown Boston, and that was by public transportation. There was no place to park within a ten-block radius. She had one week to prepare. The next morning, on the way to work, she dropped the letter off at the post office. She knew that Carlton would get it within two or three days.

Robin and Sandra had developed a plan for the fiftieth "Turning." They agreed to work with the travel agent in Atlanta because she gave them an excellent deal, and Sandra's mother was getting psyched about getting evolved. If you're going to do a fiftieth "Turning," the best person in the world to have on your team is a drama queen. They knew that if Sandra's mother got involved, they would have to do very little work. All they had to do is keep her on track with their ideas. It was a little less than two years before the "Turning," but they knew because of the price of this event they would need to get information out to their invited quests well enough in advance so that they could make the deposit and monthly payments. Everyone put her list together and sent them off to Sandra's mother; there were more than four hundred people invited.

CHAPTER 22

Robin wasn't feeling very good about herself. She met Jack for the first time about four years ago and thought that by now everything would be running smoothly. Robin had held up her end of the bargain but felt that Jack was falling short on his end. More and more she began to believe that she'd made a pact with the devil.

When they met, Jack was always able to convince her that although the schedule was a little behind, it was all going to work out fine and all she needed to do was trust him. Jack was almost seventy years old and he still possessed a smoothness that convinced Robin each time that it was all going to be okay.

She told Jack about the "Cruise to Celebrate Life," which was going to be the major theme for the fiftieth "Turning." He had a faraway look in his eyes and finally said, "That sounds like a great idea." Robin left Jack the way she always did, confused and angry. When was she going to get it through her thick head that this man lied to her, and as a result she has had to lie to one of the people that she loves most?

Rosa sat on a bench in a corner at the train station, reminiscing about her life. She had every right to be angry; she had every right to want revenge.

The two o'clock train came through the station picking up a small number of passengers. Rosa sat quietly in the shadows. She had been very creative about her attire for this event; it was important that everything went smoothly. She thought by now that she might lose her nerve, but sitting and waiting only made her more determined to get this done.

At about 2:10 the station began to fill with high school and junior high school kids coming home from school. It was a Friday before a school holiday, and they were extremely excited and a bit more agitated. She knew that the anticipation of a week's vacation would make these young people bounce off the walls on the way home. Out of the corner of her eye she noticed a thin frail man leaning against a pole, waiting for the train. She looked again because she wasn't sure, but the third time she recognized him. It was Carlton. His skin was drawn; he looked like a little kid in his father's suit. Because he refused to admit that he was HIV positive, he would not get treated. The virus was taking a major toll on his body. He was on his way to meet the imaginary Dr. Mendelson. The next train would not arrive in the station for another seven minutes. Rosa had seven minutes to position' herself and pray that things would go the way she wanted.

Young people were still streaming into the station from every direction, running laughing and playing. As the station filled, she got up from her seat and began to mingle in the crowd. The space got tighter and tighter as more people entered the station. She realized that there were far more people in the station than this one train could accommodate. That meant that everyone who intended to get on board would have to jockey for position. Carlton needed to make this train if he was going to be on time for his appointment.

Rosa looked at her watch; the train was due in three minutes. There were three young men standing in front of Rosa, playfully punching and pushing each other. One of the young men fell back against Rosa, who made it a point to speak loudly to the woman next to her and said, "This situation is dangerous. These kids are playing, the train is coming through; anything could happen."

Rosa felt the vibration and heard the squealing metal against the rails as the train rounded a turn and headed for the station. She moved closer and closer to Carlton. He was oblivious. He, like everyone else at the station, was fixed on getting as close as possible to the white line to board this train. Rosa didn't want to be too close to the white line, just close enough to make her move and then walk away. As the train moved toward the station she heard two loud blasts from the train's horn. The conductor could see the danger in the crowded station ahead and therefore issued a warning.

The young people continued to laugh, play and push their way toward the front. The train was about one hundred yards from the station's platform. Rosa got closer to Carlton. He was standing on the white line; one wrong move and it would be over. She watched the train carefully. Rosa's plan had to be timed exactly. The station was tightly packed, and people were shoulder to shoulder in the crowd. She had to stay close enough to Carlton to be able to put her hands on him when the moment came. She kept her eye on the train and on Carlton.

Just as the train reached the crowd, Rosa reached out, put her hand in the middle of Carlton's back, and pushed with all her strength. Carlton fell forward onto the train tracks. Some in the crowd began to scream, some were frozen, while others started to run. The combination of squealing brakes, flying sparks, and blasting horn sent the station into total chaos. Rosa joined the crowd as they rushed to the stairs to leave the scene. It was done!

Once outside, she could see emergency vehicles coming from all directions, lights flashing and sirens blaring. By the time the police got to the scene at least half of the crowd was outside talking about the incident. The crowd that was left in the station was being held for questioning. You could tell by the way the police handled the situation that this was going to be ruled as an accident.

Rosa walked up the street with four other women who had been at the train station. They were looking for the nearest taxi stand to share a ride home. The women talked about what a horrible accident it was and about that poor man laying on the tracks. Rosa thought to herself, *If only they could know what a flaming asshole that poor man was.*

When she got home, she ran a hot bath. While waiting for the tub to fill, she looked in the mirror and wondered who that woman was looking back at her. The makeup that she used in her disguise was perfect; it made her complexion appear five shades darker, and the short Afro wig gave her flashbacks of the early 1970s. As she washed her face she wondered if Carlton had a painful death, who would miss him, and what her total net worth was now. She smiled.

That evening she sat in her bed reading *How Stella Got Her Groove Back* for the fourth time. She still couldn't figure out how a woman under forty, with a tight body, living quite nicely and having no visible money problems could lose her groove in the first damn place. Rosa was forty-eight years old, HIV positive, with a dead asshole husband, a pretty decent man in her life, and now financial stability. She thought to herself, *Now damn it, that's how you get your groove back!*

That evening she drank champagne, played some old music, and danced like she had never danced before. She watched the eleven-o'clock news; there was a four-sentence report on the accident. She knew she would have to wait to be officially notified of Carlton's death and that she couldn't talk to anyone about it before then.

At ten o'clock Saturday morning she got the call to come identify and claim the body. She tried to convince Carlton Jr. that she didn't need his help, but he was determined to go with her. He said he wanted to make sure that his father was dead. Before going to view the body she called the Sister Circle. Each of the sisters wanted to know what she could do to help. Rosa told them she would get back to them as soon as she knew for sure.

Tracy was the most verbal of the group. "Well I'll be damned; he got hit by a fucking train."

There were many people who wanted to kill Carlton. Now they no longer had a chance to do it themselves. It really didn't matter as long as he was dead.

On the way home, after identifying the body, Carlton Jr. said, "You know, Mom, if the train hadn't gotten him, I would have. I was determined to see that man dead."

Rosa felt relieved; at least her son wouldn't go to jail for murder.

CHAPTER 23

They wanted to postpone Sunday dinner while Rosa buried Carlton, but Rosa asked them not to. When they got together that Sunday the mood was somber, almost as if they were having their own personal wake for Carlton.

Finally, Rosa stood up and said, "I don't see why y'all sitting around here moping. Nobody in this room liked his ass, including me. I'm not mourning; I'm not crying. It's over; he's dead and I'm moving on with my life."

She turned on the stereo. "Now let's talk about something pleasant."

Rosa told the sisters about the discussion she and Jeffrey had and how the possibility looked good that they might be able to have a great and full relationship.

She said that after talking to Carlton's family in the Midwest there didn't appear to be any reason to have a funeral. Carlton's family made it clear that they were not coming to Boston, and she couldn't think of anyone in the area who would be interested in coming. Rosa and Carlton Jr. decided to have his body cremated.

One of the things that Rosa dreaded most was cleaning out Carlton's apartment. She said that she would go to the apartment and retrieve all of the important documents and hire a cleaning company to clean out the rest. The look on her face indicated that one of them needed to go with her.

"Well, since I have a set of keys I'll go with you," Tracy said. Rosa and Cynthia didn't say anything as they waited for Tracy to tell them why she had a set of keys to Carlton's place.

Tracy told the story from beginning to end, and they sat stunned while they listened. Tracy was really going to have Carlton killed. She said the only thing she was angry about was losing $2,500 in the deal.

They called Robin and Sandra, just to make sure that they knew what was going on. When they told them about Tracy's plan to kill Carlton, and her $2,500 loss, Robin said, "I don't believe that Tracy should take a loss all by herself. We all wanted him dead; she was the only one with the balls to plan it. If we do this right, we will each take a $500 loss and give Tracy the credit for having enough balls for all of us." They agreed.

At eight o'clock Monday morning Tracy met Rosa in front of Carlton's apartment. The only thing that Rosa wanted was the legal documents; everything else in the apartment could be done away with. When they opened the door it was clear that someone had been there before them. Most of the furniture, artwork and appliances were gone. However, the desk and file cabinet were still there. Rosa held her breath as Tracy helped her look through the cabinets.

They found several folders that they thought held pertinent information, but to be on the safe side they took everything that remotely resembled some documentation that Rosa would need.

After a little thought, Rosa brought it to Tracy's attention that the locks to the apartment had not been tampered with; whoever cleaned out the apartment obviously had a key. Tracy thought about Ramon, but remembered that Ramon left Boston with her $2,500 two days after she had given it to him. All he wanted was to get away from Carlton in one piece and would not have taken the time to clean out the apartment.

It dawned on her that the only other person with a key was Jake, and he was just the kind of snake to use every opportunity to take whatever he could whenever he could. Tracy asked Rosa if she wanted to file a police report, but Rosa said she only wanted to finish Carlton's business affairs as soon as possible. The cleaning crew was due at noon to remove everything from the apartment and dispose of it however they chose.

After going through the folders, everything that Rosa needed was there. The investments and real estate were all in Carlton's name, but Rosa was the beneficiary of everything he owned. As she went through his file folders and his mail, she saw deeds and documents indicating that Carlton owned much more property than she realized.

That evening Rosa called Robin and told her what she found. Robin suggested that she hire an attorney to sort out the business end of Carlton's life. Once that was done, Robin said she would then take the data and determine Rosa's net worth. She warned Rosa not to spend money that she didn't have yet, because it wasn't clear how much debt Carlson had.

Sandra's mother was working overtime on the fiftieth "Turning." She was now close to seventy-five years old but still looked great and was very energetic. She often said that she didn't have anything else to do and that this had become a hobby. Invitations to the "Cruise to Celebrate Life" had been mailed for almost six months now, and many of the sisters had gotten calls from friends telling them that they wouldn't miss it. They had about 160 deposits for a cruise that was not scheduled until December 3, 2000. They were scheduled to sail on the Royal Caribbean Ship, Empress of the Seas.

Rosa named herself entertainment coordinator and said for the first time in her life she would have the opportunity to show her creative skills. Once the travel package was put together, they requested five top-of-the-line cabins on the sundeck; they were the most expensive cabins on the ship, but well worth it. The sisters were fourteen months away from the cruise, and all of them were trying to get into the gym as often as possible to regain some resemblance of a figure. The youngest sister was now forty-nine years old.

The Sister Circle discussed whether or not they should bring a date to the "Turning." Robin and Cynthia decided that they weren't going to bring a date, although every other week Robin changed her mind about bringing Sonny. She was still trying to determine how committed her relationship with Sonny was. Rosa made it very clear that she and Jeffrey were a couple and that he was definitely going to be her date. Sandra said she and George had been together for close to two years and she couldn't find a reason to bring anyone else. Tracy and Carolyn were still going strong, and Tracy decided that she would bring her. They all agreed that they would establish meeting times for their Sister Circle during the cruise and, short of death, they would all attend those meetings.

Rosa was like a kid in a candy shop. Whenever Rosa came up with a new creative idea for entertainment on the cruise, she would call Sandra's mother and they would get excited together. Rosa would call the travel agent to make sure that her ideas could be accommodated on the ship. For each activity she planned she got more and more excited.

It wasn't long before Rosa's attorneys put Carlton's affairs in order. Rosa now owned four apartment buildings in the South End of Boston with an estimated value of $1.5 million. Property in the South End of Boston had skyrocketed over the last few years. Rosa also owned an impressive portfolio of stocks and bonds. Carlton's debt was minimal compared to his assets. Rosa sold one apartment building to alleviate all debt. Carlton Jr. told Rosa that he could not think of leaving her as long as his father was alive; he said he needed to be close just in case his father tried to hurt her again. Now that Carlton was dead Carlton Jr. could begin to live his life. He applied to Ohio State University and got accepted.

Robin still felt that Jack was pulling her leg, but she was so far into this agreement she couldn't pull out now. She had to play it until the end. She spoke to Jack often on the phone and saw him occasionally. She was really beginning to dislike the personal visits. This time Jack told her that it was very important and that he really needed to see her.

While she sat downstairs waiting for him, her mind began to wander to their very first meeting. She smiled when she remembered that she was actually attracted to him, until she found out who he was. He did look damn good, and he was dressed as impeccably as Cynthia had told her. As they sat across from each other over dinner that evening, she looked at Jack and thought how nice it might have been for her to have had a man like him in her life. It might have made her a different woman today.

In that mesmerizing baritone voice he began to tell her of his plan. He loved Cynthia dearly and would have given anything to be able to stay with her, but age had taken a toll on his body and he knew he could no longer keep up with her. Four years before their last meeting he had been diagnosed with hypertension, which is not unusual in black people. He was taking his medication regularly and was able to conceal his condition from Cynthia.

Two years later it became more and more difficult to get and maintain an erection. He still wasn't ready to let Cynthia go and would do anything to keep her in his life, including risk his own. He did some research on Viagra and presented the concept to his doctor. His doctor was honest and told him that Viagra works for many men but that the combination of Viagra, his hypertension medication, and age would present a problem. The doctor explained that it may not be a problem right away, but over time it would definitely damage his body.

Jack was adamant about getting a prescription, and his doctor reluctantly gave it to him along with a clear warning. It was then that Jack knew he would need help to make his plan work, and he chose Robin. Little did Robin know that shortly after agreeing to help Jack arrange Cynthia's life, he would suffer a stroke. After moving into the retirement home, Jack phoned Robin at least three times before she agreed to meet with him again. It would be the first of many times that she would visit him at the retirement home.

During their last meeting he sat with tears in his eyes as he talked about his last meeting with Cynthia. He had been using Viagra for two years and at that point he could feel the damage that it was doing to his body. He said that in their last meeting all he wanted to do was look at her and hold her, but he also knew he wanted that last memory of being with her. He took Viagra for the last time on the last day of their vacation.

He looked at Robin and said, "I had to do it; I couldn't walk away without being with her one last time." Two weeks after he returned home, he had a stroke. The stroke left his left side paralyzed, and he knew that it was over.

His son came to New Jersey to help him get Jack's affairs in order, including the selling of his house. Jack moved into a retirement/rehab center shortly after that. He said, "You don't know how many times I wanted to call her and tell her where I was so we could at least talk to each other. But I knew that it was over, and I didn't want her to see me like this." He told Robin that he needed her desperately to help him keep some level of connection in Cynthia's life and that Robin's job was to report to him as often as she could about what was going on in Cynthia's life. He said that he knew the kind of man that Cynthia wanted and needed, and he spent the last ten years of his life working on developing that man. That man was going to be his son Matthew.

Cynthia never knew that Jack had two sons. Jack didn't find out about his first son until the summer of 1980. Jack's family was originally from a small town in South Carolina. In 1946 his father came to New York, got a job with the Pennsylvania Railroad Company and, by 1947, he sent for his family in South Carolina. Jack was only eighteen years old at the time when his family moved to New York.

While in South Carolina Jack met his first love, Madeline, and they dated for over a year. Madeline found herself pregnant with Jack's son after Jack had left for New York. Madeline was never able to find him. In 1979 Madeline ran into Jack's sister at a high school reunion and was able to get his New Jersey address. She wrote to Jack to inform him about their son, who was born in 1947 and was then thirty-two years old and living in South Carolina. She said that she didn't want anything from Jack; she just wanted him to know about his son.

Jack made the first contact with his son in 1980 and, after a rough start, they developed a reasonable father-and-son relationship. Over the last nineteen years Jack and Matthew learned more about each other and found that they were very much alike in many ways. Jack never told Cynthia about Matthew; it would clearly have negated his plan. Matthew and Jack looked a lot alike, enjoyed the same things, and Jack said it was like looking into a mirror. He was determined to help his son make the right decisions and learn from his father's mistakes. The relationship grew with each passing year, and Matthew began to appreciate his father's wisdom and opinions. After Matthew's failed marriage, Jack pledged that he would help prepare him to receive his ideal woman. Jack had determined that the woman would be Cynthia.

In the beginning Jack's intentions were simply to prepare Cynthia to master the dating game and find the right man, but it all got totally out of hand. He fell deeply in love with Cynthia and could not let her go, and soon it was too late. He realized that he would have to be out of the picture in order for her to be receptive to her ideal man. After Matthew's divorce, he realized that Matthew was the right man for Cynthia. Jack's health was failing quickly, and he knew he only had a limited amount of time to put them together. That's where Robin came in.

Just as Robin prepared to get deeper in thought, she was interrupted by a tap on the shoulder. The nurse told Robin that she hated to interrupt her but that Mr. Douglas was feeling a little under the weather this morning and asked if Robin would come upstairs and join him for breakfast. Robin truly hated coming to this place. Although the people were cheerful, the place put her in touch with her own mortality, and that's what she disliked most about it.

She got on the elevator, went to the seventh floor, and started down the hall to Room 702. As she moved down the long, well-lit, white hallway, everything looked the same. Only the number on the door distinguished Jack's room from any other patient's room on the floor.

Jack was sitting in bed reading the newspaper and was very happy to see her. By this time Robin was no longer in the mood for breakfast and asked only for a cup of coffee. Jack wasn't looking too good this morning; she looked at him carefully and thought that he might be more under the weather than the nurse indicated. There was a new piece of equipment in Jack's room— a large heart monitor that kept a constant beeping noise echoing in the room. Robin thought that thirty minutes of this beeping noise would drive her crazy.

Jack smiled, looked at Robin, and said, "Don't get nervous. I'm not going to check out while you're here." Robin didn't think that was very funny.

Jack went on to tell her that he felt this intense need to get his son Matthew in touch with Cynthia. He said, "I know deep within my heart that they are going to click. I need you to get Matt an invitation to 'The Cruise to Celebrate Life.' If it's the very last thing that I do I will make sure that he's there. You won't have a difficult time spotting him because we look a lot alike. I'm going to ask you one last favor: Would you be sure that she gets to meet him?"

He said, "You know, Robin, Cynthia was everything to me. If I just had to let her go to anyone else in this world, it would have to be my son Matt. He's ready; he can be everything that Cynthia needs her man to be, and I know that he'll treat her right. I need you to promise again that you'll never tell any of the things that I've told you."

At this point Robin realized that she was in too deep; she had to keep it a secret now, for she had let it go on too long. She told Jack that she wouldn't tell.

He said, "There's one more thing that I need to tell you. My name is not Jack."

Just when Robin thought there were no other surprises that this man could spring on her, he told her that his name was Matthew. Jack's son was named after him. "Jack" was his middle name, and he had used it since he was a young boy. But actually his name was Matthew Jackson Douglas.

"Everything else that I have told you is true," said Jack. "I haven't kept anything else from you. Please, Robin, make sure that they get together. I love them both dearly. They both deserve to be loved, and they both deserve happiness in their lives. If you can just get them together, everything will work out."

She said, "I'll do everything humanly possible to get them together; you just make sure that Matthew makes the trip."

He extended his hand. Robin couldn't help but embrace him. He looked so frail and helpless sitting in that bed. She was so happy that Cynthia would never have to see Jack in this condition.

Tuesday morning, as Robin prepared to leave for work, the telephone rang. It was 6:15 in the morning. She wondered why would anyone call her that early in the morning. She dashed back to the telephone and caught it on the very last ring.

The voice on the other end said, "Good morning. Is this Robin Connors?" "Yes."

The voice said, "I'm sorry to inform you that Mr. Matthew Douglas passed away quietly in his sleep late Monday night."

Robin wasn't a very religious person, but she stopped to say a prayer for Jack and to pray they she would be able to put Matthew and Cynthia together.

It was now June of 1999. Their lives had changed in so many ways, but the bond and the closeness of the sisterhood was still strong. Rosa had turned into a real fly girl; no one could outdress her, and for most events Jeffrey was attached to her hip. Carolyn and Tracy talked about getting married. Tracy truly believed that Carolyn was going to be her life partner. Sandra had begun to spend most of her time with George. Although her eyes often wandered, she thought that at her age she needed to be monogamous.

Robin and Sonny were still going strong, although no one could define the relationship. Robin said that she was getting tired of waiting for Sonny to make her his woman. Most of the time he acted as if she was his woman. He treated her very nicely but would not make the verbal commitment; and that's what Robin needed.

Cynthia was still hanging out with Richard on occasions. He was a nice enough man, but his baggage was just too much to carry sometimes. When he wasn't wallowing in self-pity, they would hang out and have fun. When he began to sing his "woe is me" song, she had to send him home. At fifty-two years old, she could still spark the interest of men in her general age group, sometimes even younger. She still enjoyed flirting and would do it quite often. When Robin and Cynthia got together, they made flirting an art form. Robin would take flirting to the bitter end; Cynthia was much quicker at letting a brother know that it wasn't serious.

Six months away from the "Turning" meant that they needed to think about putting their wardrobe together. In order to do this they had to know the itinerary for the trip. They decided to kill two birds with one stone: go to Atlanta to set the final agenda for the cruise, and do some southern-style shopping.

Their first day in Atlanta was a nightmare; they had forgotten how hot it can get in Georgia in July. At this point in their lives all of them were in various stages of menopause. They made a pact years ago that they would go through it with as much style and grace as humanly possible.

They checked into the hotel at about noon. Sandra was due to check in at 4 P.M. While looking out of the suite's window at the gorgeous view of the city of Atlanta, Tracy mentioned how fortunate they were, compared to their mothers' generation. They agreed.

"I've been working all of my life, but I've always worked for myself," said Tracy. "We are at a point where we can continue to work, but why not work for ourselves? Why not look at what we want to do in the next stage of our lives as a business venture for the Circle?"

Robin's eyes brightened. "Now that's what I'm talking about," she said. "We know how to make money, and we've proved that. We all want to keep busy because we are far from being old. Why not make money together? We're young enough to do it, and we can afford it. The question is, what will the venture be?"

They had four days together. Between the Scotch, wine, and laughter they figured they would come up with something.

At 5:15 P.M. Sandra, her mother and George entered the suite. Sandra's mother was very accustomed to them when they got together in the Circle. George acted a little frightened as the sisters screamed and hugged each other.

Robin noticed George standing in the doorway and said, "Y'all need to stop 'cause y'all scaring this brother." George stood there smiling.

Sandra introduced each of them to George. A very pleasant brother, he shook their hands as he told them how pleased he was to meet them. They told him they had heard very good things about him and hoped that he was as good as Sandra thinks he is. In a slow southern drawl and with a crooked smile, he said, "I try." They made George a cocktail, put him in the corner and decided that they needed to get down to the cruise business.

Sandra and her mother brought the sisters up to date on the cruise plans and showed a picture of the assigned ship, the Empress of the Seas. They were to arrive in Florida on Saturday, December 3. The ship was scheduled to leave port at noon on Sunday. So far they had one hundred sixty-two passengers confirmed. Sandra could tell that George wasn't interested in this conversation, so she excused herself and let him know that she would see him later.

Rosa couldn't wait to tell the sisters about her entertainment plans. She had arranged a bon voyage party at the hotel on the Saturday evening before they were to leave Florida, with activities for guests to introduce themselves to one another and make new friends. The party would be a casual function, so no one would need to unpack for that evening. At the end of the cruise Rosa planned a talent contest for the new friends; first-place prize was $1,000. A continental breakfast was planned for 9 A.M. Sunday morning, and the buses were to leave for the port at 10:30 A.M. The ship had planned a bon voyage party for Sunday morning, so the sisters and their guests would also participate in that. At one o'clock they were scheduled to have brunch on the sundeck; and the rest of the day would be free time.

Robin was still adamant about not bringing Sonny on the cruise. She said if she wasn't bringing Sonny, then Cynthia couldn't bring anyone. She considered Cynthia her running buddy when it came to pulling the men. Cynthia agreed to go solo with her.

One of their scheduled ports was the island of St. Martin. Rosa had done her research and found that on the Dutch side of the island was a place called Orient Beach, where clothing was optional. She said, "Y'all talk big shit all the time about being liberal and down for fun. Let's see how many of you old-ass sisters are gonna get butt naked on Orient Beach. I'm definitely going to be there, and if I'm there you know Jeffery is."

Sandra said, "I don't know about being butt naked on the beach. Do you all realize that I just turned fifty years old?"

Tracy said, "Everybody who will be on that beach with you will be at least fifty. I don't know about you, sister, but I'll put my fifty-year-old shit up against another fifty-year-old's shit in a minute."

"Yeah, but fifty shows no mercy," said Sandra. "No matter what you do the years take a toll on your body. The shit that used to sit up is now hanging down, the shit that used to be flat is now round, the shit that used to be tight is now loose."

"Yeah, and she shit that used to be wet is now dry," Tracy added. They all laughed until they had tears in their eyes. Rosa said she wanted to know what was this cellulite stuff and where did it come from.

Robin said, "Well, I've got that shit too. I work out every day. I don't understand where that shit comes from either, but it's on there and it won't come off."

Sandra said, "You know, y'all, I'll be the first one to tell you that I don't like the way gravity takes its toll on your body over the years, but I've accepted that. I ain't crazy about the wrinkles and the menopause, but I've accepted that. What really pisses me off and I cannot accept, is the way the world wants to view you at fifty years old.

"I am a living breathing person, and I need and want love and affection. I need and want to be admired in some way, and I want to be dated and pursued. I want a closet full of lingerie, and I want to look as good as I can at fifty. And, damn it, I refuse to let the world determine that I don't need those things anymore. Now my son and I had this discussion the other night, he really pissed me off because he said, 'Ma, you don't need no man.'

"Before I could catch my tongue I asked him, 'Who the hell do you think you are to tell me what I need.' I apologized for that, but it just pissed me off so bad. Young people have got to understand that we need the same shit that they need, and you don't stop needing that shit at fifty, sixty, or even later than that. As long as I'm breathing I want company."

"I hear what you're saying and I agree with you one hundred percent," said Tracy, "but the problem is, you still have these old-ass women who buy into that shit. And as long as they are buying into that shit, we look like something is wrong with us. All I can say is that the world better stand up and recognize that there are far too many women turning fifty now, and far too many of us ain't ready to sit up in a house and wither away. We're out here, we're in numbers, and we're living life and having fun."

Rosa said, "You know, I work with a bunch of women in my general age group. Most of them will tell you that they don't need a man; they had a man and he did them wrong, so every man in the world is no good. They don't realize that they are the only ones paying the price for not living life.

"The difference with us is that we've all had bad relationships. Lord knows they couldn't have had a worse relationship mine. But I'm not throwing in the towel. It took a while for me to do it, but I picked myself up, dusted myself off and got back in the game. Now it may be in our best interest that some of those women ain't ready to get back in the game again, because there would be too many of us out here. So I say let's have a toast to all those women at fifty or older who are too old, too fat, or too damn angry to get back in the game."

They cheered and lifted their glasses for the toast. They spent the rest of the evening laughing about life and talking about the brothers. Before they knew it they were quite tipsy. They decided to turn in so that they could get an early start on shopping the next morning. They all needed a new wardrobe because most of them had outgrown their old one. Rosa said that she would finish the itinerary tomorrow when the sisters were sober enough to appreciate it.

Robin had been Cynthia's shadow since Cynthia and Jack parted company. For some reason Robin was all over Cynthia as they shopped, picking out outfits she thought looked good, and telling Cynthia what to buy and what not to buy. It was clear that she was much more concerned about Cynthia's wardrobe than her own. They bought a little bit of everything that day. Robin said their wardrobes would not be complete until they came to New York for the finishing touches.

After dinner they went back to the suite to get comfortable and resume their Sister Circle. Sandra wanted to tell them a little about George. He was definitely a country boy with a slow southern drawl; he didn't always have a lot to say, and he did whatever she wanted him to do. He had been married before and had two children that were now adults. He didn't mind spending money and obviously had enough to keep up with Sandra. Sandra said that she was very straightforward and direct when they began dating because she didn't want to spend a lot of time waiting for them to learn how to please each other. She told him exactly what she wanted, and George was willing to comply. Although she dated other men occasionally, George was the easiest and the most consistent.

Tracy sprang the news that over Thanksgiving she and Carolyn had decided to have a civil ceremony and become lifelong partners. The Sister Circle jumped and squealed with excitement;

she was the first one in the group to get married in a very long time. Rosa wanted to know if this now meant that Carolyn would become a part of the Sister Circle. Tracy clearly let them know that Carolyn understood how important the Circle was to Tracy and did not want to infringe upon Tracy's personal time.

Nothing would change; the Circle would continue as it always had.

Rosa said that she was just enjoying life. "Y'all don't know how good it feels to roll over in the night and have a warm black man laying next to you. When Carlton left, I resolved myself to being alone. When Jeffrey came into my life, it was one of the best things that ever happened to me. Jeffrey is not a jealous man, and he gives me plenty of room and freedom to do the things that I want to do. He knows about and fully understands the Circle and encourages me to keep my connections. And when I leave Jeffrey by himself, I don't worry because he's never given me a reason to."

Financially, they were all secure and having fun and determined not to allow fifty to put them in a rocking chair.

CHAPTER 24

For the next few months life went on as usual. On at least two occasions Robin checked to see if Jack's son had registered for the cruise. Both times they had no record of him. She figured she would try one more time. She called the travel agent again and asked her to check the roster for a Mr. Matthew . . . . She realized that she didn't know his last name. The agent told her that there were two Matthews registered—one from South Carolina, and the other from Canton, Massachusetts. Robin hoped like hell that the Matthew from South Carolina was going to be Cynthia's knight in shining armor.

Tracy and Carolyn's civil ceremony was beautiful—odd, but beautiful. The reception was definitely a classy affair that included china, crystal and waiters. Tracy wouldn't have had it any other way. She looked happier than the sisters had seen her in a long time. Throughout the evening Carolyn and Cynthia glanced at each other, as if they were trying to remember where they had met. Cynthia knew who Carolyn was; she was waiting for Carolyn to figure out who Cynthia was. Finally, toward the end of the evening Carolyn sat down beside her.

"Cynthia, do you remember me?" Carolyn asked.

"Without a doubt I remember you. The question is do you remember me?"

"Cynthia, I thought about you often after Wesley and I got married; it was a big mistake. We stayed married for a little over a year. I wanted Wesley because he was hung like a horse, but it wasn't long before I realized that it wasn't enough to make me want to stay. I had been struggling with my lesbianism for years and wanted to make it go away. I thought Wesley was going to be the one to help me do that. Wesley was a nice person. He deserved better than that, so we got divorced and both moved on."

"We all make mistakes; the important thing is that we moved on with our lives," Cynthia said with a smile.

Tracy, Carolyn, Rosa, Jeffrey and Cynthia had an eight o'clock flight out of Logan Airport on the morning of December 3. In order to be on time Cynthia made sure that everything was packed and ready to go the night before. The limo was scheduled to pick her up at six o'clock in the morning. She was sitting back having a glass of wine and listening to some easy music when the telephone rang. It was Robin. She asked her a million questions about the outfits she intended to bring. Cynthia assured her that everything was in order and she was ready to go. It began to bother her that Robin felt so compelled to look after her all of the time. She needed to know what was going on in her head.

Cynthia was up bright and early, feeling real good about this trip. She checked and double-checked her luggage. As she moved through the house engaging all of the security devices that had been installed, she thought of Jack. *Wherever he is he must feel secure that nothing could come in or out of this house without being detected,* she thought.

By the time that they got their luggage checked, and boarded the plane it was 7:45. Cynthia knew that it would be real easy for her to nap from Boston to Florida. She settled in to do just that. She began to think of Jack. She closed her eyes and could smell Sandalwood. She could hear his deep baritone voice whispering in her ear. She could feel his arms around her as she drifted off to sleep. Before long they were landing in Florida.

They checked into the hotel. Both Tracy and Rosa felt a need to include Cynthia in their plans for the rest of the day. She declined because she didn't like the third-wheel feeling. Robin was due to arrive that evening; then she would have her running buddy.

As they sat in the lounge having cocktails, Sandra said that she had a feeling this trip was going to be something special. Cynthia told her that it was definitely going to be special because they would get to celebrate the fiftieth "Turning" together. Sandra said, "Even more than that. Something special is about to happen; I can just feel it."

By six o'clock, Robin arrived at the hotel. After she checked in and put her luggage in her room, she went to find their travel agent to see if Matthew had arrived. She was told by their agent that Matthew Simmons from South Carolina had not arrived. Her heart sank. It was going to be now or never. She had no way of contacting Matthew; he had to be on this trip.

The sisters all got together for dinner at seven o'clock. The bon voyage party started at nine. They found a great restaurant that was within walking distance of the hotel, had a leisurely dinner, then strolled back for the party.

At the bon voyage party, they mingled as much as they could, meeting new people and embracing folks they hadn't seen in a while. They promised everyone a good time, and they knew they would deliver.

Rosa was busy making sure that everyone got their snapshots taken, and the travel agent was busy handing out agendas and directions. Tracy and Cynthia noticed that Robin seemed to be a little preoccupied. Robin spent a lot of time scanning the crowd. When Tracy asked her what she was looking for, Robin said she wasn't looking for anything in particular but was just trying to see who the players were going to be. She said, "It's really important to watch the players in a game, 'cause you got to pace yourself. By the end of this reception I'll know who I'm aiming for."

At two o'clock in the morning, folks were still celebrating, so Rosa warned the group that they had an early start in the morning and they couldn't wait for those too hung over to make the bus. She suggested that they all go to their rooms and get a little sleep so that they could be dressed and ready for continental breakfast at nine.

They headed toward their rooms laughing and joking along the way. Robin seemed to have lost a little of her spirit for the trip. Cynthia thought this would be the ideal time to talk to her. She followed Robin to her room.

"Robin, you've got to tell me what's wrong." Robin began to get a little teary-eyed, so Cynthia sat her down for the conversation.

"Cynthia, I really want you to have a good time on this cruise, and you don't know how badly I want you to find the man to replace Jack. We haven't had a lot of luck with that. I know how you felt about Jack, and I know about the hole that was left in your life when he went away. Although you try to hide it, I know you well enough to know when you're thinking of him, and it makes me sad. I believe that I might be able to help you find his replacement, and I'm not going to rest until I do."

"Robin, why do you feel so compelled to help me find Jack's replacement?" Cynthia asked.

Robin wanted so badly to tell Cynthia everything. She wanted to spill her guts and tell her how she and Jack had planned for his replacement. She wanted to tell her that Jack monitored her life for years through her. She wanted to tell her that his name was not Jack, but Matthew. The one thing that she didn't want to tell her was that he was dead. She knew she couldn't do it; it would hurt Cynthia too badly.

It looked like Matthew wasn't going to make the cruise and Jack reneged on his deal. If Robin could dig Jack up she would kill him. All she could say was "Cynthia, because you're my friend and I love you. I want to help in any way that I can."

Cynthia hugged her and told her that she really loved her too, and if she really wanted to work at finding this wonderful man for her, she wouldn't get in her way. "But whatever you do, don't bring me no six-legged toad." They both had to chuckle because that's what Robin thought Jack was when she first met him.

The next morning they were among the first few passengers to board the ship and were given directions as well as an escort to their accommodations. The sundeck was an excellent choice; it allowed the sisters to stand on the patio and watch all the other passengers board. There was a row of cabins specifically reserved for the Sister Circle.

Robin stood on the patio watching the passengers board, again looking for Matthew. After about an hour of boarding, the captain's voice came over the intercom to let them know that the ship would be departing in fifteen minutes. She watched the dockworkers prepare the ship to leave port. Robin finally sat down looking quite dejected.

"Cynthia, we're going to make this a damn good trip in spite of it all." Cynthia had no idea what she was talking about, and she knew Robin wasn't going to tell her.

As the ship pulled away from the pier you could hear champagne corks popping; confetti was everywhere and folks were cheering. They were on our way to the Caribbean.

Cynthia's first order of business was to put away some of the thirty different outfits that Robin insisted she bring. It took about an hour to do this. Robin was in and out of her suite dozens of times. Finally, Robin said that she was going down to check the log to see exactly how many people decided to join them on this celebration.

For a brief moment Cynthia thought about Jack. She still wondered where he was, how he was doing and if he ever thought about her. She pushed the thought from her mind; this was going to be a time for fun. She put on a caftan and some sandals, sat on the sundeck, and watched the port move off in the distance.

Robin came back with a level of excitement that you would only see on a child's face at Christmas. She hugged Cynthia and said, "Cynthia, it's gonna be all right. This is going to be the trip of a lifetime; we got plenty of stuff to do." There were obviously a lot of single men on this ship; that's the only thing Cynthia could think of that would excite Robin this way.

Robin sat down and breathed a sign of relief. Matthew Simmons was on board. She didn't know what he looked like, but she knew that she would be able to find him. Then she thought about how would she introduce herself? She couldn't tell him that she was sent by his father, and she couldn't let him know how much she knew about him. That was the least of her problems. Once she found him she'd know what to do.

Cynthia intended to get dressed only for dinner; she was going to relax until then. Again, Robin was in and out of her cabin. Finally, Robin said, "Get dressed, girl." Robin went to the closet, found an outfit she thought Cynthia needed to wear, and threw it on the bed.

"Now, you knew when you came on this trip that we were coming without a man and that we were going to be running buddies and run this shit together. So come on, let's go."

Cynthia thought about her agreement with Robin and wondered what kind of drugs was she on when she told Robin that she'd be her running buddy on this trip. She reluctantly got up and began to dress. Just as she had finished dressing, Robin came in to tell her that she needed to change her shoes. Then Robin wanted to fix Cynthia's makeup. She finally looked Cynthia up and down and said, "Okay, you're good to go." Cynthia told her that she felt like she was in a military inspection. Robin laughed and said, "Come on, girl, we got work to do."

Most of the passengers had gathered in one or two lounges for the bon voyage party aboard ship. As they moved through the ship Cynthia ran across quite a few people that she knew, one in particular was Derrick. They dated a little after college but nothing ever materialized. He was looking a lot better now than he did then. She thought to herself, *I might get back to that.* Robin was constantly pulling her to move on. On the way down in the elevator, Robin kept reminding her that she agreed to meet new people. Once in the lounge, she had to get Robin off her back; so she told her that if they were going to work this room together, Robin should start on the left side and Cynthia would work the right side. When they met in the middle they would move to the next lounge. Finally, there was something they could agree on. She went off to do her thing.

Cynthia was working the room pretty good, smiling, chatting, flirting and meeting new people. Working a room can get pretty tiring and it didn't take long before she knew she needed at least one glass of wine. She grabbed a seat at the bar and ordered her standard glass of wine. As she waited for the bartender to bring the drink, a gentleman walked up behind her and, in a deep baritone voice, ordered a cognac. Her heart started to race; this man sounded so much like Jack. She didn't want to look up, knowing she would be disappointed, but she couldn't just walk away. As she reached into her purse to pay the bartender, the man with the deep baritone voice asked if she would let him buy the drink, in celebration of the "Turning."

He was about six feet two inches tall. He had a beautiful dark brown complexion, and his hair and mustache had hints of gray. He had a bright contagious smile, and he instantly captured her attention. He told her that his name was Matthew

Simmons. He was from South Carolina and owned his own security company. He had just accepted a new job and felt that he needed a little vacation before he started. He said that it was going to be very difficult for him to leave the South, but the job was well worth it. Cynthia introduced herself, giving him only as much information as he needed. He sat down beside her. They talked about his new job, his profession, and his move north. Soon he realized that she wasn't giving up much information about herself, so he began to ask questions.

"The one question I didn't ask that I probably should have asked first is, Are you married, or did you bring your man on this trip with you?"

"No, I'm not married," she answered. "I came on this trip with the sisters in my Sister Circle."

"So, you belong to this famous Sister Circle. I'd like to know a little more about it," he said with a smile. She began to explain the concept of the Sister Circle and who they were. He sat there smiling. He was actually listening.

"It sounds like a wonderful idea, and it sounds as if you and these sisters are very close," he said.

"It was a pact between women that was made in college, and we work hard at keeping the friendship strong and honoring the pact," Cynthia added.

"Hopefully between the Sister Circle, the 'Turning,' and within these next six days I could get to know a little more about you," he said.

"I could certainly arrange that," she said with a smile.

They were constantly being interrupted by friends and well-wishers. Finally, Matthew said, "This is your time and there seems to be a lot of people who want to get your attention. If possible, may I take you out for drinks this evening after dinner?" Of course she agreed. He handed her a piece of paper and a pen and said, "If you let me know where to find you, I'll pick you up at ten." He picked up the paper, told her he looked forward to seeing her at ten, and turned to walk away.

Cynthia watched him as he was leaving the lounge. He moved with a strong level of confidence, and he was exceptionally well dressed. You could tell by the fabric and the cut of his clothes that he knew quality merchandise. She wasn't the only one watching him; half the women in the room were doing the same thing. *This might be a challenge*, she thought. Robin finally caught up with her at the bar.

"Girl, there are some fine brothers on this cruise; and this sister is gonna have fun."

Robin ordered a drink and sat with Cynthia while she finished her glass of wine. Robin began telling her about some of the brothers she met, where they came from, and what they did for a living.

"Have you been sitting here all of the time? Did you meet anybody?" she asked impatiently.

"I met several people, smart ass, but there is one brother that I am going to have drinks with this evening," Cynthia answered.

"Well, all right. What's his name?"

"His name is Matthew Simmons."

"Well, I'll be damn," Robin said with a big grin.

Cynthia asked her if there was a problem, and she quickly replied, "There's no problem." She grinned again.

Robin began thinking to herself, *After all that worry and aggravation, trying to figure out how to put these two together, Cynthia meets Matthew and doesn't even need my damn help. I just hope this shit works, cause I'm tired of messing with it.*

By 7:30 they were all dressed and ready for dinner, sitting around laughing, joking and having cocktails. Tracy said that after dinner she planned to go to the casino. George and Jeffrey said they would go with her because they had been eyeing the casino since they boarded the ship. Robin stood up and put Cynthia's business in the street with the question "Where is this brother going to take you this evening?"

Everyone stopped to look at Cynthia. She said, "Okay, everyone, I will be having drinks with a brother named Matthew Simmons, and I don't know where we are going. But it won't be far; after all we are on a cruise ship." Everyone laughed.

The eight o'clock seating for dinner was full. Cynthia kept scanning the room looking for Matthew. She began to think how eerie it was to meet a man that so closely resembled Jack; and, even more important, he took an immediate interest in her. She remembered the promise she made to Jack the last time they were together, that if she thought she met a brother who had some of the qualities she was looking for, she would give him a chance. After a very brief conversation with Matthew, she felt that she really needed to give him a chance.

They finished dinner about nine o'clock. Cynthia went along with the others to watch them throw their money away, but her mind was on Matthew. She was hoping that Matthew was as smooth as he appeared to be, that they could hold each other's attention, and that he would be able to fill the void in her life. After a few minutes in the casino she went back to her cabin to freshen up a little before Matthew arrived. He had begun the pursuit, and in her attempt to be cool she had to make sure that she did not make the brother think she wasn't interested. But she also didn't want to seem too eager. At ten o'clock on the nose she heard a knock on her cabin door. When she opened the door all of her cool went up in smoke. She didn't feel bad, because he lost his cool too. They were standing there grinning at each other.

He took her to a small lounge not far from the casino. There was a very nice jazz combo playing. The only light illuminating the bar was strings of white Christmas lights strategically placed around the room. Cynthia and Matthew headed toward the rear of the lounge almost as if they were going into hiding. They found a spot in the corner and ordered drinks. He was a cognac drinker. She had only known one other cognac drinker.

He told her that he had been divorced for about five years. He and his ex-wife struggled hard over the years to keep the marriage together, but finally realized that it was just a poor fit. He and Cynthia talked about growing up and laughed about the fashion fun and styles of the 1970s and 1980s. They talked about children and why she chose not to have any; he said that he could definitely respect her decision. They talked about dreams and aspirations and what brought them to where they are today. They talked about likes and dislikes, and it certainly appeared that they had a lot in common. He had an excellent sense of humor and was very quick-witted. Cynthia was once again mesmerized by his deep baritone voice.

They talked about the qualities needed in a mate. Things were matching up quite nicely. He said, "You know, Cynthia, from our conversation it seems as if we might be quite compatible. But there is something about me that I think you need to know."

Cynthia thought to herself, *Oh shit! Here it comes.*

He said, "I'm fifty-four years old. I've been a lot of places and I've done a lot of things. I know what I'm looking for in a woman and I know it's difficult to find, particularly because of the kind of man that I am. I'm very straightforward; life is much too short to sit around and wonder about things. Women are sometimes offended because I get right to the point. Hopefully, that won't offend you.

"I'm not apt to spend a lot of time trying to mold or remake a woman; she either has it or she doesn't. When I find the woman who is compatible, I'm prepared to do whatever is necessary to get her attention. There are still so many things that I want to do and places that I want to go, and I would really like to do it with a person who appreciates me and some of the things that I do."

She sat smiling as he talked to her. Finally, he asked what the smile meant. She told him that she was smiling because he sounded like a recording of the things that she has said to men in her life. She told him that straightforwardness was something that she admired in a man, but that it was not easy to find.

Cynthia continued: "I'm a relatively independent person. I don't require an awful lot out of the man in my life. Marriage has never been on my top ten list of things to do, but I won't tell you that I will never consider it. The man in my life needs to be open and honest; he needs to have a quick wit and a wonderful sense of humor. I believe that laughter is a healing and spiritual force and should be shared with someone you care about. He needs to know what he wants and have the heart to go get it. He needs to be slow and easy because I don't believe rushing into anything ever has a value. He needs to be patient; anticipation is a wonderful aphrodisiac. He needs to be verbal both in and out of bed. A wise old friend once told me that a brother who can't get into your head should not be given the privilege of getting into your panties. He should be prepared to take directions occasionally, and I would certainly be prepared to take directions from him."

At this point he was smiling. Cynthia said, "This probably sounds like a laundry list, and I guess it really is because I've had fifty-three years to put it together. There is some room for flexibility, but not a whole lot."

Matthew said, "I know that this has been a long planned major celebration for you and your sisters, and I've just met you today, but I've always believed that there is a natural order to things and that you are sometimes given a gift when you least expect it. I'm not sure what kind of relationship we could have, but I am sure it's worth investigating. The selfish side of me would like to get as much of your time over these next six days as possible."

She agreed with his assessment of the possibility of a relationship. She too had a selfish side, and that side would make sure that he got as much time as he wanted. Matthew led her to the dance floor. When she put her arms around him she knew instantly that this was a perfect fit.

He held her mesmerized most of the evening; she thought she'd never hear a voice like that again. He resembled Jack in so many ways. She tried hard to push that thought out of her mind.

It was a beautiful evening. As they walked along the deck they both marveled at the magnitude of the ocean and how insignificant they were in the greater scheme of things. They were talking as if they had known each other for years. He knew more about her in a short time than most men knew after a year. It wasn't long before they found themselves on the sundeck. She invited him to her cabin. It was three o'clock in the morning. They sat on the patio sipping champagne. The air was filled with an ocean mist. She was so thankful that Tracy came along for this trip, because Cynthia's hair was going to be in rough shape in the morning.

The ocean air began to change and the temperature dropped a few degrees. Matthew stepped inside the cabin and came back with a blanket.

"We're going to be a little creative with this, since we only have one blanket," he said. He sat in the lounge chair, parted his legs and motioned for her to sit between his legs. As she sat between his legs and rested her head on his chest, she was once again in her favorite position. As they snuggled under the blanket they watched the sunrise. She thought to herself, *This has all of the makings of an excellent relationship.*

Matthew asked about her schedule for the day. She told him that she had made arrangements to have breakfast with the Sister Circle and that the rest of her day was free until they docked in St. Martin.

He said, "Cynthia, it's 6:30 in the morning, and I'm sure we both could stand a little nap before going to the beach this afternoon. So how about this? I've agreed to have breakfast with my buddies, and you with your Sister Circle. I'll meet you back here at 11 A.M.; we'll take a nap until the ship docks in St. Martin, and then we'll head off to the beach."

She was sure he was waiting for a reaction from her, but she'd always had a pretty good poker face. He said, "I know what you're thinking, but napping does not mean having sex. Napping means that I will just hold you in my arms while we both relax and actually take a nap. I really don't want to miss any time with you."

She thought, *I'll be damn; he's reading my mind.* Cynthia agreed to meet him at eleven o'clock.

He said, "Cynthia, we have spent the whole night together and have talked about almost everything there is to talk about. What I'd really like to do now is kiss you good morning."

He pulled her close and gave her a soft, slow, passionate kiss, the kind that makes your head light. Matthew certainly knew how to get a sister's attention.

When he left, she realized that it was much too late to get a nap in before breakfast at nine o'clock. She had just enough time to take a hot shower, convince Tracy to do something with her hair, and get dressed. Tracy came to her suite and worked wonders with her hair. She said, "I don't know what you heifers were doing last night, but all of y'all got some fucked-up heads this morning. What happened to you last night; we couldn't seem to find you"

"Matt and I spent all of the evening together until the early morning."

"I hope you got some condoms."

"It wasn't like that; we're not there yet."

"Girl, I don't understand. I ain't never seen anybody hold pussy as long as you do."

"It's not a matter of holding it, but it is mine, and I use it only when I'm moved to. You know my motto, a brother has got to talk to me and get in my head first."

"What's the matter, the brother ain't a good talker?"

"It's just the opposite, the brother was an excellent talker, and he was definitely in my head. With this man it's just a matter of not wanting to be too easy."

"Girl you're fifty-three years old, ain't shit easy for you.

They all met on the patio right before breakfast; everybody was upbeat and having a wonderful time. Everyone seemed to have a special interest in what Robin and Cynthia did last night. Cynthia told them that she ran across a brother who could definitely hold her interest for the rest of the cruise. Robin said she had narrowed it down to two different brothers but had not decided which one she wanted to spend her time with.

Rosa reminded them that they really needed to get a little Sister Circle time in. They agreed to hold the meeting in Rosa's room at seven o'clock that evening.

When they sat down for breakfast Cynthia realized that she was quite hungry. They laughed and joked as they always do, and at times they got pretty loud.

Rosa had been very busy checking with folks to be sure that they had met their cruise/talent show partner. Some folks were real serious about this talent show; you could catch them practicing on deck or in the lounge. Then there were those who knew that they really didn't have a talent and figured why embarrass themselves. Rosa said at this point she had seven acts who wanted to appear in the talent show.

After breakfast the sisters chatted for a moment and then went their separate ways. Cynthia didn't realize how tired she really was until she got back to her cabin. It was quarter of eleven, and Matthew was due at eleven. She just hoped that she could stay awake that long. He arrived promptly at eleven o'clock, and he was looking better that morning than he did last night.

Matthew said, "I know that we are both very tired. So I suggest that we pass on some of the preliminaries and take off our clothes so that we can get a nap before leaving the ship."

He took off his pants and shirt down to a pair of tan silk boxers; this man was matching from head to toe. Cynthia could tell that he was reasonably comfortable with his body, and for a fifty-four-year-old he looked pretty good. At that moment she thought she really should have spent a little more time in the gym. She undressed down to a red teddy and didn't dare look in the mirror. She had to remember that she was fifty-three years old and no longer had the body of a thirty-year-old woman. She knew she had to rely on her many other skills and talents to keep this man interested.

As she lay down beside him she could feel the warmth of his body as he pulled her closer. He asked her if she had ever been spooned. She thought to herself, *Oh shit, here comes the kinky stuff.* She told him that she hadn't, and he let out a thunderous laugh.

He said, "I can assure you that it's not kinky. I'm very creative but not kinky. I find the spoon position very soothing and comfortable."

He told her to roll over on her side with her back facing him, then he cuddled in very close, with all the right parts touching. He was right; it was very warm and soothing. Cynthia had definitely been spooned before; she just didn't know that there was a name for it.

He pulled her closer and continued to talk to her in that warm baritone voice. Most of the morning there had been a faint aroma haunting Cynthia. As she drifted off to sleep she recognized it as Sandalwood.

They were warned before they got to Orient Beach that they would have a short period of time to decide whether or not they were going to get naked. There were about fifty people who arrived from the cruise ship together, and they all stood huddled in a circle trying to decide. For the few who decided not to get naked there was another portion of the beach available for them.

The brothers seemed to take to the concept of being naked a lot quicker than the sisters did, and clothes were flying everywhere. Matthew said, "This is what we came for, so let's do this. I think you might even enjoy it."

Cynthia looked around the beach one last time before she began to take off her clothes. She realized that her stuff wasn't so bad. They found a spot, put down their blanket, and took off their clothes. She rolled onto her stomach to enjoy the sun.

Matthew went to investigate the activities on the beach. As he walked away she thought she wasn't sure what else the brother could do but that he could damn sure walk away nicely.

Fifteen minutes later he returned to tell her about a great idea. He said, "They have dinghies and sailboats in a little hut on the beach, and they will take us to any of the little islands around the beach as well as provide a box lunch for the day. I have taken the liberty of hiring a dinghy with a boxed lunch and a bottle of wine. We are going to a more secluded part of the island where we can get some sun, talk and enjoy a good lunch."

As they walked down to the shore Cynthia intentionally put a lot more emphasis on her posture. She stood up tall, pulled her stomach in, and decided that she and her cellulite were going to move across this beach with a little attitude. She began to strut like she owned the place.

They enjoyed the warm Caribbean sun while they laughed and played in the salt water. She never learned to swim; the last thing that a young girl wanted back in the 1960s was to get her hair wet. Matthew was a very strong swimmer. Cynthia lay on the beach and watched him move through the water effortlessly. It had been a long time since a man could hold her attention as long as Matthew had. She especially enjoyed his candor. Neither of them knew where this relationship would go, but they both saw something special in it. The thought of another long-distance relationship had both pros and cons. The pros were that it allowed her to continue to be independent and heightened the anticipation of the times that they could spend together. The con: at fifty-three years old, she really didn't want a twice-a-year relationship again.

He had most of the qualities and traits that she was looking for in a man, but she wondered if he was an easy lover. So far he had certainly shown patience and said all of the right things. He was an excellent kisser. At that moment she noticed him coming out of the water. He was clearly blessed with all of the necessary equipment to be a great lover. It was at this moment that she could no longer justify not being intimate with Matthew; everything seemed to fit so easily.

He sat down and offered to put suntan lotion on her body; this would be an excellent time to see what kind of hands he had. She gave him the lotion and rolled over on her stomach. He proved to have just the right touch. As he put the lotion on her back he said, "Cynthia, this is one of those moments when I need to be direct." She told him to feel free. "My intent is to rub this suntan lotion all over your body to include your breast and buttocks. If that's a problem, you need to let me know now." She smiled and told him that there was no problem and that he should continue.

After he finished, it was her turn. She said, "Before I begin to apply this suntan lotion, how inhibited are you?" He let out a thunderous laugh and said, "Cynthia, there is nothing on this whole body that you can't touch whenever you want."

She applied the suntan lotion and lightly massaged his body. He had some pretty tense muscles in his back and shoulders. She decided that she would work on those later; besides, the texture of the suntan lotion really wasn't appropriate for a massage. They both agreed that the Caribbean sun felt wonderful on the body, and they talked about the freedom they felt lying totally naked in the sun. She had to admit that she really enjoyed it.

The day was winding down, and they had forty-five minutes before they were to board the busses back to the cruise ship. As they walked along the beach, Matthew reached for her hand. She hadn't held hands with a man in almost thirty years; she smiled because it was refreshing. She told him that the last thing that she thought she would be doing at the age of fifty-three was strolling along the beach naked, holding hands.

He chuckled and said, "You never know where life is going to take you; you just have to be prepared to go."

When it was time to leave, neither of them really wanted to put their clothes back on. She threw on a beach cover-up, and he put on a pair of shorts.

They realized that they both had friends who expected to spend some time with them on this cruise, so they were willing to give each other up for dinner. Matthew walked her back to her cabin, and they agreed to meet at ten o'clock that evening. He gave her a deep passionate kiss as he tenderly rubbed her back and neck. Her knees got weak.

Dinner, as usual, was loud and full of laughter. The topic, of course, was the nude beach and all of the events that had occurred. Sandra said she was really surprised at how comfortable she felt being naked because it wasn't about your body and how good it looked. There were all types of bodies on that beach—big, fat, tall, short, young and old.

Cynthia's sisters wanted to know if she and Matthew had a good time. She told them that it was a beautiful day and a wonderful experience with a man that she could really get into.

Tracy said, "I'll be damn; that calls for a toast. Cynthia has found a man that she could get into." Everyone at the table laughed. They decided that they would continue that conversation later in the Sister Circle.

Later that evening they lounged on the patio outside of Rosa's room. "We're gonna start the Circle with Cynthia and Robin, because they are the only two sisters who came on this cruise without a man," Rosa joked.

Robin was spending time with a brother named Frank. He was from South Carolina and was possibly a friend of Matthew. Frank had just gotten divorced about a year ago. "He'd been with a woman for years who didn't do much of anything," Robin said. "She only knew the missionary position and had a schedule for sex. So I knew it wasn't going to be hard to get his attention. I turned his ass out quick, fast and in a hurry. I've never had a long-distance relationship, but this might be the one."

"Shit, just yesterday you told us that you were in love with Sonny," Tracy joked.

"Yeah, I think I am, but my grandmamma always told me that it's a poor rat that ain't got but one hole to go to. Once I got this new brother over his shyness, I realized that he may be a keeper."

Even at Robin's age they were all very much in awe of Robin. She did what she felt and didn't particularly give a damn how other people felt about her. Cynthia was next on the agenda.

"Matthew has been divorced for about five years, and recently took on a new job. He owned his own security company and just got a major contract in Connecticut. He was very attentive and an excellent kisser," Cynthia said.

"You mean y'all spent a whole day butt naked on the beach and that's all you know," Robin said laughing. "Cynthia, you're not going to find a more romantic environment, and you already told us that the brother has gotten into your head and that you're into him. None of us know what's going to happen with these little relationships once this cruise is over and, more importantly, we're not thirty years old anymore. I'm gonna tell you this, and I've told it to you before, you need to learn to seize the moment."

Rosa was having the time of her life; every time the sisters saw her and Jeffrey the two were holding hands and cuddling. "Sisters, I never dreamed that life could be this good; to be with a man and not be in fear is such a wonderful thing."

Their discussion topics shifted to their plans for retirement, to the state of black women, and to the talent show. They planned to meet for lunch on Friday at noon.

Matthew arrived promptly at ten, looking just as good in his clothes as he did out of them. When Cynthia opened the door, he stepped inside and closed the door behind him, pulled her into his arms, and said, "I want you to know that my intentions this evening are to get totally into your head, and hopefully that will lead us where we need to go." He wanted to take a trip to the casino; there were a couple of people he wanted her to meet.

"These boys are a little off the hook. They are newly divorced and wild, so hopefully you won't be offended by anything that they say or do," he warned.

When Cynthia and Matthew got to the casino, he grabbed her by the hand and walked her over to a blackjack table to meet three black men, neatly dressed, having loud fun and talking trash. The loudest brother got out of his chair and proceeded to walk around her, looking her up and down. He said, "All right, now we can understand why you don't have time for us."

Matthew pulled her close to him and said, "Y'all my boys, and I just wanted you to know why y'all shouldn't come looking for me." They all started laughing. She wondered which one of these men had gotten Robin's attention.

While strolling on the deck Cynthia and Matthew heard some 1970s music and followed it into one of the lounges. They didn't know who these brothers were, but they were definitely crooning. Matthew ordered a cognac neat, and she had a glass of wine. He moved his chair close behind hers and lightly massaged her shoulders, neck and arms as they listened to 1970s love songs. Matthew guided her to the dance floor and whispered in her ear, "Today has been one of the most unusual days of my life. I spent four hours naked on a beach with an enchanting woman whose body I'm eager to explore." As they held each other close and moved to the beat of the music, she could feel his body begin to react to their closeness.

"Both of us came on this trip with a laundry list of characteristics that we wanted in a mate, and I believe that we are compatible in many ways. I think it's time to find out if we are sexually compatible," Matthew whispered in her ear.

She had to smile because if there were clear outward signs that a woman could show when aroused, he would have known it. He certainly had her attention. They headed toward her cabin.

Earlier during the day when she was applying suntan lotion to his body she sensed a little tension. She told him that she had just the thing to fix that. She invited him to lay across her bed while she massaged his body with "joy." Getting naked wasn't difficult for them, after all they had been naked for most of the day. She directed him to roll over on his back and spread-eagle. She waited to see if he would follow her directions. He had no reservations and did exactly as she asked him to do; he trusted her. As she finished the massage, he suggested that she allow him to return the favor. She rolled over on her stomach, and he began the massage. It was very clear that he knew what he was doing.

He said that he wanted to massage her back in a very different way, and all he needed her to do was follow directions. He rolled over on his back and directed her to lay on top of him with her knees on either side of his hips. He said, "Cynthia, I know what you're thinking. We will use a condom, and this position will not be used for penetration."

She could feel the strength in his hands as he massaged her back in this position. His hands moved up and down her back in a steady rhythm from her buttocks to the nape of her neck while she rested on his body. He talked to her softly in that deep baritone voice and told her to breathe deeply and relax. She thought she knew her stuff when it came to a massage, but this was the most sensuous, erotic back massage she'd ever had. At this point she was totally open to whatever he wanted to do. They were both quite aroused and knew that they would need to slow this down a little.

There were several outdoor Jacuzzis on the deck below them. He suggested that they go out and enjoy one. She knew exactly what he was doing; he intended to use anticipation to the fullest extent. This wasn't new to her; it was the kind of game that she and Jack played often. It was a quiet night and there was only one other couple in the Jacuzzi; they left shortly after Cynthia and Matthew arrived. As he kissed her passionately in the Jacuzzi she could feel his hands gliding over her buttocks and thighs. She put her arms around his waist and lightly massaged the small of his back; they seemed to know exactly how to touch one another.

He said, "Baby, you've got excellent hands, and you're going to make anticipation very difficult."

He asked her to turn around with her back facing him; he just wanted to caress her body. As she turned he pulled her closer and began to massage her stomach and abs. When his hands moved to her inner thigh she had to catch her breath. He slowly moved his hands from her inner thigh up to her abs, over her breast and back down again. She closed her eyes and went with the feeling. With very little direction, her legs began to part and she could feel herself getting lost in the moment.

His hands moved between her legs with a very light touch, and a tingling sensation moved up her back. Of all the things that he could have done next, he began to sing to her. Of all the songs he could have chosen, he sang "Starship" by Norman Connors. Her heart almost stopped; that was the song that she and Jack listened to most often. While Matthew sang softly in her ear, she drifted from the past to the future and back into the past again. She was sure that he could tell by her reaction that he not only was into her head, he also touched her body and mind.

He took her out of her trance by turning her around to face him. "Cynthia, I don't know the reason that we've been brought together, but it's very real and we're going to have to deal with it."

She kissed him the way she enjoyed being kissed. She ran her tongue along his lips, down to his neck and onto his chest. He put his head back as a sign that she had free reign to explore his body. She put her hands into his bathing suit and massaged his buttocks. He let her know that he enjoyed it. She then moved to his testicles, which were warm and firm, and she gently caressed them. He was back to a full erection. She lifted her left leg and straddled his penis, having pulled aside her bathing suit, allowing his erect penis to rest against her vagina. They gently moved with each other. At that moment she got a Wesley flashback; this was how she achieved her first orgasm over thirty years ago. Cynthia and Matthew both knew that they couldn't do this very long and needed another diversion.

Finally, she said to Matthew, "It is very clear that you know how to play this game."

He smiled and said, "Yes, I've played this game often; however, you don't appear to be a stranger to the game yourself and have proved to be a formidable partner. Since we both know the game and know that we can play it well, let's cut to the chase. We can always play this game again tomorrow."

They headed back to her suite to take a shower. Afterward, they spent the next ten minutes rubbing oils and lotions on each other's body. Now she knew that she had skills, but she didn't realize that he was equally skilled. She had been taught well and she knew what made a man's body feel good. Somewhere and somehow Matthew had been taught equally well, because he damn sure knew what to do to make a woman's body feel good.

Matthew was not a small man, and Cynthia knew that she had to exercise her rights of control, at least in the first sexual encounter. She had been taught early to use the first sexual encounter as a gauge to determine how she would need to handle her partner. She began to massage his penis and testicles. She could tell he was working hard to maintain control. Without warning, he sat up and lifted her onto his lap. At that moment they both remembered the condom.

As she straddled his lap, he said, "Baby, I look forward to the time when we are in a totally monogamous relationship and we will no longer have to stop to find a condom."

Once the condom was in place she remounted his lap. She took her time because she needed to gauge his body. As she slowly lowered her body onto his penis she recognized that this was going to be a tight fit. Once in position, she allowed him to take control. She let him set the style and rhythm; and, as expected, it was slow and easy.

They responded to each other perfectly, both physically and verbally. He seemed to anticipate her every move. He was an extremely observant lover and seemed to know what she needed and when she needed it; he read her body well. He cupped both breasts in his hands and began to play around the nipples with his tongue and then slowly moved her to the bed. Once on the bed he spoke softly in her ear.

"Cynthia, this is your show. You tell me how to please you, and I'll do whatever it takes." She told him that so far he was doing an excellent job, but if she felt the need to give directions she certainly would.

At fifty-three years old, she'd had her fair share of lovers, but never anyone that was even close to Jack. It wasn't very long before she realized that Matthew Simmons was giving Jack a serious run for his money. Damn this man was smooth! Soon her head began to feel very light, and she was oblivious to the world. She opened herself in a way that she hadn't done for anyone since Jack. Matthew was right there on time. She experienced her first earth-shattering orgasm since being without Jack, but there was something very different about this one. She knew that it was coming but she had no idea of the intensity. She instinctively braced herself and it clearly showed as Matthew felt the tension. He said, "Relax, baby, and let it go, because I intend to bring you here as often as possible."

Her head got light, and an orgasm swept over her body, but this one was different; it seemed to be endless. Just as she thought that she might lose consciousness Matthew joined her. As he held her in his arms she felt a series of vaginal contractions that were much like the aftershock of an earthquake. He obviously felt it too and let her know that it was a pleasing sensation. Little did he know she had no control over these contractions. He began to talk to her in her left ear, and she had to interrupt him to let him know that after an earth-shattering orgasm she became deaf in her left ear for at least ninety seconds.

She was working very hard not to let Matthew know the effect that he had on her. He was the second man she'd ever known who could keep her in a state of constant arousal. She couldn't help but lie in his arms and wonder where this relationship was going.

They spent a very intense night together; he had unbelievable control and was able to achieve an erection with very little foreplay. By ten o'clock the next morning they both regained consciousness.

He said, "Baby, I've been with many women in my lifetime, and some of them professed to be great lovers, but you have been the only one who could keep me physically and mentally aroused for almost twelve straight hours. That's a little frightening."

She told him that they both have a reason to be a little frightened because never has she wanted to keep a man's attention both physically and mentally for twelve hours. They both had to chuckle. She looked at the clock and realized that they had missed breakfast and, if they didn't get moving, they were going to miss lunch too. They made a date to meet at the outdoor buffet at one o'clock for lunch.

She took a long hot shower, trying to charge her body with some imaginary energy that was coming from the showerhead. Neither of them had gotten very much sleep that night, and she definitely needed Mary Kay's help that morning.

By 12:45 she had finally gotten herself together. She checked on Robin before she went to lunch. Cynthia asked her what her plans were for the day. Robin said that she was supposed to meet Frank for lunch at one o'clock at the outdoor buffet, but she knew that she would be running a little late. Cynthia told Robin that she would try to find this Frank and let him know that Robin was on her way. She asked Robin to describe him. Robin said that he was about six feet tall, very dark with salt-and-pepper hair, and a fraternity brand on his right arm.

At the buffet, Matthew told Cynthia that four of his buddies came on the cruise with him. She met three in the casino a few nights ago. It seems as though the fourth brother was infatuated by a woman on the ship and was classified as missing in action.

Cynthia asked him if the brother's name was Frank. Matthew wanted to know how she knew. She told him that one of the sisters in the Sister Circle had also been missing.

"I finally caught up with her this morning, and she asked me to give a message to Frank that she would be a little late for lunch."

At that moment, a brother who fit the description of Frank walked over to their table. Matthew told the brother to have a seat and introduced him to Cynthia. Cynthia told Frank that Robin would be a little late for lunch. Frank looked a little surprised, and Cynthia felt the need to let him know how she knew Robin.

When Robin arrived, they waived her over to the table and she joined them for lunch. During the course of the conversation Frank asked Matthew what was the probability that two brothers like them, who didn't even want to come on the cruise, would run into two fine sisters?

Matthew said, "You know, man, it's a small world."

Robin chimed in with a sly smile: "It's a lot smaller than you know." They chatted for a while and agreed to meet that evening before the talent show.

When they left the table Matthew looked at Cynthia and said, "Baby, that brother looks beat. I've known Frank all of my life, and even though he's having a good time, it looks like the brother hasn't slept in days."

Cynthia said, "I've known Robin most of my life; and if I know her the way I think I do, the brother hasn't slept in days. Robin's a bit of a rough rider, and I'm sure that brother's catching hell trying to keep up with her."

"Well, baby, I wouldn't worry about that because Frank is a notorious rough rider himself. That brother will ride it even if it ain't moving." They both had to laugh.

By five o'clock that evening they were sitting in the lounge preparing to have their first evening cocktail. They were all having a good time laughing and dancing. Most of the contestants for the evening's talent show were bragging about how good their act was and how they were certainly going to take home the thousand dollars. When it comes to talking trash and selling wolf tickets, no one can do it better than black people.

Cynthia noticed Tracy sitting across the room from them, deep in thought. Cynthia walked over to sit with her for a moment, just to make sure that she was okay. Tracy said that she was doing fine, but she was a little concerned about Carolyn. Tracy said she seemed to be disconnected from the group and wanted to spend more time alone than Tracy had expected. Cynthia told her that maybe Carolyn felt that she needed to give her more time and space to be in the Sister Circle and that's why she wanders off by herself.

Tracy said, "Well, maybe you're right. I could be reading more into this than there is."

Matthew and Cynthia instinctively knew that they would be spending the night together, so it wasn't a surprise that he had an overnight bag in his hand when he arrived to pick her up. He joined them for dinner, and she told him that he was the only brother in her life who has had the privilege of meeting all of the sisters in the Sister Circle. He smiled and said that he felt privileged.

After dinner they met Robin and Frank and settled into a booth in the back of the lounge to watch the show. There were nine acts scheduled; the first three were dancers. Next was a duet, then a trio dressed like the Supremes. Then there was a brother who played the piano while a sister sang. The sister wasn't a bad singer; the brother just couldn't play the piano. Then a very serious and dramatic sister got on stage and began to recite a poem. If there had been points awarded for drama, she definitely would have won.

Then there was Tracy and her partner, John, who played the alto sax. The brother was playing the hell out of that saxophone, nice and smooth. Tracy sauntered onto the stage, looking like a diva. She pulled up a stool. The audience started cheering. She told the audience that she only recently was introduced to the spoken word, that this was her first piece, and she hoped everyone *could* appreciate it. She dedicated the piece to all of the women in the world who felt that they had been misused or taken advantage of by a man. She titled it "He Didn't Take Nothing from You":

All of a sudden, out of the blue,
Brother packed his shit because he's leaving you.
He said, "It ain't you, baby, I just need a little space,"
Which he didn't need last month when he was living at your place.
Now you down and out and feeling real bad,
But you can't miss a brother that you never really had.
You settle in for the long heartache;
You moan and whine and re-evaluate.
Ali comes on the air; now she's the last thing you need
'Cause she can only tell you how to beg and plead.
Can't live without you, cry without you, sleep without you, eat without you, be without you, die without you.
Damn it, get a grip!
'Cause he didn't take nothing from you that you didn't want to give.
He didn't take nothing from you to make you not want to live.
He didn't take nothing from you to knock you off your feet.
He didn't take nothing from you to make you incomplete.
He didn't take nothing from you that you won't give again.
He didn't take nothing from you that you won't give to another man.
Now you knew he had a woman the day you met that man.
He told you he was leaving 'cause she just didn't understand.
You took that as a victory; your ego began to show,
But a brother won't leave a woman unless he got someplace to go.
You can't be mad with a brother when he says he's got to leave.
You can wallow in self-pity, beg, cry and grieve,
But there's a well-known fact that you just didn't see:
Why the brother gonna buy the cow when he can get the milk for free?
Step up, young girl, take your place in this game.
Don't try to give the brothers all the blame;

'Cause he didn't take nothing from you that you didn't want to give.

He didn't take nothing from you to make you not want to live.

He didn't take nothing from you that should send you on this trip.

He didn't take nothing from you.

Damn it, girl, get a grip!

Life is yours to live whichever way you choose,

But don't get mad and fall apart when in the game you lose.

You allow yourself to be devalued, mistreated and abused.

You allow yourself to be redefined by videos, music and the news.

So get a grip, move on!

But first you must understand

You cannot be validated by the presence of a man.

Hold on, my Nubian sister, you're gonna take this emotional ride.

You're gonna take it again and again and again

Until you finally decide

That you control your relationship; it's in the men you choose.

But in the end it's always the same.

They didn't take nothing from you.

Tracy and her partner won first prize and announced that the $1,000 prize money would be donated to a young student at the Berklee College of Music in Boston.

Everyone was busy celebrating Tracy's win and didn't notice when Carolyn left the lounge. The ship's air conditioning must have been working overtime because the lounge began to get quite chilly. Cynthia snuggled in closer to Matthew for warmth, and Sandra asked George if he would go back to the cabin and get a shawl for her shoulders.

When George returned with the shawl, he seemed a little agitated. He took Sandra over to the corner and whispered in her ear. When Sandra returned to the table, she asked Cynthia to step outside the lounge for a moment. Cynthia excused herself and followed Sandra outside.

"Cynthia, I think there might be a problem," she said. "George has had a few drinks, so he got a little disoriented when he was looking for our cabin. As he was wandering around he came across Carolyn standing in front of a cabin with a man. He said the brother was all over her, and she wasn't resisting. He said that he watched for a moment just to be sure that it was Carolyn. Both of them had their hands all over each other, and they finally went into the cabin together."

Sandra asked George to keep it to himself because she was sure there was an explanation, but deep in her heart she knew that Carolyn was doing Tracy wrong. Sandra, Cynthia, and George agreed to keep this to themselves, at least until after vacation. Tracy had been having such a good time, and they didn't want to spoil it.

It was getting late in the evening, and Rosa reminded them that the Sister Circle was scheduled to meet over lunch at noon the next day. Matthew and Cynthia decided to take a stroll on deck to enjoy the warm Caribbean evening. They ended up back at Cynthia's, sitting on a chase lounge in her favorite position—between his legs with her head resting back on his chest.

He put his arms around her and said, "Cynthia, unfortunately we've only got a few days left to this cruise, and I truly intend to make the best of them. I believe that we have more than just a passing affair; we need to determine the next move in this relationship."

"It was definitely more than a passing affair because I don't believe that an affair comes with the kind of intensity that we have experienced," said Cynthia.

Her primary concern was that she was not interested in a long-distance relationship. South Carolina was a long way from Boston.

"If that's your only concern, we can certainly fix that," said Matthew. "I'm scheduled to move to Connecticut around the fifteenth of December because my contract with the new company begins the first of the year. Connecticut will put me an hour to an hour and a half away from Boston."

She told him if that was the case, there really was no reason that they could not continue to cultivate this relationship.

"There is one thing you should know," he said, "I'm looking for a monogamous relationship. I don't necessarily have to be married, I've done that before. But I do know that the woman in my life has to be my woman. I would like for both of us to get tested so that ultimately we can do away with the condoms. I need to feel completely connected to you."

She told him that it sounded like an excellent idea.

He said that although he would not have an official address until after December 15, his cell phone was always on. In celebration of his new address he wanted to invite her to spend Christmas in Connecticut with him.

"If you are ready for company by Christmas, I'll be there," she said.

"Baby I will never consider you company. As far as I'm concerned you have become a significant part of my life," he said softly and sincerely.

"We will spend Christmas together whether it is in Connecticut or Boston; we would definitely spend it together," she said.

"You know, baby, we've been teasing each other all day," said Matthew, "and I've had an erection on at least four different occasions during the course of the day, and that's pretty unusual for me. Women usually don't move me quite like that. Last night I allowed you to be in control because I felt that's what you wanted. It's now my turn."

At about four o'clock in the morning, as she snuggled close against his warm body, she was deaf in her left ear and gasping for breath. Matthew certainly knew how to take control. As Cynthia drifted off to sleep she had a feeling that she hadn't had in years, and this time she intended to keep it.

Cynthia was the last one to arrive for lunch. When Cynthia sat down at the table, Tracy started laughing. All eyes were on Cynthia, and she knew what that meant.

Cynthia said, "I have only one thing to say, and that is if I did not love you heifers there is no way in the world I would have walked away from that gorgeous naked black man laying in my bed."

"Good for you, I'm glad the brother's keeping your attention," Robin said.

"Frank seems to be keeping your attention too," Rosa said.

"Yeah, he's all right. I really like the brother, but I'm not so sure that he's the man for me. I find myself thinking about Sonny too much," Robin admitted.

"Robin, you're going to have to make up your mind what you want to do. We'll always be here for you, but we can't help you make your decision," Sandra added.

Tracy said that although she was having a real good time, she was a little concerned about Carolyn. There seemed to be something on Carolyn's mind. Sandra and Cynthia glanced at each other quickly. As long as Tracy knew that there was a problem they felt as if they didn't need to intercede. They would wait it out and see what happened.

Tracy changed the subject and told the sisters she had been making notes and thinking about ways in which they all could go into business together. They listened intently.

The Captain's Dinner was an excellent ending to the fiftieth "Turning." Tracy wanted to be the one to thank everyone for joining the sisters. She told the guests that the sisters in the Sister Circle were all retiring this year and were preparing to launch a joint business venture—a health and social club for women over forty. The health spa would operate through dues and provide aerobic workouts with an Afrocentric touch, body sculpturing, strength training, saunas and massages. The sisters intended to bring women over forty out of their dull lives into a vibrant social environment.

Rosa, Jeffrey, Tracy, Carolyn and Cynthia were scheduled on the same flight out of Fort Lauderdale to Boston. They were all seated in the same area and began to settle in for the long flight home.

"Cynthia, are you going to be okay?" Rosa whispered.

"I'm going to be more than okay."

"It sounds like you and Matthew have arranged to make this relationship happen," Rosa said.

"I think you're right, Rosa. We are planning to spend Christmas together."

"Oh shit, don't tell me that it's another one of those Christmas-and-July relationships," Tracy joked.

"No, Tracy. Christmas is just the beginning. Matt will be moving to Connecticut, about an hour and a half away from Boston. So we'll spend a lot more time together."

CHAPTER 25

It would have been easy for Cynthia to immerse herself totally in Matthew, but a part of her knew that if it was too good to be true, it probably wasn't. Matthew was everything she thought she needed in a man. This was the first time since Jack that she had been totally enthralled with the company of a man. Matthew did all the right things at the right time. The only other person who could hold her captive was Jack, but that seemed like ages ago. Matthew finally completed his move from South Carolina to Connecticut and settled into a two-bedroom townhouse in North Stonington, a small obscure town. North Stonington was very close to his new assignment. He needed to be close, at least for the first year; he was on twenty-four hour call.

Matthew had been in the security business for many years and was considered among the best in black-owned and -operated security firms. He was awarded a $22 million contract with one of the largest casinos on the East Coast.

It was early Tuesday morning, the day after New Year's. Cynthia was headed back to Boston. It was time to reconnect to the real world. She and Matthew had just returned from the Sister Circle's fiftieth "Turning." The cruise was one of the best ideas the Sister Circle had in a long time. As the sisters boarded the cruise ship, everyone seemed to believe that Cynthia would meet that special man. Even Cynthia's wildest imagination could not have prepared her for Matthew. She promised herself that she would not compare him to Jack, she would not wonder where he came from or how he got here. She would just bask in the joy of having him in her life.

The traffic was relatively light that particular morning. Her mind wandered to the most recent set of events that had an impact on the Sister Circle. Over the last three weeks each of them needed to make a decision that could change their lives. The first Sister Circle meeting of the year was scheduled for Sunday at Tracy's house, and it was guaranteed to be intense. There was a lot to share, and in some cases, there were things to disclose.

The traffic began to tighten considerably as Cynthia got closer to Boston. Driving in Boston was like playing an interactive space video game. As she dodged the aggressive space aliens and maneuvered closer to home she couldn't help but wonder about the pending joint business venture the Sister Circle was about to begin. This new venture would take a lot of time, hard work, and a significant financial commitment. Money would not be a problem; they were all financially stable. The question in Cynthia's mind was their ability to give up valuable time to make this venture work. Everyone had either retired or was in the process of retiring, and felt committed to making this plan work. She would have to see just how much work had been done over the last three weeks. Everyone had an assignment.

When she entered her house through the back door, a series of beeping noises made her aware that she needed to deactivate the home security system. As she punched in the appropriate codes she thought about Jack. The security system was a gift from him, and it made her feel safe every time she entered her home. She found that over the last several weeks she thought about him less. Matthew had proved to be an excellent replacement. Once she unpacked her bags and got comfortable she knew that the next order of business was to reconnect to the Sister Circle. She got on the phone with each of them. Everyone was excited about the next Sister Circle meeting scheduled for Sunday. Everyone had taken her assignment seriously and was prepared to report on her findings. It looked like their next business venture was shaping up nicely. Sandra and Robin were coming into town Saturday morning especially for this meeting.

While in the process of preparing for bed that evening Cynthia thought about Wesley. She was scheduled to have dinner with him on Friday evening. Upon returning from the cruise she had received a letter from him stating that he wanted to meet with her. She didn't know what to expect from this meeting, but she knew she had to see him if she expected to totally commit to Matthew. That evening the erotic dreams returned.

Sunday's Sister Circle promised to be an unusually long meeting. Everyone had something she wanted to share, so they scheduled dinner for four o'clock to ensure that everyone had time to say what was on her mind. They began to gather at Tracy's house about 3:30 and immediately began the cocktail hour. After about an hour of laughing, joking and reminiscing, Rosa got serious.

"I can't begin to explain my feelings as Jeffrey struggled for life in the hospital," said Rosa. Shortly after returning from the cruise Jeffrey had to be rushed to the hospital after experiencing flu symptoms and a seizure.

"I was finally experiencing happiness with a man for the first time in my life, and it paralyzed me to think that I could lose him. Jeffrey and I finally realized that time was not promised to any of us; it was given to us one day at a time. Because we are both HIV-positive, simple ailments can sometimes become critical. We both take our medication regularly and keep in contact with our doctors, but we can't forget that the virus is with us. So Jeffrey and I decided that we will be getting married next month. Whatever time we have, we want to spend it together."

That announcement called for a toast, and a loud celebration began.

"Sisters, there is something else that I want to share with you," Rosa said. "I haven't shared this with anyone, including Jeffrey, but I can't keep it to myself any longer. I only ask that it never leave the Sister Circle."

They all agreed to keep her secret within the Circle. She continued: "When I realized that all of you were moving on after making good financial investments, I panicked at the thought of not being able to financially keep up with the Sister Circle. I thought about it for weeks. Carlton would not pay child support and refused to help in any way. The only thing he gave me was the HIV virus, and he would have to pay for that."

Rosa went on to tell the Circle how, when and why she planned and executed Carlton's murder. When she finished her story, the room was silent and she waited for a reaction.

After what seemed like an eternity, Tracy finally said with a smile, "I ain't mad at you. The only reason I didn't have it done was because you beat me to it. I said it then and I'll say it now, that motherfucker needed to die." The rest of the Circle remained silent.

Rosa continued. "I'm not asking anyone to condone or agree with what I've done. I know that I will have to answer for my actions, even if it is not on this earth. I only ask that you try to understand why I did it."

The room remained quiet until Robin reminded the sisters of the thirty years of commitment they had to each other. She reminded them that it was not their place to determine punishment or grant forgiveness; that was left to the Almighty. She then asked if there was anyone who could not keep Rosa's confession within the Circle.

Tracy said, "What confession?" The others joined in to say that they hadn't heard a confession, either.

Cynthia felt that she needed to lighten the mood a little. She told the sisters that she finally found Jack's replacement. The sisters stood to give her a round of applause. Everyone felt that it was long overdue. Cynthia went on to say that she finally wanted to have a man, this man, around more than twice a year and that she and Matthew would spend as much time as possible together. She didn't know where this relationship was headed. But she knew he made her happy, and she was determined to do the same for him.

As Cynthia looked around the room she realized that these were her sisters, the people who would be with her through the good and the bad. These were the people she could trust. She realized that this was her opportunity to unload some of her personal baggage. Baggage she carried alone for many years—the haunting memory of the abortion. The memory remained dormant most of the time. On rare occasions Cynthia would watch a mother comfort her child with a look of total commitment and unconditional love, and for a brief moment Cynthia would wonder if she had made the right decision. It never took her long to snap out of it, but those brief moments were still there. She felt this was the time to share this experience with her family. She proceeded to tell them of the shock of her unplanned pregnancy. She spoke about her feelings as she planned for the abortion, and she talked about how deceitful she felt in keeping the information from Jack. When she finished telling her story, she walked over and held Rosa's hand.

"Well sister, it looks like you'll have company on Judgment Day, when we both have to account for our sins." At that moment Cynthia realized that she was guilty of murder too. It didn't make a difference how it happened, murder was still murder.

After composing herself, Cynthia told the sisters about her recent dinner date with Wesley. She finally got a chance to know a little about the Wesley as an adult. She had to admit that he still excited the hell out of her, but she had learned to control that. He had matured quite nicely, was very articulate, attentive and had a great sense of humor—three of the traits that Cynthia needed in her man. He was still very elusive. They spent the evening talking about their lives and life decisions. Far too many years had passed between them and they both would always wonder "What if." She walked away from that dinner with a tingle in her panties, a smile on her face, and enough information to manifest several new erotic dreams. Cynthia and Wesley promised to keep in touch. That evening the erotic dreams intensified.

Sandra had a difficult time determining whether or not to take Jason back. She remembered the hurt she felt when he cheated on her, and she promised she would never allow herself to be in that position again. Jason said he wanted to come home and was willing to do whatever Sandra wanted in order to prove his love for her. He wined and dined her, made passionate love to her while he apologized, and recommitted over and over again. She knew that he was the only man that could stir passion in her, but she would never be able to fully trust him again. She finally decided to take him back but he would still have to pay for his indiscretions. She just hadn't determined how.

Tracy made it clear that she didn't have any significant drama in her life at this time. "I've decided that I can't share my woman, especially with a man. I've waited most of my life for that special person and I thought Carolyn was it. Although I love Carolyn and she says that she loves me, I cannot tolerate the thought of her being touched by a man, even if it is only on occasion. I'll keep searching; I know that special person is out there. Now sisters, I have to admit that there is no real drama in my life right now; however, if they parole that motherfucker that killed my mother, I'm gonna keep my promise to kill him."

Robin stood up, moved across the room, and sat down facing Cynthia. She looked around the room at the other sisters and said, "I think it's time. I've got a lot of shit that I need to unload and I'm counting on the strength of the Sister Circle to hold us together after I tell you what I've done."

Robin continued: "When we returned from our fiftieth 'Turning' I knew without a doubt that I loved Sonny and wanted to be with him. I was prepared to do whatever it took to make that happen. The week after the 'Turning' I was on a business trip to New Orleans. I got in late and noticed a small Creole restaurant across the street from the hotel. I went in to have some gumbo and a glass or wine before turning in. I sat quietly in the corner having dinner and reviewing the evaluations of my last seminar. I noticed an elderly woman behind the counter watching me as I finished dinner. She was a short round woman wearing a soiled apron that advertised the daily special. She watched me with soft and tender eyes, much like my grandmother used to do. When I finished my gumbo, she came over to clear the table and softly said, 'Child, I've been watching you for a while and I know what's going on in your life; it's written all over your face. You're in love, and you don't know what to do about it. There's one thing I can tell you, you're gonna have to go get that man. You gonna have to bring him to you.'

"I had been in the restaurant for less than an hour and wondered how this woman could read me so clearly in that short period of time. I asked her to have a seat; I wanted to know more about her. She sat across the table from me and asked me to hold her hand. I was hesitant to reach out to her, but her eyes told me she was a friend. Her hands were thick, warm and well-used. Hard work was not a stranger to this woman. As I held her hand she read me like the *New York Times.* She told me things that I hadn't even admitted to myself. Finally, I pulled my hand away. She was scaring the hell out of me. She told me that she was the granddaughter of a voodoo priestess, but she was not a practitioner. She, however, did possess the ability to read others, and what she saw in me made her want to help. She gave me a small envelope and told me that the contents would encourage my man to make the right commitment. She told me to use the contents to make tea; it could be served hot or cold. She guaranteed me that it was not voodoo; it was just a little something to help him make up his mind."

Everyone was listening intently. Robin went on with her story.

"Shortly after returning to New York I invited Sonny over for dinner and served him a large glass of iced tea with his dinner. Within a week he told me that he loved me and was prepared to take our relationship to the next step. I'm not proud of the way I got his commitment, but I got it. So, hopefully, we may be planning a wedding in the near future."

Everyone in the Sister Circle was stunned. Rosa said, "I don't know a lot about voodoo, and I can't say whether voodoo was used in this case, but I can tell you that you better be sure that this is what you want. Voodoo is a dark and scary practice and can backfire on you."

"I guess I'll have to take my chances," Robin said. "There is one more thing that I would like to share with the Sister Circle, and this is the hardest thing I've ever had to do."

She began to pace the room as tears welled in her eyes. "Cynthia, I love you dearly, but I have lied to you for the past ten years. I knew much more about Jack than anyone would have expected. Before anyone comes to a conclusion, please just hear me out."

Robin went on to tell the Sister Circle how she met Jack and what he wanted from her. She told them his true identity, that Matthew was his son, and explained why she agreed to help him make his plan work. She told them about her visits to the rehabilitation center and how she couldn't bring herself to tell Cynthia about his death.

Cynthia sat with her head in her hands. The sisters could tell she was crying. As the tears rolled down Robin's cheeks she got on her knees in front of Cynthia and asked for forgiveness. Robin told her that both she and Jack believed that they were protecting her. She told Cynthia that Jack loved her more than he loved himself and felt that she deserved a younger man who could make her happy. She said that Matthew didn't know about Jack and Cynthia, and Jack wanted to keep it that way. As Cynthia and Robin cried the room was silent. Robin was crying because of her deception, and Cynthia was crying because she never got to say good-bye to Jack.

Tracy was the first to speak. "What are we going to do about Matthew? He deserves to know the truth."

"What if he can't handle the truth? It could mean the end of what seems to be a perfect relationship for Cynthia," Rosa said.

Cynthia was visibly shaken by what she just heard. She wiped the tears from her eyes and held Robin in her arms. "Robin, I honestly believe that both you and Jack were trying to protect me. Protection was not what I needed; I really needed honesty. Matthew and I both needed honesty before we committed to our present relationship. I'm not sure how he will handle this information, but he has to know and he has to know now."

Robin said, "Cynthia, I think I should be the one to tell him. After all, the agreement was only between Jack and me. Matthew needs to hear the whole story."

Cynthia thought about it for a while and finally agreed. Robin agreed to come to Cynthia's house next Friday to tell Matthew the story, and Cynthia would give him the opportunity to make a decision about their relationship based on the new information. It was going to be a long week for Cynthia, and she prayed that Matthew could handle all that Robin had to say. Cynthia didn't want to lose him.

This had been one of the most intense Sister Circles ever, but they knew that in spite of what they had heard and what they felt, they were going to stand by each other.

Matthew and Cynthia had agreed that they would alternate between Boston and Connecticut during the weekends. It was Matthew's turn to come to Boston. She called him on Wednesday to let him know that they would have company for dinner Friday evening. Matthew was excited about his new contract and the promise that it held for even bigger contracts in the future. He told Cynthia how much he missed her and how he couldn't wait to see her on Friday. He told her that every moment that he spent with her made him know that she was the one for him. She assured him that she felt the same. She could only hope that he would continue to feel this way after dinner on Friday.

Cynthia took a little extra time preparing dinner. She had become a fairly decent cook over the years and wanted to be impressive with this dinner. Matthew arrived a little earlier than expected and they lounged on the sofa as he held her in his arms and recapped the week's events. He said he always wanted her to know what was going on in his life, and he always wanted to know what was going on in hers. As she sat between his legs with her head resting on his chest she could hear his heart beat strong and steady. She closed her eyes and asked the Lord to please let Matthew be strong enough to overcome this hurdle that was about to be placed in front of them.

After about fifteen minutes, the doorbell rang. *It couldn't be Robin; she had her own set of keys,* Cynthia thought. Cynthia turned on the security camera and saw Robin standing at her door, looking as if she carried the weight of the world on her shoulders. Cynthia opened the door, embraced Robin and asked why she decided not to use her keys this time.

Robin said, "After all that I've done, I'm not so sure that I still deserve the privilege." Cynthia assured her that they would get through this somehow, someway; it would all work out. They sat through dinner making small talk. Cynthia decided that she would let Robin make the first move.

After dinner and over cocktails Robin said, "I really need to talk to both of you." She began by telling Matthew how happy she was that he was in Cynthia's life and what a difference he had made. "I've got to be honest with you, Matthew, and believe me, I'm not very proud of this." She began to tell her story.

Matthew sat quietly sipping cognac and occasionally shifted in his seat. It was clear that Robin had his undivided attention. Robin was pacing the floor with tears in her eyes as she apologized again for her deceitfulness. All she ever wanted to do was to make sure that Cynthia was happy. Matthew could see how upset Robin was, and he stood to comfort her. He finally moved to the sofa, where Cynthia had been sitting quietly. He reached for Cynthia's hand and pulled her into his arms. He thought, *How much should I tell them?*

Matthew and his father had spent many long hours together while Jack was in rehabilitation. For the first time Jack opened up and told Matthew about his life. He told Matthew about his love for a younger woman and how she would have been the perfect mate for him if he were younger. He never told the woman's name, but Matthew saw the sparkle in his eye every time he talked about her. He was told by the nursing staff at the rehabilitation center that a young woman would visit occasionally, and Matthew thought that she was the one. He never felt a need to meet her. He respected his father's privacy.

As Jack's condition began to deteriorate he talked more about Matthew's need to find his perfect mate before it was too late. Jack kept trying to convince Matthew to book passage on the "Cruise to Celebrate Life," the Sister Circle's fiftieth-year celebration. Matthew was busy negotiating his present contract with the casino and tried to convince his father that he couldn't take a vacation until the contract was signed. Jack kept pressing.

Toward the end Jack was heavily medicated. He finally told Matthew that his ideal woman would be on this cruise, and it may be a once-in-a-lifetime opportunity for them to meet. He told Matthew that he didn't need to know her name, but he would know her when he met her. He asked Matthew to keep an open mind and not be swayed by any past relationships that either of them might have had.

Jack's final words to Matthew were this: "Son, I missed my chance to be happy for many years because I didn't know where or how to go in search of that special person. I've done the work for you, and I ask only that you go on that cruise, meet her and accept her into your life." Jack made Matthew promise to be on that cruise. It was the last promise Matthew made to his father.

Matthew now understood what his father had done, and a part of him resented his father's manipulation. But a larger part of him knew that his heart was deep into his relationship with Cynthia and he didn't want anything to interfere with that. Matthew decided to keep his own little secret; no one ever had to know that he was aware of his father's manipulation. He only hoped that Cynthia loved him enough to look past all of this.

As he held Cynthia in his arms he could feel the tension in her body. He asked Robin for a moment of privacy. Cynthia held her breath. He sat on the sofa and asked her to sit between his legs with her head resting on his chest, her favorite position. He needed to talk to her.

"Baby, I don't know why we were put into this relationship. And, to be honest, I really don't want to know. I do know that I enjoy every moment with you and would never want to be without you. There has been nothing said this evening that would make me change my mind. Most couples come together by chance. We were put together by a person who loved us both and knew what we needed."

Cynthia could finally breathe. Matthew was in for the long haul. Robin was relieved to know that she had not ruined the perfect relationship and that finally Cynthia could be happy. The faith, strength and love of the Sister Circle remained tight, and they were poised to enter the next new venture.

Printed in the United States
131061LV00003B/31-78/A